D0389064

INVASIVE

ALSO BY CHUCK WENDIG

THE MIRIAM BLACK SERIES

Blackbirds
Mockingbird
The Cormorant
Thunderbird

THE HEARTLAND SERIES

Under the Empyrean Sky
Blightborn
The Harvest

OTHER NOVELS

The Blue Blazes
Double Dead
Unclean Spirits
Atlanta Burns
Star Wars: Aftermath
Zeroes

NONFICTION

The Kick-Ass Writer

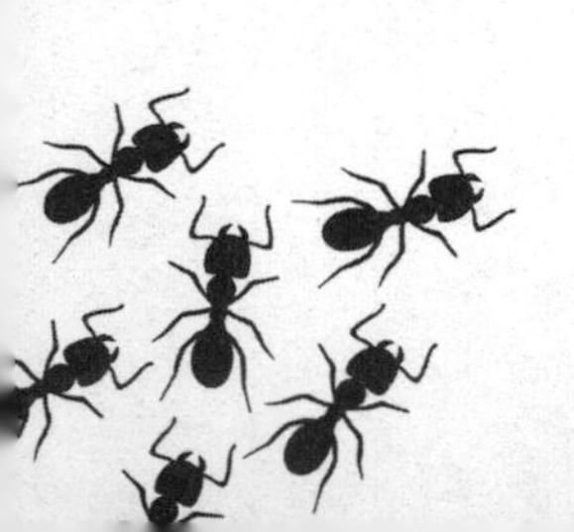

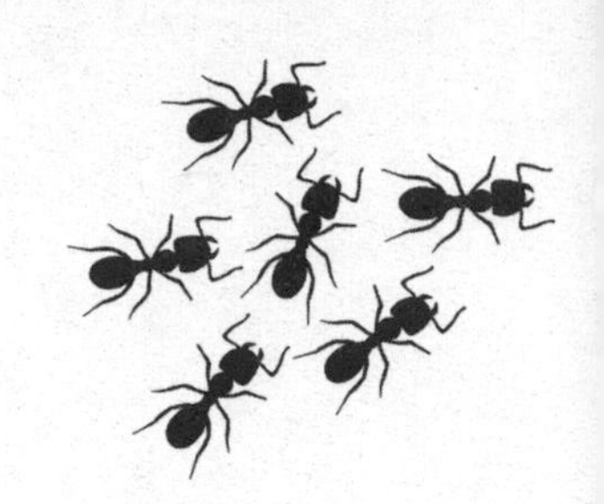

INVASIVE

CHUCK WENDIG

HARPER Voyager
An Imprint of HarperCollins*Publishers*

This is a work of fiction. Names, characters, places, and incidents are products of the author's imagination or are used fictitiously and are not to be construed as real. Any resemblance to actual events, locales, organizations, or persons, living or dead, is entirely coincidental.

HarperCollins books may be purchased for educational, business, or sales promotional use. For information, please e-mail the Special Markets Department at SPsales@harpercollins.com.

FIRST EDITION

Designed by Paula Russell Szafranski
Ant illustrations © by Stephania Hill/Shutterstock, Inc.

Library of Congress Cataloging-in-Publication Data has been applied for.

ISBN 978-0-06-235157-9

16 17 18 19 20 RRD 10 9 8 7 6 5 4 3 2 1

To Gwen Pearson and the fine folks at the
Purdue University Bug Barn

The future is a door.

Two forces—forces that we drive like horses and chariots, whips to their backs, wheels in ruts, great froth and furious vigor—race to that door.

The first force is *evolution*. Humanity changing, growing, becoming better than it was.

The second force is *ruination*. Humanity making its best effort to demonstrate its worst tendencies. A march toward self-destruction.

The future is a door that can accommodate only one of those two competing forces.

Will humanity evolve and become something better?

Or will we cut our own throats with the knives we made?

—Hannah Stander, in her lecture to students at Penn State University: "Apocalypse versus Apotheosis: What Does the Future Hold?"

INVASIVE

PART I

FORMICATION

formication (n)

1. the sensation that ants or other insects are crawling on one's skin.

1

Terminal F at the Philadelphia International Airport is the end of the airport, but it feels like the end of the world. It's a commuter terminal, mostly. Prop planes and jets hopping from hub to hub. The people here are well-worn and beaten down like the carpet underneath their feet.

Hannah's hungry. A nervous stomach from giving a public talk means she hasn't eaten since lunch, but the options here late at night—her flight is at 10:30 P.M.—are apocalyptic in their own right. Soft pretzels that look like they've been here since the Reagan administration. Egg or chicken salad sandwich triangles wrapped up in plastic. Sodas, but she never drinks her calories.

She's pondering her choices—or lack thereof—when her phone rings.

"Hello, Agent Copper," she says.

"Stander. Where are you?"

"The airport. Philly." Uh-oh. "Why?"

"I need you to get here."

"Where is 'here'?"

He grunts. "Middle of nowhere, by my measure. Technically: Herkimer County, New York. Let me see." Over his end comes the sound of uncrumpling papers. "Jerseyfield Lake. Not far from Little Hills. Wait. No! Little *Falls*."

"I'm on a plane in—" She pulls her phone away from her ear to check the time. "Less than an hour. I'm going home."

"How long's it been?"

Too long. "What's up in Little Falls?"

"That's why I need you. Because I don't know."

"Can it wait?"

"It cannot."

"Can you give me a hint? Is this another hacker thing?"

"No, not this time. This is something else. It may not even be something for you, but . . ." His voice trails off. "I'll entice you: I've got a cabin on the lake with more than a thousand dead bodies in it."

"A thousand dead bodies? That's not possible."

"Think of it like a riddle."

She winces. "Nearest airport?"

"Syracuse."

"Hold on." She sidles over to one of the departure boards. There's a flight leaving for Syracuse fifteen minutes later than the one leaving for Dayton—the one she's supposed to get on. "I can do it. You owe me."

"You'll get paid. That's the arrangement."

She hangs up and goes to talk to an airline attendant.

* * *

Boarding. The phone's at her ear once more, pinned there by her shoulder. It rings and rings. No reason to expect her to answer, but then—

"Hannah?"

"Hi, Mom."

Everyone moves ahead toward the door. Hannah pulls her carry-on forward, the wheels squeaking. She almost loses the phone, but doesn't.

"I wasn't sure it was you."

"You would be if you turned on caller ID."

"It's not my business who's calling me."

"Mom, it is exactly your business who's calling you."

"It's fine, Hannah, I don't need it." Her mother sounds irritated. That's her default state, so: situation normal. "Are you still coming in tonight?"

Hannah hesitates, and her mother seizes on it.

"Your father misses you. It's been too long."

"It's a work thing. It's just one night. I've rebooked my flight. I'll be there tomorrow."

"All right, Hannah." In her voice, though: that unique signature of sheer dubiousness. Her mother doubts everything. As if anyone who doesn't is a fawn: knock-kneed and wide-eyed and food for whatever larger thing comes creeping along. What's upsetting is how often she's proven right. Or how often she can change the narrative so that she's proven right. "We will see you tomorrow."

"Tell Dad good night for me."

"He's already asleep, Hannah."

* * *

In flight the plane bumps and dips like a toy in the hand of a nervous child. Hannah isn't bothered. Pilots avoid turbulence not because it's dangerous, but because passengers find it frightening.

Her mind, instead, is focused on that singular conundrum: How can a cabin by the lake contain a thousand corpses?

The average human body is five eight in length. Two hundred pounds. Two feet across at the widest point. Rough guess: a human standing up would take up a single square foot. How big would a lake cabin be? Three hundred square feet? Three hundred corpses standing shoulder to shoulder. Though cording them like firewood would fill more space because you could go higher. To the rafters, even. Maybe you could fit a thousand that way . . .

She pulls out a notebook and paper, starts doodling some math.

But then it hits her: Hollis Copper was dangling a riddle in front of her.

Q: How do you fit a thousand dead bodies in a cabin by the lake?

A: They're not human *bodies.*

2

She rents a little four-door Kia sedan just as the place is closing. Smells of cigarette smoke smothered under a blanket of Febreze.

It's late April, and the drive to Little Falls is long and meandering, through thick pines and little hamlets. The GPS tries to send her down roads that are closed (BRIDGE OUT) or that don't seem to have ever existed. She's tempted to turn it off. Not because of its inefficacy, but because she knows it's tracking her. Passively, of course. But where she goes, it knows. And if it knows, anybody can know.

She grinds her sharp spike of paranoia down to a dull knob. She is always cautioning her parents not to give in to that anxiety. (Let's be honest, the horse is miles out of the barn on that one.) That is a deep, slick-walled pit. Once you fall into it, it's very hard to climb back out.

She leaves the GPS on and keeps driving.

After another hour, she sees the turn for Jerseyfield Lake. It's another hour to the cabin. The pines here are tall, like a garden of spear tips thrust up out of the dark earth. The road is muddy, and the sedan bounces and judders as it cuts a channel through the darkness.

Then, in the distance, she sees the pulsing strobe of red and blue. As she approaches, a cop stands in her way, waving his arms. He's mouthing something, so she rolls down the window to hear: "—back around, this is a crime scene. I said: turn *back* around, this is not a road, this is a private driveway and—"

She leans out the window: "I'm Hannah Stander." Her breath puffs in front of her like an exorcised spirit. It's cold. The chill hits her hard.

"I don't care if you're the Pope," the cop says. He's got a scruffy mustache and beard hanging off his jowls. "You need to turn around."

"She's with me," says a voice from behind the cop. And sure enough, here comes Hollis Copper. Tall and thin as a drinking straw. Hair cut tight to his head. Gone are his muttonchops; now there's just a fuzzy, curly pelt on his face.

The cop turns. "She law enforcement?"

"Yeah," Copper says.

"No," Hannah says at the same time.

The cop gives an incredulous look. "You know what? I don't give a shit. Park over there—" He flags her toward a puddled patch of gravel tucked tight against a copse of trees whose leaves are just starting to pop. She eases the sedan over there, cuts the engine, meets Hollis. She thanks the cop, still standing next to a cruiser and a couple of black SUVs. He just gives her an arched brow. "Sure, honey."

"He's an asshole," Hollis says, not quietly. "This way."

They head across the limestone gravel toward a pathway cutting through the trees. She can make out knife-slashes of moonlight on distant water and the shadow of a small black cabin. Its windows and doorway are lit up like the eyes and mouth of a Halloween jack-o'-lantern.

"I'm not really law enforcement," she says.

"You're a consultant for the Federal Bureau of Investigation. That makes you law enforcement to me."

"I don't enforce the law."

"You investigate breaches of the law. That's the first step of enforcement."

She knows better than to get into a semantic argument with him. "It's not human bodies, is it?" she says.

He cocks his head at her. "Nope."

* * *

The smell is what hits her first. It forces its way up her nose before she even crosses the threshold of the cabin. It's not one odor, but a mélange of them competing for dominance: a rank and heady stink like mushrooms gone mushy; the smell of human waste and coppery blood; the stench of something else behind it, something pungent and piquant, vinegary, acidic, tart.

It does nothing to prepare her for what she sees.

The dead man on the floor has no skin.

He still wears his clothes: a fashionable hoodie, a pair of slim-cut jeans. But his face is a red, glistening mask—the eyes bulging white fruits against the muscles of his cheeks and forehead. The skin on his hands is gone. The upper arms, too. (Though curiously, the skin at the elbows remains.) Where the present flesh meets exposed muscle, the skin is ragged, as if cut by cuticle scissors. It looks like torn paper. Dried at the edges. Curling up.

There's one body, she thinks. *Where are the rest?*

It takes her a second to realize she's looking at them. The little black bits on the floor—hundreds of them, thousands—aren't metal shavings or some kind of dirt.

Insects, she realizes. Ants. Dead ants, everywhere.

"What am I looking at?" she says, putting on a pair of latex gloves.

The question goes unanswered. Hollis just gives her a look. He wants *her* to tell *him* what she sees. That's why she's here.

"No tech," she says. No laptop, no tablet. The cabin is a single room: cot in the corner with a pink sheet on it, galley kitchen at the far end, a cast-iron pellet stove against the far wall. No bathroom. Outhouse, probably. (She's all too familiar with those. Her parents had one for a number of years because they didn't trust any plumber coming into their house.)

If there's no tech, why is she here? She takes a gingerly step forward, trying not to step on the ants. They may contain vital forensic data.

But it's impossible not to step on the ants. They make little tiny crunches under her boot—like stepping on spilled Rice Krispies.

She looks up. *Oh God.* What she thought was a pink bedsheet on the cot is no such thing. It *was* a white sheet. But now it's stained pink. The color of human fluids.

She looks over at Hollis. He gives a small nod. He's got his hand pressed against the underside of his nose to stave off the stench. She doesn't even notice it now. Curiosity's got its claws in.

The sheet on top, the one stained with fluids, is lumpy, bumpy, oddly contoured. She bends down, pinches the edges with her fingers, and pulls it back.

Her gorge rises. This smell won't be ignored. A wall of it hits her: something formerly human, but something fungal, too. A sour bile stink filled with the heady odor of a rotten log. Her arm flies to her nose and mouth and she chokes back the dry heave that tries to come up.

Under the sheet, she finds a good bit of what remains of the victim's skin. All of it clipped off the body in tiny swatches—none bigger than a quarter, most smaller than a penny. Tattered, triangular cuts. Half of it covered in striations of white mold—like fungus on the crust of bread. The white patches are wet, slick. The air coming up off it is humid.

Amid the hundreds of little skin bits: More dead ants. Hundreds of them.

Hannah pulls out her phone, flicks on the flashlight. The light shines on the glossy backs of the ants, each a few millimeters long. Many are covered with a fine carpet of little filaments: red hairs, like bits of copper wire. Some of those filaments are covered in the same white fungus.

And in some of their jaws—their prodigious jaws, jaws like something a morgue attendant would use to cut through flesh and bone—are snippets of dried skin.

Hannah's head spins as she tries to imagine what happened here. A man dies. Natural causes? Falls forward. Ants come in—

A memory passes over her like the shadow of a vulture:

She's young, not even eight, and she's out at the mailbox (before

Mom chopped the mailbox down with an ax), and she pops the lid and reaches in—suddenly her hand tickles all over. Hannah pulls her hand out and the tickling bits turn to pinpricks of pain. Her hand is covered in ants. Little black ones. Dozens of them pinching her skin in their tiny mandibles. She screams and shakes her hand and ants are flung into the grass as she bolts back to the house, forgetting to close the barbed-wire gate—Mom would give her no end of dressing down over that because you never leave the gate open, never-never, ever-ever, because then anybody can get in . . .

She stands up. The smell recedes. She gently sets the sheet back over the battlefield of ants, fungus, and human skin, then turns to Copper. "Is this even a crime scene?"

"That's what I'm waiting for you to tell me."

She looks around. The pellet stove is cold—the air here almost the same temperature as outside—but she sees ash spilled on the floor in a little line.

Hannah takes a knee next to the body. Most of the skin on the scalp is gone, as is most of the hair. The skull underneath is exposed: pinkish-brown, like the sheet on the cot. But no sign of injury. No broken bone. "Any injury to the body?" she asks, taking a pen and poking around.

Hollis tells her no, nothing.

The dead man's ears are gone, mostly. Holes leading into the side of the head. As she nudges the skull with her pen, more ants spill out of those canals. All dead. Were they eating the brain, too? Or just trying to nest in there?

The dead body doesn't bother her, but that thought does.

* * *

Outside, the air is cold and crisp—like a hard slap against her cheek. She paces out front a little. After a few moments, Hollis joins her, thumbs a piece of hard gum through its foil backing, offers it to her. She takes it. Wintergreen.

He pops a piece into his mouth and gives a hard crunch. "What am I looking at in there?"

"I don't know."

"You're supposed to know."

"I don't see any tech inside. I don't see any . . . anything. There's no *there* there. This isn't my world."

"Just tell me what you saw."

Is he asking because he knows something she doesn't? Or has Hollis Copper lost a step? She's heard rumors. Last year's fiasco with Flight 6757 was hell on him. Brought down by hackers, the story goes. Nobody brought her in to consult on that one—to her surprise.

Whatever it was, Hollis had to take some time off before the NSA lobbed him back to the Bureau like a hot potato. When he came back, he seemed the same at first, but something lives behind his eyes now.

"Again, I don't see any tech. But who doesn't have a phone? Everyone has a phone. You didn't find one?"

He shakes his head.

"How'd you even find this? This is way off the beaten path."

"Cabin's a rental. And nobody is renting it. The owner got a call from someone across the lake, said he saw lights here. Thought it might be squatters."

"But the dead man in there isn't a squatter."

"Why do you say that?"

"He's got money. The boots are Lowas. Boots for rich-kid backpackers. Three hundred a pop, easy."

He snaps the gum. "You got a photographic memory I don't know about? Or are you just a boot fetishist?"

"I hike. Those are hiking boots. Overkill, really, and whoever that corpse was, he didn't get much use out of them. And his jeans are fashionably ripped, not worn from use. The vest is nice, too—an Obermeyer. Also not cheap. I'd say the vic is a young man. Under thirty, at least. Probably not under twenty."

"Agreed. Go on."

"The owner found the body?"

"Uh-huh."

"He see anybody else here?"

"Nope."

She *hmms*. "He complain about an ant problem?"

"No. But he did puke."

"I don't blame him." She pauses, considers. "It's early for ants."

"What?"

"Ants hibernate over the winter. Argentine ants, carpenter ants."

Hollis blows a bubble. "It's spring, though."

"But spring in upstate New York. Snow belt." Something nags at her. "When did the owner find the body?"

"This evening." He looks down at his watch. "*Yesterday* evening. It's already past midnight. Jesus."

"The man was dead when the owner found him. The ants were dead, too?"

"So he says."

A thought occurs to her. Hannah heads off the meager porch at the front of the cabin and stoops by a small bundle of early greens growing up out of the limestone gravel. Little yellow flowers sit on top, withered and cold. She rubs her thumb across a burgeoning, uncurling leaf. Wet. Cold. Not icy. Not yet.

Over her shoulder, she says, "Was there a frost the night before?" It would make sense. Last expected frost date around here is probably what? May 3?

Hollis says he doesn't know, and calls over to one of the unis. The officer walks over, says there was a cold snap, so maybe. Copper comes up behind her, towering over her. "Yellow rocket," she says, indicating the plant. "One of the first blooming weeds of spring. You can eat it."

"Your parents teach you all this stuff?"

"They did." She starts to stand—but then she sees it.

"Look," she says, pointing to the ground. A footprint. In a patch of shining mud next to the driveway, away from the stones. "Pointed toward the lake. Could match the Lowas on the victim's feet." Hollis snaps his fingers, tells one of the cops to get pictures and a preserved mold.

The cop who comes over is the same one who tried to shove her off—the jowly, scruffy one. "Is this even a crime scene?"

"Just get the damn print," Hollis says.

"Yeah, yeah, sure, all right. Relax."

Together, Hannah and Copper head down a set of stairs—stairs that aren't stairs so much as a collection of flagstones stuck haphazardly in the earth, leading down to a narrow dock jutting out over the lake.

Hollis pokes around while Hannah stands and takes it all in. The moon is just a scythe hook over the dark lake—a bitten fingernail left on a blanket of stars. She tries to piece together what happened while Hollis walks out over the dock, his boots clunking on the wood as the whole thing bobs and plops against the surface. Eventually he returns, empty-handed. "Nothing."

She stares at a fixed point on the horizon as she tells the story: "Our victim comes to the cabin. Doesn't settle in for long, because he's still got his vest on, his boots, everything. But he feeds the pellet stove, starts to get warm." A thought occurs to her. "Did you check the outhouse? Did someone use it?"

"We checked it, but nobody used it."

So she continues: "Somehow he dies. I know, that's a big *somehow,* but it's all we have. A health issue, maybe. Carbon monoxide poisoning. Or something more sinister than that? He dies there on the floor. And the ants come in—this is a rainy area this time of the year, and ants tend to come indoors when the weather is cold or rainy." Like the mailbox from her memory: it had rained the night prior, hadn't it? "They have no food and choose him as their meal. But then, of course, nobody's feeding the pellet stove. The stove goes out. The chill creeps in. Cold snap. Frost. The ants perish. And here we are."

"Sensible. And still doesn't give us the answer to the question."

Is this a crime scene? Or is it something else entirely?

"The ants," she says. "They might hold the key. Ants have two stomachs. Crops, they're called. One for food for themselves, one for food for the colony."

"So, the ants might have forensic value."

"It's something. Obviously you're going to do further analysis—a tox screen and all that."

"We will. I'll contact someone in the Bureau who might be able to help on the forensic side." He flinches. "It's pretty nasty in there. Ants pulling all that skin off. At least he was dead when they did it."

She thinks but doesn't say: *We assume he was dead when they did it.*

Maybe he had a heart attack or a pulmonary embolism. And along come the creepy crawlies. What's that old song? *The ants go marching one by one, hurrah, hurrah . . . The ants go marching one by one, hurrah! hurrah! . . . The ants go marching one by one, the little one stops to suck her thumb, and they all go marching down to the ground to get out of the rain . . .*

Then they start to bite.

Even in the cold, she starts to sweat.

What she says to Hollis is "I'd like to handle it."

"You're not in forensics, I'll remind you."

"No, but I have a friend who's a forensic entomologist."

"You sure? I thought I was interrupting a vacation."

Visiting my parents is about as far from a vacation as Pluto is from Earth. "It's fine. Put together a package ready for travel—ants, fungus, skin sample—I'll book a flight to Tucson. Ez Choi teaches bug science at the state university."

"That Arizona State?"

"No, it's—" She tries to draw it up from memory. "The other one. University of Arizona."

"We'll have to ship the package separately, if that's amenable."

"It's fine by me, thank you."

"Then go forth and do the work of the law, Ms. Stander."

"Will do, Agent Copper."

3

She sleeps in the rental car because it's too late to get a room anywhere and her flight to Tucson is early. Her sleep is restless—she's shaken by forces unseen, the threat of the future, the threat of the open door. The threat of anything and everything. A sword above everyone's heads, held by a thread. A plane hacked by hackers, crashing. Terrorists using homemade drones as bombs. A world pinned by global warming, the lack of resources plunging the planet into another Cold War—or worse, an active global conflict.

Hannah moves her hips. She bangs one knee on the stick. She bangs her other knee on the underside of the steering wheel. It's 4:00 A.M. *This is my job,* she thinks. To imagine the worst. To look far down the road to see what's coming: What technology, what social system, what change to nature will humans face? Will it elevate and evolve us? Or will it destroy us?

Or worse—and here is the crux of her work—*Will we use it to destroy ourselves?* Her brain follows the yellow brick road all the way to Oz—except this Emerald City is shattered, with spires of broken glass, skyscrapers like jagged shards. She looks ahead to see what risks await: the threat of artificial intelligence, the danger of hackable cybernetic implants, the permutations of robots as part of daily life. Will they put us out of work, will we rely too much on them, will the laws be fast enough to catch up with what they can do, will artificial intelligence one day take control of them and decide that we are the greatest threat to robotic "life"? GMO crops that don't feed us and brain modifications that allow us to read each other's minds and mass extinctions—a drain-swirl of improbable but possible scenarios.

At some point, her mind quiets down long enough for her to sleep. But her dreams are thick with terror—in the darkness of slumber she smells that foul piss-vinegar odor. She smells the earthy, turned-soil stink of fungus on skin scraps. She reaches into a mailbox and returns an arm covered in ants. She tries to scream but the sound is caught in her throat. She tries to flail but her arm is stiff and her feet are rooted to the ground. Her family's farmhouse sits in the distance. Somewhere a goat bleats, then screams. The ants begin biting. Ripping bits of skin off like pulling the wet label off a sweating beer bottle—bit by bit, in larger strips and curls, in worthless, gummy swatches. Until soon her arm is just bold vermilion—red and raw like a steak cut right from the cow. Lush, blood-slick meat braided with bruise-dark veins.

Finally she screams—

And screams herself awake. Here she is. In the airport rental lot. She sits up. Her hair is matted to her forehead with sweat. She looks at her arm. She's got three scratches down the length. Nothing serious. No blood. Just raised red furrows where her nails must have done their work.

She looks at the time. She's running late.

With a growl of frustration, Hannah gets out of the car and rescues her carry-on from the backseat. She'll call the rental place, have them find the car parked in the adjacent lot. She rushes to catch a shuttle bus.

* * *

The shuttle is slow. The lines through security are long, too long, and because she's only a consultant with the FBI and not actual FBI, she is afforded no privilege with the TSA. She has to go through the cattle chute like the rest of the traveling herd.

The plane leaves without her. They rebook her on an afternoon flight.

She calls her mother.

"You're not coming, are you."

"It's work," she says. Her stock answer.

"Your father wants to see you."

"I know."

"He needs to see you."

"I know."

"No, you don't know." A sigh on the other end. Mom's voice softens a little: "Is it important, what you're doing?"

I don't know. "Yes."

"Do you need to warn us? Is something going on?" Her work always leads to that question.

"No. This is just standard. It's a . . ." Her mouth forms the word *murder,* but she has no evidence of that. It doesn't even add up yet. She says, "It's an ongoing investigation."

"You didn't tell me about last year. The plane."

"I didn't know about the plane."

"Terrorists can hack planes and crash them into the ground? What have we done to ourselves, Hannah? We've made it all too complex. Too complex to live."

"I have to go, Mom. I'll be in Tucson a day or two and then—"

"Don't say it. Your mouth shouldn't make promises the rest of you can't keep. We will see you when we see you."

"I love you guys."

A pause.

"We love you, too, Hannah."

* * *

The flight is a roller-coaster ride. Bucking like a horse, then dropping like the horse got shot. (Here, a sudden, unexpected memory: The way to drop a whitetail deer is a lung shot. Take the air out of it and it'll fall right where it stands.) The turbulence doesn't bother her, even though her stomach takes every bounce and dip a half second later than the rest of her. But all along the way she ponders how you'd hack the plane in flight. She's not a hacker, so she doesn't have the skills, but if she did . . .

The systems are all bound together. That's the problem. That's the vulnerability with planes. The cockpit, the Wi-Fi, the Jetway controls, they're all braided together and plugged into one another. The systems are not islands. Which means if you're really savvy, you can find your way to one system and burrow a hole—programmatically speaking—to another. Connect to the Wi-Fi, and someone of genuine talent could punch a hole into the flight systems. Even easier, though far more conspicuous: rip off part of the armrest and access the plug with a cat-5 Ethernet cable (one that is perhaps modded) and connect to a laptop, and it gets even easier because Wi-Fi has its own security protocols in place. They don't expect you to go in this way because only workers do that—which means one fewer locked door standing in your way to the flight systems.

Then from there, what? Take control? Set the autopilot? You'd have to know how to fly a plane, somewhat.

Or you just tell the systems to drop you out of the sky like a stone.

That scares her. The fragility of the thing. All the systems together. Vulnerability to people with terrible agendas.

She obsesses about this for a while when she should be obsessing about one dead man and a thousand dead ants.

They land in Tucson.

* * *

Another car rental. A Nissan. It's hot here—not even May and it's in the midnineties. Everything feels dry. The heat, squeezing her like a lemon. The air, a vampire sucking her dry. It strikes her that Arizona and its two principal cities are settlements of great hubris.

Once at the hotel—a Marriott across the street from the university—she texts Ez, tells her she's in town. Hannah gets settled in and then—*bing*. Ez doesn't respond until suddenly she does:

Ez: i'm downstairs

(The text followed by a trail of emoji: hearts, smiley faces, high-fiving hands that also look like *Praise Jesus* hands, and for kicks, a tiny little cartoon ant standing on her hind legs.)

* * *

They go to a nearby pizza-and-beer place with a name as honest as it gets: Pizza & Beer. Ez sips a craft beer—something called Dragon's Milk—and Hannah goes with a glass of wine.

Ez is a little slip of a woman. Chinese descent, first-generation American. She's got a Mohawk (presently hot pink and flopped over like a wilted flower) and the sides of her head are shorn down, the stubble dyed a deep viridian. Her nose is pierced. Her eyebrow, too. Her lip. Her arms are inked with swarms of bugs: honeybees, ants, praying mantises, all woven in and around vines and leaves. Her makeup is thick, matching her hair: rich green lips, green eyebrows, a pink blush. None of it should work together and yet, on her, it sings.

She's the opposite of Hannah in many ways: Hannah is tall. Dirty-blond hair long, pulled back. No makeup. As a kid she always told her father, *I'm plain.* He always said, *Plain is pretty to me,* and then he'd kiss her brow.

"Dead ants," Ez says, pulling a slice of sausage, pepper, and onion away from the pie. "Ants who apparently were munching on itty-bitty snippets of human skin." She chews a glob of cheese like it's a wad of gum. "Cool."

Hannah laughs. "Yeah. Cool."

Ez nods. "Okay, so, the thing is? Ants don't really do that. The skin-nibbling thing."

"It wasn't just the skin, though," Hannah says, pulling a slice for herself. "It was fungus. Fungus that had grown *on* the skin."

"I saw that. What's super fucking kooky about that is, that's how leaf-cutter ants work. Leaf-cutters literally scissor bits of leaf off with their mandibles, then carry those bits back to the mound—their nest—and use them to form a substrate for fungus. Then they bring more leaves to feed the fungus. It's mutualism. They grow the fungus. Nurture it."

"Like farmers."

"They are farmers. A lot of ants are. Some herd aphids like livestock and—who does this sound like?—drink their milk."

"Do they wear little cowboy hats?"

Ez claps her hands and squeals. "God, I wish! How fucking *amazing* would that be? Little ants with cowboy hats. Riding on the backs of beetles." She freezes, eyes wide. "I could do it. *I have the power.*"

"Ease off the throttle, Dr. Frankenstein. One step at a time." Hannah chews her pizza and around a mouthful of crunchy green pepper says: "So, what we're dealing with are leaf-cutter ants. Except given the early season and the frost, they didn't have any leaves to munch and so instead they found our victim?"

"Maybe. But New York isn't home to any leaf-cutter ants."

"So, what's that mean? Invasive species?"

"Or a new species."

Hannah raises an eyebrow. "Is that likely?"

"It's not impossible. Earth is home to more than twelve thousand species of ants. If you weighed all the ants and all the humans, the ants would weigh more. We discover new ant species every year. And not just in weird places, but all over." She sighs. "That said, *disappointingly,* an invasive species is way more likely. Think of how Africanized bees invaded from South America. It was only twenty or so hives that were accidentally released, but bugs get busy fast. It's why they put the *fun* in *functional* when it comes to the lab: you can breed generations of them like boom, boom, boom." With each "boom" she snaps her fingers. "And ants can be invasive—take the 'tawny crazy ant' around here. One of our mandates is to study those little fuckers. They're tiny and they move like lightning. One day nobody knew what they were. Next day they were here in the millions. They get in everything: industrial machines, electronics, cars. And if they get electrocuted, they release a swarm chemical that tells all the ants nearby to swarm. So they do. And they all get electrocuted and release the signal and whatever machine or electronic gadget they've swarmed is suddenly ruined."

"And the ants just keep coming?"

"All the ones nearby. The machine fritzes and then the waves stop."

"That sounds terrible."

"Uh, yeah, terribly *amazing,* you mean. They're resistant to a lot of poisons and they're persistent—even if you kill them today, unlike other ants they won't find a new way forward. They're like zombies at a fence—they just keep swarming until they're climbing over a field of their own dead. Brilliant little buggers."

Hannah cocks an eyebrow. Again that image hits her: ants swarming her hand as she pulls it out of the mailbox. "They're a pest, though."

"They are. Cost millions of dollars a year. But that's on us, not them. They don't know they're a pest. They're just living."

"Like us."

"Yeah, but *we* know that we're a pest."

Hannah offers up her wine. "That's as good a toast as any."

They clink glasses. "It's good to see you, Stander," Ez says.

"I missed you, Ez."

Ez shows all her teeth in a big madhouse smile. "Missed you, too, Stander! *Missed you, too.*"

* * *

They talk for hours. About books (Hannah reads only nonfiction, Ez seems to read every epic fantasy novel she can shove inside her eyeholes). About school (both attended Cornell University for graduate studies). About family (Ez talks to her parents nightly, Hannah does her best with hers). The two of them get a little fuzzy with all the wine and beer. The pizza ends up a demolished mess.

Outside, Ez steals a quick cigarette ("I know, I know, don't give me that look, *Mom,*" she tells Hannah) and asks: "So, you doing okay?"

"I'm good."

"'I'm good,' she says in a way that indicates she is not necessarily doing that good. C'mon, Han. You can tell me. Panic attacks?"

"Under control." *Mostly,* she adds inside her head. "I see the giant bottomless chasm of worry over *there* and I stay over *here.* It'll never go away, but I can choose to not go falling down in there."

"You take meds for it yet?"

"No," she says firmly. Too firmly, maybe. "I don't trust meds."

"Says the woman who just downed, like, a half bottle of zinfandel."

"Pinot noir. But that's not medicine."

"Beer is my medicine. When the world seems dim and all seems hopeless, a little buzz from a top-shelf bottle of beer will set everything back on its axis." Ez drags off the cigarette and blows smoke from both nostrils. Then she indicates the cigarette. "These are not my medicine. These are my poison. And yet: I smoke."

"We all do things we know we're not supposed to. And vice versa."

Ez squints and scrutinizes. "You say that like it means something more."

"No, I just mean . . ." But her words die in her mouth.

"Go on. Tell Dr. Choi what ails you, child."

"I told you about Dad, right?"

"Yeah. How's he holding up?"

Hannah sighs. "I think he's fine. There most of the time. But of course he won't touch medication—"

"You understand the irony of what you just said."

"It sounds like irony, but it isn't." She hears a bit of steel in her voice—a coldness, an anger, and she quickly bites it back. "If I'm ever sick-sick, I'll take meds, trust me. I don't consider general anxiety disorder to be a sickness. It's a thing I can deal with all by myself. Alcoholics don't need medicine to stop drinking. I don't need medicine to stop worrying. But for Dad, this is bigger than that. And Mom doesn't want any kind of medication in the house."

"You could sneak him something. Exelon, maybe."

"What are you, a pharma rep?"

"My aunt was on the stuff and then, you know, *died*." Ez makes a face like she just licked a toad's belly. As if the very thought of death is both distasteful and inconvenient. Which, Hannah supposes, it is. "Hospice said we were supposed to flush her meds, but we kept them because—well, I don't know why. We just did. So, I still have the Exelon. I could get it for you."

"I'll think about it." If she ever tries to sneak her dad any kind of meds—even an aspirin—her mother will kick her outside the gate and lock it behind her.

"You gone home to see him?"

"No." She must make a face. Ez seizes on it.

"That's it. That's what's bugging you. Going home."

"Well."

"Am I right?"

"*Well.*"

"I'm totally right."

"Going home means . . . going home."

"Ooh, a tautology."

"But true just the same. I don't like home. I left home for a reason. But Dad is there . . ."

"Held there like a princess by your tyrannical mother."

"She's not tyrannical. She's a good woman. Just broken."

Ez shrugs, puts out her cigarette. "We're all a little broken."

"I think she's a lot broken. But she's my mother and he's my father and they're good people even if they're getting it wrong." *I just can't bring myself to get home.* Something always ends up getting in the way. Sometimes it's random. Other times, she wonders if she orchestrates it so she has to stay away.

Ez does a Chubby Checker twist on the cigarette, then picks it back up and tosses it in a nearby trash can. "I'm going to go pay the bill."

"Let me. The Bureau can pay."

"I don't think America's tax dollars should go toward paying for my beer tab, Stander. I'll take care of it."

* * *

Ez drops her back at the hotel, a three-minute drive. Hannah gets out and asks, "You're okay to get started tomorrow?"

"This morning I got a box full of dead ants, human blood, and fungal skin remnants. Santa was good to me this year."

"You're weird."

"*You're* weird."

"Fine, we're both weird."

That exchange: Not the first time they've shared it. Won't be the last.

4

It's 3:30 A.M. when her phone dings.

She's asleep—the hotel bed isn't comfortable and she needs to use three pillows to give her the support of one real pillow, but everything has caught up with her and she's down. The phone dings again and she swims up out of that dark place, hand pawing at the side table. Knocking the alarm clock over. Finding the phone. She winces against the glow.

A text:

Ez: i'm downstairs

She thinks: *Stupid phone.* It's recirculating yesterday's text for some annoying reason. Digital detritus washing back up on her shore. But then the phone vibrates and dings again, making her heart jump.

Ez: get dressed and meet me out front. asafp.

* * *

Hannah staggers downstairs in last night's clothes, which smell of wine and garlic and a hint of cigarette smoke.

Outside, the early-morning Tucson air is surprisingly chilly. The predawn sky is the color of gunmetal.

Parked nearby is Ez Choi's little two-door Honda. Hannah pops the door and sits and Ez gives her a look.

"These ants don't exist," Ez says. She chucks Hannah a folder sloppily stuffed with pages and printouts.

Hannah lifts the manila folder and shuffles through the pages, trying to make sense of what she's seeing. Images of DNA sequencing, a spreadsheet of various codes and descriptions, some macro snapshots of the ants. One of those photos is a portrait of sorts: a dead-on shot of an ant's face. It's shaped like a Satanic black heart: what would be the two top curves are instead pointed, almost horned—this from the antennae. The jaws at the bottom close tight like a pair of serrated scissors tapering to hooks. Dead black eyes. Little hairs all over. Black, shiny, demonic.

"I went back to the lab last night," Ez says, breathless with what seems to be excitement. "I had a few minutes, so I started pulling out samples. Next thing I knew, it was hours later. Your dead guy's blood was a cocktail of tryptase and histamine, which is in line with anaphylaxis."

"An allergic reaction."

"An allergic *over*reaction, but yeah. And I checked the skin samples: unnatural swelling beneath the subdermal layer, which is consistent. So I cracked open one of our little ant friends. It's a stinging ant."

"Do leaf-cutters sting?"

"They do. A lot of ants do. They're Hymenoptera—same order as wasps and bees. Fire ants clamp down with their jaws, but the pain comes from the sting. We've got these ants locally, the Maricopa harvester ant—"

Suddenly, movement by the car door. A hand comes down against the passenger-side window, and Hannah's heart hops into her throat—she feels at her side for a knife or pepper spray or her keys, but the only thing in her pocket is a hotel key card and it makes her feel suddenly naked. There, at the window, is a man: scruffy, older, lizard-like skin, eyes pinched behind folds of flesh. Half his face is red with some kind of dermatitis or eczema.

Her window starts to buzz down. She looks to Ez in panic.

Ez says, "It's all right." Then, louder: "Hey, Carl."

"Oh. Hey! Hey, is that you, Ezzy?" His voice is hoarse. An esophagus abraded with the sandpaper of a hard life.

Ez grunts as she leans across Hannah and hands out a crumpled wad of money. Hannah spies a few one-dollar bills, a few fives. "It's me, Carl. Here's some cash." But before he takes it, she jerks the money back. "Ah, ah, ah. You know the drill with this."

He chuckles—a raspy, wheezing sound, like air whistling through an old rusty pipe. "Don't buy liquor."

"Are you going to buy liquor with it, Carl?"

"No?"

"Are you lying?"

"Maybe."

"No liquor!" she barks, then hands over the money. "Go on, get out of here, you old scamp." She shoos him away and he kisses his calloused fingers and blows her a kiss. Hannah smells his breath: it smells, contrary to her expectations, herbaceous. Like basil or oregano. His laugh can be heard trailing away as he shuffles across the parking lot.

"That's Carl," Ez explains. "He's local homeless. Nice guy. Drunk, but not a creeper. We gotta watch out for him on really hot days. Try to get him into shelters with AC."

Hannah releases a stuck breath. "You were saying something about a . . . a harvester ant?"

"Right! The Maricopa harvester. The venom in a harvester ant is the most toxic in the insect world. Its LD50 value—the median lethal dose—is through the floor: 0.12. The lower that number, the less of the venom it takes to actually kill somebody. And 0.12 is freaking low, Hannah."

"Deadliest ant in the world and it's right here in your backyard?"

Ez snaps her fingers. "See, that's the thing. It's not the most lethal because it kills the most people. It's aggressive, like the fire ant, but it's rare—you don't see many around. Which means people don't get stung all that often. Fire ants are all over the damn place and, so, technically super deadly. A hand grenade is more lethal than a single bullet, but most people don't have hand grenades."

With fingers like forceps, Hannah pinches the bridge of her nose. She runs through this in her head and asks, "Why are you telling me all this?"

"Look," Ez says, grabbing the folder and thumbing through the pages. She finds what she's looking for—a close-up image of a skin fragment. It's so close-up it almost looks topographical. Ez stabs down with a finger and says, "I scraped away the fungus—which, by the way, is *Candida*, just old-fashioned, old-timey yeast—and underneath I found marks. Lines and dots, lines and dots." Sure enough, on the skin sample: a small horizontal red line and a red raised dot beneath it. "Like with fire ants, you have the line from where they get a good mandibular grip—*chomp!*—and then they do some insect yoga and curl their bodies inward to jam their little stinger into the flesh. Injecting venom."

"These ants stung the man. They didn't just bite his skin."

"They definitely stung him. And the venom of these weird little monsters is as bad as the harvester ants'. It's almost the same venom: amino acids, peptides, polysaccharides. Plus the toxic, allergenic proteins *and* the alkaloids that both poison the victim and send up a chemical signal to the rest of the nearby ants."

"So, somehow, harvester ants made their way to New York State, to a remote cabin by an even more remote lake, and—"

Ez laughs: an unhinged, wild sound. "No, you don't get it, Stander. It looks like a leaf-cutter ant and has the venom of a Maricopa harvester. This is what I'm saying: no ant like that exists."

"Guess you got your wish?" Hannah says. The smile across her face is not meant to demonstrate happiness, but rather to temper the shock of the absurd. "Maybe you can name it after yourself."

"It's a new species, all right. But not one that appears in nature."

"I don't follow you."

"This ant isn't natural. This ant was *engineered*."

5

The sun isn't up yet and Hannah is pacing the hallway outside Ez Choi's office in the faculty science building. Her boots echo on the cheap tile. Her phone is pressed tight to her ear—it's only 5:30 A.M. here in Tucson, but it's already 8:30 back on the East Coast.

"Pretend I'm dumb," Hollis is saying. "In fact, don't pretend, because when it comes to this sort of thing, I'm pretty goddamn stupid. You are telling me that our victim was killed by ants? And that these ants were made—genetically engineered, in fact—by persons unknown?"

"I think so."

Silence on the other end. It goes on long enough that she's about to continue, but then Hollis makes a sound: a long, nasal sigh. "God damn it."

"Yeah."

"My gut had it right."

"I'm sorry?"

"Bringing you into this. I knew things didn't add up. I checked my gut and my gut told me to find you in my contact list. When the going gets weird, the weird needs Hannah Stander."

This sticks Hannah with a swirl of complicated feelings. On the one hand, it's good to be wanted. On the other hand, is that what she wants to be? Spooky Mulder? She tells herself: *This is just part of the gig. It's what you get when they introduce you as an FBI futurist.*

Hollis is saying: "Are you listening to me? Did I lose you?"

"Sorry, I think I dropped the signal there for a second," she lies. "What were you saying?"

"I asked how your bug friend knew the ants are a GMO."

"She said she found genes—indicator genes, marker genes. Labs use them in genetic engineering to determine if a modification in a plant or animal was successful. If they're still present after breeding, then that gene mod is viable."

"So. The next question: Who did this?"

"I don't know. I don't know how we'd even find out. The ants got there somehow. This was purposeful. Are we sure they're what killed him?"

"Blood tests suggest our victim died of shock—though whether from anaphylaxis or having his skin bitten off by tiny insects, I don't know."

"It's officially a crime scene, then."

"Looks like murder."

Murder by genetically modified organism, she thinks. The future really is a door. And it looks like ruination is winning.

* * *

Ez comes back with breakfast tacos—chorizo, egg, cheese. She sits at her desk, hunched over like a starving person, while Hannah picks at hers.

Hannah's too wound up to eat. Her mind races with a grim, disturbed excitement. She expected that any GMO angle in future crimes would be somewhat obvious: a murder over a seed patent, or someone modifying a bacterium to create a rampant superbug—some new strain of tuberculosis or cholera.

This, though? Ants? Insects?

It's like Ez is reading her mind. Around a mouthful of breakfast taco she says, "You know, this shit is unprecedented."

"I was just thinking about that."

"That's a good thing."

Hannah arches an eyebrow. "How so?"

A hard swallow and Ez explains: "This isn't the work of one

person. It's not like some loony white guy who can go pick up an AK-47 at a gun show, or some foreign terrorist who cooks up an amateur bomb so he can duct tape it to his body and run up alongside a city bus. This takes resources. This takes *infrastructure.* Modifying organisms is a game of inches—you tweak little things here and there. But those ants? They're a huge leap forward. Like I said, *unprecedented.* There's hardly anybody out there with the money and the talent to do this. Your range of suspects will be a lot smaller than you think."

It hits Hannah then: "Companies patent their creations, right?"

"Yeah." Ez looks up at the ceiling, and it's almost like she's watching a lightbulb click on over her own head. She hurriedly wipes her mouth on a napkin. "Holy shit. They do. That might be the key. Compare the DNA sequence and the particular marker genes—see if anybody else is using them."

"Like a stamp."

Ez grins. "Like a *signature.*"

* * *

The university lab is makeshift: one wall is a bookshelf, except on it are wooden frames instead of books. Hannah pulls a few out while Ez works on her computer. Under the glass of each are dead bugs. Butterflies. Scarabs. Something called *dermestids,* which are a kind of beetle.

Next to the shelf is another set of shelves, these ones lined with terrariums. Hannah sees a caterpillar in one, crawling up a leaning stick. From the back corner of the same cage dangles a cocoon—or is it a chrysalis?

Her eyes glide over each terrarium: she sees huge cockroaches in one, and crawling beetles and worms in another. As she moves downward, Ez calls over: "The bottom two shelves are all spiders, by the way. If you're squeamish."

Spiders have never really bothered Hannah. But these spiders are a step above. Tarantulas, mostly. Some of them are fuzzy—some of them are so fuzzy the description has to be upgraded to *downright hairy.*

Ez says: "I can take one out if you wanna play with it. We have a Chilean rose tarantula in there named Delilah. Her little legs on your hand feel like the tickle of Q-tips."

Hannah laughs. "No, I think I'm good." She sees one terrarium with what looks like a very real human skull inside—and, she thinks at first, no spider. But then she peers into the skull and sees the gangly, bristling limbs of something hiding in the eye socket. Wisps of white, diaphanous web drift from the holes like the ratty curtains in a gothic house. Webs surround the skull, too, stretched across the floor of the terrarium—barely seen, each as thin as a whisper.

One of the legs recoils as Hannah gets close to the glass.

"I can't let *her* out," Ez says. "That's OBT."

"OBT?"

"Orange Bitey Thing. Okay, actually it's the orange baboon tarantula. *Pterinochilus murinus.* One bite from that grumpy bitch will put you in the hospital. And she doesn't warn you before she attacks. If I wanna move her from one terrarium to another, I gotta use a special suit. Hip waders and gloves and a mask. *Just* in case."

"Wow."

Ez snaps her fingers and gestures over her shoulder. "Go look across the room there."

Hannah does. Parallel to Ez's desk, stands a metal rack full of plastic Tupperware-style dish bins that slot into tracks, each open bin hanging above the next. It hits Hannah that these are probably from the cafeteria: bins, rack, and all. She pulls out one of the bins like a drawer—and almost screams.

Ants. Little ants like black pinpricks. Swarming over a couple of dead crickets and little ampules of goop that looks not unlike pink Silly Putty. Inside is also something that looks like a beaker sealed up with cotton balls at the top. At the corners of each bin are smeary, dark-stained piles. Scattered about, too, are these round black discs—like hockey pucks with holes in the side.

Suddenly Ez is hovering near her. "You found Antlandia!" she says.

Hannah swallows. Feels the ants crawling on her even though they aren't. "I don't get it."

"Don't get what?"

"Are all these bins full of ants?"

"Cool, huh? Each is a different kind of ant. Argentine. Odorous. Carpenter. These are the elegantly named 'little black ants,' aka *Monomorium minimum*."

"How are they not swarming all over the lab?"

"Fluon. Liquid Teflon. Spray the edges of each bin and they can't get past. Occasionally one or two sneak out, but for the most part it contains entire colonies. And by the way, these black discs? Formicariums full of colonies and queens." Ez taps the top of one of the hockey pucks. Ants suddenly stream out, carrying what look like little white eggs.

"What's the dirty stuff in the corners?"

"Midden piles. Ants are tidy little fuckers. They clean themselves religiously—so perfectly, in fact, that nanotech designers are trying to figure out how to mimic their cleaning habits to keep microscopic devices clean. The ants take out all the trash and dirt—oh, and their colony mates' corpses—and put them in what are essentially little anty landfills."

"Is that why those ants were cutting skin and carrying it away?"

"Doubt it. Probably a food source. But hey, anything's possible in the wild, wacky world of inventing entirely new animals."

While Ez goes back to work, Hannah pops open her laptop and researches who in the world—publicly, at least—is attempting to genetically modify insects or other invertebrates.

Globally, only a few meaningful players emerge. Most companies are understandably focused on modifying crop plants: corn, wheat, and soy in particular. Agriculture is big business. It's good money and, when the patents run out and the modified seeds go global, it has the potential to be good for the rest of the world. (Hannah knows it also has the potential to harm the rest of the world.)

Whatever the case, those doing work above the cellular or plant level are few and far between. She's peripherally aware of some of these players. Rumors have long suggested Monsanto is working on genetically modifying honeybees to protect them from colony collapse disorder, though the company has just as long denied it. Empyrean AgroScience, GmbH, a German company, has begun initial steps in modifying an insect known as the European corn borer, a moth whose caterpillars destroy cornstalks by boring tunnels through them. The company's goal is to create a self-destroying insect: the first generation breeds aggressively with borers in the wild and passes along a lethal gene that wipes them out.

Other companies like Agra-Sci, Johnston Hybrid, and Mar-Gene, Inc., are like Monsanto: rumored to be working on genetically modified honeybees, but they deny, deny, deny.

Scientists at various universities have modified insects and even fish and mice—usually only for a single nonreproducible generation and frequently only to make them glow fluorescent. (Hannah imagines a bunch of mice escaping their confines, glowing blue or green from jellyfish genes. How long would it be before the average homeowner found a bioluminescent mouse scurrying across the bedroom floor—or a whole colony of rats glowing green inside a city Dumpster?)

But do such laboratories have the resources to pull off creating a new species? That takes money. And time. It takes *systems.*

And it's not like murderers would be making their work public.

Unless they are.

It strikes her: the Cartagena Protocol on Biosafety.

* * *

It takes some finagling on a late-night conference call to get what they need. Ez and Hannah sit in the university lab (with Ez's teaching assistant, a peppy preppie named Hank), with Hollis on the other end on speakerphone.

"I don't know anything about any of this," Hollis says. One of his favorite refrains. He likes to reassert how he's old school and doesn't know a damn thing about hackers or genetics or any of this crazy stuff. Hannah thinks it's an act. "But looks like there's a database of GMO organisms. A product of the Cartagena biosafety protocol."

"But the United States never ratified that," Ez says.

Hannah answers this one: "And yet, a lot of American companies want to do business overseas. Which means they have to be on the books."

"And in the database," Hollis says.

Ez asks, "You can get me access?"

"Already did. Check your e-mail, Ms. Choi."

"I think you mean *Doctor* Choi," Ez says, giving Hannah a wink before wheeling around to open her e-mail.

"Apologies, Dr. Choi, for any injury I have caused."

"Relax, *Agent* Copper. I'm just fucking with you. Oh. Here's the e-mail." She gives a double thumbs-up. "If there's something to find in here, then I will jolly well fucking find it."

6

Hannah's hands are slick with blood.

Wind whips the meadow grass around her feet. The knife in her right hand—a folding gut-hook knife, a Schrade—is greasy with red.

A body lies before her. Human feet—one dirty brown shoe knocked off, a corpse-black toe poking through a hole in the fraying sock beneath. But she spies white fur, too. White fur spattered with red.

The air is thick with the smell of animal waste. The sound of a fly wing hums near her ear.

Dad stands nearby, the breeze lifting his wisps of white hair like the seeds blowing off a dying dandelion. He's got a rifle in his hand. A .30-30 lever-action. Held across his chest, across his heart, like a gate closing a road. "What did you do?" he hisses.

She gasps as hands shake her awake. It takes her a second to get her bearings—the grass is gone, no carcass at her feet. Instead the light is garish, bright: the harsh fluorescence of the university lab. A face roving into view: Ez. She wears a look of concern.

"You okay?" she asks.

Hannah tries to answer, but her words are sticky, tacky, incomplete. She swallows and gets some saliva to her tongue and tries again: "Fine."

"You passed out hard."

"Sorry."

"You still sleep with your eyes open sometimes, I see."

She blinks. It's like blinking past sand. Hannah pats her pocket, but she didn't bring her wetting eye drops with her. She should have, given how dry the air is here. "Sorry. It's not often, just . . . sometimes."

"I found something."

Hannah stands. "Show me."

On the screen is a database. It's clumsily designed: utilitarian and ugly. Ez says, "The key is, like we said, those marker genes. They're unique."

"A signature."

"A fucking *signature*. Nobody else uses these markers except—"

She hits a key.

Nothing happens.

Ez mutters something under her breath. "I swear, if this thing crashes on me again . . . It's amazing how the scientific community somehow maintains such outmoded, antediluvian technology to keep themselves afloat—oh!"

The database pulls up one entry: Arca Labs.

"Arca?" Hannah asks. "Is that—"

"One of Einar Geirsson's many boo-jillion-dollar companies? It is."

Hannah remembers. "The mosquitoes. That was them."

"*Aedes aegypti*."

"Same gene markers?"

"The very same."

"Shit."

7

Einar Geirsson—a billionaire contemporary of Elon Musk and Steve Jobs (maybe even *Iron Man*'s Tony Stark)—has houses all around the world, but his chief residence is in Hawaii, on the island of Kauai. Arca, one of his many companies, sits on a private island—the Kolohe Atoll—west of Kauai, a couple of hundred miles past Niihau.

Hannah can't just drive over and knock on his door.

Days pass. Ez continues studying the ants. Hollis works to open lines of communication with Einar and Arca. Hannah, for her part, feels adrift. She spends her nights reading about Einar Geirsson and his companies. She also spends time reading about ants, an unpleasant subject that leads to uncomfortable dreams. Hard not to wake up in the middle of the night with the feeling of them all over her, skittering over every inch of her skin.

She tells Hollis she should go home. But Hollis says she should stay there. In case Ez has anything. And a flight to Hawaii from Arizona would be easy.

Does she even *want* to go home? She's been avoiding it for so long . . .

Hannah spends her mornings hiking Sabino Canyon—she tries to outrace the heat, though she never does. The third morning, she's running the overlook above Sabino Creek. Down below, the cottonwoods are at the start of their bloom: clusters of fat red flowers dangling down, waggling in the breeze like chastising fingers. *Tsk, tsk, tsk.*

And then, down there in the creek, walking around: a whitetail

deer. A doe with her belly hanging low. Hannah stops. Watches for a while as the deer stoops and drinks, tail flicking. A few flies buzzing around her hind end. Ripples radiating out from around her legs.

Hannah's right arm tightens a little. Her trigger finger twitches.

An absurd muscle memory—even back then, even when she was a child, she wouldn't have shot a pregnant doe. Her mother would have stripped her hide for that. But still, seeing an animal like this, it's like the ghost of a memory rises up and she hears her mother's voice: *Deer that size would fill the freezer for winter.*

Suddenly, a buzzing at her hip followed by a quick chirping ring. Her phone. Hannah's surprised she gets a signal out here, but she grabs it and answers it and by the time she looks back up the doe is bolting—two splashes and an arcing jump before the deer ducks down through the underbrush and is gone.

It's Copper. "They're stonewalling. Asking for a warrant. Their representative—some cocky prick someone-or-other named Espinosa—says they're a private corporation, they've done nothing wrong, and until there's a formal connection . . ." He sighs.

Above Hannah's head, a pair of vultures orbit each other as if bound by a single axis. "I feel like I'm in a holding pattern."

"Because you are in a holding pattern. We all are."

"Maybe you want to send someone else to deal with this."

"So far, we're not sending anybody." A pause, like he's considering his next words. "Hannah, I understand you had plans to go home, but this kind of thing? It's why I need you. It's why we pay you. Unless you want us to pay somebody else."

She knows the Bureau has other people like her on its payroll. Futurists aren't common, but they aren't rare anymore, either. The FBI also has a stable of hackers, philosophers, authors, other professional miscreants, and future-facing weirdos. If they can't get her, her stock sinks. If she bails on this, she bails on future consults.

"It's fine. I'm in." Her own words sound stiff and angry because, she realizes, she feels stiff and angry. It's not Copper's fault. He

needs what he needs. She is a tool and he needs her to do a job, end of story. She decides to switch tacks. "You find anything else about the body? You didn't just call me to deliver this non-update, right?"

"Oh, there's more. First up: We found something in the lake. A container."

"What kind of container?"

"We don't know, exactly. It's not typical for anything. It's a lab container used for shipping. Picked it up on the lake floor not far from the dock. Weighted down with rocks."

"Send me a photo. You get an identity on the body?"

"No. We still don't have a national database of dental records or DNA, and with no idea of who he was in the first place, we don't have anywhere to start. We're having someone work on a potential facial reconstruction. The nose is a problem, since it was mostly gone, but the reconstruction'll give us *something* to feed to the recognition software."

"Fingerprints?"

"I might remind you he seems to be missing those, since an unholy colony of demon ants nibbled them off."

"You might still be able to find them. Ez found bite-and-stinger marks on a few individual swatches of skin. Go through the skin samples. One by one. See if you can rescue a fingerprint."

"That's grisly. I like it. I'll get the lab geeks on the job."

A rustle down below. Hannah leans over the short stone wall framing this part of the overlook. A rangy coyote slips out of the brush, loping along. It looks up and sees her. It watches her watching it. A moment of recognition between them, then the coyote moves on.

"What else did you find?"

"Found more boot prints leading down to the lake. The print is one size down from the victim's Lowas. The gait is off-kilter, too. Sometimes it leans in on the outside of the foot. Sometimes has a tilt inward."

"Huh. Okay." *Same boot, but not on the victim's feet?* It's an answer that only conjures more questions. "Something in the gait, then. Ill-fitting shoes. Or a physical disability, maybe."

"We'll keep on it. Just wanted you to have the update. Feels like not much, but we're getting closer. And we'll get you closer, too. Arca will open up to us somehow. Even if we have to pick up a battering ram to make them do it."

But she doesn't want a battering ram. She wants a scalpel. "I'll talk to you later, Agent Copper. I'll call you if I think of anything. And send me a photo of that container!" She hangs up her phone, waits for the e-mail from Copper, but her signal isn't robust enough to download any image. Above her head, the vultures are gone. A plane draws contrails across the sky like a pair of chalk lines.

* * *

Back at the hotel she pulls up the e-mail. Sees not one photo of the container but several. Some of the photos are washed out, but they serve her purposes: The container is a metal box. Lined with rubber and what looks like Styrofoam. Inside the container are chambers separated out by plastic dividers. Hexagonal. Like honeycombs for bees, if the bees were the size of a rat.

That night, she does dinner with Ez at a nearby taco joint, and she shows the entomologist the photos. "Looks like a cryo container," Ez says. "We use them sometimes."

"You do?"

"Yeah. Ours aren't exactly like that—the honeycomb design is different. Ours are cylindrical. This is custom, maybe. But the overall idea is the same. They probably had smaller containers inside those chambers. Around the cylinders you pack in liquid nitrogen. The dry vapor keeps everything chill; then when you open it—boom, thaw. And the buggies warm up."

"Like they're hibernating?"

"Almost. More like suspended animation. Easy enough with ants or other buglets. Bigger animals are still a challenge, though I'm pretty sure someone figured out how to cryo-freeze a pig and revive it." She looks down at her taco and raises a curious eyebrow. "Now I want a pork taco. You into *al pastor*?"

* * *

Hannah's heading back to the hotel—walking, because the evening is cooling down and night is bleeding into the sky and the happy (if idiotic) voices of students from the university carry—when her phone rings.

She answers it. "Hi, Mom."

"You haven't called."

"I know. I'm sorry. It's this case."

"This case. That speaking engagement. An appointment. A conference. We've stopped expecting that you'll make any time for us. For your father."

"Hey, can I talk to him?"

A hesitation. "He's resting."

"Is he?" That would be strange. He usually stays up watching all the late-night shows. "Is it the medication? Oh, right, it can't be." A sudden knife-stick of guilt in her gut. That was a petty barb and she knows it.

"He's not doing well enough for a call," Mom says. Her words are rushed. Hannah knows she's lying.

"I'll try tomorrow," Hannah says.

"If you have time, dear."

Hannah sits back in her hotel room, chewing a fingernail and stewing. She bites the nail down to the quick and tastes blood. The panic hits her like a wave she wasn't facing: *Antibiotics are becoming useless. Superbugs are rampant. Even a small infection can end your life. You're bleeding and it could become infected and just because you had to chew your stupid fingernail you could lose the finger or maybe the hand or maybe your life and then—and then!—what happens to the world when antibiotics fail us all? Everything from heart operations to getting a tattoo will go from being rote explorations of the human body to perilous trips like the first pioneers crossing the badlands . . . Once antibiotics go, everything goes. Maybe that won't be the first domino to fall. Maybe it'll be the one where we lose all the honeybees, or maybe it'll be when we lose all the ice caps, or, or, or—*

She's sweating even in the conditioned air of her hotel room. Her chest tightens. Her arms feel loose, rubbery. Her eyes are watering. Her jaw is so tight she could crush a Brazil nut between her back teeth. *I'm having a heart attack.*

No. She's having a panic attack.

She lies back. Tries to breathe. In through her nose, out through her mouth. Her fingernails are digging into her palms and it takes truly heroic effort to relax her hands enough that her fingers straighten. She repeats her mantra in her head:

The future is a door.

The future is a door.

The future is a door.

She pictures the door: A black rectangle at the end of a white hallway. A silver doorknob. Bright light shining in around the edges.

The door is unknowable. It is perfect in its uncertainty. It isn't an answer. It remains a question. The world's destiny is not set. Her life is not ending.

The future is a door.

Hannah looks up. Night has settled over Tucson.

She clears her mind and looks out her window for a while. In another hotel room, a woman unpacks a suitcase with meticulous attention. Lifting up shirts and skirts and dresses, placing them on hangers, picking off bits of lint with pinching fingers. It's calming to watch someone else go about her life. Focusing so much on little things.

The suitcase looks fancy. Not black like other suitcases, but patterned. Probably monogrammed. Maybe even custom-made—

Something nibbles at the back of her mind like a dog biting at an itch.

Custom suitcase. Container. Ez said the container was like the ones they use, but not the ones they use. She said it could be custom.

She texts Ez:

Hannah: You said the container could be custom?

Ez: weirdest way to ask for a booty call ever, H

Hannah: Do you think Arca has proprietary cases?

Ez: would make sense yah

Hannah: How do I get Einar Geirsson's email address?

Ez: hes my boyfriend so hold on let me just grab it from my contacts list

Ez: einargeirsson@hot-icelandic-billionaire.com

Hannah: Ha ha.

Ez: i met him on tinder LOL #blessed

Hannah: So what you're saying is, I have no way of getting his personal address.

Ez: gaaahd hannah jeez let me Google that for you

Ez: btw my autocorrect capitalized Google but not hannah but don't feel bad because corporations are people now and people are basically just bugs

Ez: oh holy shit isn't this your lucky day

Hannah: What is it?

Ez: einargeirsson@einargeirsson.com

Hannah: Ha ha again. I'll see if I can find a company address for Arca.

Ez: hannah i'm not fukkin kidding that is his email address

Ez: he has it right on his goddamn website which by the way looks like the website youd find for a model

Ez: smoldering sexy pics of einar in fancy suits

Hannah: That's really his email?

Ez: so his website says though i gotta warn you it probably gets read by some assistant and by assistant i mean some well-paid cat

Ez: a cat who probably just says FUCK THIS and bats it into the mouth of a shredder with an inconsiderate paw

Ez: a beautiful Icelandic cat

Hannah: You're weird.

Ez: NO YOU ARE WEIRD

Hannah: I guess we're both weird. You rock. Love you. Talk to you tomorrow.

Ez: don't forget to tell my boyfriend i miss him

Hannah sits down, cracks her knuckles, and composes an e-mail.

Mr. Geirsson:

My name is Hannah Stander. I serve as a consultant for the Federal Bureau of Investigation and we have been trying to contact you regarding a recent death. A man died, killed by what appears to be anaphylaxis as the result of multiple ant stings.

Tests reveal these ants to be genetically modified. They possess indicator genes that match those of your modified aegypti mosquitoes. We believe they came in this container (see attached photo). We further suspect this container is unique to your company. Custom made.

I would like to visit Arca at your earliest convenience. The alternative solution is for actual agents of the Bureau to make that visit instead. Once that happens—meaning, they procure a warrant—this becomes a far more serious investigation.

I hope you will read this and take it seriously. I certainly do.

Thank you for your time and consideration.

(I'm also attaching the phone number and e-mail address of the agent in charge of this investigation, Hollis Copper.)

Regards,

Hannah Stander

She hesitates. It's a fool's errand, flinging an e-mail like this off into the ether. But the hell with it.

Hannah hits Send.

* * *

Hannah tosses and turns.

She hears a *tink-tink-tink*. Above her somewhere in the dark.

She closes her eyes but tilts her head up to listen. Again: *tink-tink-tink*. A little pitter-patter.

Then, much closer: a *tap*. Like the sound of a drop of water hitting the pillow next to her.

Hannah groans, fumbles for the bedside lamp. There must be a leak from the floor above. She gets the switch and ocher-yellow light fills the room. Everything is washed out as her eyes adjust.

She squints at the pillow.

A dark shape is there.

An ant.

She thinks: *This is both creepy and ironic*, an ant here in the room at the same time she's investigating a murder involving ants. But then she looks closer. Its face is familiar. The corrupted heart shape. The demonic barbs at the top of its head. Serrated mandibles open and closing. Antennae tickling the air. It's one of them.

Another sound. Above her once more. *Tink-tink-tink.*

Hannah looks up. There's an air-conditioning vent. A small black speck is crawling out of it. Another ant.

Another two come out. Then another four. Then ants are pouring from the slots. They spill out as Hannah scrambles off the bed, slipping and slamming backward, her shoulder cracking hard into the wall—

I wrote that e-mail.

I shouldn't have written it.

Now they're coming to kill me.

The ants sweep over the edge of the bed, hungry jaws working, antennae seeking the air—*seeking her.* She screams as they spill toward her. Her legs kick out and she propels herself toward the far wall, pointing herself at the doorway out—but there, something underneath her feet. She dances away from it.

Black water spills out from under the door.

No. Not water.

A spreading pool of insects. Black and shiny. She feels them on her now, crawling up her bare feet, skittering up her calves and her thighs—

A pinch of skin, a sharp stick like from a thumbtack—

And she wakes in her bed, screaming, the sheets tangled around her. She's slick with a patina of sweat. Hannah paws at her arms, her legs. Nothing. She quickly flips on the lamp, looking around—

Nothing.

No ants.

Just a dream.

"Stupid brain," she says, almost laughing, almost crying.

8

Up before dawn, hounded by the dream from only hours before, Hannah comes out of the shower, serpents of steam released when she opens the door.

Her phone is lit up with a new text message.

> **Hollis:** Whatever you did, you did it. Aloha, Ms. Stander. Enjoy Hawaii.

PART II

ANT COLONY OPTIMIZATION

ant colony optimization (n)
1. a metaheuristic algorithm that utilizes the swarm intelligence behavior of simulated "artificial ants" to search out optimal paths or outcomes for problems.

9

Sitting alone on a private jet feels apocalyptic. Like Hannah is the last person in the world. The plane has pilots, of course, but it is only her back here among the beige leather seats, the small tables, the little kitchen.

Outside the window, wisps of cloud whip past. Down below she sees where the crooked line of North American land meets the deep cerulean of the Pacific. The crinkle-cut margins of the shoreline look not unlike the way the ants scissored through the victim's skin.

Hannah grabs a wrapped sandwich and a Boylan cream soda from the kitchen, then heads back to her seat. The sandwich is labeled WESTPHALIAN HAM, GRUYÈRE, CONCORD GRAPES, MICRO-WATERCRESS, STONE-GROUND MUSTARD.

While she eats, she researches Arca and its founder and CEO, Einar Geirsson. The plane has Wi-Fi, and she has a fairly good feeling that whatever she looks up, Arca will know. But her goal here isn't occulted, and so she figures: *Let them look.*

She pulls up Einar on her MacBook. This isn't the first time she's seen a photo of him, but she's never really taken a good look. He has been a fixture of innovation for the last six, maybe seven years, but most of what ends up online is the results of his efforts, and not him. He tends to avoid the spotlight and media attention.

So it's surprising that his website looks, as Ez pointed out, a lot like a portfolio for a model: so many pictures of Einar, always with the wind-tousled swoop of his sand-blond hair, the boyish cheeks, the Puckish grin. Those eyes: not quite blue, not quite gray. Still as the frozen water of a deep lake in winter.

Images of Einar surfing, diving, cooking, playing acoustic guitar. Images of him helping scrub black goop off an oil-sodden pelican, walking the line at one of his manufacturing facilities, peering soulfully at a mosquito trapped in amber.

It all feels so artificial, so manufactured—and yet, could he be sincere? His website calls him an *altruistic capitalist*. He's quoted as saying, "Changing the world for the better is more important than changing my financial fortunes. But I believe that doing the right thing is also a very good way to get rich."

So far he hasn't been wrong. He first filled his coffers with the profits from a game he designed with ten other people, his first and only release. Dragonsdoor: a massively multiplayer open world. Changeable and buildable. Hannah doesn't know much about it, but she knows that if you walk into any Walmart or Target you can buy the game, toys, T-shirts, beach towels, snack foods. Einar no longer owns the rights—he sold the game and the company he formed to produce it years ago. But it's still a machine.

Since then, he's used the billions of dollars he made on it to jump-start a series of projects: desalination plants, solar batteries, wind energy, nanotechnology, and, of course, plant and animal genetics. Not to mention smaller endeavors: a company devoted to sustainable, free-trade coffee; a micropress publishing company meant to release free scientific data and plans unburdened by copyright or patent; a tiny South African software company that makes a free meditation app for every phone, tablet, and computer platform. He's recently begun dropping hints that he has a self-driving car in production. (This is tied to the secret factory he is rumored to have built in Wyoming.)

He believes that innovation in technology and science will save the world. According to him, nanotech will compensate for antibiotic immunity. Desalination will solve the fact that global groundwater has been on the decline for decades. Wind and solar—installed aggressively and made attractive to buyers—will fix the screwed-up climate before the damage is irreversible.

The future, it occurs to Hannah, does not frighten him the way it frightens her. That worries her. Someone with his power and experience shouldn't have such raging optimism—and deception by powerful men is a danger as persistent as global warming, famine, or disease.

And yet the work he's doing is unparalleled. His companies are literally changing the world. Nobody else invests in these future-forward technologies like he does. Most Fortune 500 companies run on business models reliant on maintaining the status quo. But Geirsson never flinches in the face of global troubles.

And yet, can you really trust someone with that kind of money? With that kind of *power*? It appears as though Einar Geirsson represents evolution. But what if he's secretly betting on ruination?

* * *

They land at a small airstrip on the south shore of Kauai. As soon as Hannah steps off the plane, a hard wind lashes her in the face. The airfield is dark, but saturated with a red, rust-like dust as far as the eye can see. In the distance, a few palm trees sticking up past bent guardrails give the only sign that they're on a Hawaiian island and not Mars. That and the chickens: a scattering of hens and roosters mill about.

Nearby on the tarmac sits a black Lincoln Town Car, the tires and bottom of the car airbrushed with red dust. The driver—an older man with chubby cheeks and the cast of a native Hawaiian—shows Hannah a big set of bright white teeth and waves her on. She looks behind her, back at the private jet: Nobody sends her off. The pilots remain in the cockpit. She gets in the car.

"It's a short drive," the driver says, looking back at her over the seat. Still that beaming smile. Like this is the best job in the world. Maybe it is. Einar is known for paying his employees well. He's *also* known for working them to the bone: he's notoriously judgmental of employees who want to take time off for the birth of a child or the death of a parent. A quote from Einar that Hannah read on the airplane: "We're here to change the world, *not participate in its tedium*."

"Thanks for driving me," Hannah says.

"My name's Pono," the driver says. He holds the wheel with one hand and puts his other hand over his shoulder so she can shake it. "You're lucky. A guest of Mr. Geirsson. He lives here, you know."

"I know. Up north?"

"North Shore. Not far from the Kilauea Lighthouse. It's beautiful up there. He's got horses. Garages for these fancy old cars. Little movie theater. Plus a little airfield and a helipad." She wonders suddenly why she didn't fly in there. Pono seems to sense her hesitation and adds, "He's very private. Very private. But it's beautiful. Really. I haven't been up that way in a while, but . . . beautiful, just beautiful. He's even got these toilets imported from Japan. They do everything." A throaty chuckle in the deep of Pono's chest. "I'm surprised they don't give you a handj—" He clears his throat. "Ma'am, I am sorry. That was not appropriate. That's not appropriate language for a driver. I won't—I shouldn't—please don't tell anybody I said that."

She laughs. It's been a long flight, but the sun is warm, and Martian landscape or no, she's in Hawaii. "It's fine, Pono. You live around here?"

"No, I live in Lihue." He still seems embarrassed or worried. "How about you? Where are you coming from?"

"The mainland. Bethesda."

"Oh, good, good." He turns around like he wants to say something. Then he faces forward. Then he turns around again. "Just a tip? We don't like it when you call it the 'mainland.'"

"Oh. Now it's my turn to apologize."

"It's no big deal. It's just—we're *kama'aina* here. This *is* our mainland, you know? It's where we're from."

"So, what do you call it? The States?"

He clucks his tongue. "See, that's a whole other problem because Hawaii is a state, you know? So it sounds dismissive to call it that. Like we're somehow not really officially a state."

“You don’t want to be a part of the country, but you don’t want to be told you’re not a part of the country?”

Pono snaps his fingers. “Bingo! You got it.” Another low chuckle. “We Hawaiians are hard to please, huh?”

“Being hard to please just means you know what you want, and that’s a good thing.” Those words belong to her father, and to hear them coming out of her mouth churns a sudden high tide of guilt in the well of Hannah’s gut. She misses her father, suddenly. Grief to join the guilt, hand in hand, driving off the cliff like Thelma and Louise.

Outside, the car passes guardrails painted with the unearthly umber dust. Signs of the Hawaii she imagines pop up here and there—more palm trees, purple bougainvillea on the roadside, a blue pickup truck bounding along in front of them loaded down with surfboards and scuba gear. More chickens, too, scratch and peck about.

“What’s with all the chickens?” she asks.

“Ah. Yeah, yeah, those are the Iniki chickens. Hurricane Iniki came in and wiped out a buncha chicken cages in ’92, set a lot of birds free. They went feral and kept breeding. Invasive species, they say.” He shrugs. “At least they eat the centipedes!” Then Pono says, “Here we go,” and turns the Town Car down a little dirt road, Lokokai, that runs parallel to the rocky shore. Pono gets out.

At the end of the road sits a small condo building and a gravel lot. “Tomorrow,” Pono says, grunting as he bends over to pull her carry-on out of the trunk, “I’ll pick you up. Bright and early. *Ka puka ’ana o ka lā*. Sun comes up, I get you to the boat—”

“Boat? I’m going by boat?” She feels her middle clench up. She doesn’t like boats. “I thought—a plane or helicopter . . .”

“No, no.” He waggles his finger like a metronome. “Where you go, only Mr. Geirsson goes by helicopter because he has a permit and his own pilot.” Of course he does. “Kolohe is a protected atoll. Only permitted so many flights in and out per month. So, boat ride.”

“I don’t like boats.”

He laughs and shrugs. “I’m sorry. There’s food in the fridge. I’ll see you tomorrow morning. Sunrise!”

“Sunrise it is.”

He drives away, leaving clouds of dust trailing behind him. Hannah is alone.

* * *

Sunrise. Bleeding across the horizon like a slit throat. Pono picks her up, drives her to a nearby marina.

Groggy, she heads down past men and women hauling fish off a boat, onto the dock and into coolers full of misting ice. At the end, a man in a pink aloha shirt and loose-fitting black pants stands straight as an arrow shot into the ground. Chin up, eyes down, dark features. On the boat, another man—older, white mustache—stows an extra life jacket. The captain, she guesses. He gives her a smile and a nod.

The other one, the man in the pink shirt, takes off his sunglasses and offers a hand. “Ramon Espinosa,” he says. “Ray. You must be Agent Stander.”

Hannah shakes his hand. He gives hers a good squeeze. Her knuckles grind together like they’re in a millstone. “Not an agent,” she says. “Just a consultant.”

A wry smile. “Right. Of course. This is our ride. “Behind him, a luxury catamaran. Blue and orange. Name across it: *The Damselfish*. “That’s the captain up there. Captain Dan Sullivan.”

“Ms. Stander,” the captain says, and ducks belowdecks.

“You ready?” Ramon—Ray—asks.

“I am.”

“Good.” He gives her one last look like he’s sizing her up. “I assume you can get your own bag. Third-wave feminism and all that.” A stiff smile, and he precedes her up the ramp and onto the boat.

This should be fun, she thinks.

* * *

Hannah almost drowned when she was a little girl. Her mother insisted she learn to swim, and Hannah did not want to. The water terrified her. It seemed endless and unknowable. It contained *multitudes.*

But her mother had other ideas, and one day threw Hannah into the reservoir. The dark water felt like it was trying to swallow her up. Hannah struggled. She felt hands reaching for her (fish, probably, or just tangles of weeds or even old fishing line), and she took in mouthfuls of water. Her mother said she didn't almost drown, but to a little girl it sure felt like almost drowning. Eventually she learned to swim, when she got older, but not eagerly and not easily, and even now that old fear of the water rises inside her like a surfacing beast.

The ocean beneath the boat unsettles her. She imagines what lurks down there. The sea is a poorly understood ecosystem. Every year someone pulls up some creature that nobody ever knew existed—hellish jellyfish, parasitic nematodes, alien crustaceans, pyrosomes. She once saw a documentary about the Humboldt squid—a massive thing, more than six feet long, aggressive enough to attack and maul an unsuspecting diver with tentacles lined with razored suckers.

But her fear, she knows, is part of the problem. Man knows next to nothing about the ocean. And because of that, he doesn't respect it, and he is ruining it with overfishing, pollution, global warming, toxic algal blooms.

And so, as Hannah sits alone on the deck of *The Damselfish,* she fears both what the ocean is (a hungry mouth) and what it will become (a dead place). Even though the day is beautiful and the ocean is a blue like she's never seen, Hannah feels herself teetering on the edge of full-blown panic. To the right of the boat—is that starboard? she thinks so—they reach the end of the island of Kauai. There stand the swoops of the jagged peaks and cliffs of the Kokee Mountains; Hannah tries to concentrate on them instead of on whatever is going on inside her head. The shape of them calls to mind the teeth in a deer skull grown over with moss—nature reclaiming a creature in death. *Death.* That puts her right back to it. Obsessing over the future. Over the end of all people and all things.

Instead, she just closes her eyes.

It's a long, choppy ride. Several hours in, her head starts to feel disconnected from her stomach. And closing her eyes isn't helping.

When she opens them again, she sees Ray standing over her. "Getting seasick? I can get you a bucket. Anything for a guest of Einar's."

She frowns. "It's not seasickness." But she doesn't owe him an explanation.

"Well, whatever existential dread you're suffering right now, you don't have to sit out here. You can go belowdecks. There's a bar. Some salads, sandwiches, wine, whatever. It's nice. You should check it out."

"I'll stay up here." She's not sure why. Is she paralyzed by fear? Or is she trying to face down that fear? She tells herself the latter. "What's the agenda? When I get to the island."

"Well. We'll get you settled in. Get a meal. Give you the tour. Then it's on you. Poke around. Ask questions. Maybe just leave everyone the fuck alone and go enjoy a little bit of an untouched tropical paradise."

"Okay," she says, not sure how else to respond. "Will Einar be there?"

"Will Einar be . . . ? C'mon, no, of course not. He's one of the busiest guys in the world. He doesn't have time for . . . *this*." Ray stands there, and she feels his impatience and irritation. The man makes these little noises: microsighs, the whisper of his fingertips against each other as he fidgets, a small grunt. Finally he sits next to her. "It's bullshit, you know."

"A whole lot of things are bullshit," she says, seeing in her mind's eye her mother wincing at the vulgarity. "So I need you to be more specific."

"You. This. The reason you're here."

"The murder."

"It's bullshit."

"Murder is never bullshit."

"I just mean—ants? Really. You're saying ants killed this guy and that we were the ones who—"

She keeps staring out over the ocean. "I'm not saying any of those things. We believe ants were at least in part responsible for the man's death. We believe those ants were genetically engineered. And the marker genes present in those ants are the same ones present in your mosquitoes."

"Those mosquitoes have saved lives."

"I'm sure they have."

"If we could bring them to Florida—or even here, Hawaii. Dengue's bad news. They call it breakbone fever for a reason." He scowls. "You get this . . . pain behind your eyes, like someone's got their thumbs back there trying to pop them out of your head like corks. Comes with a fever, headache, chills, sweats. But the hell of it is how your bones hurt. Your arms, your legs. It feels like someone is pulverizing them. Crushing them like big rocks into little gravel."

"You've had it."

"Damn right I have. Doing relief work in Haiti a few years ago. We're trying to do good things. And you're standing in the way."

"I'm not standing in anybody's way. I have a job to do and that job is a fact-finding mission. I'm not an agent, as has been discussed. I'm here just to rule out involvement by Arca—"

"You're the enemy is what you are."

"I'm sorry you feel that way."

He shrugs. "Good luck with your investigation, Ms. Stander." He walks off, whistling. She's about to go after him.

Instead, she pukes over the side.

* * *

Hannah is leaning over the edge of the boat. Breathing in and out. Her brow is wet but her lips are dry. It's then that she sees it. A line above the horizon. A small bump. Seven hours so far on this boat and that's what she gets: a bump.

She looks around. That island is alone. No neighboring islands to be seen.

"The Kolohe Atoll," Dan Sullivan says, startling her. He comes up, arms crossed and chest out like all the water and all the sky is his domain. He's not a big man—average in most ways. But he's got that captain vibe about him. "Kolohe—Hawaiian word. Means 'mischief' or 'mischief-maker.' A trickster."

"That's comforting," she says, her guts plunging down when the boat goes up and slingshotting up when the boat drops back down.

"The legends about the atoll are not too dissimilar from those about the Bermuda Triangle. Boats trying to avoid it crash here. Ships trying to land here can never find it. And sure enough, there are a few wrecks out there. One on the island, too—an old Japanese Zero that went astray, got lost, and crash-landed."

Hannah lifts an eyebrow. "Are we going to crash?"

"I sure hope not!" Captain Dan lets loose with a big belly laugh. "I don't truck with legends and stories. None of that *red sky, no bananas on board, look I see a mermaid* nonsense for me. I'm an old tour captain. I use things like *science* and *my brain* to get through each trip."

"You give me hope for the human race, Captain Dan."

He just laughs as the boat surges closer, cutting through the churn with great big belly flops. "You want a soda? Protein bar?"

"I'm good."

"Just be happy we didn't hit any of the weather."

"Weather?"

"Some coming in over the next few days. Don't worry, we'll get you out of here before it hits."

Soon evening settles in. As if to spite Captain Dan's insistence on ignoring superstition, the sky has an eerie red cast to it. She tries to remember if it's *red sky at night* or *red sky at morning* that sailors caution against—not that it really matters, because a red sky whenever carries its own sinister feel.

The island looms closer, and Hannah starts to get a sense of what it looks like. Flat for the most part, as most atolls are—though she knows this isn't entirely an atoll. It's part coral, but also born in part from a geological shift. The very edges are reef, but the inner ring of the circular island is pushed and bundled like the dough in an uneven loaf of bread: puffing up at the center, but burned thin at the margins. From here she can see the rise in the earth—dark stone and ground riddled with trees and white dots. Birds, she thinks. The white dots are seabirds. Thousands of them.

The boat moves alongside the edge of the ring-shaped island. Here the sea becomes calmer—and Hannah breathes a sigh of relief.

Ray emerges from belowdecks. "There it is. Kolohe."

"You come here often?"

"You hitting on me?" He rolls his eyes. "No, I don't come here often. Couple times a year."

"What is it exactly that you *do,* Mr. Espinosa?"

"Like I said, it's Ray. I'm a liaison."

"With whom do you liaise?"

A cheeky smirk. "With whomever I please." But then his face darkens. "Right now, you're my job, Hannah Stander. To make sure you don't mess things up here."

"I have no intention of ruining what you're doing here."

"I hope that's true. I'm sure our lawyers would be more than happy to eat you up the way you say those ants ate that dead man."

"He was alive when they ate him."

"All the more like lawyers."

Suddenly, Ray is jostled aside as Dan shoves his way in between them. "Oops," the captain says. "Sorry, Mr. Espinosa."

"Dan, don't fuck with me. I'd hate to have to tell Einar."

The captain shrugs. "I'd hate that, too. I'll be sure to apologize to him directly the next time we play poker. Next Wednesday, I believe."

Ray looks suddenly humbled. His nostrils flare in anger, but he looks away.

"We're ready to pull up and dock," Captain Dan says.

10

A narrow dock framed by sea-licked rocks leads to wood decking lifting across the flat beach and up toward the rise of swollen island that rings the center of this not-quite-atoll. As Hannah pulls the wheels of her carry-on over the lip of the catamaran, someone comes down the dock to meet them.

She knows his face from the research materials: Dr. David Hamasaki, a small man with round cheeks lifted by a beaming smile. One thing the photos didn't quite show: he has a mullet. He walks like he's perpetually falling forward, or like maybe the world is forever dragging him from place to place.

"Hi, hi, hi," he says upon reaching them. He grabs Hannah's hand and gives it a warm shake. "I'm Dr. Hamasaki—David, David, you can call me David."

"I'm Hannah Stander. Consultant for the—"

The man waves her off. "I know who you are, no need for that kind of introduction. We don't get many guests out here. Particularly ones with your . . . request." His accent is a little bit New York. He sounds like a Jewish guy from Columbia she dated once.

Before she can respond, Ray steps up next to her. In a droll, disdainful voice, he says, "Hey, *Dave*."

"Fuck you, too, Ray," David says. His eyes tighten, and the smile gets broader, almost a little feral. "You finally gonna pony up or what?" He puts out his right hand and pats it with the back of his left.

"I got your money. Can we get off the dock first?"

"Don't think I'm going to let you forget." Hamasaki turns to

Hannah: "Sorry about that, sorry, sorry. Ray over there is a Miami Dolphins fan. I, on the other hand, know that the Dolphins are a worthless agglomeration of wasted football talent and that the New York Giants are supreme. We had a little bet as to who would finish the season stronger and, well . . ." He starts heading up the dock and across the beach. As they walk, he asks, "Who's your favorite team?"

"I don't really follow sports."

From behind them, Ray says, "Of course she doesn't."

Anger flares in her, but David waves it off. "Ignore Ray. If I said that Ray was a Neanderthal, actual Neanderthals would thaw themselves from glaciers just to make me pay for the insult. Neanderthal man was actually quite smart. So, careful of your step here."

The walk gets steeper and the flora gets thicker as the decking ascends up through a copse of barrel-bellied palm trees. Even the brief shade from the sun is welcome.

They get to the top of the hill, and Hamasaki steps off the walkway and into the underbrush. It's cooler and shadier, like a rain forest. Not far away, Hannah spies a small wooden fold-up chair sitting between two palms. She remarks upon it: "What's that?"

"That's my spot," David says. She can't tell if he's being defensive about it or not. "I like to come here, drink my coffee, and just sit for a little while. Because look, look." He sweeps his hand. "You can see the whole island from here."

She steps forward. He's right—from here, you can get a good look at the island. In the middle of it all: a bona fide blue lagoon. So blue it looks fake, like Windex. Out past the beach, she sees dark mottled shapes beneath the water.

"Are those whales?" she asks.

He gives her a look, like, *Please don't insult my intelligence.* "That's the fringing reef. Makes it hard to bring boats in—where you came in is the only place that works unless you've got yourself a little shallow raft or something. But that's good, it means this place isn't, you know, all that spoiled yet. We still have some species that you can't find anywhere else on this planet. The Kolohe finch, the Kolohe duck, the alkali noctuid moth." His fingers fritter in the air like he's trying to pick the point out of the ether. "This is a special place. A pure place. And it's kept that way by being unfriendly. Paradise is precarious. Just one little thing . . ." He mimes a little shove. "Can push it into imbalance. It didn't take much to screw up the Garden of Eden. Do you understand?"

He's telling her the same thing that Ray did: *You're not welcome here.*

"Let's remember," she says crisply, "that Eden wasn't disturbed by outsiders. The destruction of paradise was from within. I'm not here to hurt anybody or destroy the company. But someone is dead and something strange is going on, and right now, it connects here."

He sighs. "Of course. I will help you in any way that I can."

"The way you say that sounds like it comes with a caveat."

"It does. I don't know that anybody else here will."

"I can deal with that."

"Good." His smile—which has never wavered, which has remained plastered to his face not in a pedantic or sardonic way but rather in an almost avuncular manner—broadens. "Let's go get you a room in the dorm, see the lab, meet the team."

11

They come up out of the rain forest. What rises up from the shade of the island reminds her of Luke Skywalker's house on Tatooine.

"They're called mod-pods," David says. "Module-Pods. That's their official name. One of Einar's friends from college invented them. They're 3-D printed buildings." He rubs a chin wispy with little hairs. "Actually, I'm surprised Einar hasn't gotten into the 3-D printing gig yet."

"He will," Ray says, coming up behind them, looking at his phone. The 8-bit chirps and warbles of some kind of game rise from the device as his thumbs make quick work.

The lab—with a modest sign reading ARCA in Futura font above the double doors—is a chain of these modular pods: one round plastic dome after the next, linked together by telescoping tunnels and pressurized doors. Some pods are larger than others, some have a different arrangement of windows (round portholes or rectangular wraparounds that look almost like windshields), some seem to have HVAC split systems. A few in the back look particularly large—two, maybe three stories tall.

"We don't call them mod-pods, though," David says. "We call them bubbles. The lab bubble, the dorm bubble. Pretty cool how they build them. These robot arms work along these two axis poles—rotatable—and the nozzles and lasers print a flexible honeycomb skeleton of stainless steel. Then it adds layers of plastic, then insulation, then more plastic. I've seen some that spray in concrete, too." As he talks, he moves his hands around like it's

happening in real time, his own limbs turned into imaginary maker bots.

"Impressive," Hannah says. She has her doubts about 3-D printing. If people think that hacking intellectual property is a problem now, just wait till what they're hacking isn't books and movies but entire blueprints. Third world countries might benefit from 3-D printing, particularly using stolen intellectual property and forbidden patents. They could build cheap, storm-resistant structures or make new farm equipment or—

"You okay?" David asks her.

"Just lost in my own head," she says. Then, given the company she's in, she decides to float a more honest answer: "Dreaming about the future. The good stuff and the bad stuff."

He chuckles. "We like to think it'll be a dream, but it's good to remember it could be a nightmare, too. That's why we gotta do good things now. Make good decisions. Try to move the rudder long before the boat ever gets near the iceberg, right?"

Ray grouses: "Can we just go inside?" He pockets his phone. Hannah assumes he lost his game.

* * *

They pass through an empty reception area bubble.

(David says: "I don't even know why we have this area, to be honest with you." Ray answers: "Because it's what Einar wanted, David." To Hannah, David mutters: "A familiar refrain.")

The second bubble serves only as a fork in the road.

Go left, David points out, and you head toward the living quarters: the dorms, the kitchen, the rec area. "Bathrooms and showers," Ray adds.

Go right, and you head toward Arca proper: the labs, the offices, the conference room, the science library, the cafeteria.

The living area is open. The lab area is protected by RFID locks. "Everybody who works here gets a wristband with a chip in it.

Silicone-encased. Water resistant, but not waterproof. We can code who can get through which door from the main computers in the lab."

"Not everybody has access to every bubble?" she asks.

David says, "We have thirty-three people here, but some are just support staff. Two cooks. Two janitorial. One maintenance. The cooks don't need to go deep into the labs, and only one of the custodians is trained to handle hazardous or biological containment—not that we have that problem around here." He seems suddenly defensive. "Anyway. Let's get you set up."

David hard-charges into the living area. Ray follows behind Hannah. They pass through a rec room lined with severe-looking European couches, a bookshelf holding hardcovers, ratty paperbacks, board games like Settlers of Catan, a whole shelf of vinyl records, a small metal bucket with LEGO bricks in it, and a coloring book. *Is there a child here?* Hannah wonders.

David talks as he walks: "This is the rec room. You know, just a hangout space. Though sometimes people hang in the dorms, too. Play cards, music. They're pretty soundproof." He changes the topic so fast she feels like she just fell out of a moving car: "We won't have a badge for you, so when you go to the labs or the caf you'll need to have one of us with you. But that should be no problem, no problem at all."

Directly connected to the side of the rec room is a small kitchen bubble. Narrow fridge, microwave, a set of burners, cabinets. Past that: the dorms themselves. David points down the long hallway, its edges crinkled like the elbow in a bendy straw. "See here, these doors?" All along the cylindrical hallway are narrow, windowless doors. "Fourteen rooms. Seven doors on each side, usually two to a room, though there's four beds in each room because they're bunks. At the end, bathrooms and showers. Communal and unisex."

"Okay," Hannah says.

"It's dinnertime in the caf."

"It's a little early yet. I could use a shower."

"No time. Unless you don't want to eat."

"I . . . want to eat." She's exhausted. But she's hungry. And it would be best to get to work.

"Let's eat," Ray says.

* * *

The cafeteria is the first bubble heading toward the labs. David moves his wristband with its diamond-shaped swatch of white plastic toward the RFID lock, and the door opens onto a room holding five long, heavy tables. While everything else in Arca has been austere, this room is not: the tables are a burnished red wood and Hannah sees centerpieces of white orchids, palm fronds in bronze vases, a ceiling fan, and an outrigger canoe propped up against the curvature of the far wall. The windows—round portholes—are open, letting in a breeze that smells of salt air and flowers.

The kitchen is open air, on the side of the room opposite the decorative canoe. Dinner is serve-yourself, though she sees a couple of cooks working behind the scenes—one who looks like a stout, linebacker-bodied native woman and the other a wan wisp of a man.

Those in attendance—maybe twenty-five people—turn, juddering their chairs to see who's coming in. Judging by the looks they give her, they know who she is and they are not pleased to see her. But judging by the looks they give Ray, they don't want to see him, either.

Interesting, Hannah thinks.

David Hamasaki, his smile never wavering, claps his hands. "Everybody, our guest has arrived. This is Hannah Stander of the FBI—"

"Consultant," she asserts, but David doesn't correct himself.

"She's going to be with us for the next two to three days, and she'll go back on the boat with some of you who are cycling out of the lab rotation. I expect all of you to give her your attention when she requires it so she can make the best assessment possible for the Federal Bureau of Investigation."

A few people lift their chins or offer a small wave in greeting. Most don't do a damn thing. They run the gamut, though Hannah can tell most of these folks are scientists and not support staff. A few are even in their lab coats. Most of them are young.

David pulls up a chair for her at one of the tables toward the canoe. "This is us," he says, smiling warmly and patting the chair: a move that is either pedantic and condescending or genuinely welcoming. She can't quite tell yet.

They join a narrow-shouldered, big-hipped woman with punky bleach-blond hair; a severe-looking Indian man; a scruffy, average-looking white guy with a muss of hair, dark stubble, and horn-rim glasses; and an impossibly tiny Filipino woman with a disdainful set to her lips and a pair of hot-coal eyes searing holes right through Hannah.

Before Hannah even sits, the little woman twists up her face and says, "*Kalokohan.*" It's said so vehemently she's amazed the woman doesn't spit afterward.

"I'm sorry?" Hannah says.

The man in the glasses smiles. "It's Tagalog for 'trivial.'"

"It's Tagalog for '*bullshit,*'" the woman corrects. Then she offers up the fakest smile Hannah has ever seen. "Hello, I'm Dr. Mercado."

David laughs nervously. "Nancy is our team lead." Then he goes on to introduce the others, all project leaders:

He points to the one with spiky bleach-blond hair. "That's Kit Reed, leader on the *Aedes aegypti* mosquito project. Next to her"—he points to the stone-faced Indian man—"is Ajay Bhatnagar, project leader on what we call the 'pollinator project.' And the man who has clearly forgotten to shave yet again is Will Galassi, head of Special Projects. We are missing one person, though—"

As if on cue, a big-bellied, blush-cheeked man in a pink polo and a rumpled lab coat comes bolting through the doors that lead deeper into the labs themselves. He's got a mess of dirty-blond hair, the curls kept tight to his bowling-ball head. "Sorry! Sorry," he says, adjusting himself as he sits. "Hey, everybody. Hope I didn't miss anything." Before anybody can speak, he turns to Hannah. "You must be the lady from the CIA—"

"FBI," Hamasaki corrects.

"Right! Right. *Right.* I'm Barry."

"Dr. Barry Lowe," Hamasaki says, more formally.

Then, in what must be his version of a deep, sultry soul-singer voice: "Or as they call me, *Barry Love.*" He laughs big and bold: a kind of donkey bray. When nobody else laughs with him, he clears his throat into his fist and says, "Sorry. I'm head of the sustainable edible insect project and—"

A flash of movement on his shoulder. A burst of green. Hannah pushes her chair back in startled surprise. It's a praying mantis.

Barry rolls his eyes and smiles in an *aw-shucks* way. With a lift of his finger he teases the mantis onto his hand. "This is Buffy." The mantis tilts its alien head.

"Well, hi," Hannah says. All eyes are on her now. These people do not like her. They do not trust her. *And,* she reminds herself, *one or more of them may be involved in creating those ants.* She remembers a day way back when, after she left her parents and moved in with her aunt, Sugi, when nothing felt familiar, and the woman's three dogs—two mastiffs and one Chihuahua—stared at her as if she were a trespasser whose smell did not belong. She'd waited for those animals to decide one day they would tear her apart. This feels very much like that. Better then to just cut to the chase. "So, what exactly is bullshit?" She remembers suddenly that Ray used the same word. *Bullshit.*

Dr. Mercado—Nancy—seems surprised at her boldness, and then answers: "Your reason for being here. You really think we're capable of doing what you're implying? Creating a whole new ant species out of *thin air* is just not possible. Ask Ajay."

Dr. Bhatnagar barely moves his facial muscles when he breathes loudly through his nose and says, "We have focused on modifying ants to serve as a replacement pollinator. Ants indeed go from flower to flower, and the fine hairs that cover many ants do indeed carry pollen." His face shows a faint veneer of distaste as he adds, "Problem is, the kind of ants that would be best geared toward pollination often secrete a natural kind of antibiotic that damages the pollen and makes them inefficient pollinators. We tried to remove the antibiotic, but that makes them particularly susceptible to disease—and so the quest continues." He offers a polite, sad smile before staring off into the middle distance.

"What you found? Those ants?" Nancy says. "They were not engineered. That is foolishness. It's a new species. It has to be a new species."

"The ants had your signature genetic markers," Hannah says. "The ones from the mosquito project. I brought the data with me on a USB. You can see for yourself."

"Your guy, Agent Copper, has already sent them ahead," Kit says. She's got a hint of a Jersey accent. "I'll be honest: those look like our markers."

Nancy scowls. "*Looks like* our markers doesn't mean they *are*."

"Are they proprietary?" Hannah asks.

"They are," Nancy answers.

"Could they be stolen, then?"

"Impossible."

"Im*probable,*" Will says. "But that's not the same as impossible. Wouldn't take much to sneak." To Hannah, he says with a small smirk, "We do not hire dummies, after all. A lot of those people sitting at those tables graduated from some of the best programs in the country—in the *world*."

* * *

After dinner, Hannah heads to the dorm they assign her and starts unpacking her bag.

"Hey, dorm buddy," says a voice from the doorway. It's Kit.

"I can ask David if he can give me another bunk—"

"Psssh." Kit waves her off, then starts kicking off her Tevas. "My tiny messy bunk room is *your* tiny messy bunk room. A minor inconvenience that will surely reveal itself to be an unplanned delight. Besides, you're out in a couple days, right? Out with the off-islanders?"

"I am." A reminder: *I am on a time limit.*

"Good."

That word. A bit too sharp. A bit too happy-to-see-Hannah-go.

And it's then that Hannah understands why she's in a bunk and not on her own. It's not just a space issue. Here, Kit can keep an eye on her. The question floats to the fore of her mind: *What do they have to hide?*

"Besides," Kit says, "that way you'll beat the weather."

"Captain Dan said something about that. What weather?"

Kit stands there, arms crossed. "It's the start of typhoon season in these parts, so we get some whopper storms out here."

Just then, David Hamasaki pops his head in. "Kit, can we talk?"

"Sure," Kit says.

The two of them give Hannah a look before they exit. She decides now is a good time to ask: "David? Real quick. I know my cell doesn't have a signal, but—"

"We have three satphones, but they float around, so you'll have to track them down. Sometimes they're in the lab?" The lab to which she does not have access, she reminds herself.

"How do I contact someone off-island?"

"Try yelling really loud," Kit says.

And then the two of them are gone, leaving Hannah feeling all the more alone on an island with no friends and little contact. She gets suddenly dizzy, as if plagued by vertigo, even though she's standing here on solid ground. Hannah feels immediately small: this island is nothing more than a speck on a map surrounded by blue, and she is just a speck upon that speck.

* * *

Hannah has to stand outside with the phone. Some bubbles have exits at the back (in case there's a fire), and David pointed her to one of the doors placed just before the bathrooms.

Now she stands under a canopy of palms and calls her mother. It's almost four in the morning back in Ohio, but Mom barely sleeps.

But the phone just rings and rings. Hannah leaves a message: "Mom. It's me. Everything's fine. I'm on an island. I'll call you." She thinks of adding *Love you,* but she holds back.

Then she takes a chance and dials Hollis.

He's awake. Either up early or never went to bed. "Stander. You kicking back on a beach somewhere, sipping a Mai Tai?"

"Oh, sure. Just like spring break. I won the wet T-shirt contest." She clenches her jaw and says, "I'm just checking in, letting you know I got here all right. I haven't gotten too deep yet. But nobody here seems to think it's even *possible* to have engineered those ants in the way that they are."

"And do you believe them?"

"I believe some of them believe that. But somehow, those ants exist, and it's not by divine intervention. How are things on your end?"

"Nothing here yet. No movement on the body ID. Techs have gone through a little over half the skin samples, though. Maybe get a print by this time tomorrow if we're lucky."

"And if we're not?"

"Then it's all down to you, Stander. Just gimme a reason to send a team to Hawaii to knock on Einar Geirsson's door."

"Will do."

"One more thing, Stander."

"What's that?"

"Don't forget that one of those people you're with could be a murderer."

She flinches. "Thanks for that reminder."

"Just doing my part of the job."

12

Kit lies facedown on her bed. She's snoring in a deep bass rumble.

Hannah is awake. Eyes open. An orange ring of light creeps in around the plastic shutters in the porthole window. She fumbles for her watch. Six in the morning.

She sighs. She knows how lying there awake will end: with her plunging into the icy waters of her own mind. A willful, anxious descent.

She wills herself out of the bed.

Once showered, she gets dressed—sensible white T-shirt, jeans—and she smells it: coffee.

Adjacent to the rec room is the little kitchen, and there's Will Galassi. He's got a Bunsen burner out and it's hissing blue flame under the bell of an onion-shaped glass container. Water bubbles and then rises up into a glass hopper above it. He sees her and gives her a small grin. "Early riser, too?"

"Not usually *this* early," she says. "Jet lag."

"Ah. Jet lag's a monkey on your back." He begins to pour the coffee. "You want?"

"I don't just want it, I need it."

"I can relate." He pours the both of them cups.

His coffee makes her normal Starbucks brew taste like the charcoal filter you'd use in a freshwater aquarium. She makes an *ahhh* sound.

"Welcome to my world: Tahitian vanilla and small-batch home-brew cocktail bitters and dragon tongue beans." He grins. "Since we're both up, would you care for a tour of our work? Wanna go see some bugs?"

* * *

The lab is huge: two pods married together. A pair of conjoined bubbles. It's easy for Hannah to see how a couple of dozen people could be in here at a given time, all of them working side by side. Right now, there's only a young woman with bright eyes and freckles as big as ladybugs. It looks like she's testing equipment.

Everything in the lab is clean and spartan. All the equipment looks new—some of it cutting edge. Hannah sees a genetic piezo-electric microdispensing station, a handful of 3-D printers, a massive thermal cycler against the back wall. One wall has a series of thin robotic arms mounted to the counters. Two of them end not in hands but with what look like repeating pipettes.

Will holds up a pair of black goggles affixed to a white helmet, which is itself connected to a series of cables. "Oculus Rift VR. We're also getting a HoloLens in here. We take the microscopic space and make it macro—so we can literally operate in that space. Using those arms." He gestures toward the robotic limbs.

"Impressive," Hannah says, and it is. But she's wondering: How does this help her solve a murder?

Will unlocks another set of double doors with his wristband and leads her through a small collapsible hallway to another staging room, this one with three doors. "Choose a door."

Hannah points to the leftmost door.

"The left door. The sinister door. The word *sinister* comes from *sinistra* in the Latin, which means—"

"Left, yes, I know." She gestures for him to open the door. He does, and she sidles through and—

"Hey!" Barry says, wheeling around at the intrusion. He shakes a jar of what look like stinkbugs at them, and it sounds like the rattling of some strange, alien musical instrument. "Holy crap, guys, come on in, come on in. People don't visit here very often." He says that last sentence like he's surprised.

The room is a smaller bubble: utilitarian and plain, with metal shelves forming a horseshoe shape against the curvature of the walls. On those structures, Hannah sees opaque plastic bins big and small. Dark mass fills them and she already understands what she's seeing: containers brimming with dead bugs. Another doorway sits at the end of the room, closed.

Near Barry's hip is a little table with tiny plastic cups. In each of those cups, Hannah sees more stinkbugs. The cups are notated with marked numbers in black ink, one through six.

"You guys wanna do a taste test?" Barry asks.

"I'm good," she answers. "I still need breakfast and I'm hoping this isn't it." Barry laughs at that, because he seems to laugh at everything, until she adds, "So, this is part of Einar's vision, huh?"

That's when Barry gets deadly serious. "Don't joke. People joke, but this is no joke. The world is home to a lot of starving people. Famine's the real deal. Global warming makes it worse, and then we're losing pollinators, so finding a new source of protein is a real important struggle. Insects are cheap, sustainable, and, if I do my job right, tasty."

"I wasn't trying to poke fun," Hannah says. "I apologize if I came across that way. I just mean—it's a room full of dead bugs. We think the future is robots and hovercars and maybe it's really here."

"It is," Barry says. "It really is." But then he snaps out of super-serious mode. "You think the dead bugs are cool, you oughta check out the live ones—" He starts to reach for the door just past the shelves, but Will stops him.

"Barry, I'm going to take her to the next rooms."

Barry nods. "Those guys get to do the rock-star work, you'll see. It's really something!" He smiles at her, but Will is already leaving and Hannah has to hurry to catch up.

As they head back into the room with the three doors, she says, "So. Einar."

"What about Einar?"

"First, you all call him Einar."

"He asks that we call him by his first name."

"He's an easy boss, then?"

Will smiles and chuckles softly. "That would not be how anyone describes him. Einar is incredibly serious and driven. He honestly wants to save the world. And that means he runs us pretty hard. Work weekends. Little vacation."

"I read he expects parents of newborns to take as little time off as they are legally afforded."

"That remains a controversial point, but it's true."

"I want to talk to him. They told me I likely wouldn't be able to, but . . ."

"He doesn't come here except for quarterly reviews, where we have to do our song and dance to demonstrate our progress. That was just a few weeks ago. He won't come back soon, and who even knows where he is in the world right now? Sorry to disappoint." He directs her through the next door.

When she steps through, she instantly *feels* the sound vibrating her back teeth. It goes all the way through her, from the soles of her feet to the top of her head. A thrumming hum that almost makes her dizzy.

This bubble room has been specially made—*printed,* she reminds herself—to accommodate hives of honeybees. Long channels of translucent material run from floor to ceiling. The walls squirm: thousands of bees vibrating, dancing, dipping and diving, and pulling themselves back out of the hexagonal honeycomb chambers. She heads over to one, pressing her hands against it: the vibrations carry all the way through her palms to her elbows. Little white blobs hide within the bee throng: *baby bees,* she thinks. Larvae. Along the edges of the glass and behind all the insects are combs of gooey gold. Honey.

Will walks next to her, reaches down below one of the windows, and pulls out a clear plastic drawer like a file box. Inside, Hannah sees racks and rows of honeycombs. Bees dancing. Honey oozing. A memory hits her like a splash of water: *Running behind one of the generator sheds, stepping on a hole, yellow jacket wasps pouring out, darting in and stinging her, three dozen stings, two weeks of misery, and Mom told her she still had to do her chores . . .*

"You okay?" he asks.

"Yes. Yeah." Hannah forces the memory away. "So, how does all this work? Bees make honey from pollen. Where are they getting it?"

"On the other side—I can take you out there eventually—you walk around and you'll see these tubes, these plastic tubes that open up to the air so that the bees can go to the flowers. We've nearby guava, pineapple, ohi'a lehua, and so on. Ajay harvests the honey. There's some in the kitchen if you want a taste."

"What's the end game here?"

"With the bees? To make a stronger honeybee. A bee with a stronger immune system against varroa mites and other parasites. Or, alternatively, to dampen the aggressive response of African honeybees." Hannah knows that African honeybees evolved in an area where their honey reserves were persistently plundered by other animals, and so they developed a fast, brutal response. They're hard to domesticate in terms of food production.

"Any luck so far?"

"Not really. We've gotten some foreign genes into queens, but while we've had the *Apis mellifera* genome cracked for well over a decade now, we still haven't puzzled out the intricacy therein. Bees' immune response is coded in there, but how that interacts with brood disease or mites, we just don't know. You want to go see the ants?"

"I do."

Back out of the buzzing, humming room. Toward the other door. But Will stops before he opens it. "I have a confession," he says. "I'm a fan."

"A fan of . . . Charlize Theron? The X-Men? Mumford & Sons?"

"You. I'm a fan of yours."

Hannah takes a half step back. "I don't follow."

"I read your work in *Wired*. I watched your TED talk—"

"TEDx."

"And some of your university talks are on YouTube. It's insightful stuff. And it aligns with things I already believe, which, admittedly, means I'm leaning into confirmation bias. But it's smart. You're smart."

The feeling that goes through Hannah is a strange one: she's honored and pleased. And yet, it still feels creepy. Despite being in the public realm, her work has always been small and—to her, at least—unexceptional. And oddly, curiously, paradoxically private. "Thank you" is all she can muster.

"I think about the future a lot," Will says. He leans backward without looking and taps his wristband against the lock. "Let's see some ants."

The door hisses open. Hannah's breath is snatched away by the dueling forces of wonder and fear. The whole room is one big ant colony.

In the other bubbles, the walls curve down with little adornment. In this pod, the walls are unseen, hidden behind what Hannah guesses is about six inches of dirt and then another clear plastic layer. In that dirt an ant colony works. All around her. Left, right, above her head. It exists in all directions but down: her feet still stand on the textured floor common to each pod within Arca Labs.

She feels ants crawling over her skin—*formication*. Tingling, tickling, an invisible sensation but no less real. Minimovies of fear play out in her mind: the plastic suddenly cracking as the colony crashes down upon her, dirt in her eyes, ants in her hair, her ears, her nose—

She takes a sharp breath. *Stop it, Hannah. Get it together.*

"Beautiful, isn't it?" Will asks.

"It is." She asserts that for herself and for her own well-being. And in truth it really is a beautiful thing. This room is a feat of engineering, entomology, and even art. It feels like being underground. The sophistication of the ant colony is laid bare: the labyrinth they've built, the ants of different sizes and different purposes moving silently through the passages in an almost arterial movement. The entire nest gives the sense of a circulatory system: the churning of life through tunnels and chambers. "What species is this?" she asks.

"*Pogonomyrmex badius.* Florida harvester ant."

Harvester ant. She hears Ez's voice in her head: *The venom in a harvester ant is the most toxic in the insect world.* Didn't the venom of the modified ants closely resemble that of the harvester? She asks carefully, "Those are highly venomous, right? The harvester ants."

"Hm? They do have a very painful attack—the sting is vicious. I've gotten hit and it swells, grows hot, starts to secrete fluid. Painful for a few days. Though the really venomous ones are the Maricopa harvesters. And even though it hurts, these little guys aren't aggressive. You have to *really* provoke one to get a sting."

She steps closer to the plastic—closer to the ants. Behind the clear wall, they dance through their maze. She spies them carrying little bits of something to a small, dead-end chamber. *Seeds,* she thinks.

"That's one of their granaries," Will says, standing suddenly and unexpectedly near her. She didn't even sense him approach. *I'm off my game,* she thinks. Must be the jet lag. "They're seed collectors. That's what they harvest." He bends one knee and leans down to open a drawer just below the colony, pulls out a magnifying glass—a jeweler's lens—and presses it against the plastic. "Here, take a look through. You'll get a better glimpse."

Hannah takes the lens, presses it against the plastic, gives a look. In the tunnels, the ants move fast—so she repositions herself over the granary instead. There, little red ants carry seeds into the storage area. The movement is slower and easier to see. "They seem to have seeds near their mouths but not *in* their mouths."

"In their mandibles, yes. But on the ventral side of the head you'll see a collection of long hairs—those are psammaphore hairs. They form a kind of basket that the ants use to carry those seeds. Or sand, or other particulate matter. It's those hairs we're focusing on as being valuable for pollination. As the ants go to claim seeds from plants, they pick up pollen. Ideally. Though now we're thinking we'd be better off looking for nectar-drinking ants."

"Are these harvesters native here?"

"No. No ants are. Hawaii and the leeward chain have no native ants."

"Why bring them here? Aren't you going to destabilize the environment?"

Will shrugs. "It's always a risk. Same with the bees. The harvesters are incredibly inoffensive, though. They're not a pest insect. They don't attack, and they don't hurt the wildlife—if anything, they help propagate new plants through seed carrying. Hawaii, though, right now is plagued by two invasive ants—fire ants and crazy ants. So we're thinking of starting a new program to create beneficial ants who will be armed with the ability to incapacitate the nests of these other nasty invasives."

For a moment, they're quiet. Hannah can hear the tiny *ticka-ticka-ticka* of the ants' legs. It's all around her. "Let me ask," she says. "You and Ajay are on these projects? The ants and the bees."

"Ah. Well."

"No," she says, pretending to just now remember. "That's right, you're . . . what's it called? Additional projects?" She gets it wrong deliberately, hoping he'll correct her.

He does. He fidgets with his eyeglasses as he says, "No, it's called Special Projects."

"And what are those?"

A cagey smile. "If I told you, they wouldn't be quite so special." A slick line. It feels practiced. It's also a diversion.

She's about to pursue it further, but just then: A faint vibration in her feet. A distant pulsing *whup-whup-whup*. "I didn't think anybody could get here via helicopter," she says.

"That's true. Which means it isn't just anybody." She realizes what this means even before he says it: "It's Einar."

13

With the sound of the helicopter, Arca Labs goes from quiet and still to a wasp nest knocked out of a tree with a rock. Bodies moving in hallways. Throwing on lab coats. A buzz of unfocused panic.

Hannah enjoys observing the sense of agitation that Einar's visit—presuming it really is him, of course—has caused. She stands in the reception area, waiting and watching. Will is with her. He's trying to play it cool, but he's failing: his Adam's apple twitches with nervous swallows, and his right hand taps out a staccato drumbeat against his pocket.

Ray comes up out of the lab, still buttoning up a billowing white shirt underneath a jacket. "What are you doing? What are we doing? Where's David? Shit."

David Hamasaki comes out next, his head and chin leading, the rest of his body pinwheeling to catch up. He's smiling, but it's strained, like a cord pulled too tight and about to snap. "Okay, okay, Einar likes someone to meet him down by the helipad, so let's go." He's out the front door, Ray glued to his heels.

Will gives her a small smile. "We could wait here—"

"No, I'd like to see the helipad." Hannah strides out the door.

Outside, the day is warming and the wind coming off the ocean is assertive—it gives her a little shove as soon as she steps out of the trees, following Ray around the left side of the building along a small decking walkway. This walkway descends through the trees toward the massive lagoon in the center of the island. Out there, tucked behind a small black rock cliff and a trio of bent, splayed-out palms, is a helipad.

Hannah can see a helicopter there—black and gray; almost insectile. Rotors red like they tasted fresh blood. She doesn't know much about helicopters, but reading about Einar took her to an article about this very one: it's a Bell 525 Relentless. The ultimate in luxury helicopter rides. This chopper isn't even on the market yet.

Next to the helicopter, a pilot stands with his hands clasped behind his back. Between Ray and David she sees two figures walking up from the helipad: A tall, thin, pale woman. Like a human scalpel—like a vampire. Next to her, the man himself.

Ahead she hears Ray curse under his breath. "Fuck. We were too slow."

Einar Geirsson marches right up. Ray and David greet him, but he ignores them entirely. Next thing Hannah knows, he's reaching out to her. A gentle kiss on each cheek, light as moth wings fluttering. She wants to pull away, but by the time the urge reaches her it's already over.

"Hannah Stander," he says, a bit of his accent turning the words just so. "Einar Geirsson. An absolute pleasure."

"The pleasure is mine," she answers. It strikes her that what makes him handsome is his little imperfections. His nose is thin and just a bit crooked. His lips are thin. He carries about him the air of a strange, unknowable predator: beautiful like a spider or a wolf.

"Let us walk," he says. And then he's moving toward the labs and the crowd turns to follow him the way goslings follow their mother goose.

She is swept up in it. "I did not expect to meet you," she says, working to catch up and match his strides. "I was told you'd remain off-site."

"Ah, but how could I? Your report troubled me like a bad dream, and so I had to come. If such trouble is afoot, how can I stand back and ignore it?" He snaps his fingers. "Do you know what to do if you are sailing and you meet a rogue wave? You do not turn your side or your back to it. That is how you capsize. No! You meet it head on. You cut the wave in half. Rising truly to the challenge."

Ray juggles himself forward and says, "Einar, I just want you to know that everything here is under control."

"Of course it is," Einar says. "I trust you implicitly, Ramon. Hannah, this is my assistant and bodyguard, Venla Normi."

Hannah turns to the vampire—who hides behind a pair of massive-lensed sunglasses—and says, "Good to meet you, Ms. Normi."

The woman says nothing but gives a short, clipped nod.

Now they're back at the labs and in through the front. Einar continues his unstoppable march—this time in the direction of the dorms. "Venla, please have someone here get my bags from the Bell. I'd like to have a quick run and a soak." As they move through the rec room he says to Hannah, "I am here for the duration of your stay, Hannah. I will help facilitate your investigation to the maximum degree of which I am capable. Consider me your humble servant in this."

"Thank you," Hannah says, feeling both drawn in by him and pushed away. She can't settle on whether he's doing this to her as a favor, as a PR move, or as something deeper and more protective.

"You are comfortable here?"

"I am."

"Everyone has been kind?"

"They have."

"Kindness is sadly underrated. Have they been helpful?"

"Also yes."

"Good. You and I will meet at dinner to go over your findings. Seven P.M.? We will eat after the others so that we may have privacy to discuss your case freely."

Before she can respond, he makes a fast beeline for the back exit beyond the dorms. He opens it with his own wristband RFID tag, and then disappears down another walking path toward a small domed house about a hundred yards away.

Hannah almost goes through the door after him, but Ray catches her elbow. "Uh-uh. Not you. We don't follow that far."

David says, "Nobody but Venla goes to his yurt."

"And me," Ray says.

David gives him a wilting look, like, *Really?* And Hannah wonders when the last time was that Ray was really on the inside. Because suddenly it looks a whole lot like he's on the outside. The outside of the scientists here, and the outside of Einar's inner circle. Which, from this vantage point, isn't even an inner circle so much as it is a two-person cabal. Maybe less, even. A star chamber for one: Einar all the way down.

* * *

I'd like to have a quick run and a soak.

That gives her the idea. Croissant half out of her mouth, Hannah sits on her cot and stands to pull on a pair of running shorts and sneakers. She draws her hair back into a ponytail as she hastily chews the pastry.

Kit comes whirling into the room like a tropical storm. "Shit, shit, shit, was not ready for our surprise visit. Will there be an inspection again? This soon? Should've known. Einar always says he believes unpredictability to be a virtue." She's talking to herself, it seems, because it's like she suddenly realizes Hannah is there. "Oh! Oh. Agent Stander. You going running?"

"I am."

"Einar's on the path."

"I know."

Kit narrows her eyes. "We aren't supposed to run when he does."

"I'm not like the rest of you." It sounds cockier than she means it, but she lets it lie just the same. "It's fine. I'll leave him alone."

There: A tiny flinch in Kit's face. Like she knows something but is afraid to say. It's barely perceptible, but Hannah catches it.

"Have fun," Kit says.

Hannah gets up and heads to the front reception area. Venla is standing by while one of the interns grunts and hauls bags into the area one by one. "Where are you going?" Venla says, looking Hannah up and down like she's some homeless person who wandered into a cocktail party. Her lip curls into a dismissive sneer. Her accent is sharp like a hook. Finnish, maybe.

"For a run."

"No. Einar has the path. He has it for one hour."

"I won't be long and I won't be in his way."

"But I will be in *your* way," the woman asserts. She steps in front of Hannah, hands flexing like spiders doing calisthenics. Suddenly Hannah remembers: assistant *and* bodyguard. The woman moves like a spring ready to uncoil into a wire lash.

Hannah feels her own body tense up. "Are you threatening me?" she asks Venla. "That wouldn't be an act of good faith, would it? Threatening a consultant for the FBI."

"It is no threat. It is a promise. Remember you are a guest here."

"And you are a guest here, too. I've seen the lease agreements. Einar co-leases this island with the United States government. It would be a shame if that agreement had to be reviewed because of this mess."

"Little consultant," Venla hisses. "This is cute. That you think you have this kind of power. That you think Einar's money would not buy him whatever he wants. I could break both of your legs on the White House's front lawn and Einar would write a check and make it all go away. He could make *you* go away."

"Understood," Hannah says, then heads back into the dorms. She hears Venla cursing at the boy to hurry up with the bags.

Hannah moves quickly. As soon as the door hisses shut behind her, she jogs through the length of the dormitory branch—past the rec room, the kitchen, the dorms, to the communal bathroom. The woman she saw earlier in the main lab—the one with the big eyes and the ladybug freckles—is in one of the open shower stalls. A lone wristband is sitting next to the faucet by the sink. Must belong to the woman.

Hannah darts in. She yells over the sound of the shower spray. "Hi, David said I could have this." She scoops up the wristband.

The girl turns around, startled. "Hey, I need that back," she protests. "I have to be back in the lab in fifteen."

"What's your name?"

"Lila."

"Lila, I'll be back in ten." It's a lie.

"Oh . . . okay." Worry falls across the girl's face.

Hannah hears Venla barking at Kano to move faster. She hurries back out of the bathroom and to the side exit. Then she pops it with the RFID tag on the wristband and she's out.

* * *

She runs. Feet echoing along the synthetic decking.

Running has always been clarifying for Hannah. People think they're being funny and ask, *What are you running from?*, and she always tells them, *I'm running from death.* Though the real answer is quite different: *I'm running toward answers.*

Running moves blood. Heart to brain. It clears clutter from her mental table. Makes way for new thoughts, ideas, conclusions.

Her legs churn and burn. Through the trees. Past a spray of orchids. Past a couple of fat-bellied bottle palms. Under the hanging blossoms of a guava tree. As she moves, she hears the buzz and tap of honeybees. The path winds and slaloms—down through the flora, along the lagoon, and then back up along a volcanic ridge where seabirds nest. She can see the Pacific Ocean stretch out like a plate of dark glass.

Then she sees him. On the far side of the island ring, Einar runs at a steady clip, a hard pace. That far away, he's just a small silhouette against the wide-open sky. She barely knows why she's out here, except that Einar is a mystery. He wasn't supposed to be here—and now he is. Could he be tied to the murder? Nobody else is supposed to be out here when he is, and that tells her maybe, *just maybe,* there's something worth seeing.

Hannah runs harder, putting more power in her own legs, the

sweat dripping off her brow and into her eyes. Down the ridge once more, to the beach. She looks up again and—

Einar has stopped.

Hannah blinks against the sun because she's seeing double now—Einar's silhouette splitting and becoming two, two shadows reaching across to each other and—

No. It's two people. There's someone else standing there. Then they're moving, disappearing down the second elevated rise, through a small gateway formed of swaying palms.

Who was that? Nobody else is supposed to be out here.

Again Hannah runs. She rounds the northern bend of the island, pumping her legs harder. They must still be a mile away. She can run a mile in eight easy, but now she pushes herself to do it faster. The walkway winds around volcanic rocks jutting up like dragon fangs, and then begins to ascend up the next ridge—

Her foot hits, slips on a scree of whispering sand—

Pain as her ankle twists. Everything whips up past her as she falls. *Wham.* She lands hard on her side and she curls her leg inward. It takes her a few seconds to stand back up, but when she tries to put even a little bit of pressure on the foot—it's a mistake. Another sparking snap of pain. She's twisted it. Or worse.

Stupid, stupid, stupid.

She's miles from where she started. Miles back to the lab. Hannah guesses that she's roughly at the midpoint of her run, so going forward or going backward, it's all the same distance. All she can do is urge herself forth, gingerly limping.

When she crosses the top of the ridge, she sees Einar. He's ahead by a good ways, running back to the labs. She thinks to yell to him, but why? Instead, she keeps moving toward where she last saw him. Where did he go? With whom did he meet? Someone else might still be up here. The back of her neck goes suddenly cold.

She hears a scuffing sound. A rasp of what may be a shoe against rock. She stops. Sucks in a quick breath and holds it.

The sound of wind through palm fronds. The crash of sea against sand and rock. The warble of seabirds.

Then, another footstep. A shape ahead of her, moving through the trees—

"Will," she says, surprised. And suspicious. "What are you doing out here?"

He gasps, clutching at his chest in his own surprise. "Oh God. Agent Stander. You scared the crap out of me."

"It was you." *You that Einar was meeting with.* She sees Will has come from a set of steps leading down through the dirt and the porous volcanic rock, toward the sea. "What's down there? It's Special Projects, isn't it?"

"Hannah, I can't talk about this."

"I'll go have my own look," she says, and starts to move around him.

As she limps past, his hand falls on her elbow. Without even thinking, Hannah darts out her other hand, catches his thumb, and bends it as far back as it will go. Will drops to one knee as if there's nowhere else to go, a susurrus of air whistling through his clenched teeth. "Leggo leggo leggo."

She lets him go. He pulls his hand away and shakes it. Then an odd sound bubbles up out of him: A laugh. A little unhinged. "You're really something," he says.

"I am. Now I'm going to keep walking." She turns to head back down the path, though *walking* was an overpromise. The only verb on which she can truly deliver is *hobble.*

Will trails after. "It won't matter. You can't get there."

It's then that Hannah sees the elevator platform ahead. It's industrial-looking—not modern, not chic—built out of heavy wood and a metal frame on a braided stainless steel cable. She instantly recognizes a RFID reader pad next to it.

"I'm guessing this won't work," she says, holding up the borrowed band.

Will shakes his head. "No."

"I could take yours." She nods toward his wrist.

"You could, I'm sure." He leans into a personal plea, and Hannah isn't sure if it's sincere—or if she's being played. "But Einar will fire me. And do understand that when I say *fire me,* I don't just mean from the work I'm doing here. I mean that he will fire me from a cannon into a rock wall. Come back to Arca with me. Talk to him about Special Projects. Let him tell you."

"What's down there, Will? What is Special Projects?"

"It's not what you think. It's nothing concerning your investigation."

Hannah looks one more time to the elevator—it appears to drop down over the side of the cliff. It can't be more than thirty feet down. She thinks, *I could climb it.* She's done free-climbing. But as she eases her weight, the pain in her ankle reminds her: *You're not going anywhere.* "Fine," she says. "I'm going back." *If Einar won't help me, I'll try to call Hollis, see if he can't grease the wheels.* That is, if they let her have the satphone again. What if they don't? Her heart stutters in her chest at the thought.

"Are you okay?"

"I'm great."

"Your ankle—"

"Is tweaked. It'll heal."

"I'll go with you."

What, so you can keep an eye on me? He's eager. Too eager. "No."

She limps on ahead and makes him follow behind. The walk back is arduous—a misery on her ankle. The journey made all the worse because the two of them are silent the whole way.

* * *

Hannah is on the satphone, with Hollis on the other end.

"We got data on how the package got to the cabin," Hollis says.

"The package. You mean the ants."

"Yeah. Closest traffic cams were twenty miles out, but on one we found a low-rent shipping courier—a local knockoff of FedEx called, hold on—" She hears the whisper of paper. "Quick-Fix Ship, Inc."

She leans against a palm tree, pulling her leg up as high as it will go. The on-site nurse gave her an ankle support brace—simple neoprene but with a closable cuff. She holds an ice pack against it. The nurse wouldn't commit to a sprain or a strain—said it could be a mild injury, but it also could be from overuse. Tendinitis, maybe. Only a doctor would know for sure. "So what else? Where'd it come from? Who sent it?"

"We don't know who sent it. Credit card they had on file was bullshit—literally John Smith. What's interesting is everything else."

"Tell me."

"They told the delivery guy where to find a key to the cabin—under a rock off the west corner of the porch. They gave him an explicit time to deliver the package, and instructions to abandon delivery if anyone was present."

She furrows her brow. "So—what? Setting a trap?"

"Sounds like it. Here's the other thing: this package came from Hawaii."

"Kauai."

"No. Big Island. Town called Hilo. Still, it's close to Arca."

"Hollis, Einar's here."

A low rumble in the back of Hollis's throat. "Well, we did suggest that one of the world's benevolent billionaire geniuses is somehow responsible for murdering one dude in a cabin with killer ants. I imagined he'd take that seriously."

"I know." Deep breath. "He's hiding something from me. Special Projects here on the island."

"I'm sure he's hiding all kinds of things from you, Hannah. Guys like that don't get to *be* guys like that unless they have secrets piled up behind vault doors like so much gold."

"I'll ask him at dinner tonight."

"Dinner. Well. Aren't you fancy."

"I am. The fanciest." She winces as pain cranks her ankle and sweat drips down the bridge of her nose. "I'm so fancy I have to go and take a proper shower before I grill him about Special Projects."

"Keep on sniffing, Hannah. We're close on this. Kick the tires, shake the reeds, and whatever other metaphors you prefer. You come home in—thirty-six hours now? Make your time count."

14

The cafeteria is empty but for one man and a spread of food. Einar sits like a benevolent king: his arms out, palms up like he's Jesus welcoming the sinner to a meal. He stands as Hannah enters and gives her a light, almost airy embrace. "Please," he says. "Sit."

She does. The smell of the food is intoxicating. Einar identifies plates as his hand passes over them: moonfish sashimi, shoyu ramen with pork belly, grilled Pacific blue marlin, steamed breadfruit, tofu in something called a huli-huli sauce. Finally, his fingers (wiggling like he's playing the piano) hover over what she first believed to be simple sushi: a slice of fish over rice, wrapped in a belt of nori.

But then she realizes: that's not fish.

"Spam," he says, with an almost childish delight. "Spam musubi is a Hawaiian treat. Sold most everywhere. Spam became popular during World War Two—"

"I want to know about Special Projects."

His hand stays hanging in the air above the plate. The corner of his mouth fishhooks into a wry, playful grin. "Yes, I was told you went for a run today."

"I followed you."

"And dodged Venla. To that, I must offer—" He brings both hands together in a gentle round of applause. "I apologize if she made undue threats. If I am being honest, while she is very good at her job, she is growing overprotective."

Because you're sleeping with her. She can see that now. The faint,

pained look on his face. A tiny sigh of regret. That isn't why she's here, though. So she says again, "Special Projects."

"The Cove," he says.

"I'm sorry?"

"That is its nickname. The Cove. You saw the elevator—it goes down the side of the cliff—but did you see any buildings down there?"

She hesitates. "I didn't."

"The building is inside the rock. Inside a small cove up against the sea."

"A good place to do sensitive work. I want to see it."

His face freezes for a moment. "Tomorrow morning. I shall arrange—"

"Tonight. Now, in fact." Her heart is like a speed bag under the pummeling fists of a prizefighter. The less time she gives them to clean anything up, the better. Who knows how much time has already been wasted? What they've already been able to hide?

Einar taps the side of his thumb against the plate. "It would be a shame to waste all this dinner." She's about to protest when he adds: "So, we will pack this up and have them bring it to Special Projects. We can eat there."

* * *

The sun bleeds into the ocean as they walk.

Einar carries a flashlight—not yet necessary, the bulb still dark even as evening starts to soak the sky. He tries to get Hannah to sit in a wheelchair (they have one in nursing), but she insists on making it her own way.

"The pain," he says. "Inside of the ankle or out?"

"Outside."

"Good. Inversion sprain, then. Grade one, very mild. Probably go away on its own—though since you insist on agitating it . . . Maybe take it easier?"

"I will . . . try."

She hobbles along and he keeps a measured pace. "I watched your talks," he says suddenly. "Will encouraged me to take a look."

"Oh. And? Your thoughts?"

"I quite liked them. I consider myself something of a futurist, too. Though, obviously, I do not remain content to merely watch the future approach. My hand is an active one, not passive. Not that I am attempting to diminish your accomplishment. The work of those who *do* is only made meaningful by those who *study.* Someone must always be there to ask if we chose our actions correctly, and the critical conversation is an essential one."

"You seem to believe that the future will be on the side of the angels."

"Only if we make it so. We must be active participants in creating a future. We cannot be only prophets. We can divine whatever we want in the guts of a pigeon, but unless we work to make the future we see true, then we will likely never see it made so. You say that two forces race toward the open door—"

"Evolution and ruination."

"Angel and demon, yes. But to me it's not which one wins. It's which one we *let* win. We are the ones urging them forward. The one that makes it through wins because that is the beast we backed."

"Insightful."

"Is it? I'm drawing upon you for inspiration. You have framed it in ways I had not previously considered. And for that: *brava*."

As they walk beneath palms, through the darkness of the shade, two red birds dart through the underbrush. Honeycreepers, she thinks. Chasing each other out of territory, perhaps, or for mating, or for some other birdly reason that remains unknown to man.

Einar asks, "Do you find your outlook complicated by your childhood?"

"I'm sorry?" she says, suddenly feeling off guard.

"Your parents were hard people."

The warm air goes cold quickly as a chill slides over her. "How do you know about my parents?"

"You submitted to a background check before coming here."

"I did no such thing."

"You did with the FBI, and the FBI granted us access to those results."

She stops walking. The foot belonging to her sprained ankle hovers an inch over the walking path. "That's private."

"What I do here is private, too. Journalists around the globe would offer a tithing of blood to see what I have going on. And my competitors would cut throats just to get a peek. You are here because I trust you, and I trust you because your background check helped me to trust you."

"Fine," Hannah says, her voice stiff. She keeps walking. "I can appreciate that."

"Your parents—they believe the future is on the side of the devils, don't they?" He watches her as she stumbles along. The way a hawk watches a mouse.

"They are fearful of what is to come, yes."

"They are not doomsday cultists but . . ." He searches the air as if hoping to find the words he's missing. "What is the term?"

"Preppers. Doomsday preppers. They're survivalists."

"Right. Yes. They believe the world will end sooner than later. Potentially in their lifetimes—or yours."

"Correct. Some believe in a very specific end—reactor meltdown, governmental takeover, comet, famine, polar shift."

"Hm. In what end do your parents believe?"

Hannah's not used to talking about this. She wants to shut the conversation down. "Unspecified."

"Certainly enough signs of doom to warrant it," Einar says. "Global warming, for one. Greatest challenge of our lifetime. And it only complicates preexisting water crises. Food crises. Wars between nations."

"Yes." He's right. What else is there to say?

"Was it strange?"

"Was what strange?"

"Living with them. These people. With these ideas."

"It wasn't strange then. I grew up with it."

"The famous question posed to the fish: 'What temperature is the water today, fish?' And the fish answers: 'What's water?' It was normal until it wasn't."

"That's right."

"You were homeschooled early."

"How do you know that?"

He smiles. "My background checks are thorough. I know they homeschooled you. And I know at a point you left. To stay with your aunt Susan. Mother's sister, yes?"

Hannah feels pinned underneath a glass slide, with Einar's microscope pressing down so hard against her the whole thing splits and shatters. "Yes." If he knows all this, he must know everything.

"Why'd you leave?"

"That's not really your business."

"We're just talking."

"No, I'm just talking. You've got your scalpels out. And I don't feel like being dissected. I'm here because the FBI trusts me as a consultant to look into matters of peculiarity. Matters like this business with a dead man killed by genetically modified ants. Ants that contain a proprietary marker gene identical to the ones used at Arca Labs. My history isn't what's under the glass, Mr. Geirsson—"

"It's Einar, please—"

"What's under glass is you and this place and what you do here."

He laughs and touches her arm. "Of course, Hannah. Of course. I did not mean to pry. My brother says I am like a hound on the scent of blood—I keep pursuing it past the sense of reason or social grace. I find you fascinating, is all."

And I find you fascinating, she thinks. A strange man with untold money and power. Possessing a charisma that is both magnetic and repulsive in equal measure, flipping back and forth effortlessly and unpredictably.

* * *

The elevator is just a platform with a metal frame around it—*A cage,* Hannah thinks. As it descends past the black wall of the cliff, she hears the surf pounding the side of the island below with merciless reiteration—a fuss and crash, fuss and crash. As the elevator moves, the sea spray mists them.

They drop toward darkness, the setting sun on the other end of the island now. Down here, the black rock and the depth of the grotto deepen the shadows. Hannah's pulse kicks in her neck as she feels the cove looming—a monster awaiting, a mouth hungry to swallow them up.

But when the elevator platform rattles and bangs to a stop, Einar steps out and flips a switch and the cove is suddenly awash in light. Strings of bulbs are driven into the rock with metal pitons. Hannah sees a steel walkway—a bridge dangling from braided cables—drawing them farther into the grotto. Beyond that is a building that looks like it's made from the same plastic as the mod-pods, though the shape is considerably different. It's a cylinder, like a long tube driven into the rock.

"Did you build this right here? Right in the cove?"

Einar smiles. "We did." He points to a few vertical bands along each side of the cove—straight lines gouged into the rock as if by a massive blade. "That is where we anchored the 3-D printers—and the robotic arms did the rest. They could operate only during low tide, so it took considerable time and resources."

Astounding. She almost says as much, but she is wary of feeding the man's ego. Instead, she nods and offers a stiff smile, hoping that the awe she feels remains hidden behind the mask of her face.

In the cylindrical structure is a door, and Einar walks over to it. He has no wristband, she notes for the first time, and yet the door opens for him. Just as, she realizes now, the elevator did. *Is he micro-chipped?* she wonders.

Inside is a whole other lab. Along the edges of the cylindrical room are three rings of steel mesh platforms, each with a set of curving steps connecting them—and one more set of steps leading to the floor. All along the way are glass containers of arthropods. As they descend she sees tarantulas, centipedes, butterflies, even a paper wasp nest. All in different ecosystems: simulated rain forests, deserts, swamps. It's less a lab and more a zoo. Another doorway sits at the bottom of it all—down there, she thinks, is below sea level.

It's as if Einar is reading her mind. "The cylinder is designed to withstand the pressure of the ocean—both the water pressure and the push and pull of the tides. But," he says as they reach the bottom of the room, "you'll notice those massive . . . what's the word? Shutters. Up there around the top floor, just below the door where we entered."

She looks up and sees them—shuttered metal vents. All along the circumference of the room. "What are they?"

"If you were to push that red button there—" He points to a junction box hanging on the wall, an oddly industrial feature in this room. On it is a comically large red button. "The room floods. Below our feet is more grating, and if the need arises, we can then flush and pump the seawater back out, though it would take time to do so."

Her middle tightens. "Why would you need to flush this room? What exactly is Special Projects?"

"Military applications for genetically modified insects."

The ants. That's what they are, aren't they? He all but said it. They're a military project. Her palms go cold with a slick sheen of sweat. "That doesn't seem like you. Goes against your ethos."

The man smiles, a lean, tilting smirk, as if he's pleased she knows him that way. "As you well know, I co-lease this island with the United States government. Our last president extended American territory to these islands, and so the deal I made that allows Arca Labs to work here, isolated, is that I was also to create a division to study and potentially design insects that could be used by the military."

"You're creating weapons."

"Ah." He thrusts his finger up in the air. "That is what you would assume and that, I hope, is what the government assumes as well." He leans in now, and with a conspiratorial whisper says, "But that would be an incorrect assumption."

"I don't understand."

"Military application. It's an ambiguous term, isn't it? The government wanted weapons from me—their first example and stated desire was that Arca create for them a weaponized mosquito, a sterile insect who is a carrier of genetic disease. But that isn't really how it works, and I said as much. I did note you could create a mosquito which, upon biting, passes along new genes to the bite recipient—genes that would make the victim more susceptible to disease."

"Something like what happened with Japan and China in World War Two."

Einar seems pleased by her knowledge. "Yes. Unit 731."

Unit 731: a Japanese biowarfare unit that used disease-infected insects (fleas and flies, primarily) to deliver pathogens to unsuspecting Chinese. Hannah read that they reportedly planned to attack the West Coast of the United States with plague-infested fleas, but the war ended before that attack.

"Regardless," Einar continues, "when I began to research the mosquitoes, what I found more interesting was a different mechanism: mosquitoes who *can* breed, but who pass along terminator genes. Genes that carry to the offspring and ensure that only one more generation can persist. The modified *Aedes aegypti* mosquito."

"Not exactly a military application."

He shrugs. "I would disagree. Studies show that populations driven by certain environmental miseries—famine, disease, water shortages—are more susceptible to violence. Sometimes this violence is random, like when a heat wave strikes a city and the crime rate spikes. Sometimes this violence is controlled: A dictator takes power under the auspices of repairing whatever misery governs the people's lives. And inevitably, that dictator leads his people into deeper misery and worse, war. Modifying a mosquito—"

"Means getting rid of mosquito-borne diseases and, ideally, taking one war-driving factor off the table."

"Correct."

"It's pretty brilliant. Are your other projects here so suspiciously benign?"

He laughs. "They are. We have not yet made a weapon. We have spiders and silkworms spinning thread whose tensile strength and overall toughness is higher than steel, higher than most polyaramid filaments, and is totally organic. Most people don't know that spiders spin several different kinds of silk: for predatory capture, for nest construction, for parachuting. We've only just begun to map what can be done with them. Structures. Armor. Surgical applications on the battlefield. But it doesn't end there. What about honeybees who can detect bombs or other hazardous materials? Or insects genetically designed to have susceptible, controllable nervous systems—making cybernetic enhancement all the easier to perform?"

"Like creating remote-controlled bugs. I've read about flies, caterpillars, cockroaches that are designed accordingly."

"Right. Right! This, *this* is where the future of animal-machine hybrids begins. So much potential. So much promise."

"All under the pretense of military application."

He pouts. "No pretense about it. Remember, the Internet was a military application. And now look at how it's changed our culture."

"And the ants?" she asks.

"The murderous ants? The ones that purportedly left a body behind? Are you asking if they are a product of Arca Labs?"

She tenses. *Is he toying with me?* "Don't play coy. Of course I'm asking that. It's why I'm here."

"No, Hannah. We have not created ants for military applications, nor have we created those specific creatures. Despite the presence of our genetic markers, they are not ours."

"How do you explain the presence of your indicator genes?"

He sighs, furrows his brow, and seems to consider his answer. "We're looking into that. My best guess? They were stolen. We have a rotating team of scientists, many of them young, fresh with advanced degrees. They sign legal paperwork and we check those leaving the island for contraband, but no barrier is truly impermeable. One of my rivals would pay well for my secrets. Even better for something so marked as one of our indicator genes."

"You're saying this is corporate espionage. By a rival."

"Not necessarily. But it may have begun there."

"Your enemies hate you that badly? To engineer some sort of demon ant? With stolen indicator genes? I can believe all manner of corporate sabotage, but this seems to be on a whole other level."

Einar puts his hands behind his back. "Hatred is quite a powerful thing. It rarely begins as hatred. It starts as something else. Something smaller, more intimate: jealousy or greed or self-doubt. In biology, one thing can evolve into many. But in this case, the reverse is true: all those negative emotions evolve into one thing and one thing only—hatred."

The two sit quietly for a time, each regarding the other. Over his shoulder, she spies the last set of doors—ones that remain closed, beyond which she expects are the unseen experiments of Special Projects. She's about to ask if he'll open them when—

Bang. She startles.

"Our dinner has arrived," Einar says. Above them, chefs and waiters have entered, bringing with them the tantalizing smell of island food.

* * *

Dinner is elaborate. Drinks and food. Sweet and sour. Salt and spice. He opens a bottle of wine, a Château de Beaucastel, and offers her an Icelandic spirit—Brennivín—that tastes of caraway and anise.

(Einar says it is sometimes called the "black death," not because of its taste but because Iceland once tried to dissuade its drinkers during a period of temperance, putting a skull-and-crossbones logo on all the bottles.)

Soon she's heady—everything soft and buzzy, her lips gone numb while her teeth feel oddly electric. She feels distracted by him. Or worse, seduced. Like a magician's misdirect—look over here at the shiny thing while the trick happens plain but unseen in the other hand. Just the same, she falls into it as Einar tells her his story. He talks about growing up wealthy in Iceland, but then leaving his parents behind and traveling the world—young and dumb, seeing everything with bright eyes and empty pockets. He worked on a South African fishing boat (and once fought off pirates). He was a janitor in a Russian orphanage. He helped run a Malaysian dodol factory—"Dodol is a chewy candy," he explains. "Sticks to your teeth and gums like glue." He says that's where he developed a taste for the durian fruit, a fruit that (by his estimation) smells like a dead man's mouth and tastes like onion custard. She wants to enjoy his stories, and she does. But she also worries—*What am I missing? What am I not seeing?*

Einar tells her: "I saw a man die on the streets of Paris. An Ethiopian man—by some reports a male prostitute, but the law found evidence only that he worked in a local warehouse. Two skinheads came up to him. One grabbed him by the back of his head and neck. The other plunged a broken bottle into his throat. They ran off, cackling like crows. I raced over and he died in my arms. It was that moment that turned it around for me. I decided I had to make the world better, not worse."

"My father killed a man," she says. It is a story of public record—if he truly has investigated her fully, it would've come up. She tells herself that she tells him to help secure his trust—or, alternately, to make herself seem vulnerable to him. Some men become more brazen when they sense vulnerability in a woman. It leads them to make mistakes. Suddenly she worries that's why he told her about the Ethiopian man—has he been herding her toward this conversation? Is he manipulating her, or is she manipulating him? Doesn't matter. Too late now. Einar watches her, waiting.

"A local man. A vagrant, you'd say, but that's not really accurate. He was a farmhand, lived in the area. Alcoholic. Drank too much and ate too little, and one day his sodium went out of whack. His liver was already in bad shape and the man lost a bit of his mind and memory and never really got it back.

"We lived way on the edge of town. Maybe even past it. Not even a town where we were—just a zip code for mail." *And one day, after Mom ripped out the mailbox, it wasn't even for mail.* "We had fences and cattle gates. A long driveway and a distant house. Animals. Gardens and greenhouses. A backstop for shooting practice. It was isolated enough and mysterious enough that I guess some locals developed legends about what was up there—a cult or a conspiracy or, at the least, a passel of gun nuts waiting to bring down the government. Most folks probably knew those were just stories, but not Roy. That was his name: Roy Peffer. One day he decided to cut through our fence and . . ." The words wither in her mouth as the rest of the story plays out silently behind her closed eyelids.

"The man attacked you," Einar says.

"He did."

"And your father shot him?"

"He did."

"So you saw a man die, too."

"I did."

"That must've been hard for you. You were young?"

Not yet a teenager, she thinks. But she says, "I want to see what's past the doors."

A stiff smile. "Of course, Hannah. I'll open the doors. Feel free to explore. I will make us coffee? A bit of a pick-me-up?"

She nods and takes the deal. They walk to the door, and he

opens it to reveal a hallway with multiple doors off it. He explains nothing, and leaves her to it.

Tipsy but not properly drunk, Hannah steps forward. The doors slide closed behind her. She's alone. For a moment, that gives her relief.

But then, a septic dread. The hallway is lit only by emergency lighting. Anyone could be waiting. Anything. The hairs on her arms stand at attention as she imagines ants moving behind the walls, underneath the grates, above her head . . .

She moves forward, the pain in her ankle dampened by the alcohol. She peers into the first room. As soon as she steps in, the lights flicker on. Bright, bold fluorescents. She blinks, lets her eyes adjust—

She sees a white room with a steel table in the middle and three Plexiglas walls—cages—that at first blush seem empty. But then she notices the little black shapes forming a small mist—a faint gray cloud that shimmers and shifts like a specter shuddering in the cold.

Mosquitoes. The *Aedes aegypti.*

The Plexiglas walls end before the ceiling—a fine mesh, like mosquito netting, finishes the distance. On the table is a smaller clear plastic box with a rubber fontanel on the side. Through which, Hannah thinks, you could thrust an arm. To determine bites? To test some kind of insect repellent?

She continues down the hall. Another door is a bathroom. The next door is a supply closet.

Then—a smell. Strong. Pungent. A whiff of soap and citronella. The odor crawls up her nose like a pair of hungry worms.

The next two doors lead into the same lab. She steps in and lights cascade on. This room is as big as the main Arca lab, and at first glance empty. A lab at the end of the world.

Then she spies, there on another steel table, a container. Styrofoam. A rim of black rubber separating the two halves. Like the one they found in the lake.

Hannah dry-swallows. She steps deeper into the room, her footsteps echoing. Over at the box, her fingers find the edges, tracing along the dark rubber. She starts to lift up, and it resists, so she urges it harder, and the lid pops—

"There you are."

"Jesus," she says.

"Apologies," Einar says, holding up both hands in a beseeching gesture. "You were gone awhile, and the coffee is done."

She looks down at the box and sees smaller containers tucked away between plastic dividers. These are cylindrical, not hexagonal. This isn't the same as the one in the lake. This is generic. Like all the others. Like the ones Ez uses.

Relief moves over her like the touch of a ghost, and she shudders in spite of it—or because of it.

"Find anything?" Einar asks.

"Nothing out of the ordinary," she reports.

* * *

Back at the table, a small coffee press—an AeroPress, he says. Next to it, a small electric kettle and a hand-grinder. Einar presses down on the plunger, extracting coffee into a small cup—"Espresso," he says. Hannah takes it to her chin and steam rises to her lips. "You saw the mosquitoes, then."

"I did."

"I hope your government lets me use them one day."

"I thought you had a partnership with them."

He fills his own demitasse and sips the black brew. "Sadly, not on this. Panic and fear drive today's discourse, I'm afraid. Releasing a modified mosquito has people afraid that we're going to give them all cancer or turn them into the blood-sucking equivalent of Spider-Man, I suppose. Science is trumped by ignorance when the ignorant are given a vote. We have the program in other parts of the world: South America, Madagascar, the Philippines. One day, perhaps we will convince your country it is safe. Maybe when dengue fever finally becomes a true epidemic in Florida, Louisiana, even here in Hawaii."

"Often that's when we wake up—just as we're on the cusp of disaster."

He offers up his demitasse. "To the cusp of disaster, then."

"Indeed." She clinks cups.

15

The memory of bedding Einar (or his bedding her) lingers through the first hour of sleep: his hands were slow and confident; his mouth eager, with his lips forming a sticky trail along her breast and down her side and between her legs; her pushing on top of him and the movement of them together, that and the half drunkenness making her feel swimmy, dizzy, giddy. But as deeper sleep draws her down, darker dreams take their place. Dreams of gagging, hacking—Hannah coughing so hard she sees stars, spitting up a phlegm-slick knot of squirming ants over her tongue and down her chin to the ground. Twin streams of them crawling out her nostrils. Bending forward, arms covered in biting mosquitoes, blood running off in watery rivulets. The ground covered with mealworms, wet and writhing over a field of their dead.

A distant echo of her father's voice. A gunshot. An animal scream.

And then she's awake.

"You," comes a voice. Venla. Hannah glances at the clock: just past midnight. Where's Einar gone at this hour?

Venla stands by a wardrobe made of red koa wood, hanging up shirts with an almost laser-guided precision.

Hannah's in a yurt. Einar's luxury yurt—two words that are so absurd together she can barely think them. Round walls framed in a crisscross diamond pattern of wooden slats, covered over with white leather.

Hannah sits up in the bed—a bed that so perfectly straddles the line between comfortable and supportive that she's not sure she has

ever met its equal—and Venla pauses in her task and walks over. The woman leans over the footboard, hands gripping the posts like each is a throat she'd like to choke.

"You fucked him," Venla says.

"That's not your business," Hannah answers. She eases the sheets to the side instead of pulling them tighter. Immediately she feels self-conscious. She decided to sleep with him because, or so she tells herself now, she hoped it would get her in his circle of trust. The closer she is, the more he might tell her. And that means the closer she gets to solving a murder and understanding this case. Last night, though, no such logic was present—all she could think was how long it had been, and how through the drunkenness (or because of it) she wanted him without mercy, without reservation, without caring about consequence.

"All things Einar are my business. You got drunk. He took advantage. It happens. You are not the first."

"I wasn't drunk. He didn't take advantage."

But now she's cursing herself. Because what Venla is saying is what everyone will say. She's here to do a job. Unburdened by bias. Even the *appearance* of having slept with Einar undermines her effort. The fact that she really *did* is just icing on that judgmental cake.

Venla stares down at her like Hannah is a piece of fast-food trash thrown from a speeding car. "Whatever helps you sleep at night, Ms. Stander. But please to be advised: Einar is my business. If you dim his light or damage his shine in any way, I will see it. And I will act."

"He's thinking of firing you."

Those words slip out of her mouth unguarded, and she immediately curses herself for letting them go. It's petty, catty nonsense. It isn't her style. And yet, the woman's scrutiny has left her feeling vulnerable. Cornered, like an animal. And cornered animals bite. Apparently with venomous passive-aggression.

The blow lands hard. Venla seems staggered by it. Her hands uncoil from the bedposts and she stands up straight. Looking off at nothing. Her lips move as if to speak, but the words are silent.

"Good luck with your investigation" is all she says. Venla snatches up a small bag from the corner of the room, and then leaves Hannah alone. In a luxury yurt that's not her own.

* * *

It's still night when Hannah heads back to Arca Labs, taking a few hasty minutes in Einar's bathroom to freshen up. Her messy tangle of hair will only reinforce the inaccurate narrative of her and Einar hooking up. She can't have that.

As she scrambles to make a hasty exit and head back to the labs, she begins to realize that she just complicated this investigation. Because she was drinking. And because—what? She thought she could make a power play? Use sex as a weapon? Or just because she wanted it and *at the time* figured, *I'm an adult woman in control of my sexual destiny; I can do as I damn well please.*

Did she seduce him? Or did he seduce her? Was it a seduction at all?

Damn it.

Hannah stalks the trail heading back toward Arca, ducking under palm fronds and pushing through dangling curtains of flowering vines.

Back at the pod, she grabs several more hours of witless, restless slumber. She floats in and out of sleep, recounting her mistakes—not just sleeping with Einar but every foolish thing she's said or done in her life and her career.

She draws herself out of bed in the morning (though she'd far rather hide under the covers and avoid the scrutiny that daylight will afford). In the rec room, she grabs a cup of coffee from a percolator. Will is nowhere to be found. Neither can she see Venla or Einar. Others are already in there, and she feels their gazes burning holes through her. Kit makes small talk, and Barry tries to crack jokes with Ajay (who stares back, implacable as the flat face of a tall cliff). Suddenly Ray is up behind her, and he says, sotto voce: "You bang him?"

"Jesus, Ray."

"You wouldn't be the first. The man is basically a pussy magnet. Handsome, but not too handsome. Rich enough to buy his own moon base. I'd fuck him if I could."

She wheels on him. Some of the coffee splashes up over the rim. She lies when she says: "I didn't. We drank. I fell asleep. End of story. Okay?"

"You're saying he showed you his Special Projects but not his 'special projects,' huh?" He waggles his eyebrows and smirks.

"You know," she says in a voice loud enough to be heard by all, "you told me people wouldn't like me here, but I think what you mean is, people don't like *you* here. Do they like you anywhere, Espinosa? I bet you don't have many fans."

"Ouch. Wasp has a sting."

She pushes past him.

He calls after her: "Got my eye on you, Agent Stander." Then, to the others: "The fuck are you looking at?"

She goes into the dorms, and Ray trails after. Without looking at him, she asks, "Where's Einar?"

"Hell if I know. I'm a liaison, not his schedule monkey."

"Where's Will?"

"I don't know that, either. I don't run this lab. Talk to David—"

As if conjured by his name, David appears out of the room in which Hannah was staying. Why was he in there? Looking for her? Looking to see if she wasn't there? Looking through her things, meager as they are? Paranoia seeps into her. She's off her game. Unbalanced and feeling it.

"Agent Stander, I was looking for you," Hamasaki says. "The storm that's coming is expected to make it here a little sooner—the weather system is spinning off the coast of Japan faster than we figured. Means the boat will be here this afternoon instead of tomorrow morning. Should be around four P.M."

Suspicion besieges her further. Is this even true? *They're trying to get rid of me.* She says as much: "You're kicking me out?"

"No, no, that's not it—but the boat won't make it back for a few days after that, and we've got people going off-island. This is your window."

Her heart suddenly feels like it's in a vise. Anxiety. Panic. She knows it. She mitigates it. The fear dogs at her just the same: *I'm not doing enough, I haven't solved this, we're no closer now than we were before . . .* "Where's Will?"

"Special Projects, maybe?" David says. Then, before she can ask more questions, "It's been really good having you. See you at lunch, Agent Stander."

* * *

Hannah starts packing. She doesn't have much to pack, but it gives her something to do while she fumes at herself, at the storm, at Einar, at everyone and everything.

Real quick, she flips the top of her laptop open to check her e-mail, types in her password (*compsognathus*), sees a message pop up from Hollis.

Call me. 911.

Laptop down, back to the door—

Kit almost runs headlong into her.

"Hey," Kit says. "You okay?"

"Fine," Hannah says, and she hears her own voice and it is most definitely not fine.

"Hey, don't listen to anybody around here. It's all bullshit, just office gossip. We're a bunch of weirdos trapped on an island with each other. Look, I'll be honest with you, I fucked Will a couple times when we first started, and that was a big dramatic how-do-you-do—not between him and me, because we're goddamn adults, but with everybody else. Gossip like that chums the waters and brings the sharks out in everybody—"

"I have to make a call. Where's the satphone?"

"Oh, uh, check with David. His office, probably."

"Thanks."

* * *

No wristband anymore. Can't get back into the labs proper. She has to wait till someone shows—and of course it's Kit. Kit, to her credit, plays it cool. All she asks as she opens the door for Hannah is "You seen Kano, by the way?"

Hannah says no.

"I need his help—there's a fluorescent out in the main lab."

They head into the lab wing. Hannah says, "If I see him, I'll tell him. Let me ask you something real quick."

"Shoot."

"You're the head of the mosquito project."

Kit smiles. "I am. And now you want to know why it's down in Will's kingdom. Or why I didn't tell you that."

"Well. Yeah."

"I didn't tell you because it's not my secret to tell. And as to why it's down there?" She lowers her voice. "I don't know. After Einar's last review, he yanked the project out from under my feet and stuck it with Will. No idea why. Will didn't know, either. Einar called it a 'necessary professional rearrangement.'"

"Do you have any theories as to why?"

"Maybe he doesn't think I'm good enough. Maybe he's a sexist asshole, of which there are many inside the vaunted halls of research." Kit shrugs. "It sucks, but what can I do? I still do backup research for it, and I'm the one scouting out which countries we can try to hit up next for the mosquito release. But that's not my jam. I'm a scientist. I want to make science, not phone calls."

Hannah parts ways with Kit, collects the phone, and heads outside. She paces the walkway as she makes the call to Hollis.

"Finally," he says. "Hold on, I'm looping in Ms. . . . sorry, *Dr.* Choi." Moments pass. A few clicks. Then: "Ez. You there?"

"You bet," comes Ez's voice. "Hannah on the line?"

"I'm here," Hannah says.

"We found a print," Hollis says.

"*I* found a print," Ez says.

"Yes, Dr. Choi found a print."

"Were you able to run it and find a match?" Hannah says.

"We did, and it's a real nut-kick. You know the name Archer Stevens?"

She does. Billionaire. Old money. Made *more* money off oil, then had a come-to-Jesus moment about global warming and the conflict in the Middle East and swore off the stuff like an addict in therapy, transitioning his entire financial world to supporting renewable energy, battery storage in particular. In her own parlance, the man went from being a devil to an angel. Whether it was a legitimate transformation or something driven by commercial interests, she has no idea. But now liberals and hippies have his face on posters.

"That body couldn't have belonged to Stevens," Hannah says. "The age doesn't track." Nor, frankly, did the fashion sense.

"It was his son," Ez says.

"Scottie Stevens," Hollis says.

"His son?" Hannah thinks of the shoes. The vest. The jeans. Kid was rich. Makes sense. "You talk to the father?"

"That's where it gets weirder: the father's gone off the radar."

"How do you mean?"

"Nobody will say it, but the guy's in the wind. When Archer Stevens takes a piss, the world knows about it because his people let the world know about it. He's as public as they come. And he hasn't been seen or heard from in a week. Rumor is that the paparazzo bastards who hang around outside his various homes and hot spots haven't seen him come in or out."

"What do we know about him?" The wind kicks up over the ocean—the sun is hot, but the air bites with cold teeth, and Hannah can't help but shiver. Everything suddenly feels claustrophobic. She answers that question herself: "Archer Stevens is one of Einar's competitors in the energy market."

"That is correct."

They tell her the same things she already knows, then Hollis adds some personal details: "Archer Stevens. Age sixty-one. He's had a few sexual harassment claims dog him, but he bought his way out like they all do. Only one child: Scottie Stevens. Age 26. Archer's single now: he divorced his wife, Eileen, four years back and, thanks to an ironclad prenup, got to keep most of his fortune. By all reports, he's an egomaniac in person but becoming something of a corporate culture hero. Rumors say he might try to go for a turn in politics as a result."

"You talk to the ex-wife?"

"She was prickly about him. Hasn't seen him. Said he sometimes talked about breaking away and going off the reservation—'taking some time for himself,' he called it—but he never did it. There's something else, though."

"What?"

Hollis says, "Stevens sits on the board of directors of a lot of companies. It's public, but not that public, and most of the culture hero stuff going around about him tends to ignore this. One of the boards Archer Stevens sits on? You know BHW? Blackhearts Worldwide?"

"Private military contractors. PMCs."

"Right. He's on their board with a couple of ex-VPs from other companies, an NRA lobbyist, one of our shittier attorney generals, and so on."

Problem with all of this is, how many of these bits are puzzle pieces that fit, or pieces that don't belong? She turns around. Makes sure nobody is out here with her. She feels eyes burning the back of her neck like sniper scopes. "You think Einar did this to him? Or did he do this to Einar?"

"Maybe this is how billionaires wage war on each other."

She tries to draw the narrative. "Stevens was just into clean energy, right? No genetic anything?"

"That's what we thought," Hollis says.

Ez adds, "Another one of those companies Hollis mentioned? He sits on the board of Mar-Gene as an angel investor. He's got money wrapped up there. *Lots* of money. He's a player in this space, just not a *noisy* one like Einar is."

"Mar-Gene is mostly plants, right? No bugs or other insects?"

"On the record, no. But entomology isn't a big community, Hannah. We've heard whispers that they've been whipping up some kind of terminator bugs: like Arca's mosquitoes, but for common crop pests. Borers and weevils and the like. One generation breeds in, and the next generation dies off."

"Archer didn't kill his own child. So that would mean Einar killed the boy to undercut a competitor." Her throat tightens at the thought: *I just slept with a man who may be a narcissistic corporate killer.* "Real talk. Is that even his speed? It seems . . . extreme. I don't get a read on him like that."

Neither Hollis or Ez can answer that, and they say as much.

Hannah hesitates, thinks out loud. "You need to check Scottie Stevens's phone. See if anything at all ties to this narrative."

"We don't know where it is."

Hannah shakes her head. She has to remember: Hollis is way behind the times, technologically speaking. Time to remind him of the reality. "Hollis, you have to sync up with the realities of modern tech. If Scottie had a newer phone—and a rich kid like that isn't running around with some clamshell ringy-dingy from 2005—then most of what he did probably kicked automatically to cloud servers. You've got his real fingerprint; now find his digital one."

Hollis says: "Hannah, this is why I love you. Old dinosaurs like me need young mammals like you."

"You need to get me paid better, then."

"We'll talk about that when you get back. Meanwhile, keep on looking. If something's going on there, you're the only eyes I got on the ground. If Einar wasn't Einar, I could probably pull the trigger now and get people on-site to tear that place apart. But we try that, we'll be hamstrung by lawyers soon as we step out of the gate. I need more. And you need to get it for me."

"Storm is rolling in. They're sending me away this afternoon."

"Then you better keep looking quick."

"I will."

Ez says, "Hannah? Stay safe out there."

"It's fine," she says. "I'm safe. I'm good. Thanks." But suddenly she's not so sure. She's got a sucking feeling in her gut, like a black hole has formed inside her stomach and is drawing all of her toward it. *I'm making mistakes out here. I'm getting sloppy.* And now time is ticking down. "Talk to you soon."

After they hang up, the satphone sits in her hand. Heavy and inert. Uncertainty courses through her. Did Einar really do this? It doesn't track. He's a man with a lot to lose. And a lot to build. This murder is petty, deranged, small. One dead son of a rival billionaire, stripped of skin and eaten by genetically modified ants? That's not something a philanthropist and billionaire benefactor does.

That's something a serial killer would do.

But then, maybe Einar is hiding in plain sight. Maybe he *is* a serial killer. What an amazing cover that would be. A man protected by industry, commerce, innovation, and all the money that comes with it. He does good things, yet he also uses that power to express the sick desire to destroy other people in the most egregious, demented way possible. A sociopath, a psychopath, a diseased lunatic clothed in the raiment of the wealthy and the benevolent.

Her thumb finds the buttons on the satphone and she plugs in the number to her parents' house. She doesn't expect them to answer, but then—

"Is that you, Hannah?"

"Hi, Mom."

"You're still out there, aren't you." Not a question. An accusation.

"I am. On the island."

"The Internet says there's weather headed your way." *The Internet says.* One of her mother's favorite sayings. Connecting online is the one guilty grid-based pleasure her parents have. They manufacture their own power, water, and food, but the Internet—and the phone line on which Hannah is speaking right now—still forms a tenuous thread connecting them to the Almighty Grid. They get it from satellite, and Hannah helped them set it up so that their web surfing is almost entirely anonymous. Using private search engines like Anonymouse, installing software like Hider-Bot, turning on two-stage identification, never entering in credit card information (not that her parents have credit cards).

Mom is addicted to the Internet, and Hannah knows why: It gives her all the bad news she so hungrily desires. All the threats about jihadists and commies and comets and water shortages, all the fearmongering about race wars and GMO corn and this or that president coming in with armed troops to take your guns away—she feeds off it the way a tick sucks blood. She doesn't believe *all* of it. But she takes it all in anyway.

(Mom almost unplugged from the Internet last year when the hackers took that passenger plane down. She told Hannah: "I read on the ConWar forums that it wasn't hackers at all, but an artificial intelligence from Iran. It was a state-sponsored terror attack, Hannah." Where people get this stuff, Hannah doesn't know. Mom disconnected for a little while, and then three weeks later was back again, drinking from the fire hose.)

"It's a storm," Hannah says. "I'm getting off-island before it hits."

"It's a tropical storm."

"I know. I'll be fine."

A hesitation. "I hope so, Hannah. We miss you." Three words. A rare showing of affection from her mother. Strained-sounding, but present nonetheless. Hannah appreciates them, even though she knows that, as with most things her mother says, they come with an unpaid, unseen cost. Subtext underneath the text.

"I miss you, too." And she does. Sometimes.

"Is everything okay?" Mom asks.

A popular question, and she knows what it means. Hannah does the reassurance tango: "Everything is good, Mom. The world is still spinning. No nukes, no biological disasters, no terrorist bio-weapons—"

"No, sweetheart. I mean with you. You sound on edge."

"I'll be okay. I'll be coming home soon."

"I hope so. You need to get here and see your father. We love you."

Why is Mom being so sweet? Hannah wants to suspect ulterior motives but cannot imagine what they would be. "Love you, too, Mom. Tell Dad the same."

"I will."

* * *

Hannah sits, puts on her running shoes. Time to pay another visit to Special Projects. It's time to get answers. Will may know who else in the world is capable of designing such a creature. Einar may know what this kind of thing would cost and who would be capable of paying the price. And if either of them is guilty, then she hopes like hell she will see it on their faces. A flinch, a twitch, a microadjustment of the muscles. Men lie. But lies are rarely perfect. Even if the words line up in a tidy row, they still skew crooked.

She gets up off the bunk. She's about to step out of the room when Ajay Bhatnagar steps in from the hall. He quickly closes the door behind him.

"Ajay—" she starts to say, but then he perforates her personal space. Suddenly she sees him as a threat. He's tall. Looks like a hatchet about to fall. He's not in a lab coat, and his black T-shirt shows off ropy muscles. Hannah's hands coil into fists.

"I looked at the samples," he says, almost in a whisper. "The ants. I got one of the carcasses from Dr. Mercado. The files, too, from Dr. Choi."

"Okay," Hannah says, not sure where this is going. He steps farther into the room.

She takes a step back.

He notices. It seems to shake him a little. "I'm here to help," he says. "You did not hear this from me."

"So far I'm not hearing anything from you."

"I looked at the genetic composition of your ants. They're elegant little monsters. I've only just opened the code, and already I see inside it what could be genes from marauder ants, harvesters, leafcutters. Someone of great skill crafted this creature. An artist."

"Who could be such an artist?"

"Around the world? Not many. A small list, to be sure."

He hesitates again. Something he's not saying. "What is it, Dr. Bhatnagar? I am short on time and long on a desire to get this done."

"I found genes in there that we engineered. At Arca."

"I know. The marker genes."

"Yes. But others, too. *Pogonomyrmex badius.* The Florida harvester ant—the one we have here? We've changed it. Subtly. Nothing so dramatic as the ants you found in that cabin. The gene that governs the length of the hair that runs along the body: We modified that gene for longer length of hair. To assist in pollination. That modification is present in the ant you brought us. Inert, but there." He flinches, like this wounds him to admit: "I designed that gene."

Hannah stands there, staring at him. Trying not to tremble. This is it. This is the start of what she needs. She has to call Hollis, has to convince Ajay to make a written statement—okay, no, what he told her isn't exactly a smoking gun, but it's the first firm, committed connection between the dead body and what's going on here at Arca. Her mind is a jumble of priorities and she has to focus hard and line them all up in the proper order. All her ducks in a row. (Or all the little ants . . .)

Ajay says: "You cannot tell anyone I told you. I'll lose my job. I'll lose access to the work. Arca owns it, owns the patents—"

"I understand. We'll figure it out." No need to tell him now that she *has* to tell someone. That's her whole purpose for being here.

"Tread carefully. Einar is protective of this work. Even if he isn't responsible, if he thinks this will blow back upon him . . ."

"I will. Let me ask you: Who here could have done this? Who could have really made those ants, Ajay?"

"Only one," he says. "Will Galassi. He is your artist."

The air is almost robbed from her lungs. She manages a stiff nod. "Thank you."

16

Hannah runs.

She runs despite her ankle. The pain there remains in recession—now it's only a twinge that snaps like an electric charge from the sole of her foot to the heel. It's small and she chooses to ignore it. Her mother once told her that pain has power over us only when we let it. That sometimes you have to ignore it in order to do work. In order to stay alive.

Hannah carries with her the satphone—snatched up again on her way out, not long after she returned it to its charging cradle. The day is bright, golden, blue—but out there, beyond the margins of the sea, hanging over the horizon sits a faint darkness. A coming storm.

It is now 10:00 A.M. She has six hours before the boat takes her away.

She runs toward Special Projects. Looping the island. Feet pounding the walkway boards. *Whump, whump, whump, whump.* Theories run laps in her head as her feet work. Did Einar dispatch his competitor, Archer Stevens? Or did Archer Stevens dispatch his own son—accidentally or on purpose? And where does Will Galassi fit into all this? If he truly is *the artist,* then what does that mean? Did Einar hire him? Did Archer? Or is he all on his own? She needs to see Will again. Needs to probe at his edges, see what she can tease out. And she needs to talk to Hollis, too. He can help her put the pieces together.

She looks down at the phone, and as she slows her run to a jog, she calls Hollis again. He doesn't answer, so she leaves a message on

his voice mail: "I need to talk to you. Contact me ASAP." She lets him know she talked to Ajay, then cuts herself off before the voice mail does it for her.

She runs through the trees, past the orchids. Toward the ridge that drops down to the beach, the ridge where birds nest. This morning the birds are squawking and shrieking loudly. Something about the cries is primal. It cuts right through her.

She watches one bird fly up into the sky in a clumsy spiral. Then it hitches and jerks, and plummets back to the earth.

Hannah slows to a stop. She watches birds big and small erratically flapping about. Nearby, not ten feet off the walkway, a big white bird with a long, sharp beak stabs at the ground—*tack, tack, tack*. It's got a nest nearby.

Then it shrieks and flies off.

A morbid curiosity sticks in her like a gaff hook, pulls her closer. Hannah steps off the path. The hard volcanic ground is sharp beneath her feet. The seabird's nest is a mound of dirt and pebbles—some shells, some sand, too—and she sees shapes in the center. Baby birds. Squirming about and screeching.

Another step closer and she sees.

The baby birds are bloodied. Feathers torn off in patches. Skin, too, in places. One is missing an eye. Another has its beak part of the way off. A third has only one foot—and then she sees the foot, gently sliding across the porous dark rock almost as if floating . . .

It's not floating. It's being carried.

Ants. Black ants, so black she did not see them against the surface of the volcanic ridge. Panic seizes her in a gauntleted grip, threatening to crush the oxygen right out of her lungs. Instantly, the feeling of formication trickles over her—*hand inside a mailbox, black ants showering the top of her arm, winding along the little hairs, crawling between fingers*—and she takes a quick step backward, shuddering—

Ants on her sneakers. A dozen of them. Heading toward the sock.

No, no, no—

She juggle-steps backward, almost twisting her ankle again but recovering at the last moment. She lifts her feet one after the other, shaking them, then wiping and swatting with her hands. Ants fall, tapping against the walkway, and she stomps them as they hit. She *feels* them give way—a slight pressure, then a zit-pop and a wet crush. Ants surge toward their fallen colony mates. As she staggers, the satphone in her hand slips—slick now with sweat—and bounces against a rock. The battery case on the back springs off; the batteries pop and roll.

Nearby: *thud.* A seabird—a white petrel—slams into the walkway, flapping about like one of its wings is broken. Squawking in pain.

Ants, maybe a dozen, swarm over it.

The bird stops thrashing and goes still.

More ants crawl up from the ridge and over the edge of the walkway.

Toward her. Marching in little streams. *The ants go marching one by one, hurrah, hurrah . . .* Hannah stifles a scream. The rock glistens as if wet. It's not wet. It's the ants: the sun is gleaming off their burnished black exoskeletons.

Hannah turns—she moves to the phone, but it's too late. Ants are already upon it, crawling over it. Coming toward her.

She does all that she can do now:

Hannah runs.

PART III

INVASION

invasive species (n)

An invasive species is a plant, fungus, or animal species that is not native to a specific location (an introduced species), and which has a tendency to spread to a degree believed to cause damage to the environment, human economy or human health . . . Biotic invasion is considered one of the five top drivers for global biodiversity loss. —*Wikipedia*

17

Hannah runs.

She is ten years old.

Her hands are covered in blood.

Her father is screaming her name.

Rewind.

Five minutes before. Hannah is kneeling in grass matted into mud, the tips of her shoes stuck in the wet ground. Her father is behind her to the left, rubbing circles into her back. Her mother stands in front of her. "Don't coddle her through this, Hugh."

"This is hard. You know it's hard, Belinda, come now."

"Then she shouldn't have named it."

Under Hannah's right arm, a six-month-old goat. Bucky. She called the animal Bucky because he's a funny little thing who bucks and kicks out his back hooves like he thinks he's a rodeo bronco even though he's really just a tiny goat.

In Hannah's left hand is a butcher knife.

"We can use the rifle," Dad says.

"No," Mom says. "We won't waste the bullet. And a goat's head is hard. The shot has to be just right." She leans forward, now speaking for Hannah's benefit: "Besides, she needs to know where her food comes from. She needs to feel it. This is how we eat. This is how we survive."

"It's okay if you don't want to do it," Dad says to her.

"*Hugh.*" It silences him. It always does.

The goat wriggles in her grip. Little bleats: *behh, behhh, beh.* Small hooves smooshing prints into the mud.

Mom reaches out, holds Hannah's shoulders and squeezes. It's meant to be caring, she thinks. Reassuring. "I love you. You can do this."

Hannah thinks: *It's like they taught you. You've seen Mom do this a hundred times.*

She's seen Dad do it, too—though he never seems to do it well, and he never looks happy doing it. Mom is the champion at it.

She hears Mom's voice in her head: *One day I'll die, Hannah, and you'll need to know how to do this.* A surge of sudden anger as Hannah's imaginary response rises within her: *No! One day I'll just go to the grocery store like normal people do and buy it with money I made at a job.*

Mom doesn't think that will be an option in the future, though. Banks will fail. The climate will ruin everything. Maybe superstorms. Maybe a terrorist attack. Maybe a bioweapon will go off on purpose or accidentally—or some new strain of flu will leap from a bat to a pig to people, or it'll be war or overpopulation or, or, or. An endless cascade of reasons why grocery stores may not exist in the future, near or far. A host of objections that lead to this: Hannah has to learn to kill and butcher an animal. To survive.

Eyes on her. Mom's eyes. It's a hard stare, but a kind one. Mom believes she can do this.

Hannah can't disappoint her mother. She makes a noise—an unanticipated, grief-struck cry—as her right elbow jerks hard, the arm slicing across Bucky's throat.

The goat makes a loud, ragged bleat. It's cut short quickly, but the sound startles Hannah. She does what she's not supposed to do—

She lets go.

The goat bucks and hops, jumping away. Blood soaking its white front. A hiss of arterial spray peppers Mom's face, dotting her glasses. She takes it in stride, doesn't even clean her glasses, instead growls in the back of her throat and goes after the goat. She's already talking about how she told Hannah not to let go, and she wonders aloud if the cut was deep enough and Dad is suddenly yelling about how they should have gotten out the .22 like he said, the old bolt-action in the barn, and Hannah stops listening. Even as her father reaches for her, she ducks his grip and she runs, hard as she can.

Crying. Hands bloody. The knife dropped somewhere behind her, stuck blade-down in the ground like a surrendering flag.

18

This is how we survive.

Feet on the walkway: pounding with the surf, thudding with her heart. She thinks: *I dropped the satphone. I need it.* But it's too late to go back.

Hannah heads in the direction of the Cove—Special Projects. Maybe Will is there. Or Einar. They'll know what to do. Won't they? Are they prepared for this? Or the darker thought:

Did they make this happen?

She rounds the low point of the northern tip of the island, and as it starts to rise back up again, skids to a sudden halt—

A body. On the decking. Fifty feet away. Facedown. Hannah calls out before she even sees who it is—

The body moves. Shifts. She puts more gas in her tank and hard-charges toward the figure, her ankle sending out pulses of pain with increasing frequency.

It's Kano. The young man. His body moves again. But it's not his body moving. It's his clothing. A ripple of shirt fabric and then ants stream out from underneath the sleeves and the neckline and the bottom hem. They move in little rows, carrying bits of something. *Carrying bits of Kano,* she realizes. Swatches of him. Skin bits, chewed raggedy. Marching them in the other direction.

She winces, knows she shouldn't do it, but reaches out with a long arm and grabs a hank of his hair and lifts up his face—

It peels away from the deck. Sticky blood pools. Around the top of his face is a reverse superhero mask: all the skin around the eyes and the bridge of the nose has been clipped away. Ants dangle from

the wet muscle and fleshy edges like sailors hanging off the lifting stern of a sinking boat, their jaws holding them there like little vise grips.

They begin to drop off his face: *tick, tick, tack,* one by one.

And they begin to move toward her.

They *all* do now: they leave Kano's feet and begin to swarm toward her. Antennae searching the air. Heads up. Jaws working.

Hannah turns, falls on her ass. She begins to backpedal as they stream closer and closer, too fast, a sudden carpet of them rising from his body and moving like a rippling tide. She tucks and rolls off the walkway, then uses that small momentum to get to her feet.

Behind her, the sound of more shrieking, warbling birds.

Ahead, the ants pour forth. The trail of them goes all the way to Special Projects. Through the trees. Off the walkway. A little crooked stream of skin flags carried onward. The wind dies back and she suddenly smells the stink of piss and voided bowels. Her stomach churns.

She thinks: *Go back the other way.*

But the ants are coming from that direction, too. They're *everywhere.*

So as the ants *tick-tack-click* toward her, she takes a running jump and vaults over the walkway—and over the ants. She lands heel-first in a patch of sand, and almost goes akimbo. But somehow she leans forward, her arms reaching out for balance—and she makes another jump—

And jumps over the edge and into the blue waters of the lagoon.

INTERLUDE

HOLLIS COPPER

Hollis tries calling that number back, but nothing. Doesn't even ring. He tries the numbers of the other phones there, and still, nothing. He e-mails Hannah with the same message he sent her before:

Call me. 911.

Then he tries to e-mail David Hamasaki—he keeps it brief. *Have Hannah call me ASAP.*

But that e-mail goes out and bounces right back: No server, SMTP not found (whatever that means), blah blah blah.

He listens to Hannah's message again: *I need to talk to you. Contact me ASAP. Spoke to Ajay Bhatnagar. He said our ant contains more than just Arca marker genes. It contains other proprietary material . . .* Then she ends it, and that's it.

It's been a hard year for Hollis Copper. The world doesn't even know how hard it was. Most folks in this country think the downing of Southwest Flight 6757 is open and shut. And the politicians like it that way because that narrative is easy: domestic terrorists sought to bring down the plane (so goes the story) in order to start a new civil war in the country. Tea Party types. Wack jobs. It had a chilling effect on a lot of the hard-right rhetoric, which Hollis thought was a pretty good side effect—but the other effect, the one that scares him blue, is that Congress used that as a battering ram to gain greater domestic surveillance powers.

Which, of course, is how all this started in the first damn place.

It wasn't any domestic terror group that brought down that flight. It was a self-aware surveillance program designed for the NSA. And a group of hackers Hollis recruited helped bring that artificial intelligence down. (Or so he hopes. He still wakes up with the fear that the program, Typhon, is out there somewhere—hiding in networks like a forgotten disease ready to one day roar back and kill them all.)

Hollis went through hell to make all of that happen. Got his ass kicked raw in some horror house in West Virginia. Then had to endure six months of secret tribunals just to figure out what happened (and he's not sure the entire picture is clear for any of them to see). Not to mention watching how the government spun the whole story—and how the media helped. Now everyone is willing to give up a little more of their freedom for what they feel is protection. A snake biting its own tail. Chomp.

So, Copper going back to the FBI was supposed to be like a vacation for him. Back on the job. Working again as an agent on things he *understood.* Crime is easy to figure out. Even serial killers have an ethos. A blueprint of some kind: emotional, intellectual, whatever.

But now he's worried.

On the desk in front of him lie file folders of all the staff present at Arca Labs. None of them has pinged his radar. None are criminal. None have demonstrable mental health issues—or at least issues that have left a paper trail. Though he hasn't done a deep dive. He doesn't even have the *resources* for a deep dive. The NSA might.

It hits him. He doesn't need the NSA. He just needs some old friends.

Hollis picks up the phone, punches in a number.

A gruff voice answers: "I'm told this is Hollis Copper calling me, but that can't be right, because the Hollis Copper I know wouldn't ever want to talk to an old crazy man like me."

"And yet here we are. Hello, Wade."

Wade Earthman grunts and chuckles. "Hello, Hollis."

"I need a favor."

"I like favors. Especially when it means the Federal Bureau of Privacy Invasion owes me one. What do you need?"

19

Hannah breaks the surface. Gasping for air. Blinking salt water out of her eyes.

From here, for this moment, everything is calm. She can hear only the water lapping at her neck and cheek. The sound of wind. Her panic starts to recede, swallowed back down into her belly like a mouthful of stomach acid.

But then another sound: birds squawking.

And something beyond that: someone screaming.

Anxiety rises up in her, a red dragon with burning breath. It threatens to sink her like a stone. *Get control of yourself,* Hannah thinks.

She dives again, and swims hard—arms out, joints burning with the exertion. Pushing herself through the space. She tries to discern just how bad this is. How many ants could there be? Who did this? This is an attack. On Arca Labs. Or Einar.

Above her: a shadow. Hannah halts her momentum and corkscrews her body so she's looking up—

A human shape. Floating there, cruciform. Nearby bobs a round shape like a basketball. No. Not a basketball. A helmet. The pilot's helmet. The helicopter.

She realizes she hasn't seen the pilot since he landed. He's been here, at the helicopter, all along. It's big enough to sleep in. And now here he is, dead in the water. Blood drifts off him like plumes of purple ink. And little shapes—struggling, paddling black insects.

Hannah tries not to scream. Bubbles release from her nose and between her teeth as she squeezes her eyes shut and swims on.

Soon the ground is beneath her. Her palms flat on reef and pebble. With both arms she drags herself out of the water, her knees and legs under her as she gasps for air. Ahead of her, the beach. Beyond that, the first ridge and Arca Labs. She looks for ants. None here. Not now. Good.

A plan starts to form. Get to Arca. Bring everyone into a single place. What's the most protected area? The lab, maybe. Big enough to work.

Then wait. A boat will come this afternoon.

They just have to survive long enough.

* * *

The reception area is eerily serene. The lights are on. It's quiet. Hannah's almost afraid to make any noise.

The moment doesn't last.

Somewhere deep in Arca, someone yells. A panicked sound.

Hannah pushes on out of the reception area, down the tunnel to the second bubble, the bubble with two doors: one leading to the living quarters, one leading to the labs. She tries to go to the labs but—

She has no wristband. No RFID to open the door.

"Shit," she says under her breath.

To the living area, then. Good. Fine. Her laptop is there. Maybe she can get it and send an e-mail—

She steps through the door. Through the next tunnel. Into the rec room.

Three people in this room. One woman is facedown on the floor. Hannah doesn't recognize her. One of the younger workers, maybe. The girl's long chestnut hair shifts by her scalp as *things* crawl underneath.

Not far away, curled up on the couch, is the man from the cook line: pale, bleach-blond, thin, too thin. His back rises and falls. His breath is wheezing. She watches a line of ants crawl up from under his shirt, up the highway of his spine along his neck, and under his hair.

Leaning up against the bookshelf—books tumbled around him, the Settlers of Catan box overturned, its bits scattered about like pieces of a broken puzzle—is David Hamasaki. His face is a mask of ants. They tug at pieces of flesh peeling off his face. They have not yet stripped much of him away; their work has only just begun.

David's eyes rotate in their sockets. He's still alive. "David . . ." Hannah says, her voice cracking.

His gaze falls upon her. His lips work soundlessly. All that comes out is a squeaking wheeze. Hannah is paralyzed. She wants to run over and sweep the creatures off him, but if Ez is right and all it takes is one sting—one sting to paralyze, and one sting to summon the others—then she is exposed. Vulnerable. Already the ants are in this room with her . . .

A new sound interrupts her thoughts—banging from the other bubble, from the dorms. Thumping. Mumbled yelling. Not one person. Several. Hannah envisions the scenario: survivors running to the dorms, closing the doors, locking themselves in. The doors are pressurized, maybe the ants can't get in there. Which leads to the question: How did they get in here at all? *HVAC,* she thinks. Air-conditioning.

Air-conditioning.

The ants in the cabin died because of a late snap frost.

There, on the wall—a fire extinguisher. One in every bubble. More, probably, in the labs proper. Hannah creeps around the edge of the room. Above her in the vents she hears a sound: a *tick-tick*. More ants. She turns, sees the black shapes pushing their way out of the vents. Squirming, wriggling. Some creep along the curved wall and ceiling. Others just drop, pitter-pattering against the carpet.

She moves fast, grabs the fire extinguisher off the wall. She hopes it's the right kind—a CO_2 extinguisher, because the CO_2 liquid expands very rapidly to become a gas. And as a result, it gets incredibly cold. If it's just a chemical powder, it won't work.

She wheels, backs herself against the curvature of the wall. Her finger tugs the ring and then she squeezes the trigger. A cold blast of CO_2 hoses down the space in front of her. Wisps of cloud dance in the air.

The ants ahead are covered in a rime of white. They turn in dizzy circles. Some list like drunken sailors and topple over onto their backs. The others just stop moving. They freeze in place, mandibles wrenched open. Only their antennae twitch in what she hopes are their death throes.

A brief, if difficult, choice pings Hannah's radar: Save David now? Hit him with the extinguisher? Or save the others? The decision is easy and quick: the others can help her. She opens the dorm door—

Ants crawl the floor, the ceiling. Not a swarm—there are several inches between each of the insects. They walk with little urgency. Meandering. Searching. Content to roam and rove.

Two more corpses toward the end of the hall, near the door. Nobody Hannah immediately recognizes. But closer is the nurse, against the wall, lying on her side. Snot running out of her nose. Blood from where the ants are peeling the skin off her hands and face.

Hannah feels ants on her feet, crawling up her legs, and she spins around—but there's nothing there. Formication again. A sensation driven by fear.

Calm down, Hannah. She holds up the extinguisher as someone pounds on one of the dormitory room doors. Someone else hammers on another door on the same side. Nearby on the wall is another fire extinguisher. Good.

She plucks the second extinguisher from its bracket, tucks it under her armpit. Then Hannah wades into the hallway, using the first extinguisher to blast the ants ahead of her and above her. Gouts of CO_2 in white dragon's breath. *Whoosh.* Ants fall from the ceiling, writhe on the ground. Others start to head toward her. She sweeps the geysering trail of carbon dioxide across the floor, freezing the demon ants where they move. They twist and curl in on themselves.

Hannah backs up against one door. She hammers an elbow into it and yells, "Open the door. It's Hannah."

Fumbling on the other side, and it suddenly hisses open.

"Oh, holy hell, thank God," she hears Kit say, and the woman throws her arms around Hannah's shoulders.

"No time for that," she says, handing Kit the other extinguisher.

Behind Kit, Ray steps out. "Jesus tits," he says. His face is ashen. He sees the ants on the ground and staggers back. He looks like he might puke.

More ants stream toward them, but Hannah hits them with the CO_2. *Pssh, pssh, pssh.*

Hannah extends an arm and bangs on the neighboring door with the side of her fist. "C'mon, we have to go."

The door judders and slides. Ajay and Nancy Mercado emerge. Nancy sees Hannah and her face scrunches up like a squeezed fist. "*You.* This is your fault, somehow. *Tanga. Kainin mo tae ko!* You brought this on us—"

Ajay steadies her. "We have to go, Nancy. We have to—"

"Shut up." The little woman pushes past Ajay, and her face is a rictus of inchoate rage. "You brought this to our door. You—"

A black shape lands atop the tightly bound hair on Nancy's head. One of the ants crawls out across the Rubicon of the woman's hairline.

"Nancy," Hannah says in alarm. "You have—"

"I said to shut up! Listen to me—"

The ant opens its mandibles and bites down. Hannah backhands the woman. Nancy cries out.

Hannah shows the woman the back of her hand. A smashed ant—wet and black, a droplet of mucus flecked with ground pepper—hangs there.

"Oh" is all Nancy says.

"We need to go," Hannah says. "Stick close. You see the ants, say something. Kit or I will hit them with the fire extinguishers. Ready?"

They move.

* * *

In the next room, they see David. The attack on his face and hands continues. For a moment, in the stunned silence, they can *hear* the ants working on him: the faintest sound of chewing. Moist clicks. Some have managed to pull off bits of skin no bigger than a child's fingernail. They carry them back up toward one of the HVAC vents.

"We need to save him," Nancy says.

"He's dead," Ray answers. "We gotta move."

Hannah shifts from foot to foot. "He's not dead." She thinks to add but doesn't: *Not yet*. What happens if they pull him back? Just because he's still breathing doesn't mean he'll make it. What does the ant venom do? On the exposed parts of his skin she can see little red blisters. The marks of their stings, she suspects. With that much of their toxin pumping through him, is his death inevitable? Or can they forestall it? She asks, "What about EpiPens? Could they work?"

Ajay says, "Maybe. If this is anaphylaxis, it couldn't hurt."

No time for further discussion. Hannah turns the extinguisher toward David. It hisses as it exhales its icy breath. The ants shake and shudder, falling from him like climbers off a mountain. She turns it away from his face—now red and chapped from the CO_2—and blasts his hands. The ants there fall away.

"Let's grab him," she says to Ray.

Ray gives her a look. "You sure about this?"

"No. But we have to try." To Kit: "Be ready."

Kit nods.

Hannah and Ray step toward him. Hannah tucks her own extinguisher under her arm and the two of them reach for David, hands tucked under his armpits. They start to lift him up. Hannah feels something moving under his shirt and she knows it's just an illusion, a delusion, another fear sensation—

But then Ray cries out. David's body drops, hits hard. Ants begin to stream out from his sleeves and pant legs. Ray curses and throws himself backward. "They're on me, shit, they're on me." He raises his hand to smack at the ants that Hannah sees are now crawling up his fingers, toward his wrist.

Ajay catches his hand. "No! Kit, quick."

Kit blasts Ray with the extinguisher, and the ants drop. Hannah uses her own on the ants pouring out of David's clothing, stopping them in their tracks.

But then the streams of CO_2 gutter and sputter. It's running out of juice.

Ray is standing there, stock still, growling through gritted teeth: "Are there any more? Any on me? *Are there any more on me.*"

"No. No. I got them," says Kit.

"We have to go," Nancy says suddenly. Her voice is small and afraid. "We have to leave him."

They all know it's true.

The choice is made. They leave David Hamasaki to die.

INTERLUDE

HOLLIS COPPER

Still no contact with Arca Labs or the Kolohe Atoll. And Archer Stevens is still missing, too. His son, dead. Hollis chews on that for a while. Maybe Archer did it. Maybe he killed his own kid. Why? Does that even make sense? Hollis sits at his desk, his knee jumping like kernels of popping corn in a hot pot.

The phone rings. He hauls it to his ear. "Go."

"Got something," Wade growls. "Two of those scientists ought to earn a second look from the likes of the Federal Bureau of Assholes, I think."

"Who? And why?"

"William Galassi and—shit, I don't know how to pronounce this name, but Ajay B . . . Buh-hat-nuh . . ."

"Bhatnagar. He's Indian."

"Fry bread Indian or naan Indian?"

"Jesus, Wade."

"C'mon, Copper, I'm just fucking around. I did the research, remember? Guy's from Chennai. Rich family. You want to hear about him or about Galassi?"

"Go with Galassi. What's his deal?"

Wade snorts hard, like he's sucking a booger back up into his sinuses. "Galassi's got an 'incident' from way back. Private school days. High school. He, ahh, tried to poison a classmate."

"What?"

"Looks like he had a bully—boy was a senior while Galassi was a—let's see here—a junior I guess it was. Wasn't your normal

everyday bully, but one of those who gets on you like a bad smell. Boy named Charlie Irvin. Charlie hurt Galassi at one point, enough to send him to the hospital with a broken thumb. But you know how it is: they treat bullies like they're just as much the victims, so the boy got suspended. Then, when he came back, Galassi used a poison—oleander, the report says—on Irvin. But the bully survived. Whether because Galassi used a low-potency dose on purpose or just fucked up killing him, I can't tell."

Hollis asks the obvious question: "How'd we miss that?"

"It was buried. Wasn't in a place you'd look. An old archived external hard drive from the Columbus, Ohio, police department."

Columbus. That's where Galassi grew up. This is a juvenile record, and Hollis knows that with a lawyer and some paperwork, you can get those expunged. But *expunged* doesn't mean *erased*. Paper trails exist. Data trails do, too, clearly. Either Will had lawyers handle this, or this is Einar's hand trying to sweep it all under the rug. Whatever the case, someone thought it was gone.

And Wade the hacker just proved that it wasn't.

Instead he asks, "Galassi ever do time for it?"

"Nope. Parents are old money and got a good lawyer, by the look of it. And it never got into the news. Galassi did a year's worth of community service. Was treated as a youthful fuckup."

"Shit." Hollis's nostrils flare. "Bhatnagar?"

"That one's even more fun. Not a crime, but a censure. A scientific censure driven by some civil rights watchdog group. He did kind of a caste-based eugenics research paper. Seemed to feel that the only people allowed to work in genetics should be the genetically pure. It got circulated, dumped him in hot water."

"What kind of hot water?"

"Censure is formal, but no formal effects, I guess. Mostly just made it hard for him to get a job."

Bhatnagar's only been working for Einar for five years now. This explains why his career record before that was spotty and inconsistent. Copper's best guess is that Einar saw past the censure straight

through to Bhatnagar's skill set. The controversy, like Galassi's crime, could be buried.

Hollis thinks both men are problems. *Ajay is a racist. Galassi tried to kill a classmate.* Are either of those things enough to indict?

No. But enough to make Hollis wonder. And worry.

"Thanks, Wade."

"So, I can chalk this up as an official favor?"

"You can."

"You're a peach, Hollis Copper."

"The peachiest." He hangs up the phone, then picks it back up and books a flight to Kauai, ASAFP: as soon as fucking possible.

20

Moving out of the living area and into the labs feels like an out-of-body experience. Hannah leads, and the others follow in a cluster facing outward. Their movement is slow and deliberate. Nancy's the one who opens each door with her wristbound RFID chip.

The labs are eerily still and quiet. Only hours before, Arca was a functional place. Now all they can hear are the ants crawling on the walls and in the ducts. They see them, too: crossing in front of them or above them in trickling columns. One of the lines of ants is carrying forth tiny, wrinkled bits—she knows what it is. Skin. The only question is to whom those morsels of flesh belonged.

The cafeteria makes that answer both easier and harder to answer.

"Oh God," Kit says, covering her mouth.

They'd been eating breakfast when it happened. Chairs are overturned, food is on the floor. Bodies sit slumped against tables or on the ground with their arms splayed out as if reaching for something or someone. Hannah wonders: Did the ants come out of the vents here, too? Did those gathered think that the ants crossing the carpet were Arca's own harvesters? Did someone laugh it off or try to crush one or brush it away?

Now the dozen or more who fell to the ants are covered by them. Black, writhing masses of insects. The *sound* is intense, like a thousand little rats chewing drywall into a wet paste. She shudders. The way the ants swarm, the way the bodies shift beneath the throng . . . It's not just that the victims are still alive. It's that the

sheer weight of the ants is making them move: the rise and fall of the swarm on still-living bodies.

The air draws into Hannah's lungs and stays there—it's like she cannot release it. She feels a kind of existential panic. Not just a panic for her or those around her, but for the fragility of life. It's the same feeling she gets any time she passes roadkill on the highway shoulder—a deer blasted into two halves by a speeding Peterbilt or a possum practically erased, all its margins ruined by a half ton of speeding Detroit steel. Life is woefully short. Flesh is vulnerable. The only future we're all guaranteed is one where everything ends.

Hannah and the others stand at one end of the cafeteria, knowing their only goal is to get to the other end. The ants, well involved and industrious, have not yet discovered them.

"What the fuck do we do?" Ray asks.

"I don't know," Hannah says. It's not the answer she wants, and all her muscles tighten.

"We leave," Nancy says. Quiet as the others, as if fearing to spook the ants into swarming toward them. "We go back the way we came. The helicopter—"

"The pilot is dead. I saw him in the water."

"Then the boat. We go to the boat."

"Boat's not here yet. Won't be for four or five hours."

"Not that boat. There's another one. A blue-water fishing boat we keep at the Cove. Diesel. We have it just in case."

Ray says, "I'd say this is damn sure a *just in case* kind of moment."

"There may be others here," Hannah says. "Some of them may even be in the lab. We can't just abandon them."

"We can," Nancy insists. "And we must."

"I agree," Ajay says. "We have a real chance here. To survive."

Ray scowls, casts about an angry glare. "No, Hannah's right. We gotta look. She looked for us and now we're out here."

That surprises Hannah. Earlier, when he suggested they leave David there, she thought he was just another self-interested survivor. *Like my parents,* she thinks. Over time she's come to feel this way about Mom and Dad: so interested in their own survival, they've completely rejected the existence of other human beings. Community means nothing, only the survival of the family unit matters. And it always makes her wonder: Would they save themselves before saving her? *Put your oxygen mask on first before you help your children . . .*

"You're just doing it for your boss," Nancy says.

"He's your boss, too. And I'm not doing it for Einar only. I'm doing it for . . ." Ray's voice trails off. "Barry."

"Barry? Why Barry?" Nancy asks.

"Because he's right there," Ray says, pointing.

Sure enough, across the room, through the door leading to the lab: there's Barry's face. Peering through the porthole glass, moonlike. He smiles—a desperate, mad smile.

"Shit," Nancy says.

"We need to get across there," Hannah says, suddenly irritated at Nancy. "My extinguisher's almost out. I don't know that we can do it with just yours, Kit. Any ideas? We can't just run for it."

But nobody has time to answer. Because across the room, the door opens, and Barry bolts like a tumbling boulder straight into the cafeteria, screaming as he runs.

* * *

The vagrant runs right toward Hannah across the meadow, the tall grasses blowing. He's got something in his hand. A knife, maybe. It's Roy. Roy Peffer. The town crazy. Weirdo. (Everyone makes up stories about him—but Hannah isn't supposed to know those stories because she's not supposed to stay in town long enough to talk to the others.) Roy is saying something as he runs, yelling it, but the wind carries his voice back over the field, to the fencerow and beyond.

Everything seems slow. His running. His yelling. Hannah's heart—a fast beat slowed to a crawl. It was such a nice day, too.

The sound of a gunshot.

Roy Peffer hitches, his left shoulder—no, his right, because he's facing her—dips down, but he keeps on keeping on for another three, four steps. His hip pivots as his one leg gives out. Whatever's in his hand goes spiraling. He falls as the blood starts to spread across his breastbone. Then the grass swallows him up. Disappears him as if he never existed at all.

Hannah blinks.

All of it is gone. She's in the cafeteria at Arca Labs and Barry Lowe is charging into the heart of the room. He's got something in his grip. Something heavy that needs two hands to carry. *Another fire extinguisher,* Hannah thinks, but then Barry whips around and what emits from his extinguisher isn't a cold white cloud meant to put out fire but *fire itself.*

Great bursts of flame sear the air. Barry screams, "Come on come on come on!" He moves in a half circle, turning his fire toward the ground and, *whoosh, whoosh,* spitting more fireballs. Above his head, a white particulate dust shimmers in the air like the faintest snow.

Kit gives Hannah a look, and they nod to one another. Fire extinguisher up, Kit moves into the room, discharging CO_2 at any ants that come toward them. The others follow close after. As they get nearer to Barry, Hannah taps Kit on the arm and gestures behind them, and Kit circles around to the back, covering their rear as Barry handles what's ahead of them.

Together, they move toward the lab through a gauntlet of black ants and human bodies. Some of the ants are charred and smoldering. Some have not been tempted from their human prizes. Hannah doesn't think Barry burned any of those poor souls, though she wonders if there'd be a mercy there. One victim lies with her head to the side on the table—Lila. The girl with the ladybug freckles. Her tongue is thrust out and resting on her lower lip. It's covered in a rime of dry saliva. An ant dances on the end of it. Another ant skitters up her nostril.

The girl's eyes blink.

Hannah chokes back a sound as, behind her, Ray urges her forward. They move to the lab door. It hisses open and then shuts behind them.

Hannah shudders. She can't shake the feeling of ants crawling all over her. She can't shake the image of that girl's face. Staring at Hannah as the colony claims her and all her freckled skin as its own.

21

The door that leads out of the cafeteria doesn't go right to the labs. It goes to another of the telescoping tunnels, and the lab is still another door away.

No ants here. Not a single one.

Barry is bent over, hands planted on his knees. Gulping for air. At his feet is what he had been carrying: a metal container with a plastic nozzle sticking out like a mosquito's proboscis. The nozzle's end is puckered with white powder. Jutting up from the bottom at a forty-five-degree angle is a metal rod duct taped to the base. At the top end of it, taped into its U-shaped bracket, is a lighter.

Impressive, Hannah thinks. *An improvised flamethrower.* She remembers making all sorts of weapons as a kid. Spears. Traps. A bang-stick out of a broom handle, a spring, a ballpoint pen, a shotgun shell. The only flamethrower she'd ever made was the simplest kind: a can of hair spray and a Bic lighter. Mom encouraged everything but that one. *Fire,* the woman said, *isn't something you control, no matter how much you think you do.*

Hannah crawls out of her own memories and looks up to see ants swarming on the other side of the cafeteria door. Lines of them crossing the glass of the porthole window, meeting each other in the center. A bullet hole in glass, engineered in reverse.

But they're not coming in.

She says as much aloud.

"Yeah," Barry says. "I sealed off the lab HVAC vents. I'll show you." He gets up with a grunt and blearily heads toward the lab entrance.

"This is fucked," Ray says. He grabs Hannah by the elbow. "This is them, isn't it? These are your monster ants."

She nods. *My ants. My demon ants.*

"Thanks for saving our cans back there."

"Thanks for backing my play."

Nancy gives them both a look like a pair of hypodermic needles.

"Fuck you, Nancy," Ray says.

"Fuck *you,* Ray." Ahead, the door opens for Barry. "We could've gone for the boat. Or even just waited in the ocean till this all blows over."

"We saved Barry."

Kit jumps in: "I think Barry saved *us.*"

Barry gives a goofy smile, but one tinged with lunacy and exhaustion. Then, suddenly—movement near Hannah's elbow. Something skittering. She gasps, pulls away—just as Barry reaches in and scoops up Buffy, the praying mantis.

"So," Barry says, smacking his lips together. The mantis runs up his hand and perches on the pad of flesh at the bottom of his palm. "Here's the sitch. I locked down the HVAC vents from here to the back of the lab—into the bee room, the ant room, and my lab. I also sealed the doors to the bee room and the ant room because I can't control the exit points. Bees and ants have a way out, which means our new invasive friends have a way in."

Hannah asks, "How are the vents sealed?"

"Electronically," Ajay answers.

Barry nods. "Yup. I used the network to seal them off. It means it's going to get hot in here. No AC."

"Phones?" Hannah asks. "We could use the satphones from David's office." Even just saying his name, she sees how the others react. Grief and shock warring in their eyes. He meant something to them. Nothing will bring him back, though, so she says: "David is gone. We have to accept that and move on."

"Yeah, yeah," Barry says, swallowing hard. "Okay. Okay. The phones are a problem." He reaches into one of the lab counters and

pulls out the two remaining satphones. Hannah doesn't understand the problem until he flips his hand. The back of each phone is open. The battery packs are gone.

"Somebody did this to us," Ray says. "On purpose."

"*Putang ina mo,*" Nancy says. "Who?"

"It's Will," Ajay says. "Will did this. I *never* trusted him."

"You're fucking nuts!" Kit says. "Will is a puppy. He's one of the few nice guys I've met. Maybe *you* did it, Ajay. Maybe it's one of us in this room."

"Maybe it's Einar. He's not here, either," Nancy says. She throws up her hands. "I see that look. Don't be naive. He isn't like us. The way he watches people. He's like that praying mantis. Cutting people apart as he looks at them. Ready to take your head if he needs to."

"Everybody calm down," Hannah says. "Doubt and suspicion won't help us. We need to focus on next steps."

"Maybe it was you," Nancy says.

"It wasn't me, Nancy."

"Oh, sure. You come waving your hands around, talking about some ant we made, and then next thing we know: Here they come. Marching into our lab. Killing us off one by one. Guess that was just some kind of coincidence, hm? Or *maybe* you came here planning on killing us all in order to cover up your own—"

"*Whoever did this,*" Barry yells, "they *also* sabotaged our satellite."

"That means no Internet?" Hannah asks.

"Bingo was his name-o. Means no communication off the island at all. Except for what's at the Cove."

"I told them about the boat," Nancy says, sour-faced.

"The boat has a radio. That's our only shot."

"Why is the boat all the way out at the Cove?" Hannah asks.

Kit runs her hand through her hair and sighs. "Best place to dock it. The dock here is right on the fringing reef. The tide goes down and the boat will sit on the reef and hurt the coral—or the boat hull."

"Our priorities as I see them are as follows," Hannah says. "We need to get to that radio so we can send out an SOS and get word out to Captain Sullivan. If Dan docks and comes onto land without warning, the ants will take him. We need to get off the island, either with Sullivan or using the Arca fishing boat, or both. We have—" She looks at her watch. "About five or six hours before a storm is coming in, right? And Sullivan should be here in around four hours. Any of this not making sense?"

"Sounds legit," Ray says. Everyone else seems on board. Nancy grumbles but nods.

"Good. That means we've a very short window to create favorable conditions for our survival and escape. Let's figure out how we get clear of this island alive."

22

Prepping for the apocalypse means a lot of planning.

Much of Hannah's childhood was spent on exactly that: running drills for the end times. When the Shit Hits the Fan, you need gear. You need your bug-out bag. You need a bug-out vehicle and a bug-out location. And if your original home is compromised, you need an INCH—an I'm Never Coming Home bag. A way to survive on the fly.

By the time she was eight, Hannah knew all the exits in her home. Knew to watch the perimeter. By the time she was ten, she could whittle, could do minor rewiring of electronics, could reload ammunition, could clean and strip a gun and put it back together, could start a fire without fire-making material. By the time she was twelve she knew how to kill and butcher her own meat. She knew how to suture wounds. Knew how to make a shelter. How to forage.

She was always poised on the edge of Armageddon. Listening and waiting for everything to fall apart, for the first sign of the last days: an earthquake, a volcano, a mushroom cloud, a gunshot, the airplane of an enemy nation. At night, outside was silent (but for the cacophony of crickets and night birds), and yet in the white noise of nature she always thought she heard things: men coming through the grass or up the driveway, a squeak of a footstep on a floorboard, distant popping like the sounds of terrorism, revolution, or invasion.

The ground beneath her was solid, but her parents taught her that one step to the left, she'd fall into a pit. They all would. The end was tantalizingly close.

Now, as an adult living and working in society, she's learned techniques for coping with the persistent fear her parents ingrained in her. Ways to center herself. Breathing. Meditating. Exercise. And yet some small part of her is always ready for SHTF: shit hitting the fan.

It hasn't come yet. She's lived a somewhat charmed life. The only incident was a man who tried to attack her at a park in Washington, D.C. He came up behind her. Grabbed for her throat. She broke his arm and ran; didn't even call the cops.

The panic from that single incident felt like a poison inside her for weeks. She couldn't sleep. Could barely eat. Mentally and emotionally she felt like a cramped muscle that wouldn't loosen.

Here in the lab, she feels that way again. Coiled like a snake ready to strike. It feels good in the moment. Later, when it's all over (if it's all over, *if* she lives through it), it'll ruin her for weeks, months. But right now, she's present and bound up with the moment.

Together, they go through the list. Hannah reads it off: "We need EpiPens. Beekeeper suits. More CO_2 extinguishers. Any of the basics we can find: flashlights, clean water, fire, food."

Barry starts rummaging through one of the lab cabincts. "Hold on." He grunts as he lifts a cardboard box and plops it down. "You want food, I got food."

Ray opens the box and pulls out a protein bar. "Peanut butter, chocolate. All right." His fingers poise to tear the plastic, but then he freezes. "Jesus fucking Christ, Barry. Really?"

"What?" Barry asks.

Hannah lifts an eyebrow.

Ray shows her. It is, indeed, a peanut butter and chocolate bar. It's also made with crickets.

Barry waves his hands. "This is what we do here! Edible bugs, man. I got the protein bars, I have a couple cricket cookies, and I have all the straight-up bug meals, too: mealworms, crickets, grubs. This is the future of eating, people."

Ray glowers. "I'd eat you, Barry, before I eat one of these things."

"Fine, starve then."

Hannah sighs. "I see two extinguishers here in the lab—"

"Those won't work," Kit says.

"Why?"

"They're not CO_2 extinguishers. They're dry powder extinguishers. The CO_2 could dick up our equipment or our experiments. But the CO_2 extinguishers still line the living area. If we end up back in there, we can grab more off the walls."

That's something. "Beekeeper suits are nearby, Ajay?"

Ajay nods. "Yes. In the honeybee room. They protect well against bees getting in the suit, but a bee stinger can still pierce under the right conditions. The ant stingers shouldn't be able to, but an ant is a fraction of the honeybee's size—I cannot promise they won't be able to get in."

The thought of being inside a suit filling with those ants almost has Hannah cry out in panic. She swallows the feeling and says, "But it should work for temporary protection?"

Ajay nods.

"Great. The first step of the plan is twofold: find survivors and get to the radio. We're still missing about half the lab, including Einar and Will, so it has to be a priority to locate the others. The fishing boat is a value add, and with that boat and Captain Sullivan coming in, we have two ways off the island. Ideally with as many survivors as we can manage. Ajay, you and I will go get the suits. Then I'd like you to stay here and study our enemy. We need to know what these things are and why they're doing what they're doing. Fair?"

"Of course, Agent Stander."

"Once I get in a suit, I'll head out to the Cove—"

"You?" Ray asks, incredulous. She looks back at him, irritated.

"I assure you, I can handle it. Who else is going to do it?"

Ray shrugs. "I'll do it."

"I don't trust you," Nancy says to him.

He rolls his eyes so hard Hannah thinks they might roll up out of his head like a couple of pebbles. "Oh Jesus. Nancy, is there anybody you *do* trust?"

"I trust *me*."

"I'm doing it," Hannah interjects. "Nancy, Kit, Barry, I need you to help Ajay figure out who these ants are, but also what will hurt them. As a bonus you can figure out how to get the satellite back online in case I don't make it to the radio."

Barry *hmms*. "It has to be a problem with the physical dish. Which means going outside—the dish is right above us. But with the ants . . ."

"No way to cut through the top of the bubble?" Hannah asks.

Ajay says, "We do have a reciprocating saw—believe it or not, it's good for cutting through honeycomb. But it won't cut this stuff. These domes are tough."

"So only way is to go out." She licks her lips. "How many suits are there?"

"Beekeeper suits? Two."

"Someone can take one and use it to go out to repair the dish."

"Ah jeez," Kit says, and Hannah again detects something of a New Jersey accent. Something she tries to hide, maybe? Why? In case it doesn't sound smart enough? "I'll do it. I can try."

"Good. You can try to repair the dish, I'll head to the Cove—"

Ray jumps in: "I said I'll do it."

"Listen," Hannah says, turning toward Ray and holding up her hands. "I get it. You think you're a hero. But I see you. The real you. You're what, Miami? Fort Lauderdale? You come from money. You clean up nice. A pretty, pretty boy. You exercise and you're in good shape. But this isn't that. You're a talker. That's no knock against you—it's your job. Me? My parents are survivalists. I grew up homeschooled on the hundred ways the world could end. I've got this."

Everyone is silent for a moment, then Kit whistles low and slow.

"Yeah," Ray says, surrendering. "You got this."

"Good. Ajay, let's go get the suits."

* * *

Before they head out, Barry unseals the door to the bee room. He reminds them that the bees have a way out—which means the ants could have a way in. Just in case, Ajay takes the extinguisher, and Hannah takes the flamethrower.

"Cornstarch," Barry says, giggling at his own genius. "Cornstarch is flammable. You didn't know that, did you? We keep it here because we were testing its pesticidal properties. But stick it in a powder pump with a bit of fire—whoosh. Instant flamethrower. All natural. Organic, actually."

Organic, all-natural flamethrower. Hipster anarchist murderers the world around would line up to buy these from Trader Joe's, Hannah guesses.

She and Ajay set out. "Ants are one of your specialties," she says. "Tell me about these ants. Our little killers."

He sighs. "I haven't wanted to be seen as overly interested. I couldn't give whoever created them the satisfaction. But of course I am fascinated. How could you not be? These creatures are marvels of biological engineering."

"They take skin. And not all of it. Why?"

He seems flustered. "I do not know. It is behavior like we've never seen. Leaf-cutters take clippings of plant matter in a similar way, but not *skin*."

"They seem to start in certain places. Around the eyes. On the face. The extremities—hands and feet. They were under David Hamasaki's clothing . . ."

Ajay stops suddenly. His eyes lose focus into a thousand-yard stare. "Yes. Of course. Like leaf-cutters. Leaf-cutters take leaves not because they eat the leaves but because it is an example of ant-fungus mutualism. Ants are very good at making relationships at the micro level—farming and milking aphids, for instance, or protecting certain plants. The acacia ant desires the nectar of the acacia tree, so the ant nests there and protects the tree from pests. I think something like that is happening here. My gosh. *My gosh.*"

"But the ants aren't protecting us."

"No. It's not us they want to protect." He licks his lips, suddenly energized. "The human body is not just the human body, Ms. Stander. We are an agglomeration of much smaller creatures: bacteria, viruses, mites. Increasingly we learn that our entire evolution has been governed and urged forth by a choir of microscopic flora. Viruses changed our DNA—and that's why we use viruses now to change the DNA of other creatures."

"I don't follow you."

"Fungus," he says, a child's light in his eyes. "We are covered in fungus. All of us. You. Me. Right now. One such fungus is *Candida.* A variety of strains, the most common being *Candida albicans,* which exists in very small levels on our skin—though if our bodies ever go out of balance thanks to disease or obesity or even overuse of antibiotics, it can turn into candidiasis. Thrush. Or a yeast infection around or within the genitals. But in small amounts, it lives on certain areas of our body. Between the fingers. The buttocks or the genitals. And between the eyebrows and around the eyes—even more so if the person wears glasses, because the heat and friction trap and encourage the growth of *Candida.*"

"They're farming the skin for the fungus," she says.

"Yes, perhaps. Like the way leaf-cutters use bacteria and the leaf mulch they steal to encourage bacteria growth. And they start at the moist parts of the body because that is where the yeast grows. The drier portions of skin they leave alone."

They don't eat us, she realizes. *They eat the fungus. And we just happen to have it all over us.* Her brain flashes back to the cabin in New York: lifting the sheet and seeing all those dead ants and those bits of skin. The stink coming off it was like sour bread baking. The air there was humid, cloying, sickly.

They head into the hive room—in here, the honeybees are acting like Hannah feels right now: agitated, ready to engage, just moments away from swarming and stinging.

"These ants," Ajay is saying, heading into the room, "they're like little pastiches. A puzzle made from the pieces of other, different puzzles. It's cliché, I know, but they're like little Frankenstein's monsters, cobbled together with the traits and attributes of other ants, *unrelated* ants, and—" As he speaks, he kneels down and unlocks one of the drawers at the far end of the bubble—a drawer Hannah expects to be filled with trays of honeycomb and honeybee just like the one Will showed her. But Ajay's words suddenly stop coming as he stares down into the drawer he just opened.

He lifts one suit up. A rumpled white beekeeper suit. It looks like the molted skin from an alien humanoid. "There's only one," he says.

Fear cuts through her. "You said there were two."

"There were. There were!"

Somebody is messing with us. But who?

"Who has keys to this place?"

He thinks. "Any of us. All of us. Me. Will. Kit, Nancy, Barry, David . . ."

Above them comes a sudden banging sound. Hannah hears more like it cascading elsewhere. In other bubble pods. "What was that?" she asks.

"I . . . I don't know."

She waits. Listens. Then she notices it—the hairs on her arms, moving gently. Tickled by a sudden flow of air. Her throat tightens and her jaw seizes. *No.* She looks up at the two vents at the top of the room. Each a square: twelve inches by twelve inches. "The vents. Barry must have opened them again."

Ajay's eyes go wide. "That means—"

"The ants can get in. If they want the *Candida* from us—can they detect it on us? Is that how they find us?"

He keeps his voice quiet, almost a whisper. "Their antennae have thousands of nerve cells. Smell detectors, chemo receptors.

They can sense changes in humidity, in airflow. We don't know how complex they are as sensory organs. But yes. *Yes,* I think so."

The lights buzz, flicker, and then go out. Arca Labs is suddenly too quiet. All Hannah hears is the buzz of the honeybees behind the wall.

"All the power is out," she says. "Grab the suit, we need to get back."

23

The hive room door hisses open. It's not the only one. Hannah and Ajay leave the hive room and see that the doors to the colony room and to Barry's room are wide open, too. So is the exit. That means all the doors must be. *Shit.*

They hear the wind through the palms outside. Ajay fruitlessly presses his wristband to the door's mechanism, but it doesn't shut. He should know better, Hannah thinks. But he's panicked. Panic works that way if you don't know how to harness it: it dulls some minds, sharpens others.

She grabs him. "We need to move."

Down through the connecting tunnel they go. Back into the lab. Panic has taken hold there, too. Everyone's buzzing about like the honeybees in the hive room.

Kit: "It's just a glitch. It happens. It'll come back on—"

Ray: "Fuck that. *Fuck that.* Somebody did this to us."

The lab is dimmer without the overheads, but the big porthole windows bring enough sunlight in—though Hannah notices now it's sunlight filtered through a texture of crawling ants. They're on the glass outside, a network of hungry insects. Legs dancing. Antennae working. Mandibles opening and closing, looking for something to *snip.*

Barry: "Maybe it's the ants. Some ants nest inside electronics, then get electrocuted, which sends up the pheromone call to the swarm—"

Hannah interjects, making her voice louder than everyone else's: "The vents are open. The *doors* are open. Someone opened them. The ants are able to get in through the vents."

Nancy shushes them. “Shh. *Shhhh.*”

Nothing at first. But then—the sound of little feet. Whispering in the vents outside the bubble.

They’re coming. Slowly. And surely.

Hannah looks up, does a quick count of the vents. Four in here. “We need to block the vents,” she says. “Now.” She looks around. There. Metal lab trays. Few inches deep. Looks like they have a big enough footprint—she claps her hands and starts handing them out. One each to Barry, Kit, Ray, and Ajay. Nancy’s far too short to reach the vents.

Those with trays scatter—stepping up on their toes to press the bottoms of the trays against the vents. Barry, Ray, and Ajay are tall enough.

Kit isn’t. She struggles to hold up her tray. The top wavers, pulling away from the vent, leaving a gap of several inches. To Nancy, Hannah says, “Step stool. Something she can stand on.” But Nancy looks throttled by the terror of the situation—she stands there, teetering, eyes wide, mouth open in a soundless *oh*.

There, by the autoclave and near the fridge, Hannah sees a cooler. A Thermos cooler, like you’d take tailgating or to the beach. She grabs it. Yells to Kit and slides it across the tile floor. It hisses as it slides, and Kit catches the cooler with the toe of her boot.

She starts to step onto it.

The tray wavers again—peeling back. Kit’s fingers scrabble against it, finding no purchase.

As Kit steps up, the tray falls out of her hands. She tries to catch it—and fails. The cooler slides out from under her feet. Kit tumbles, arms flailing. One leg kicks out as she lands right on her tailbone, crying out.

Ants start pouring out of the vent above her.

* * *

Hannah still remembers the yellow jackets. Running like a fool behind the generator shed, not realizing what she was doing or

where she was going—she stepped right on that hole. The wasps came out of that thing like demons out of hell, sensing their one chance at escape. They knew to come right for her. Her eyes swelled shut. Her throat felt tight.

It was her father who rescued her. He heard her screaming. Next thing she knew, he was swooping her up in his arms—getting stung himself—and running back to the house, calling for her mother.

Later that night, Hannah sat hunched over the side of their porcelain claw-foot tub as Mom dabbed pink blobs of calamine lotion all over her with a cotton ball. She told her mother, "I'm scared now."

Mom asked what she was scared of.

Hannah said, "Wasps. They might come for me again." She hadn't yet encountered the ants in the mailbox, but when that time came, it would only prove to her what Mom told her that night.

Mom said, "Hannah, the world is not ours. We think it is, but it isn't. The greatest lie we tell ourselves is that we are in control. Those wasps didn't care about you. Didn't care who you were or what you wanted. They're not mean. You scared them. They attacked, and that scared *you*. They're simple creatures, which is what we try to be here. Simple survives. After human beings are long gone from this planet, those wasps—and flies and butterflies and cockroaches and all the other crawly things—will still be here."

"That makes me sad," Hannah said, wincing as Mom smushed another glob of lotion against a swollen welt. "I don't want us all to die."

"I don't want all kinds of things, but that doesn't change what's true. We all die, Hannah. And when we do, it'll be the bugs that eat us down to the bone."

* * *

Kit cries out. The ants fall on her like rain. They make a sound as they fall: *pat-pat-pat, tap-tap-tap*. The woman flails, tries to scramble and stand, but as she yells—"Help! Help! Get them off!"—her words dissolve into a scream of pain.

She succumbs beneath them. Shaking. Seizing up.

Hannah springs forward, grabbing the extinguisher from where Ajay left it. She leans back, blasts the extinguisher up first—to get the ants coming out of the vent, still, and those now crawling across the ceiling—and then arcs the cold blast downward, all over Kit. It's cold, too cold, and Kit might come out of this with frostbite. But maybe, *just maybe*, Hannah can save her skin.

The ants begin falling from the vent: a hiss of raining black corpses. They fall off Kit, too. Hannah seizes the moment and catches the woman's ankle, grunting as she drags Kit back five, six feet from where she fell—

As Kit's face crosses a patch of light from one of the porthole windows, Hannah sees the sting marks up and down her face: angry, swollen blisters. Whiteheads, each filling with pus. Already Kit's breathing is a shallow wheeze. Her fingers twitch and seize as if grasping for something that isn't there. Her eyes remain focused on Hannah, even as she tries to say words that fail to come out as anything but a gassy rattle.

Hannah whispers, "I'm sorry."

Then she's up again, blasting at the open vent. More dead ants fall. But the others seem to hesitate. The edges of the vent are rimed over with foam and ice crystals. The ants don't want to push past them.

Hannah thinks. Whoever shut the power down—Will? Einar? someone else they don't know?—did it to kill her and the others. Options race laps around her head: She could put on the bee suit, but she doesn't know how and it would take too long. She could stand here with the tray and hold it, but that doesn't solve the problem of the doors. The ants above her seem held at bay by the leavings of the CO_2 foam, but the cold is disintegrating, melting, and soon the way will be open once more . . .

That's it.

Back in Ez Choi's office. The plastic bins.

Hannah: "How are they not swarming all over the lab?" Ez: "Fluon. Liquid Teflon. Spray the edges of each bin and they can't get past."

Hannah yells, "Ajay!"

"What?" He stands under his own vent, the tray pressed against it. His legs and arms are shaking. He's nervous. Adrenaline is running through him. He and everyone else will soon be worn down by it, sandblasted raw.

"Fluon! *Do you have Fluon?*"

His eyes light up. "Genius. Of course. Yes. Yes! To the left. No! Sorry. Your right. Under the cabinet—there, by the sink."

Hannah dives to her knees and throws open the cabinet. There. Fluon. Not in spray bottles like she'd hoped, but in amber bottles, all glass. She spins the cap off one—

Underneath the cap is a brush applicator. Internally, she screams at how long it'll take to get this stuff slathered around the vents and around doorjambs—but it'll have to do. She cradles one bottle under her arm and holds the other out to Nancy, who is still standing there, shell-shocked.

Hannah thrusts the bottle against Nancy's breastbone with a *thump*. "Take this. Fluon. You do the doors, I'll do the vents."

The woman's eyes flutter and focus.

"Nancy? You good?"

"Yes. *Yes*. I can do it."

"Hurry. Because they're coming."

24

It feels like the attack happened just moments ago. And also a lifetime ago.

Hannah and Nancy have drawn streaks of Fluon around every conceivable opening. Every vent and door and crack they could find. The stink of the stuff remains on Hannah's hands: an ammonia odor that conjures a swift and recent memory. It's the same stink she smelled down in Special Projects.

Will, or someone, was using Fluon down there, too.

Now Kit sits propped up in front of her. The woman's face and arms are peppered with angry red stings. Her skin is hot. Her lips are ashen. Her breath comes in sharp little intakes.

The news came back fast: the EpiPens are gone.

They had a dozen. Now they have none.

Someone stole them. The same someone who made the ants and set them upon Arca like a plague. *Damn it.* She failed. And now Kit is dying.

Nancy said it's anaphylaxis. All the signs are there. The shallow breathing, her pallor, her temperature. Untreated, she'll die. The best they can do right now is force Kit to swallow a few antihistamines. Nancy says, "It'll slow the anaphylactic reaction down. But it's a Band-Aid on a bullet hole. This could kill her."

Hannah stands up. Nancy stands with her.

"We have more EpiPens," Nancy says. "At the Cove. At Special Projects."

"I have to go there," Hannah says. She's willing to bet the stolen EpiPens are there, too. She looks to the beekeeper suit. She picks it

up, holds the material in her hand as she rubs her fingers against her thumb. It should work against the ants, shouldn't it? To Ray she says, "Put on the suit and head outside. See if you can't figure out what's been done to the power. Whether it's the breaker or the battery or what."

"C'mon, I don't have the experience with that sort of thing. Send me to the Cove instead. You take the suit. Check out the equipment."

No, Hannah thinks. Fact is, Ray isn't that smart. And Will, if he's the one behind this, is smart. Genius level. *Evil* genius level, apparently. If it's not Will and it's Einar, instead—Ray's allegiance there is tenuous. "I'm going to the Cove," she says.

"I can't do what you want," Ray says.

"You'll have to try."

"I can't—"

A scuff of a heel. A throat clearing from across the room. And then a voice says, "I'll do it."

They all wheel. There stands Einar Geirsson. Leaning against a far counter. His hair is dark, a blood-black crust. His clothes are damp and dripping.

"Einar," Ray says, a little bit of awe in his voice. Hannah knows her instincts were right on.

"Hello, everybody," Einar says, his voice raspy, tired. "Glad to see some of you are still alive. We have much work to do if we are to survive."

* * *

The story Einar tells is this:

Early this morning he went looking for Will at Special Projects. He did not find Will. What he did find was a strange-looking container.

"A barrel" is how he describes it. Plastic, like the same printing used on the pods. With metal rims and hinges. Except it did not open at the top, but along a vertical line down the center. Einar opened it.

Inside, it appeared to be heavily insulated. The bottom of the container was fitted with a tray and brackets, and below those brackets was water. Cool water.

Like the runoff from dry ice, Hannah thinks.

Above were metal racks lined with black discs. "The discs looked like hockey pucks," he says. Each disc had a small hole sealed with wax. He touched one and felt vibrations through it.

Hannah remembers seeing them in Ez's lab back in Tucson. She says, "Those discs are ant colonies."

"I didn't realize it at the time. I am not an entomologist." Einar sighs and winces as Nancy applies a wet paper towel to his wounded head. "But yes. I think so."

Ajay says, "Little formicariums. For moving small colonies with queens."

The picture forms in Hannah's mind: Each colony cryogenically frozen and kept cool with dry ice. When it thaws, the ants wake. And if the only thing keeping them in is a wax plug, they can chew through that.

"How many discs?" she asks. "In the barrel, I mean."

Einar thinks. "About twenty per rack. And roughly twenty racks."

Four hundred discs. Four hundred ant queens and colonies.

"That's a lot of fucking ants," Ray says.

Einar clutches both hands together and takes a deep breath. "It doesn't end there. There were five other barrels like it. Stored in the laboratory. Brought out from where, I cannot say. I do not know where Will would have hidden those from me. From us. But there they were."

"That's twenty-four hundred colonies," says Nancy.

"That's twenty-four hundred *queens,*" Ajay says.

A sense of vertigo threatens to pull Hannah down to the floor. If those colonies ever leave this island, it will be disastrous. Each sting is potentially deadly. And they do not merely attack humans as a matter of accident or happenstance. These ants *hunt* people. It would be an ecological nightmare. A plague on mankind.

Ray says to Einar, "I assume you hauled fucking ass out of there."

The look Einar gives Ray holds a measure of distaste. "I did leave that place. Already I saw that the ants were here, on the island. On the sand of the beach, in the fronds of the palms and ferns. Killing birds. Turtles. I saw a dead seal on the beach. From there I hurried to my cabin . . ." He draws a deep breath. "I found Venla. The ants had gotten to her." His voice cracks. "I admit, I was not brave. I did nothing for her. I ran. I ran down out of the jungle and onto the beach and into the water. I thought that the ants could not get to me out there. So it was there I waited."

Hannah gestures toward him. "What happened to your head?"

"I saw someone." He sighs. "Someone stalking around the labs. I couldn't see who—I was too far away and this person stood obscured by the trees. So I thought I had better investigate. I avoided the ants as best I could, and crept up—and this person came out of nowhere. I didn't see who it was. Something hammered against the side of my head. A rock, I think. I fell"—here he shows the palms of both of his hands: they're scratched up, bloodied—"and I again crawled my way to the beach and into the water. I didn't have to go far. Any ants that tried to follow me lost my scent once I was in the water."

"Why did you come back?" Hannah asks.

"I heard screams. They were Kit's, I believe." Again his voice cracks.

"We are running out of time," Hannah says. He seems to care about these people. Is that just a careful act? She reminds herself that he doesn't yet know what *she* knows: that the dead body in the cabin belonged to the son of his greatest rival, Archer Stevens. That is currency. Archer is a special mystery all his own and she doesn't want Einar's help untangling it. She decides to keep that information to herself. For now. (Of course all that is meaningless if he is the murderer, isn't it? Then he knows everything and she's the one behind the eight ball.)

"Yes. Hannah is right. We need to make haste. *Sá vinnur sitt mál, sem þráastur er.* An Icelandic saying. We must persevere and be stubborn enough to win. And in this case, winning means surviving."

Hannah nods. "I'm going to the Cove."

"It is dangerous there."

"The boat is there. EpiPens, too."

Einar nods. "Give me a few moments to gather my bearings and I will put on the suit and see what I can see inspecting the power supply and the satellite dish."

Hannah narrows her eyes. "You came here through the jungle. But you never got bit. How? You must have come in through the exit. The ants are out there. Hell, they're in *here* now. How did you escape them?"

A look of surprise and bewilderment crosses his face. "I honestly don't know. They seemed to ignore me. Perhaps I was moving too quickly."

"No," Ajay says, pointing a finger to his chin. "It is the salt water. The ants' receptors will not as easily be able to detect the *Candida* on our skin—the salt water masks it. Temporarily, at least."

Our skin is the fertile soil, and Candida *is the crop. The ants are just coming to harvest.*

"Hannah," Einar says, "That speaks to how you might make your way to the Cove: swim it. Not the lagoon, but the sea. It will be tiring, but perhaps effective."

"I'll do that. Thanks. Good luck here."

"Good luck to you," he says, taking her hand. "There is another Icelandic saying, Hannah. *Ég skal sýna þér í tvo heimana.*" Ray flinches at that, though she doesn't know why. Einar ignores it and explains: "It means we must survive by whatever means we can, however we must. Survival is king."

That she can agree with.

* * *

She gets a small pack ready. A few protein bars, a flashlight, a small serrated folding knife they had in the lab to cut honeycomb. Plus a little plastic honey bear filled up with Fluon. Before she goes, she takes her sneakers off and paints them with Fluon.

Barry tells her to take the extinguisher, but she declines. They need it more than she does, and she doesn't know how well it'll do in the ocean anyway.

On the way out, Ray catches her and in a low voice says, "Be careful out there. Things just don't feel right."

No kidding, she thinks. Nothing feels right. And no one feels safe—not to trust, not to stay alive. "Okay, Ray. Thanks."

"Stay frosty. Stay safe."

"I think we're well past the point of safe."

25

She stands at the door at the edge of the lab. Ants have gathered at the margins beyond, unable to pass the invisible border marked by the Fluon.

The plan is about as simple as a plan can get.

Run.

So Hannah runs. She starts with a leap over the ants massing at the borders of the door, then sprints down the hall, praying to all the gods of all the world that the Fluon painted on the sides of her shoes didn't slip down to the bottoms of her shoes, because one slippery misstep and her ankle will twist.

Boom, boom, boom—her feet carry her down the first telescoping hall, to the second bridging room that leads out to the hive room, the harvester colony, and Barry's lab. There, past them all, is the exit, and her only goal is to make it out and to the ocean beyond.

And like that, she's out. No time to stop and see if she has ants climbing up her. Her jaw tightens and her legs pump as she runs down the decking—a walkway that is covered in ants. Eyes forward. Feet moving. Ahead she sees a break in the trees—she'll take it the way you take a highway exit, and then she'll bound to the sea. But she takes another step and—

Her foot starts to skid. The Fluon isn't making her shoes slippery. All the dead ants smashed underneath them are.

Her heel tweaks, turns, and leans like a listing ship—the injury from just a day before returning like a vengeful specter. Pain screws up through her heel into her calf and she cries out, jumping off the walkway and hobbling now as fast as her ruined gait will take her.

Her foot catches on something. Everything goes blurry as the world is yanked away from her. Her elbows hit. Her forehead snaps against the earth.

Then she hears the sound. A sound like sleet *ticky-tacking* on a roof. It's loud and getting louder.

She looks, squints, sees the ground shifting. A rippling black column of ants in far greater number than she's seen yet.

No time to care about her worthless ankle. She gets her good foot underneath her and pistons it down, launching herself up. Through the brush. Her shoulder clips a bottle palm and she spins and almost falls again. The ridge drops hard to the sand below, and she has no time to make this graceful or even safe. She gets to the edge and leaps.

A twenty-foot drop.

She tucks and curls, hitting the sand hard—her body rolls forward, and she takes most of the impact on her shoulder. The air blasts from her lungs, and then she's up, clumsily staggering forward. The sea is only ten feet away. But around her she sees the bodies of birds. What few feathers are left are sticking up in bloody tufts. She launches herself over an albatross whose head is stripped raw, its eyes gone, its beak hanging off. The rest of it is crawling with ants.

And now, she realizes, so is she.

They're not on her sneakers, they're on her legs. As she books it forward, she swipes her hands fast at her legs—ants tumbling off the fabric of her pants and into the sand. The sea is only five feet away now—

She hops, flinging the black insects to the ground—

Four feet.

Ants on her hand and arm now, mandibles open—

Three feet.

She shakes her arm back and forth, ants flung to the margins—

Two feet.

Her ankle hurts so badly it's almost numb. But the ants from her arm are gone and once she's in the water—

One foot.

A tickle on her neck—

Then a pinch.

And then something far worse.

Hannah drops to her knees in the surf as a single ant jabs its stinger into her neck. Immediately the area grows warm. Hot. She feels woozy. Now here they come—the tickle of ants up her legs, this time getting under her jeans, on her skin. A hundred little legs tickling.

More pinching.

More stinging.

Her throat tightens. Everything starts to go blurry.

Hannah tries to crawl out to sea but her arms wobble and fail to respond. Her forehead crashes down into wet sand as the wave draws back, dragging her with it—then crashing back over her. Some of the ants wash away but others keep biting and stinging. She tries to speak, tries to cry out, but what emerges from her closing throat is only a teakettle whistle. Then there's salt water up her nose and down her throat and she's gagging, sputtering.

The waves roll in.

The waves roll out.

Her forearm is right in front of her, like a disconnected piece of meat—she can't even feel it now. Some of the ants get sucked out to sea, but some don't. They are tenacious, these little demons.

Then—she rolls over suddenly. Did she do that? She tries again to scream but she can't. A shadow over her, the sun behind it. Will's face roves into view. He whispers something to her: *Hold still.* He has a knife.

He sticks the blade into her thigh. She can't feel it. And then it hits her: It's not a blade. It's an EpiPen.

As her breath starts to return to her in great gulps, he bends down and presses something against her mouth. A white cloth. A heady, buzzy warmth spreads across her. Again her eyes lose focus, and this time she can't get it back. Everything goes slippery and it slides away, out to sea, out to sea . . .

INTERLUDE

EZ CHOI

The university buys spiders out of a van.

That's not a thing they would admit to publicly, but it's a true statement. It's not just spiders, either. Sometimes it's Madagascar hissing cockroaches. Or scorpions. Ez has even bought a few praying mantises and walking sticks that way.

The trick to the van is this: People buy spiders and they don't really want spiders. Either they buy them and get freaked out, or they buy a Chilean rose tarantula and realize they really should have bought a rock because they're about the same level of excitement. *Or* they buy one and get bit, or get stuck with the practically invisible urticating hairs that New World tarantulas can fling at you if they're feeling particularly sassy that day. (Ez has never had that problem, because Ez is a professional.)

There aren't many rescue organizations for tarantulas like there are for cutey-wootey little poochies. For the most part, people do what they shouldn't do: they throw them out into the wild (which isn't legal) or they kill them (which isn't legal, either).

Those who have some kind of conscience, though, first try to take the tarantulas back to the store. The store won't take them back. But the store *will* direct the unhappy owner to a person.

In this case, that person is Dallas Lardell, a bony scarecrow of a man who buys up unwanted creepy-crawlies from those aforementioned unhappy owners for dirt, dirt cheap.

Then he sells them.

Sometimes he sells them to other owners who can't afford a new

tarantula (Ez has always joked he should spray paint SLIGHTLY USED SPIDERS on the side of his minivan). Otherwise he sells them to the entomology lab.

Tonight, though, Ez is about to leave empty-handed. Dallas is pleading with her to buy another of his "many, many spiders," even though all he has are two Chilean rose and one pinktoe. Both of which are nice, but perfectly common spiders.

"You said you had *Poecilotheria regalis,*" she says, and he gives her a pinched look like she's speaking another language. Which she is, because it's Latin, so she says, "A regal parachute spider. One of the ornamentals."

"I think I did have one, but I sold it to a nice kid on a skateboard." He gives her that rictus grin of a human skull that's been sitting out in the desert. "I have other spiders. Good spiders. Look, see."

"I'm not buying these basic bitches." Ez sneers. "Ugh. Dallas, you're wasting my time. Call me when you have something with some bite, some venom. Though, no baboon spiders. I already have the Orange Bitey Thing back in the lab." People buy the OBTs as pets because they think they're cool. No urticating hairs, either. But then they get bit and end up in the hospital. Oops. "I'll see you, Spider-Man."

He tries yelling after her, but she leaves him and his ratty late-nineties minivan back in the lot and heads back to campus, stopping by one of the food trucks to pick up some fry bread and a Coke. Worry dogs her steps. The university is again fucking around with the funding for the science departments. And they're playing musical chairs with the department heads again.

And then there's Hannah. She hopes Hannah is all right.

Ez tells herself, *She's probably fine.* This kind of thing is her jam. It's the rest of life Hannah can't handle.

Ez heads back inside the lab—it's evening now, the sky gone ombré. Nobody's here, really, which makes it Ez's favorite time to be here. But when she goes to flip on the lights, the office stays dark.

Flick. Flick. Flick. She tries the switch a few times. Nothing.

The hall lights are on, so there's still power. Did both of her fluorescents burn out at the same time? Ugh, the university gets what the university pays for: not much and never enough. She steps into the room to turn on the lamp at her desk.

Something crinkles as she steps onto it.

Something that shouldn't be there.

Suddenly she's frozen in place, not sure what's underneath her foot. It feels like plastic. Like a painter's tarp.

Her eyes adjust, and that's when she sees the human shape standing ten feet away. Against the far wall, close to the terrariums.

For a moment Ez remains motionless. A grasshopper or spider in the middle of an army ant swarm knows to remain *perfectly still* because the ants detect by movement. Do nothing, and the ants continue to stream by. Move one micrometer and they tear you apart.

But she's a human and someone is in here with her and as her eyes adjust further to the darkness she sees that whoever is standing there is tall, broad-shouldered—a man, she thinks, and suddenly her brain goes to all the worst things: *campus rapist, serial murderer, a spurned student out for revenge—*

She wheels toward the door. A sharp *snap* from the other side of the room—a gunshot, but no muzzle flash, no deafening ringing in her ear—and her hand blooms with pain. She reels her hand in, resting it against her middle. The end of her arm feels like it's a roadside flare, burning hot and red.

She screams as two more shots pop, peppering the wood of the door where she had been standing only moments before. Ez dives behind her desk, her shoulder slamming hard into her chair, which rolls away with a clatter before tipping over and crashing against the floor. Her legs feel suddenly wet and she thinks, *I pissed myself,* but then she sees the darkness of the stain: It's blood. Blood from her hand soaking her jeans. All parts of her feel desperate and mad and though her life doesn't flash before her eyes, the singular regret of *Have I done enough, or is this all there is?* joins the chorus.

She hears a footstep on the tarp. He's coming closer.

The desk wobbles as she leans into it. It's an IKEA desk. She put it together herself with those godforsaken little wrenches and the utilitarian instructions. The desk is a piece of shit with an unpronounceable name. And it isn't heavy.

It isn't heavy.

Another footstep. The tarp crinkles.

Ez gets her legs under her at the same time she gets her shoulder underneath the lip of the desk. She kicks off like a swimmer. The desk judders forward, skidding across the floor as her legs push and piston. The drawers rattle open. Pens and organizers and bins fall off and crash against the floor. She screams—

And hits something hard.

Desk, meet body.

As her blood spatters the floor, she gives one last hard shove—and the silhouette falls backward, into the rack of terrariums. Ez ducks down, holds both hands over her head as the rack shakes and the terrariums begin to fall: popping, shattering, a cacophony of sound. On her hands and knees, ignoring the pain jolting up through her hand to her elbow, she scrambles forward, slipping on her own blood as she crawls as fast as she can toward the window—

More gunfire. *Pop, pop, pop.* Books leap off the wall like scared toads. One crashes against the back of her neck and her jaw snaps hard against the floor but she doesn't care, *can't* care, and keeps moving—

Behind her, the man screams.

There, by the window, a standing lamp, another IKEA find with another tongue-twisting name, and her hand skitters up the pole. Her fingers find the switch.

When the light flickers on, she doesn't understand what she's seeing. The desk is shoved up against the rack of terrariums. (*The poor spiders,* she thinks, *they don't deserve the fate that just befell them.*) A man is sandwiched in between, bent over at the waist. He's clad in black: black pants, black tee, arms painted with some kind of dark grease. Dark hair all a-muss. His face is turned toward her, cheek against the wood, frozen in what appears to be pain. His hand raises up and in it is a lean black pistol with a suppressor at the end. The barrel is a black void, a dark eye staring her down—

Then he cries out again, wincing. The hand holding the gun thuds against the desk. Ez thinks, *I really hurt him. That desk broke something inside him. Maybe an organ, maybe spinal damage . . .*

But then she realizes that's not it at all. From the back of his neck, up the far side of his head, emerges a pair of hairy orange legs. The OBT—the orange baboon tarantula, the Orange Bitey Thing—crawls up his scalp and perches atop his head. Fangs glistening. Venom in.

The man's teeth grit. "It hurts, it hurts," he keens. His eyes clamp shut.

Ez stands on wobbly legs. She holds up her hand. The middle of her palm and the back side of it are black with blood. Fresh red drips on the floor like she just dipped her whole mitt in a can of red paint. The sound that comes out of her is a wounded-puppy sound.

On the floor, scrunched up around the legs of the desk, is a blue tarp. *A murder tarp,* she thinks. He was going to kill her on it, then roll her up, take her out of here. Why? Who would want to kill her?

She staggers over to the desk, reaches out for the gun and pulls it from the man's hand. It's heavy. She points it at him. The barrel wavers and dips. "Who are you?"

"You need to call somebody. What the fuck. What the fuck." The back of his throat makes a desperate plucked-banjo sound. "I got bit. Something bit me."

"OBT," she says, knowing it won't make any sense to him. Tears creep down her cheeks. "Tell me why you're here."

"Fuck you. Fuck you. You should be dead."

She thinks: *Kill him.* Kill him for wanting to kill her. But that emotion is like a grease fire: hot and bright and then it burns itself out. The gun wibbles, wobbles, and then Ez runs out of the office, screaming for help but all along wondering: Why? Why should she be dead? Who is that man and why is she his target?

26

How much do you remember about that day?" Will asks her.

Hannah sits at the table at Arca Labs and thinks. "I remember almost making it. *So close.* I had gone to the beach and made the jump. My ankle was twisted, sprained, though I worried it was broken, and I *almost* made it."

"Then they were on you. The ants."

"Yes. And I thought I was dead." She has to take herself through it one step at a time because it's all muddy, confusing. Even existing here and now in the present is hard. *Establish a beachhead,* she thinks. "Establish a beachhead," her father would say when teaching her to play checkers and, later, chess. "Like in the war. Just get your soldiers out there in position before they die." He was never in a war, but his own father was. Her grandfather, a man who died before she was born. She has to blink hard to push those memories back. "Then you came along. You stuck me in the leg—"

"An EpiPen."

"Right. And then—"

"A cloth over your mouth."

Establish a beachhead. But what's her move, here? Tell him she doesn't trust him? That she knows he's a killer? Or keep it secret? All she says instead is:

"Why?"

"I needed you."

"*Why?*"

"Do you think I did this? That I'm a killer?" he asks.

Yes. I do. I don't trust you. "You're an artist," she says.

He laughs.

"You do think I did this."

He reaches for her throat. She pulls away, but he has her.

"I still do," she chokes past his crushing hand.

"Even though I saved you?"

Even though, she thinks, but her words won't come.

"The ants are everywhere now." He stands up suddenly, the chair legs barking against the floor. "It's going to be a global catastrophe. An ecological nightmare. Once they get entrenched . . ."

He pulls her closer. Her throat burns. She tries to pull away, but can't. *He has me drugged. My limbs won't work. What did he do to me?*

He keeps on talking. "Someone sent the colonies all around the world. Every continent. Countless countries. It's a kind of genetically modified terrorist attack. We still have time—not much, but enough—to undo what's done before they get established." He's pulling her around the table now, closer, closer, even as she gags. "But all you want to do is talk about whether or not I'm guilty of the act of creation. We're all guilty of that. Creation and destruction are our human instincts, Hannah. You know that. It is who we are. You think we'll pick a side, like we'll figure out if we're good or evil, but it's really that we're both."

He's next to her now. Bending toward her. His hand lets go of her throat and she's left gasping. Then his hand moves under her chin, lifting her mouth toward his. "Is this okay?"

"No," she says. And yet she doesn't pull away. His lips find hers. A rasp of his unshaven face against hers, red and raw—his tongue in her mouth as they lean together—something small and delicate runs from his mouth to hers.

A tiny ant. A scout.

Hannah tries to pull away, but Will's hand finds the back of her head and clamps there, a vise grip at the back of her skull. Her teeth crash against his and pain goes through her jaw as a column of ants begins to surge up out of his mouth and into her own, down her throat, and once again she can't breathe—

Hannah moans in pain. That sound becomes a sudden, mournful wail as she tries to stand. Pain crashes through her ankle like lightning and she cries out.

Vertigo throttles her. She blinks back the dizziness and leans forward and plants her hands on a wall—no, a window—to stave off the tide of disorientation.

No, it's not a window, either. Or, rather, it's both wall and window. A Plexiglas wall. At the far end there's a door, not quite three feet tall. Clear Lucite hinges. A metal lock, the knob and fixture on the other side.

It takes her a second, but then it hits her. Hannah is inside the mosquito cage at the Cove lab. Inside Special Projects. *That was just a dream.* Or a hallucination. In the center of the room she's looking into is the steel table. Under the table is her bag. On top of the table is a trio of EpiPens.

She looks around. Inside her cage, she sees no mosquitoes. Outside, though, are ants. Just a few, as they were back in Arca. Lazily moving about—a line of them here, a line of them there, winding around like crooked cracks forming in the walls.

Hannah tightens her hand into a fist and slams it against the clear wall, but she has almost no strength. Her hand falls dully against the plastic.

It must be loud enough, however, to act as a summoning. The ants begin to wind toward her. They climb up the plastic and converge into one teeming, seething mass. Up from the bottom, down from the top, in from each side. Fear twists inside her. *I shouldn't have done that.* Were they attracted by the sound? Hannah wonders. Or was that simple movement—her hand against the Plexiglas—enough to cast her scent into the air? Tears burn at the corners of her eyes as she backs away against the wall—the sense memory of them crawling all over her is renewed, as if it's happening here and now.

The ants climb up to the mesh at the top, a mesh blessedly too tight and narrow for them to crawl through. Their attempt to enter is thwarted.

She crumples, wiping away tears.

But it seems Hannah has summoned more than the ants. Will Galassi strides into the room, hands behind his back. "Hello, Hannah."

"These are yours, aren't they?" Her eyes follow a trail of the ants winding drunkenly in front of her. "These little demons."

He smiles. "*Myrmidones bellicus.* The Myrmidon ant."

"Warriors. These ants are your warriors."

"You know your mythology, then."

"And my Latin." In the myth, a Greek king, Aeacus, lost his people to a great plague. As Aeacus was one of the sons of Zeus, he asked the god to help him repopulate, and Zeus obliged. He said he would make the king's people diligent, hardy, and ready for war: and so he rose them up from ants Zeus found on his sacred tree. Men made from the smallest creatures. Industrious. Zealous. And excellent at following orders. Their exploits were told in *The Iliad:* they fought for Achilles, the brash, egomaniacal hero.

"They are my warriors, yes."

"Are you their Achilles?"

He turns away from that, almost as if it offends him. "No. I'm no hero. At least, not the kind you think." But here Will turns toward her again, giving her the side-eye.

"You can't help it. Being proud of this."

"Pride is dangerous."

"And yet, there it is. Twinkling in your eye." She presses her forehead against the plastic. The ants crawling there are reduced to blurs, and she resists recoiling. She has to appear tougher than she is. "You created them out of nothing. That takes some skill."

He shakes his head. "Not out of nothing, no. Each ant—really, every living thing—is just a series of building blocks. All the way down to the chemical level. Remix, rearrange, redo. They're not a whole new life-form, even though science would dictate they are. I consider them an *homage.*"

In the silence between them, she hears the crackle of the ants crawling.

"So why do it? Just to see if you can?"

Now he turns toward her. "No. Well." He pauses and his mouth purses. "Maybe at first. But then I started to see it for what it was: A way out. For us. For . . ." He sweeps his arms across the air above his head. "For people. Human beings, Hannah, don't you see? It's time for us to go. We need to be euthanized before we do too much damage. Nature understands that kind of sacrifice. Wolves go off to die alone, away from their pack. They know their illness or age brings weakness, summons other predators, other packs. But we humans have clung too long to this planet, and now . . ."

"We're ruining the planet. That's what you're saying."

"Of course. *Of course.*" He leans in, only inches from the plastic. "You talk about it in your own work. The race toward that one door. Angel and demon, evolution and destruction. Hannah, don't you see? The race is over. The devil won and *we're the devil.* All our sins—greed and pride and vanity and gluttony—oh, they've served us well, but what about the rest of the world?"

The ants seem unperturbed. Hannah notices that none crawl upon him. *Why?* She thinks to keep him talking so she can figure this out. "You're right. The air is sick. The oceans will boil over. Fish floating on top of the toxic algae. Bees, dead because we poisoned them. We're not good curators. But we can fix it. We've fixed it before. Look, the Dust Bowl of the thirties—that was an apocalypse. But once we committed to change—to let natural agricultural processes come back, to develop rangelands and new tree development, to—"

"*No.*" That word, sharp as a nail driven through wood. "That was small. This is . . ." He's frustrated now, nostrils flaring. He seems to find his center and speaks again: "Mankind is always going on about the things that will end us. We talk about meteors like the one that hit the dinosaurs and wiped them out. But *we* are the meteor. We're seven billion people and counting, Hannah. Breeding like rats and roaches in the walls. It's our drive. It's our nature. To keep procreating. We want more, more, more. More food, more money, more land, more everything. We're bacteria running rampant in a petri dish. We're a *parasite* in an unready host."

Hannah hears her mother's voice in her head: *The end is coming, Hannah dear. We don't know how. But ten to one says we make it happen.* "So, this is it," she says. "These ants, your little Myrmidons. You let them out to destroy the world."

"To destroy *people,* but to *save* the world. It's elegant, isn't it? A tiny little creature like the ant also possesses the largest biomass of any animal on earth. They have survived cataclysm and ruination. And they have maintained. It's perfect. If anyone deserves to end the Age of Man, it's them. They've earned it."

"You're sick." Those two words come out angry, but she's not entirely convinced. He is sick, yes. But maybe that doesn't make him wrong.

"I'm not sick. I'm clear. Clear about the state of things. Clear about our place in this world. *Clear* about what must come next if *anything* is to come next."

"Who was the victim, then? By the lake, in New York? Just a test case? Just to see?"

Will goes dreadfully silent. His mouth forms a dire line. "Aye, but there's the rub," he says. "I didn't do it. I didn't kill him. I let the ants out only after someone stole most of my colonies. I had one barrel left and I just thought . . . to hell with it." He frowns. "You know, I had a plan. Once. A well-orchestrated release of the Myrmidons: I would send them to various locations around the world, places the ants could establish strong, capable colonies. But I never had the strength of conviction to do it. Someone else did, though. I guess I should thank whoever that was."

"You're lying." But she can tell he isn't. "If not you, who? Who did it? Einar? Ajay? *Who?*"

But that is a question he seems disinterested in answering. "I have to go, Hannah," he says. "The boat is coming soon. And not long after that, a very bad storm."

"Wait." *This is a death sentence.* "You're leaving me down here to die. You said you admired my work."

He puts his hand onto the glass, like she's a prisoner and he's her lost love. "I do admire it. And I will continue to. I'm not killing you. I'm *saving* you. The ants can't get in here. You'll be clear from the storm. Ride it out. And then, whatever happens from here, I want you to tell the world. Tell them what I told you. Let them know why this is happening." He smiles: a bit cheeky now, like this is half a joke. "You're my prophet. My prophet in the truest sense of the term: a mouthpiece for all to hear the truth."

An ant dances onto the edge of his finger. Hannah watches, breathless, as it runs down the length of the digit, over the knuckles, to the hand. "It doesn't care about you," she says, bewildered.

Will nods. Then he picks up the ant with his other hand. He grabs it between thumb and forefinger. Its legs tickle the air.

He crushes it.

A rush of sound like a rain shower. Ants swarm him from the floor. They go up his body. Under his clothes. Run in panicked streams along his jawline and down his arm. All of them head toward a single terminus: the end of his hand, where he just crushed one of their own. They move in such masses that his entire hand disappears beneath them.

She sees now that there is not just one size of ant; rather, she sees two. Some of the ants are smaller than the others. A third of the size.

None of them bite. None of them sting.

Will smiles. He relaxes his hand, and Hannah watches as the ants carry their dead comrade away. Down the line, receding away from his hand: it's like watching a glove disintegrate.

"How?" she asks.

"That's my little secret," he says. "Good-bye, Hannah. I've got to go home. I hope you get to go home someday, too."

He retreats from the room, ants falling off his hand as he walks away. Hannah screams herself hoarse as he goes. She slams herself into the Plexiglas until she melts against it, collapsing into a numb, weeping heap.

27

Hannah has no idea how much time passes. An hour. Two. The minutes crawl like ants up glass. She spends time trying to kick out the door. The ants come after every kick and every slam of her good foot against the hatch and its hinges. Ants fling off to the ground with each hit, summoning more with their distress.

Eventually the pain in her ankle is too much. She sits. Simmers in futility and rage. Ants recede like a tide, gone back out to wherever it is they go.

Hannah imagines the others. Kit, dying. Einar, bleeding. Nancy, maybe overtaken by now. Stung and skinless. Will did this to them.

But that's not all of it, is it? He was telling the truth when he said someone else killed the Stevens boy. And didn't Einar say something about seeing barrels here? She looks around, straining to see. There's the door—and a big red lever next to it, which she expects opens it—but no barrels. At least, not in this room. If they were here, and what Einar told her wasn't a lie, they're gone now. Who would have taken them? Einar? Then why did he come back to the lab at all? Could there be someone else? A third party, nameless and faceless?

A sense of helplessness threatens to reach up from underneath and pull her down. And that only makes her more furious—because now she's racked with helplessness and the fear that Will Galassi may be right.

The world *is* in a bad place. Mankind isn't. Crime is down. Hunger is down. But that improvement is its own kind of strain. People have given themselves the time to breathe and a path to

do better through industry, science, technology. The more we learn, the more we burn, the more resources we chew through like termites through healthy wood. Trees and land and dirt. Sky and sea and all that dead dinosaur juice beneath the ground. We're poisoning the world with our productivity. Seven billion people—and counting.

We're not the meteor, she thinks. *We're the swarm.*

Maybe this is for the best. Let the ants come marching. Let them sweep over the world like the biblical deluge, their jaws flexing, their antennae searching, those little legs going *ticky-ticky-tack* across the dirt and the stone. She imagines it: swarming men and women in their homes, their cars, at work. They'd act like any other natural disaster: they'd take the old, the young, and the infirm first. Her mind wanders to an infant in the crib, big glassy eyes looking up at the mobile above her head, fat fingers searching as the ants come marching two by two, hurrah . . .

Hannah makes a sound: a wild, feral noise. She squeezes her eyes shut so hard she thinks they might never again open, gritting her teeth and forcing those thoughts out of her head.

She repoints her mind to something altogether more academic. The Dust Bowl of the 1930s. She mentioned it to Will for a reason. For the better part of a decade, Americans reduced a lot of the middle of the country to a dust-choked wasteland. They hurried to cut down all the grasslands, but those grasses had acted as windbreaks and kept the soil healthy and balanced. Suddenly everything dried up fast. Big dust storms—like billowing clouds from the Devil's own mouth—rolled over the land like boulders. *Black blizzards,* they called them. Everyone thought it heralded the end times. For America. Maybe for the whole world.

But action changed it. Drastic action taken in FDR's first one hundred days. The government planted more than 200 million trees. They worked to teach farmers advanced agricultural techniques: crop rotation, soil health, how to prevent erosion. The government paid farmers to learn and work the new ways. They slaughtered millions of pigs that were a drain on the region, and they fed the pigs to the hungry.

It didn't work at first. Years went by without change. But by the end of the Dirty Thirties, the practices had their effect. Rain returned to the region. The dust storms rolled back to the hell from whence they came. Life began to grow anew.

Hannah stands up. Something vibrates up through her feet—a low rumble. Thunder, she thinks. Whatever storm was on its way is almost here. She stands up on her tippy-toes, ignoring the pain in her ankle as best she can. Her fingers feel along the top margins of the glass wall—tickling the mesh as ants crawl on the other side of it. The mesh is soft metal. She can't push it out from here. She doesn't have enough leverage.

The pain in her twisted ankle is coiling around her leg and tightening, so she sits for a moment, breathing. She takes off her sneaker. Her ankle isn't swollen. It's not hot to the touch. It hurts, but it's not broken.

She opens up the laces to put the shoe back on and curses her stupidity. Shoelaces are a survivalist hack. Her parents taught her how to build shelters, bandage wounds, make rafts—all using shoelaces. Hannah's own laces are high-test: made of paracord 550. The same cords are used to suspend jumpers from their parachutes. She remembers when astronauts fixed the Hubble telescope using this stuff.

These shoelaces are going to save her life. Or end it, if it goes wrong. Because the ants are still out there, aren't they? She's going to have to work fast.

Hannah undoes the shoelace from her left sneaker. She takes each end of the shoelace, and uses her teeth to pinch the aglets tight, to little points. She stands again on her tippy-toes, wincing against the pain in her ankle, takes one of the aglets, and presses it hard against the mesh, trying to get it into one of the very small gaps between the fine wire. She blinks back sweat as another roll of thunder thrums through the ground and the walls.

Push, push. The mesh strains, tenting outward. And then: *Pop.* The end of the shoelace thrusts through.

Hannah pulls the shoelace needle back out, and then an inch over, does it again—push, push, *pop.* Back out, and again. Five holes.

The ants begin gathering on the glass wall once more. Some begin meandering across the ceiling. Walking, then pausing to detect the changes in the air. The scent of Hannah crawling along those air currents.

Hannah works the shoelace back through the first hole, and then hooks it toward the second hole. It's hard to redirect it back, and she has to squeeze the tips of her fingers on her right hand through that second hole, little pincers searching out the shoelace—

The ants gather. They creep closer. She imagines them all over her. Biting and stinging. *No.* She can't go there. Not now.

Stitch. She grabs the aglet of the shoelace, pulls it through.

Then the third hole.

She can hear the ants' little feet now. *Click, click, click.*

Fourth hole.

The ants are beginning to crawl up the bottom of the mesh. Hannah sees hundreds of them rising from the floor. Coming up the glass. Eager. Interested.

Finally, through the fifth hole—

The ants crawl up over the mesh. Hannah bangs the mesh with her hands. Ants shudder and fall. Again she hits it, again, *again,* until most of them pitter-patter back onto the floor.

But they keep coming.

The ends of the shoelace dangle through the first and fifth holes in the mesh. Hannah coils the hanging ends around her hands, then braces herself against the wall. She pulls with both hands. Muscles straining. She draws up both knees until she's suspended by the shoelace, holding tight. She gets her shins against the glass—

The ants start pouring through the holes.

Hannah pushes hard with everything, letting her weight do the job—

The mesh moves. One hard shift—a *rip* as it pulls away from its mooring. Something tickles her knuckle. An ant. No time to stop. No time to think. Just push with knees, pull with arms—

Hannah cries out as the wire mesh wrenches away and she falls backward. The flat of her back slams into the floor. The air rushes out as her lungs close like a pair of clapping hands. Her mind scrambles like a rat on fire: *Get up, get out, get up, get out.*

Ants are churning through the gap.

Hannah springs to her feet, ignoring the pain that corkscrews up through her heel and back into her ankle. She snatches up the shoelace. The ants come across the ceiling, down this side of the glass wall. *They're coming. Run.*

She takes three good steps and then springs up, grabbing the lip of the wall. Ants crush and smear beneath her fingers and palms. The Myrmidons begin to swarm her now, down her fingers, along her forearms as she pulls herself up through the gap even as she knows it's already too late, even as she feels their pinching mandibles closing on her skin like staples—

She draws herself through the open space—through a moist, squirming hole of black ants—and falls down on the other side. Her esophagus tightens like big hands are choking it shut. She gets up as her tongue swells in her mouth. Her hand hits the side of the steel table. Her legs skid out from under her.

Pain in her shoulder. Pain up her ankle. Ants up her neck. Under her ears. Under her shirt. The sound of her breathing becomes the sound of a milkshake sucked up through a bent and broken drinking straw—a wheezing wetness.

Her finger moves, an inchworm among ants— There. An EpiPen auto-injector.

Hannah rolls over—her lips fall open because she can't get them to close, but her teeth clamp and she feels the ants over her cheeks, her mouth, her teeth. A mad thought bubbles to the surface: *It's all just protein.*

She summons everything she has. Pushes all her energy into

the arm that lies flat on the floor, the auto-injector curled weakly into her fist. She draws up not just her energy but the voices of her parents, all the ghosts of those who have come and gone, all the feelings of inadequacy and fear and uncertainty about the world in which she lives, all the urges she has to live despite whatever this world will one day become, and she sings through her teeth and pushes her heels hard into the floor and—

28

A cold, electric rush punches through her. Hannah sits up suddenly, her limbs stiffening, then relaxing. All parts of her feel jittery, on edge, like she just walked away from a plane crash without dying. *The epinephrine injector worked. I am alive.*

But there's no time. She feels her face squirming and she shakes her head like a dog with an ear infection. Ants are flung from her face, and she paws at the rest still clinging to the area around her nose and eyes. Her hands come away slick and red.

She stuffs the geyser of panic back down into her gut, then grabs for the other two EpiPens on the table, tucking them into her pocket. It's time to get out of here.

Hannah barrels out of the room, still wiping ants off her arms and neck. Whatever pain she feels in her ankle is swallowed beneath the greater misery—a song sung across her skin, from hundreds of bites and stings. The epinephrine leaves her feeling hollowed out and stripped raw, both gutted and filled up with an energy as nervous and frenetic as the Myrmidons called to alarm. She turns hard to the left, heading back to the main room—the room with the winding staircase leading up to the cove. The room with all the terrariums.

When she gets there, the smell hits her like a fist. She skids to a halt.

The whole room is moving. Like something out of an acid trip, the walls shift and swell with an *arterial* pulse. Black, glistening arteries. Columns clotted with insects. Climbing down from the open door above. Through vents and out of pipes.

It's not all black, though. Hannah sees other bits amid the trails of Myrmidons: Bits of feather. Bits of skin. A piece of scalp with hair on it. At the margins of the room, along the far curve of the wall, the ants have built a mound of these bits almost six inches high. Heat and stink come off the uneven hills of sagging skin. The humidity in here is so thick, Hannah can feel it growing greasy on her already-prickling skin.

This is their nest.

Getting out means winding her way back up the stairs, past those thick columns of ants squirming like massive black serpents. *I can do it,* she thinks. She got this far. She'll just run fast. Even if her ankle snaps she'll keep pushing and pushing, because that's what she does.

As if on cue, the Special Projects lab shudders with air-splitting thunder. Thunder Hannah can feel in her teeth, thunder she can feel screaming in every ant bite and sting on her skin. And she realizes: the ants are swarming here because of the storm.

Above her the heavy shutters are keeping out the crashing sea.

Ahead of her is the big red industrial button.

It might drown her, too. But by the time that thought reaches her mind, it's too late. The heel of her hand is stabbing out—as the ants surge toward her, once again smelling the stink of her skin—and smashing the button against its frame. Above, she hears the shutters bang open.

The sea pours in.

29

The ocean burns. The salt water against all Hannah's little pricks and cuts feels like lemon juice on a paper cut times a hundred. The seawater pours over her in great pounding sheets—fists of water trying to slam her down to the metal grating of the floor beneath her feet. Already it's around her knees.

The ants collect across the gathering water like clumps of dust in puddles. They form rafts: floating black masses of insects. She thinks, *It's not killing them.* But then the water pours down over them and plunges the creatures through the froth and foam into the churning saline broth.

A sound comes up out of her: a lunatic's laugh. Triumphant and deranged. *Got you, you little bastards. Got you.*

The ocean intrudes. It rises beneath her.

And Hannah swims with it, treading water as it carries her to the top.

* * *

The day before Roy Peffer's death, Dad makes ice cream. He uses goat milk for the dairy, and to cover up some of that extra goaty flavor, he adds currants picked from the bushes along the northern hedgerow. Plus a little lemon juice (no lemons grow here in Ohio, so it's something he has to borrow from the neighbor, much to her mother's consternation). And of course, tons of sugar.

It's good. They sit on the porch, Dad with his back bowed, elbows

on his knees, like he's about to get up and spring into action. Mom sits on the rocking chair. Hannah's on the steps.

They talk about dumb stuff like what kinds of animals they see in the clouds (rabbit, hippo, and somehow Dad pretends he sees a platypus). That moves into who can make the best animal noises. They do a few rounds (the best goat, the best elephant), and Hannah does a good crow, while Dad does the most amazing horse impression any of them have ever heard, so much so that they joke he must be part horse. "A centaur," Mom says. Mom even joins in for a few rounds. Her monkey is pretty good.

Then there's silence as they sit and slurp. Hannah's got a question that's been nibbling away at her for months. So, seizing the silence, she speaks.

"Is it really gonna be worth it?"

"What does that mean?"

Hannah says, "I just figure. If everything really does go haywire"—she's not supposed to say *the shit hits the fan,* even though that's how Mom always puts it—"do we really want to be around for that? If the world is so bad, maybe it'd be better to just . . ." Here she feels Mom's gaze burning holes through her like a pair of hot needles. "Maybe it'd be better to go down with the ship."

The question has made Mom mad. Hannah immediately regrets saying anything.

But Dad jumps in: "Hannah, it's a good question. I ask myself that from time to time." That rankles Mom, but he speaks fast enough to cut her off before she can start waggling that finger of hers. "But the apocalypse isn't really an apocalypse. Not like we think of it. Doomsday is a bad name for it, too, because it asks us to believe that the whole thing will smother each of us like it's a blanket we all get trapped underneath. But it's not really that way." He leans forward even more, his knees creaking and popping. "The planet has billions of people. Now, we don't know what the end will look like, okay? Your mother and I believe it'll be an end of our own devising—a true tragedy in the Greek sense. Mankind overshoots the mark and earns its own damnation. And maybe that means global warming. And maybe global warming means—well, who knows what? Sea levels rising. Storms like we've never even imagined. Wildfires or little ice ages. Thing is, it'll end life as we know it—by which I mean, it'll end our *way* of life. But it probably won't kill all the people. Out of the seven billion on earth, what if a billion survive? Or a million? Or a hundred thousand? A fraction of what we had, but still: humanity may keep on keeping on. But the tumult that our endangerment will cause—it'll be a thing most people can't endure. And that's how people will die. But you, me, your mother? We want to be ready. We want to survive through that time of tumult. The world's going to end, but a new world will grow out of the ashes of the old, and we want to be there to help cultivate it."

Mom wears a small, satisfied smile. Her hand reaches out and takes his, gives it a little squeeze.

Hannah smiles, too, a fake one, and tells them that sounds real smart. That night, she fears the big apocalypse that's coming. The one she's not sure they'll survive, no matter what form it takes.

Tomorrow, she'll learn that it's the little apocalypses that can kill you.

* * *

For a moment, darkness. Soon the water is over her head and she swims to the door—but now it's closed, now it won't open, and a new panic hits her. She pounds on it, but that does nothing. Then she sees that red lever by the door, and she swims over to it and pulls hard.

The door opens and Special Projects disgorges her against the metal walkway leading out. Hannah gasps, pants. It's raining. Clumsy, fat drops. Storm clouds the color of diseased lungs roll in over the island from the west.

She staggers forward, the island noisy with the sound of falling rain and the crash of the surf against the walls of the cove. Hannah makes her way to the elevator just as a wave slams into the rocks.

The hard blast hits her, almost knocks her off the platform. But she hangs on.

The elevator, thank all the gods in all the pantheons, works. On the way up, she sees ants trying to come down. Trying to return home, to their nest, to their queen. Maybe not one queen, but several? She's not sure how it works, and at this point she doesn't care. She just wants them dead.

These ants won't make it. Already the rain is picking up force. A sheet of water runs down, washing one trail away. Then another. And a third. Until she can see none on the rocks at all.

The elevator clangs as it hits the top.

* * *

The cop waits down by the cattle gate, which hangs open. A wind sweeps across the tops of the tall grasses.

Hannah stands, arms wrapped tight around her chest though it's late summer and the air is warm. She's just turned thirteen a few weeks ago.

Mom: "I don't understand why *they're* here."

Aunt Sugi: "You know why."

Dad hangs back on the porch. Forlorn. Staring out.

Mom: "Do we get any visitation?"

"None officially, Bell." Bell, a nickname for Hannah's mother that nobody uses but Sugi. (Sugi, though, is a nickname everyone uses.) "But the court left it up to me and obviously, as we discussed, I'm good with it."

"I don't know what *it* means. Be specific."

"I mean—well, we'll talk about it. Maybe you come over on weekends to start. For a few hours here and there."

"That's not enough."

"But it's a start." There, in Sugi's voice, a thrust of cold steel. Icy and declarative. It's rare to hear, so you know she means business.

Mom: "We're not crazy."

Sugi: "It's not about that."

Mom hisses something then, but it's swallowed up by the susurrus of the wind through the grasses. When the wind dies back, Hannah hears: "—freedom taken away."

"You feel how you feel, Bell. We're gonna hit the bricks now."

"Can I—"

Sugi nods. Mom comes over to Hannah.

She says, "It'll be okay."

"I know," Hannah lies.

"Everything that happened, happened the way it should. I'm proud of you. Dad is proud of you."

"Why won't Daddy come over?"

"He's . . . heartbroken. Not with you. Just with the way of things."

Hannah starts to cry.

Mom doesn't hug her so much as hold her at a distance—arms out and locked, hands on her shoulders. "Hannah, you remember one thing for me. You are a survivor."

"Okay."

"Say it."

"I am . . ." But the tears grab her voice and run away with it.

"Say it aloud. You need to acknowledge it."

"I am . . . a survivor."

"Damn right you are."

A kiss on the brow, and then Sugi takes her to her new home.

* * *

The storm sweeps over the island like the wrath of a vengeful god—the sea rising up on all sides and pulling at the atoll with waves like hands. The trees thrash as if desperate to escape what's coming. The rain moves from fat, heavy drops to a cascade of water from the sky above and sea spray from the sides. Soon Hannah can barely see. She shuffles as quickly as she can down the walkway, trying not to lose her footing.

It feels like a forever journey, but eventually she finds herself at the back exit of Arca Labs.

The door is closed, which means they restored power. A small triumph.

Hannah pounds on the door as a gale wind howls. There's no response. A sick, sour feeling crawls in her gut. They're all dead. They got the power working, and now they're dead. And the door is closed and she has no wristband, no RFID tag, no way to open it.

She pounds on the door again. "Please," she says to no one, her voice drowned by the rage of the storm. "Please let me in."

Nothing. Nobody. Just the wind and the rain and the crash of the waves.

Then she senses movement behind her. She spins around, hands up, ready to claw, scrape, and punch—

A man comes at her, and she cries out—

"Whoa! Whoa. No." At first she doesn't recognize him—white mustache dripping rain, eyes blinking. He looks haggard. Captain Dan Sullivan. From the boat that brought her here. His white shirt is soaked through, and the shoulder is torn up—the fabric pulled away, part of his chest exposed. His skin there is blackened and burned, parts aggravated raw like meat. "Hannah."

Holy hell.

"Captain Dan. What happened to you?"

He staggers toward the labs and slumps up against the wall. "My boat. One of yours came and took my boat."

"Will Galassi."

He nods. "Snuck on board as I was shoring up, then grabbed a flare gun out of the toolbox on the side and—" He tilts his chin down to gesture at the burn on his chest. He looks frustrated. Mad at himself, maybe. "Knocked me right off the boat into the water. Lucky it did, too, or I might have caught fire and been burned a whole lot worse."

She looks him over like he's gotta have an ant on him somewhere.

Or like maybe he's not even here, she disbelieves it so hard. "Did you get bitten?"

"Bitten? Bitten by what?"

"We need to—" Lightning bound up with a bone-cracking boom of thunder flashes off to the lagoon side. Suddenly Hannah's shaking. And she can't stop. "We need to get inside. Then we'll talk."

"How do we do that? Place is locked up like a convent."

She starts to formulate a plan. "We go around. To one of the windows at the lab. I can see in—see if anybody is . . ." But she can't say that last word. *Alive.* "We'll see who's left. And then—"

Behind her, a vacuum pop and an exhalation of air. And there stands Barry. "I told them I heard somebody!"

30

The storm seems like a vengeful spirit, a poltergeist bringing the full weight of its spectral sound and fury against those still trapped inside Arca Labs. It bangs and howls. The cannon-fire sound of thunder from nearby lightning is followed swiftly by the bone-break snap of a tree going over. The monsoon wails: a furious, unquiet dirge.

Hannah steps into the lab, and the first thing that happens is Einar meets her, face-to-face. He breathes a sigh. "I knew you would make it back to us."

The power's on. Computers are up and running. "Kit?" she asks. "Is she still alive?"

She is.

Down on the floor, where she had been before, blankets behind her head. Her face is drained of color, her lips dark as if she'd been drinking merlot. Her eyes don't fix on Hannah, but as soon as Hannah steps up, they do move—they just look in the wrong direction.

Hannah grabs one of the two remaining EpiPens out of her pocket and jabs it into Kit's thigh. It takes a second, but then Kit's head tilts back and she swallows hard. Her eyes lose their rheumy clouds, and she takes a small breath—a mousy gasp.

And then Hannah is crying. The tears are happy in their way, but something darker lurks just below. She's tired and spent. The epinephrine charged through her like a scouring force—an abrasive sandstorm scraping her raw. She feels hypercharged and broken

down all at the same time. She knows if she doesn't get it together *right now* she'll drop into that dark well and sob until she passes out. She cries out and sucks it up.

* * *

Hannah tells them her story. She is careful to leave out the part where Will claims he didn't kill the man in that cabin in New York and that Will was no longer in possession of the colonies. For now, she keeps her story tight: he created the ants. It's not a lie. And until she has more *facts* and less *speculation*, the story remains.

The rest of them tell Hannah what happened in the labs.

Einar got the power back on, though the satellite was ruined, and nobody ever found the battery packs for the phones. Hannah wonders if Will had them stashed at Special Projects—but that lab is now underwater.

So, they have electricity, but no way to reach anyone off the island.

At least they can keep the ants out. The HVAC is locked down. So are the doors. Plus, the storm outside drove the ants away—Hannah hopes, she tells them, back to the nest. "Where I drowned them."

Barry lets Buffy scurry from the back of one hand to the palm of another as he listens. Nancy sits at a computer, tapping away.

To Einar, Hannah says, "Those barrels you saw. They're gone now."

His face tightens. "My gods."

"Did you see any strange barrels?" Hannah asks Captain Dan.

Dan tells them what he told Hannah, about Will attacking him with a flare gun. "But no, I didn't see anything like that. Hell, I didn't see any of these ants at all."

"What is he planning?" Einar asks her.

"I don't know," Hannah lies.

"We should endeavor to discover as much about his plans as possible. More specifically, about the ants themselves. We have access to the local network. Perhaps he left us a trail of ones and zeroes to follow. Could be he has hidden his research—"

Nancy barks, "What do you think I'm doing over here? Surfing Twitter?"

"Well." Einar laughs. "Apologies. Nancy, proving yet again why you are well above my intellect level."

"One thing to look for," Hannah says, "is how he protects himself from them. From the Myrmidon ants. I watched him crush one—the ants swarmed him, but they never bit. *How?*"

Ajay perks up. "What did the ants do when they swarmed?"

"Nothing. Nothing at all." Wait, that's not true, is it? "You know, they did do something. They carried the carcass of their dead colony mate away. Like some kind of ant funeral."

"Hm." Ajay turns away, lost in thought.

"So, what now?" Barry asks. Thunder tumbles above and the rain picks up, pouring down over the lab pod like ball bearings on a tin roof.

"We find out what Will was planning," says Hannah. "We need to know where he took those ants. And warn others, if possible. We see what we can scavenge from his files, and then we get off this island."

Einar says, "Someone will come once the storm abates. For now, we are safe. Relatively speaking."

"We still need to get word out. Let's see if we can get some kind of communications up and running," Hannah says. "The helicopter has a radio, right?"

Einar nods. "It should."

Captain Dan laughs. "If we're gonna go to the helicopter, we might as well just fly the damn thing out of here. I was in the Navy. Used to fly a Seasprite but ended up on a Sikorsky Seahawk."

"Then I'm up for a chopper ride," Barry says, grinning from ear to ear.

Hannah can't help it: A smile crosses her face for the first time in what feels like forever. A flutter rises in her belly like a pair of white moths chasing each other. A strange, bubbly feeling:

Hope.

But that bright cloud is painted with a dark shadow: the murderer remains at large, and with him, colonies of these killer ants.

31

Einar works through paper files in case something missed their attention, something hiding away from computer records in plain sight.

Hannah hovers over him. "Will said something to me as he was leaving. He said he hoped I would get to go home. And that he needed to go home, too. You have Will's files there. Where does he live?"

Einar stiffens, then stands. "I don't need to look in his file for that. He lives on Kauai. North Shore, or not far from it. He has a small house there, tucked away in the rain forest."

"Do you think that's where he'd go?"

"Perhaps. He has a fiancée at home."

An odd twist in Hannah's belly. *Jealousy?* "Then we need to head to Kauai."

"Yes, I suppose we do."

"Do you think he sent the other colonies around the world?"

"It seems to have been his plan. But maybe he took them home with him. Maybe that is another reason to go. Perhaps we can cut the knees out from under this biological apocalypse yet, Hannah Stander."

* * *

"Don't trust Einar," Ray says in a quiet voice, hooking her arm and pulling her toward the corner of the lab as she passes. "I've worked

with him. I've worked *close* with him. He's a genius. He's transformative. But the guy's not human."

She yanks her arm out of his grip. "You're being dramatic."

"Probably." He sniffs. "Just be careful."

* * *

Barry hands out more bug snacks. Protein bars and crispy mealworms. The protein bars taste like wall spackle, but the mealworms are like salty, greasy pork rinds. Hannah brings some to Kit, who still looks run through the wringer. "Someone needs to take care of *you,*" Kit says. The most she's spoken in hours.

"I'm fine," Hannah says. But her face tugs tight and burns. Her arms and legs are covered in angry welts where the Myrmidons stuck their spears. The ants had already started their cruel work on her hands. Her fingers and the spaces between them are raw and red—as if sliced with little slips of paper. A few triangles of skin had been cut away, and she can move flaps of flesh by poking them. "You're the one who almost died."

"I think you qualify as *almost died,* too." Kit reaches up to touch Hannah's arm, and her hand shakes. "From the EpiPen." She smiles—a weak, trembling expression. "It's actually just adrenaline, you know."

"Huh. I did *not* know that." It explains a lot.

"You learn something new every day."

Suddenly Nancy is spinning in her chair and facing the rest of them. Her eyes are wide. Her jaw set tight.

"I found something," she says.

* * *

"I thought it was nothing at first," Nancy says, circling the mouse cursor around a single file folder. "It's the recycling bin. I bypassed it because I already checked the digital trash and didn't find anything. But then I realized—"

"That's not the recycling bin," Hannah says, staring so hard at the screen the bright icons begin to blur together.

"No, it isn't. The icon has just been made to look like one."

"And when you click on it?"

Nancy demonstrates: *click-click*. A window pops up. The file folder is locked. Password protected.

Einar sidles up next to her. His fingers tickle the air as if he's already typing. "May I, Nancy?"

"Knock yourself out." She offers him the chair, but he instead stands at the keyboard. His fingers move fast. Hannah watches windows pop up and snap shut again. He switches the OS from OSX to what looks like a Microsoft installation. Then he's in the back end. Doing a REGEDIT on the registry—the cursor drifts to something-something HKEY_CURRENT_USER and he navigates submenu after submenu with alarming alacrity. As he types he talks, that crisp, curious accent accentuating every word.

"I was a bit of a hacker in my younger days. Mostly for the challenge of it—I like coding and this brand of coding is somewhat subversive. *Punk*, as it were, though aesthetically I was never really that. It always seemed to me that the hacker occupied the same niche as the American cowboy in your Wild West. Gunslingers at the edge of known civilization. Black hats, white hats. Some drawn into thievery, others taking the law into their own hands—justice both corporeal and social."

He types, then highlights a gibberish string of characters, copies it into a notepad on-screen, then more clicking and typing. Hannah thinks he's grabbed the encrypted password and is now running it through a quick-code algorithm to unencrypt it.

But as he's doing so, she notices something else. Something not on-screen.

All of them have gathered around to watch Einar at work.

All of them but two.

Ajay is gone.

And so is Ray.

She looks back. Einar has the locked file opened and laid bare—vivisected like a pigeon, guts out for the scrying. He begins to open files, flinging them to the various corners of the large screen—spreadsheets and windows populated with dense notes about genetic chains. Images pop up in quick succession: macro photography of ants. Some small, some large. One ant is almost golden in color, another as black and shining as a mirror at night. A third is red as fire. And on and on.

"These aren't Will's notes," Nancy says.

But Hannah has figured it out because the guilty ones always run, and she speaks at the same time as Nancy: "They're Ajay's."

32

Hannah grabs Kit's wristband. Did Ajay go deeper into Arca? Or out into the storm? Which would be safer? Which would he choose? Arca could still be flush with ants seeking shelter from the rain.

Finding Ajay is a priority. First, to discover what more he knows that he hasn't yet told them, but also? Because *he* might be the one who has (or knows who has) the missing ant colonies.

But as Hannah strides toward the door, it hisses open and Ajay comes hurtling toward her. He crashes into her, then spins hard against a white counter, a beaker atop it pirouetting off the corner and smashing against the floor.

No. He didn't throw himself—he was *thrown*. Ray is stepping through the door now, his once-perfect hair finally gone wild like a garden gone to weeds. His face is midsnarl. "He got bit" is all he says.

Ajay is on the ground, shaking and shuddering. A stuttering sound out of his mouth as his jaw locks and unlocks: *gg-gg-ggg*. Barry stomps on a few ants coming off him. He blasts a cloud from the extinguisher, too.

Hannah backs away, but one of the ants crawls up the back of her hand. Mandibles open, hungry for her skin (or rather, what lives upon it). She's about to cry out—

A flash of something down her arm, a tickling sensation—a green blur that she sees now is a praying mantis. Buffy scurries forward at lightning speed, scooping up the ant on her hand and tearing it in half. *Rip*.

Hannah stifles a scream as Buffy jumps off her hand and onto a nearby counter, greedily eating its Myrmidon prey.

That mantis just saved my life.

She might've needed the last EpiPen—and right now she needs that to help Ajay, to bring him back from the brink of anaphylaxis. She turns to grab the auto-injector, but—

It's gone.

Nancy has taken it. The small Filipino woman has it held tightly to her chest, like a prom date holding a beloved corsage. "No," Nancy hisses with an animal-like desperation.

"Nancy," Einar cautions.

"We need to give him the epinephrine." Hannah keeps her voice calm and measured. "We need to save his life so we can learn what he knows."

"*No.* It's our last one. One of us might need it." Translation: Nancy thinks she might need it. "We found his data. We have what we need."

Behind Hannah, Ajay's heels judder against the floor.

"Nancy. *Nancy.* Look at me. He could die without that shot. And if we want to know what happened here—if we want a complete picture of the events and a look at how to stop it—then he may know something that can help us. But he cannot give us that if his throat is closed and he dies from shock on the floor."

The woman's eyes flit like nervous flies—to Einar. To Hannah. To Ajay and back again to Einar. She looks down at the auto-injector in her hand, and slowly, her fingers start to curl away from it—

Einar says, "If you don't give it here, I'll fire you. Then I'll sue you. I have a team of lawyers swimming the oceans around me like hungry sharks. I'll be glad to chum the waters with you, Dr. Mercado."

Nancy's fingers tighten again around the EpiPen. *Damn it,* Hannah thinks. Nancy starts to back away, and Hannah moves fast. Her hands strike out like the springing forelegs of the mantis and catch Nancy's wrists. Hard.

"Hey!" Nancy protests.

Hannah hooks her leg around the back of Nancy's and *pulls.* Nancy drops backward. As she falls, Hannah lets the woman's momentum take her—and yanks the EpiPen out of her hand as she goes.

Hannah stomps over to Ajay, crouches, and slams the auto-injector into his leg.

* * *

Ajay didn't go far into anaphylaxis before Ray hauled him back into the lab, but he still needs a few minutes to shudder and shiver and work it out. The look on his face as he recovers from shock is telling.

"Where'd you go?" Hannah asks Ray.

Ray stares her down, breathes out, finally says, "Ajay ran. I ran after him."

"You should've said something."

"I didn't want anyone following."

She eyes him up. It seems like he's telling the truth. "How is it out there?"

"It's a horror show. People are stripped clean. They're dead. Everyone's dead."

Hannah flinches. Such a waste of life. "How bad is the infestation?"

"The ants? Pssh. Not too many. But some."

She has to hope that what she's learned about ants applies here, too: that these ants went back to the nest and she drowned them there. If not? That means they're still *here.* Or somewhere near.

Einar steps up to them. He doesn't even look at Ray. "Hannah, I'm sorry about pushing on Nancy. I misread the situation. You had it handled. I should have respected that."

Hannah shoots him an icy look. *You almost cost us that auto-injector.* But she guards her tongue. "It's fine."

"I think it's time to hold Ajay accountable. Will you ask the questions?"

"I will."

"Then let us begin, mm?"

* * *

Hannah is not law enforcement. Interrogation is not a thing she does. What she does is interview, asking questions not to demand answers but to see where the conversation takes them. This is her approach with Ajay. Her questions are soft and simple but probing.

Tell me about your role with the Myrmidon ants. Tell me about Will. Were you in charge or was he?

This is what Ajay tells her:

"I did not know what we were doing. What *he* was doing. Listen, Will is an artist. A genius. I hated that about him but I respected it, too. When I got a chance to work with Special Projects . . . how could I say no?"

Here, a burning stare from Kit. Hannah is reminded that Will and Special Projects stole her mosquito project away. Ajay being brought to the Cove has to sting her.

Ajay continues: "I thought it was all theoretical. Will was in charge. I wanted to study with him, but I didn't want him to feel like I was a student. I wanted to impress him. To be his equal—"

"We don't give a shit about your psychological problems," Ray says, and Hannah shoots him a look.

"The challenge was, how dramatic could it be? How far could we go engineering an insect? Something that was not precisely brand new—we are not gods creating life, not exactly—but something that would *appear* brand new because of how it was made not from a simple remix of two species but from a panoply of them. Harvesters. Leaf-cutters. Marauders. Drivers. I thought if we could crack this, it might open up the problems suffered with the pollinator project. And with my hand helping guide the project early on, it could never be claimed that it was all *Will, Will,*

Will." Will's name drips with caustic venom, practically sizzling as it comes out of Ajay's mouth.

"When was all this? When did it all start with you and him?" Hannah asks.

"A year ago. Maybe more. Eighteen months."

"He did all this in eighteen months?" Kit asks, incredulous. "How?"

Ajay offers a small, anxious nod. "Like I said, *brilliant*. I don't even know how, exactly. We started with the genome map of the Argentine ant. It was an incomplete map—so far they'd only gotten something like 216 out of 250 million base pairs with about 16,000 genes. Will and I did the rest. We already knew that the ant had 367 genes devoted to its sense of smell—compared to the honeybee's 174 genes. We knew they had cytochrome genes meant to detox the ant. But we also found genes that others had not—genes that indicated aggression, that dictated hunting patterns, breeding times and cycles. Will somehow took that knowledge and began to use it, the way you would solve a cryptogram puzzle in the Sunday paper, to decipher the genomes of other ants, too."

"Did you know he had created the Myrmidon successfully?" Hannah asks.

Ajay hesitates. She pushes. Asks the question again.

His eyes squeeze shut. "I did. One day when everyone was at dinner and I had to go back to the dorm for a moment just to get a heartburn pill—I know, Indians are supposed to be able to eat spicy foods, but I cannot abide them—there, on my bed, was a . . ." He makes a face. "Present."

Ajay describes a small Plexiglas box. Like the ones used to contain small quantities of mosquitoes or other insects. In the box was a mouse. And one of the formicariums: the black discs meant to carry small colonies.

"The mouse was not dead. It was still breathing. But most of its fur was stripped off, and half of its skin. Its whiskers twitched as the ants swarmed it, pulling it apart . . ." He stifles a sob. "There was a message on the top of the box. In Will's handwriting. It said, *We did it.*"

* * *

Hannah presses him on other questions:

Why did I see two sizes of ant?

"Some ants are polymorphic. They have castes, different sizes. Leaf-cutters have four castes: soldiers, guards, foragers, gardeners. Major, minor, media, and minim. It's the soldiers you may be seeing if you saw them in the nest. They develop as the nest matures."

How are there so many, so quickly?

"He prototyped hundreds, maybe thousands of queens. And their life cycle is tweaked—usually it's six, maybe eight weeks. This is less than a week."

So if they get established somewhere—

"Then it's over for us. They're destroyers."

They kill everything living?

"No. Just living things with the *Candida* yeast. It's not on every creature."

How did Will let them crawl all over him?

"I was thinking about that. You said they took away the carcass. The ant he killed?"

That's right.

"Ants are clean creatures. Obsessively so. They create these midden heaps—"

Hannah remembers Ez showing her the trays of ants—the corners blackened with piles of refuse and their own dead.

"—we don't know why they do it, but a good guess is so they keep pathogens to a minimum. And filth in general. An ant gets dirty, it obsessively cleans itself. It makes sense. Anything coating its antennae will limit its sensory abilities, so it is important for them to remain clean, as an ant is nothing without its senses. They carry their killed colony mates to the midden heaps, too. When some ants of certain species—like *Pogonomyrmex*—die, they release not only the alarm pheromone, but also oleic acid. That's how ants identify one of their own dead. That's how they know who to take to the midden heap."

What does this have to do with Will?

"Will may have covered himself with oleic acid. Or a mix of acid and something else. I saw that he had a few cans of Tinactin in his locker. Could be he has an antifungal in there, too. To mask the scent of *Candida*. Maybe he made it into a soap or a spray. Probably a spray. The ants crawl on him then, but do so with disinterest. They may investigate, as you suggest they did. But they would not bite."

Where would he keep that?

"I don't know! Listen to me, I don't know. You have to believe me. Maybe he kept them at the Cove. Or maybe they're here somewhere. I can't say. Because I don't know. Why are you doing this to me? I am being persecuted."

You did lie to us, though, didn't you? You knew answers to our questions and you withheld those answers. Why didn't you just come out and say something?

"I couldn't. I couldn't! Will made me complicit, but I didn't do it. I didn't do *this*. You can't hold me responsible for any of this. I won't hang. Not again."

Not again?

But that question he doesn't answer. He just dissolves into shoulder-hitching sobs. Face buried in his hands. His elbows digging so hard into his knees he's surely leaving bruises. The interview, it seems, is over.

* * *

They keep it quiet. Huddled in the corner of the lab, near the autoclave: Einar, her, Barry, and Kit. Nancy sits in the opposite corner, sullen. Ray hangs near Ajay. Watching.

They discuss what to do with him. Einar thinks he could be useful. Useful in translating his findings. Helpful in figuring out how to stop this thing.

Barry's an optimist: "Ajay's a good guy. I trust him to do what's right."

Kit goes the other way: "He's always been selfish. He hogs equipment. Secretive about notes. Don't trust him."

"I don't trust any of you," Nancy says from across the room.

Hannah turns to Nancy and starts to say, "I see irony is alive and well—" when from the other side of the room, Ray cries out. Ajay is up, a blur—something gleams in the man's hand. Even as Ray moves toward him, he's suddenly staggering back—and there's a spray of blood as Ray goes down.

Ajay wheels toward them. Feral. Like an animal forced to the back of its cage with a shock prod. A shard of glass is in his hand. Hannah realizes with horror: *From the broken beaker, the one that fell off the counter.* Nobody ever cleaned it up. Nobody even thought about it.

Ajay screams at them: "I won't hang for this—"

Hannah moves fast. Running toward him.

"I won't hang!"

She knows what's coming and she's too slow to stop it.

Ajay sticks the glass shard into the side of his neck and twists. A sprinkler hiss of blood arcs up across the wall, the window, the equipment. Ajay pulls out the glass and sticks it in again just as Hannah catches his arm. She presses her thumb hard into the center of his wrist. The glass, now greasy with his blood, falls away and hits the ground with a *kssh*.

The wound pumps fresh red. Hannah clamps her hand down, applying pressure. The blood underneath her palm is greedy and insistent. With her other hand she grabs a bunch of rubber lab tubing off a nearby counter and slides the loop down her arm to her elbow. Then she starts looking for something, *anything,* to hold against the wound. Something she can bind there to stop the flow.

Ajay starts to shudder violently. The color is gone from his face. Everything is the pallor of the inside of an ashtray. Then he starts to spit up blood.

Hannah doesn't know what that means. She's not an EMT. Her

parents ran her through homemade tracheotomies, how to get air back into a deflated lung, how to set a broken bone and keep it still with a homemade splint. But this is too big, too messy. Did he cut his own esophagus? Is there an air embolism? That can happen, can't it? She screams out for someone to get her a first aid kit.

But then someone's there, behind her. Pulling her away. It's Ray. Again and again he says, "It's over. It's over. He's gone."

Ajay is gone. He slides out of her hands. A lifeless, bleeding thing that hits the floor. Dark blood pooling.

Hannah can't look away.

* * *

Eventually Kit finds a first aid kit and gives it to Hannah. At first Hannah wants to ask, *What do I do with this?* Ajay's dead.

But then she realizes: Ray is bleeding. He held his left arm up to protect his face and the glass shard did a number across the underside of his forearm. A six-inch gash—clean, smooth, like the cut of a chef's knife.

Hannah cleans the injury. Bandages. Medical tape. All around her, piles of bloody paper towels. Ray acts like it's no big thing, so she acts that way, too.

As she's finishing up, a shadow darkens them both and there stands Einar. "The storm should pass by morning. We should spend some time tonight gathering things we need to take. Printing out Ajay's notes, for instance. Then we should endeavor to get a few hours of rest. We learn. We survive. We leave."

33

They move Ajay's body into the nursing station and close the door.

They eat protein bars and crunchy crickets and crunchier mealworms in silence. Barry says he might have some leafy greens in the back that caterpillars might eat, but Nancy says, "No. We'll all get diarrhea."

So bugs it is.

Barry stays off to the side, printing documents from Ajay's folder. By the end, he's got a pretty good stack.

Einar encourages a round of sleep. Ray says he's too hopped up and his arm hurts too much, so he'll keep a lookout for any ant intrusions. Captain Dan volunteers to join him.

Hannah's bone weary, and sleep hits her like ocean waves. She drops out of consciousness. Then suddenly she'll feel ants on her—climbing up her arms, tickling her legs, pinching the skin beneath her fingers, ripping free a mask of flesh from around her eyes and nose and mouth. Every time, she jostles awake. Gasping. Crying out. Every time she sees Ray and Captain Dan. They shush her and tell her it'll be okay.

Sleep and wake. Sleep and wake. Again and again. Hannah curls up into a ball in the corner. She weeps.

A hand on her shoulder. Captain Dan. "We'll get through this," he says. "We'll be all right."

Somehow it helps.

Hannah sleeps.

* * *

Morning. The light across the floor is a watery, washed-out pink. *A new day,* Hannah thinks. A day of escape.

Everyone wakes and moves fast. They gather their things. Take bathroom breaks. As they move around her, Hannah says in a loud voice: "We have no more EpiPens. If you get bit, that's it."

Barry says as he passes, "Sounds like something on a lab safety poster."

"Take weapons," she says. "Extinguishers. The flamethrower. Anything else you can think of."

Nancy suggests going back through Arca, just to see if anyone is left—but one step into the cafeteria tells them no. The smell there is like a living thing. Hannah feels a fist of bile forming in her throat, and it doesn't help that she imagines exactly what that regurgitate will comprise: bug parts. She chokes it down and closes the door.

Nancy does no such thing. She turns back in the extensor hall and bends over at a forty-five-degree angle to start puking. Hands on knees. When she's done, she sobs.

They go out through the back.

The storm has gone, but it has left chaos in its wake. Palm fronds everywhere. A carpet of leaves. Broken flora. Everything sodden and dripping. It's eerily quiet but for the tumult of waves. No birds. No wind. No voices. The air is surprisingly cool.

As Hannah steps outside, she looks in every direction. At the ground, in the trees, behind her to the pod. She half expects a plague of ants to come rising up. A sweeping blanket ready to disassemble them and carry them back to a new nest. But the ants are gone.

They move down the walkway, through the trees, toward the lagoon, where the helicopter awaits. The lagoon's blue waters are stirred turbid by the passing storm. Shadows moving underneath, hard to see. *Jellyfish,* Hannah thinks.

Einar points. "There. The pilot." A cruciform body bobbing a hundred yards out. "His name was Nils." He turns and walks back up the beach, away from the helicopter.

Hannah calls after him. They don't have time for this. But he ignores her. Instead, he goes to a battered bush—one whose hibiscus flowers are softened and wilted by the rain and wind. Petals like a ruined crinoline dress. He bends over and reaches out—

He jerks his hand back suddenly and Hannah thinks: *He's been bit.*

But then he laughs. With his free hand he swats at the air, still chuckling. "A bee," he calls. "A honeybee, hiding behind the flower. Clinging to the stem like a scared little thing." He turns and begins to walk back down the beach, and a shadow passes over him: a cloud gone over the sun.

Einar makes the sign of the cross, then delicately tosses the soggy flower into the lagoon. "May you pass into the next life, Nils." Then, to the rest of them, "Shall we take a helicopter ride?"

34

The *whup-whup-whup* of rotors cutting sky.

Nobody says anything as Captain Dan takes the Bell Relentless through its checks and lifts it gently into the air.

It's too surreal, Hannah thinks. The cabin is the height of luxury. A koa wood table in the center. Soft gray leather couches. Windows as tall as Hannah. The ceiling is an art piece: two curved lengths of wood laid over each other, each shaped like a smaller amoeba nesting in a larger one.

She thinks back to the Kia rental she had. The stench of cigarettes and the Febreze used to cover it up. This helicopter smells like a new car.

Einar smiles. Pride beams from him. She thinks: *He's an idiot.* No. Not an idiot—an *egomaniac.* Whether it's pride at owning this fancy helicopter or pride just for managing to survive the chaos, Einar has lived a charmed life. He's smiling, she thinks, because this only confirms for him his manifest destiny as the smartest, richest man in the room. And then she thinks: *What might he do with that pride?* Could *that* be why he's smiling? Because of what he accomplished here without ever getting caught? She reminds herself to keep an eye on him.

Whatever the case, Hannah herself can muster no such pride. Because she doesn't know what happens next. There are hundreds of colonies—maybe thousands, featuring *hundreds* of thousands of ants—missing. Taken by whom? For what purpose?

Einar slides back the top of the table in the center, and from it rises a collection of food and drink: bottled water, sodas, beers,

chips, pretzels, fancy candy bars. They pounce on this desert oasis. Twisting caps, tearing wrappers.

"It's not bugs," Ray says. It's the first thing anybody says.

Suddenly they're all talking. "What is this?" Barry asks around a mouthful. "Oh God in heaven, a dark chocolate bacon bar."

Einar nods. "Vosges chocolate. Out of Chicago. It's a bit odd for my tastes—I'd rather Amedei, as I consider them the finest chocolatier in the world—but I am glad you like it." He has a bottle in his hand, and begins pouring flutes of champagne. Hannah hears her mother's own stern survivalist voice inside her own when she protests:

"Drinking alcohol now is unwise. We need our wits—"

Kit waves her off. "I need to get crunk is what I need." She laughs around a mouthful of salt-and-vinegar potato chips. "God, I hated these as a kid. I hated these *last week*. But now it's like a gift from the gods."

"Hannah," Einar says, thrusting a flute of bubbly in front of her. "Surely we can celebrate this little bit?"

"No," Hannah says, turning it down. *I'm not interested in celebrating anything yet.* Survival here is the bare minimum, and they haven't even properly achieved *that*. "But you guys go ahead."

Einar shrugs and offers a toast:

"Skál!"

Ray reaches in for a beer, then pulls his hand back, crying out. Something skitters across the tops of the food packages.

"God *damn it*," Ray curses. "Barry, you had to bring that thing?" There, poised like a praying monk on top of a bottle of soda, is Buffy the mantis.

Barry looks stung. "What? She ate her share of ants. She did good. Didn't you, girl." He sticks out his finger and she runs up it, clinging to his forearm.

"Careful," Nancy cautions. "We might eat her if she gets too close."

Above them, the intercom crackles. "Radio's working," Captain Dan says. "Hannah, I got someone on the line for you."

* * *

The Bell's cockpit is mostly digital: four screens across, left to right. Various readouts. One satellite map. One radar. Dan looks comfortable in the seat, like he's always been the pilot of this fancy ride. He gives her a headset—and suddenly, there's Hollis's voice in her ear.

"I've never been so glad to hear from you," she says.

"I'm glad to hear from you, too, Stander." The relief in his voice is plain to hear: "Where the hell are you?"

Hannah gives him the CliffsNotes version: They left Kolohe about half an hour ago. Island overrun by the Myrmidons. Most of the people at the lab are gone. The colonies have been stolen.

"They're here," Hollis says. "On Kauai."

"The ants?" she asks, panicked. Everything feels like it's falling out from under her. *No, no, no.* "Are you there? On Kauai?"

"Yeah. They're everywhere, Hannah. People have died—" The radio crackles. His voice is lost.

"Copper?" She adjusts the headset, finds a volume control, tries spinning it up and down to see if anything happens. "Copper, you there?"

More broken words: "—Ez attacked—" *Ksssh.* "—sheltering in place—" *Fzzt, fzzt.* "—island-wide quarantine—"

And then that's it. He's gone.

She pulls off the headset. To Sullivan, she says, "Signal's gone."

"God damn it."

"The ants are there. On the island."

Sullivan grips the flight stick with white knuckles. "That means we don't know what we're flying into?"

"No, we don't." She looks out the front windshield. It's just ocean out here. No islands, nothing. Just a flat line. The white chop of the waves drawing jagged lines across the wide-open blue-steel sea. "Maybe the ants have taken down communications. Shit! I don't even know where Hollis is."

Dan says, "He could be at Barking Sands. That's a Navy base there. Got an airport, and it's snugged up against the Pacific Missile Range Facility. I'll see if I can get clearance to land there—that'll put you in Copper's lap. So to speak. But I gotta be honest, maybe it'd be best if we take this chopper to another island. We have the fuel—head past to next island over, Oahu, and—"

"No. I need to go to Hollis."

"And take all of us with you?"

She wants to yell at him, *Well, you came this far.* But her anger is irrational. She'd be putting these people in danger again. That said, she doesn't want to let them out of her sight, either. Hannah sighs and rubs her eyes with the heels of her hands. "I know, it sucks. But hopefully the base is safe. At the very least, you can . . . drop me off and then be on your way." *Or Hollis can detain you for questioning. All of you.* "I have to tell the others—"

Two of the cockpit screens suddenly go dark. "Oh, what the hell," Dan says. He gives them a bump with the heel of his hand. They flicker on, then offer up a graphical glitch before going black once again. "This is what you get flying a prototype chopper. Gimme an old-school Sikorsky any day of the week—"

Hannah shushes him. "You hear that?" she asks. She can hear a faint sparking.

He cocks an ear. "What is that?"

"Maybe an electrical malfunction."

Then both of the screens come back on. Dan harrumphs. "Guess we're back in business."

Something moves across the screen. No. Not across it.

On *top* of it.

One little ant runs corner to corner.

Hannah moves fast. She reaches down, starts trying to help Dan out of his straps. "Get up, get up, *get up.*"

The captain doesn't understand. He pulls away from her. "I don't need to get up, I need to figure out what's wrong with the—"

The screens go dark again. Below the cockpit, near Dan's legs, a panel rattle-bangs, then drops loose on a pair of hinges. A fat bulging bubble of Myrmidon ants *extrudes* out, breaking apart as it falls—

All over Dan's legs.

And up his arms.

"God damn it, shit, God damn it, get them off of me!" He starts flinging his hands, shaking them furiously. Hannah works to get the belt off him, but he's thrashing around too hard, he won't sit still—

His words of panic liquefy to a throaty shriek as the Myrmidons start biting him. The ants dot his cheeks. His lips. They clamber into his screaming mouth. It's over. Hannah realizes that now. She pivots away from the seat, launching herself back through the door. Already the others are up, drawn to the alarm of Captain Dan screaming. Einar's face is a grim mask.

Hannah never gets to tell them. The Bell shifts hard to the left. Her head cracks against one of the windows.

Moments of darkness stitched across a blurry streak of colors. Her innards do loop-de-loops as the helicopter dips and jerks. She braces herself against the wall.

Screams spin and whirl around her. Out the window, she sees those white lines of the wave tops coming closer—

We're crashing, she thinks.

And then they hit.

PART IV

COMPETITIVE EXCLUSION

competitive exclusion (n)

1. a situation in which one species competes another into extinction.

INTERLUDE

KAUAI

A boat leaves the Cove at midnight, sixteen hours before Will steals Captain Sullivan's craft, thirty-two hours before the Bell Relentless slams sideways into the storm-swept Pacific.

That boat is a blue-water fishing boat. It has a pair of Yamaha F350 four-stroke engines. The boat skips across the waves like a stone. It is a fast vessel.

In the back are five barrels. Plastic. Hinges not at the top but down the center. Barrels that break open like a chest sitting on its side.

The boat and its captain arrive at the southern coast of Kauai between 4:00 and 5:00 A.M. The captain of the fishing boat leaves one barrel behind. Open. Then the motor revs and the boat continues out into the black glass night.

5:30 A.M.

Somewhere through the haze of sleep, Makani hears it—

Nalani is crying.

It's a loud, shrill cry. And then, as fast as it starts, it stops.

The monitor blinks and crackles. Nalani is still making mewling, whimpering sounds. *Maybe she had a bad dream,* Makani thinks. She wants to just stay in bed. The alarm isn't for another hour. And then it's getting the little one off to day care and a shift at the juice bar and then picking Nalani up and taking the baby to her mother's so she can do a housekeeping shift at the Poipu Sheraton and, and, and. The day doesn't end until well into the night.

Just a year ago she would have relished staying up at night. Partying on the beach till she crawled into bed and then back out of it.

But then Nalani came along. The little one changed everything in the best way possible. *Except* for the sleeping part. The kid's got a wicked yeast infection. The ointments you get at Walmart don't do it, and the doctor—a *haole* from California, set up an office near the juice joint—said it's the humidity and heat here. So now the little girl sleeps without a diaper—which means she sometimes wets the sheets in her crib—and is on a prescription med. Makani's health insurance is shit, so it costs her almost a whole weekly paycheck once a month. It's why she took the housekeeping gig. But Nalani still wakes up in the middle of the night. Because she wants to feed. Or just wants to be held.

A bitter thought: *I want to be held, too, you know.* If only Kaleo hadn't run off back to Oahu the moment he found out she had one in the oven. Stupid *poho.* And she thought *ohana* was supposed to mean something. But Kaleo just wants to surf, brah. They're *pau*—done, forget it, piss on it.

Poor her. Poor Nalani. Dumb-ass Kaleo.

Ugh, now she's awake. Makani gets up. The monitor is flashing. And a hiss of static. Louder than usual. She staggers her way out of the bedroom and down the hall of the little house. A morning breeze comes in through the hallway—two windows anchoring each end of it make the hallway the coolest part of this dinky place. Out the windows she can hear the faint sound of the ocean—that's one of the nice things about this house. Close to the beach. Close to the dock.

Nalani's room is dark. She has to keep it that way or the little one will never get to sleep—it's, like, a shade, and then these gauzy-looking curtains, and then *blackout* curtains on top of that. She's half tempted to just get the damn windows tinted like she's riding in some slick whip.

There are gurgles coming from the crib at the end of the room. But something gives Makani's mind a little push. *Something's wrong.*

That's not one of Nalani's normal sounds. And suddenly she's hurrying over to the crib, her hands planting on the wooden rail—

She hears her little girl mewling. Right there. In front of her. In the crib. And yet—

Wait.

As her eyes start to adjust, Makani sees inside the crib. The whole mattress seems to be moving—roiling, shifting, a bulging mound of shadow. Within it, a faintly human shape. Her baby.

She reaches down, and the darkness becomes suddenly real, suddenly *tangible*—a physical, present thing. It's like plunging her hands into sand or tiny pebbles. Except whatever it is, it's moving. All around her. Not just around her, but up her arms, and her spine stiffens as she realizes that something is crawling on her—not one something, but hundreds, *thousands* of somethings, and then her mind visits back to the news story she just read about how fire ants have started to take hold in the islands. Not here, not on Kauai, but maybe they're wrong, maybe it is here—

A pinch on the back of her hand.

A sting, just after.

Then dozens of them. Up her forearms. Now her biceps. Makani doesn't scream, she just starts to say the word *no,* over and over, not because the ants are on her but because they're on her daughter and she wants her daughter to live even if she cannot—*no, no, no,* as if pleading helps, as if the ants are possessed of a merciful nature spirit.

As the ants swarm over her and rob her of her skin, she is serenaded by the sound of her little one crying. Normally it's a sound that haunts her, but here, it is a sound that reminds her until her last breath: *My baby is still alive.*

8:00 A.M.

"Moana," Pono says. "Howzit?"

He knows it's a mistake to ask. His sister, she's a big flabby wet blanket. Never a nice thing to say. Everything's junk in her life.

Just junk piling up on her shoulders. And she's secretly happy to carry it all around, pointing at it again and again so you know how miserable she is having to carry it all around.

This time is no different. She stands at the sink with a cigarette. Maybe she doesn't have much to complain about so instead she complains about him: "You *lolo.* A foolish little man, bruddah. You never home. Family means something. You always out there working and working and working for that rich *shark bait.* I should bust you up. Remember our small kid days? Our parents said we had to take care of each other. Huh? Where are you? Where are you most days, Pono?"

He wants to come out swinging. *Oh, Moana, we're supposed to take care of each other, but all I do is take care of you.* He's got a job. A *good* job. He's working for Einar Geirsson. Sure, sure, Pono's just a lowly driver—and one of a half dozen here on the island—but he's part of it. And he gets paid real nice for it, too. He gives his sister his paycheck. He tries to watch his nephews and nieces. And she just gives him humbug for it every damn time.

Outside, he hears someone yelling. Then some laughing? Whatever. These apartments down here in Lihue—somebody's always yelling at somebody. Those chucklehead mainlanders with the Jeeps and the Jet Skis are noisy like birds.

"I got bills," Moana's saying. "I got repairs. The catchment tank is leaking. My bathroom fan is buss-up."

Outside, more yelling. Whatever that's about, it's better than this. Pono smiles, nods, holds up a finger, and tells his sister he's going to check on it. She pinches her little fat eyes at him and goes back to half-assedly washing dishes.

There, by the Jeep in the parking lot. The two chuckleheads. One of them is shirtless: a tan, bronzed supermodel type of guy, always out here kicking a soccer ball. He's juggle-stepping backward, laughing. The other one is a pudgier, paler type—got on a baggy T-shirt and board shorts. Longer hair curled around his ears because he keeps forcibly curling it there, running his fingers along it and tucking it back even though it springs back out every thirty seconds.

Pono's dealt with them before. One of them is named Stav, short for Stavros, the other one is Kip, and Pono can't remember which one is which and he doesn't care, anyway. "Hey, keep it down, okay? It's early. People in this building are still asleep."

But they ignore him. Tan Chucklehead keeps stepping back. The other one is laughing, and he's saying in a ghoul's voice, "They're coming to get you, Barbara." More laughing and clapping. Like *lolo* idiots. Finally, Pudgy Chucklehead sees Pono. "Hey, man, c'mere. Look."

Pono takes a few steps, and he doesn't believe what he sees. Ants. A trail of them, about an inch thick. They clamber over each other, moving in a singular direction like a little stream of rain runoff. When Tan Chucklehead moves, they bend their path and move toward him. Both the chuckleheads giggle like they're high on *pakalolo,* which they probably are.

Somewhere in the apartment complex, someone starts yelling. A woman.

A cop car and then a fire truck go speeding by down Hoolako Street.

"Whoa, whoa, watch out behind you," Pudge says to Tan Chucklehead—and Tan Chucklehead wheels around too late to see that he's about to step into a second trail of ants. He plants one slippah down on bugs and instantly they start winding up his leg in a corkscrew trail. "Ow! Shit. They fuckin' bit—"

Tan Chucklehead sucks in a sharp intake of breath, then hops on one leg before losing his balance and going ass down. He starts flailing around like he's on fire.

More yelling in the distance. Pono starts to think something's wrong.

Pudge is still laughing. He hurries over and bends down, almost losing his footing as he starts to wipe the ants off his friend's legs—

They crawl onto him next. And it's only seconds before Pudge is making a sound like a wild pig Pono once saw caught in a barbed-wire fence. The pig thrashed around so hard it only trapped itself tighter, until its legs were up off the ground kicking the air.

Tan Chucklehead starts wheezing. And gagging. He slumps over. Shuddering.

Then one of the streams of ants pulls away, starts heading toward Pono.

Pono's no dummy, despite what his sister thinks. He turns and walks briskly back to the apartments. He's not going to run from some stupid ants. But then he hears more sirens in the distance. And someone starts screaming at the same time someone else in the complex starts weeping and calling for help.

Pono runs. He grabs his sister. Tells her it's time to go. She calls him crazy, accuses him of being stupid and high and whatever else. He asks her if the kids are in school and she says no, it's Sunday, they're at the beach.

He says they need to go pick them up. Now.

Moana protests.

Until the ants start coming in under the door. Until she sees them climbing up the screen window. The ants march into the front room. Up the walls. The ceilings. Little streams of them like arteries branching.

They head out the bedroom window and run to the car.

Noon

The civil defense sirens go off across the island of Kauai.

It is a single tone. It does not change in pitch.

This is part of the emergency broadcast system in Hawaii. They test it periodically, and it goes for a minute and then stops. Nominally, it's used for tsunamis. It's a warning sign to head inland.

This goes for longer. It is not a test.

But this is not a tsunami.

This is an invasion.

6:00 P.M.

A C-130 takes Hollis Copper to Barking Sands. He was able to call in a favor and hitch a ride on the flight carrying medical supplies and a few victuals for the military base. Halfway through the flight, they call him up to the cockpit to tell him the news: Kauai had been affected by some kind of "contagion."

Hollis asked, "What kind of contagion? What's that mean?" The two pilots looked at each other like they didn't know *how* to explain it. That's when Hollis knew. "Ants," he said.

Their eyes went wide. One pilot—young buck with apple cheeks and pinch-slit eyes, Airman Gordo Nybouer—nodded. "Ants."

"We even cleared to land?" Hollis asked.

"Yeah," the other pilot—a young brother named Duke—said. "But they're talking about a quarantine. Which means if we land, we may not get to take off again. Might be grounded for some time."

The plane lands. A hard bounce across the airstrip. On the left, Barking Sands beach and the Pacific Ocean. On his right, Hollis sees a pair of sailors striding toward the transport. Their faces are hidden behind gas-mask muzzles, their bodies clad with billowing hazmat suits.

While still on board, they give him a suit. He asks them if it's really necessary. One of them—nameless and faceless, voice muffled through the mask—says, "Have not seen any incursions of the biological entity here, sir. But just to be cautious, we recommend the suit."

The other sailor says, "But Captain Cole isn't wearing one."

Sailor One shoots Sailor Two some kind of look.

"I'm good," Hollis says. "Let's just get this under way."

6:15 P.M.

They lead him to a convertible. A cherry-red Mustang. A box-jawed man sits in the driver's seat, leaning back, one stiff arm propped up on the steering wheel as his thumb vigorously flicks through something on his phone. His hair is long in the back, almost a heat-curled mullet coming down over his neck. Captain Cole, Hollis is guessing.

"Good," the man says when Hollis gets in the other side. "You're not wearing that suit. Wear one of those, your balls will get swampy fast. That's how you get crotch rot." He frowns at the phone in his lap. "God damn it, Gunderson. You pissy little kitten." He shakes his head. "Sorry. My job here at the PMRF is to babysit a bunch of drunk, rich toddlers. We're the hottest-shit missile range in the Pacific, and I'd be all right just having to juggle dickheads from all the branches of the military and our so-called intelligence—no offense—but worse is that this base is home to executives from Boeing, General Atomics, Lockheed Martin, Sandia, Palisade, Boston Dynamics, you name it. Everybody wants a piece of me and each other. Gunderson, for instance, thinks he can just hop on his jet and take off. I'm telling him there's a quarantine in effect. Dumb fuck is stuck here."

The car revs and jumps like a nettle-whipped pony. "Sounds like fun," Hollis says.

"I'm just trying to be open kimono with you so you'll be open kimono with me." The car shoots around a bend, and suddenly they're off the airfield and coasting along the beach toward what looks like a little town. "The frisky fuck we dealing with here, Agent Copper? I'm told you know a thing or two."

"Not enough, but I know some." Hollis gives up the goods. No strategic reason to withhold information. He tells him about the dead body in the cabin, about Arca Labs, Einar Geirsson, the atoll.

"Shit. Geirsson—the billionaire? He lives here on Kauai, doesn't he?"

"It's one of his many homes."

The little town grows into view. Hollis has seen its like before. It's a base town. Gas station, barbershop with the stripy twisty pole, diner, McDonald's (there's always a McD's). And houses. Houses identical to one another except for the color of their siding. These houses are up on stilts, cars and Jeeps parked underneath.

"Listen," Cole says. "We're prepared for a certain level of shitfall. We are loaded for bear here with some top-shelf weaponization. We operate MATSS. We run and test new drones alongside UAV systems like Coyote and Cutlass. Aegis Ashore is up and running. We test and maintain damn near any kind of missile and missile system you can imagine—"

"You got any artificial intelligences here?"

"Not that I know of."

"Good to hear."

"What I'm saying is, we're prepared for someone to come along and try to knock us down or take our toys. We're ready for NBC attacks. But this is something above and beyond, Agent Copper. I don't know that we're prepared."

Hollis gets a flash of the skinless corpse surrounded by all the dead ants. *You're not,* he thinks. "Pesticides should do the trick in the interim," he says.

"Not the shit we got, hoss. We're getting reports of our men trying to use it on those damn things and most it does is slow 'em down. They stop, swarm in this squirming pile of *ant orgy,* and then they keep on coming. Like something out of a nightmare."

"Fire? CO_2 extinguishers? Poison? I'm no expert—listen, how bad is this? You got a couple ant colonies to exterminate—"

"A couple? Shit, Agent Copper, you *are* behind the times. You wanna know how bad it is, well, I got some maps to show you."

7:00 P.M.

The Roc, aka the Range Operations Complex.

Big rectangular building. Not unlike a beige shoe box, except made of concrete. On the ground floor is a big open space, where someone has set up a table. Around it are laptops, radios, a few tablet computers, some books. A whiteboard stands at one end, and at the other, a corkboard on an easel, pinned to which is a map of Kauai. Around the table mill a variety of sailors and soldiers, a woman with tired hound-dog eyes in a sharp-shouldered suit, and a nebbishy man with horn-rim glasses that fit uncomfortably on his face, given that one of his eyes is buried beneath a bulging white bandage.

Just behind all of it is a giant missile. More than twenty feet long. An SM-3, as Cole explains it. "A missile killer. A bullet you fire at another bullet to knock it out of the air."

But that, of course, is not why they're there.

Cole updates everyone. The island is in full quarantine. Folks can come in, but nobody out. The number of the dead is now just over two hundred, and the injured at twice that. They expect that number to grow, perhaps significantly. Some of the dead and wounded are due not to the ants directly, but to how folks have chosen to respond to the invasion: gasoline, fire, poison. One "numbnuts" tried to shoot them with a twelve-gauge and blew the front of his own foot off.

Cole outlines their existing response mechanisms: local police and fire are on rescue detail. The Navy here isn't geared up enough for a wide military response, nor has that been authorized, but they're running support and backup. Hospitals are staffed up extra, but Kauai doesn't have real profound medical support. They'll get military nurses and doctors to come in and do triage, but that won't happen right away.

The doctors have noted that epinephrine injectors do the trick *if* the victim is rescued from the swarming ants in time. But the hospitals are stocked with only a couple of hundred such auto-injectors. Steroids and Benadryl can help, but won't reverse anaphylactic shock. Which means FEMA will have to airdrop in medical supplies. They'll know more after midnight.

Cole does introductions.

The scrawny sort with the one eye behind a bandage: Jeff Tanzer, associate entomologist at the University of Hawaii. "Actually," he corrects, "I'm from U of Wisconsin, I'm just here lecturing. But they said you needed a bug guy." Cole starts to speak, but Tanzer jumps ahead of him: "Not that I'm qualified. For any of this. This is way above my instruction level." Again Cole starts to speak and Tanzer cuts him off anew: "And my eye, if you're asking, it's just Lasik."

"Thank you for all . . . *that,*" Cole says with a stiff smile.

Next up is the woman: Francine Roston. A representative for EAS, Empyrean AgroScience, GmbH. She says, "We have a vested interest in the Garden Isle. It has been an ideal testing ground for various GMO crops and our synthetic pesticides. In fact, I am here to note that we have one such pesticide not yet on the market—not even through testing, as yet, for the EPA's comfort level—that might work on these ants. It's a pyrethroid mix, Diazinethrin—synthesized from chrysanthemum and oleander. It's very, very safe. For us, not *them.*" She laughs, an awkward, robotic sound. "Of course, we'd need to rush approval of the pesticide—"

Cole thrusts up a finger. "Thank you, Ms. Roston." He introduces a few of the sailors and soldiers around the table: Chief Petty Officer Jana Wu; Seamen Hurwitch and Hornshaw, who helped Hollis deplane and turn out to be nearly identical gingers; and Ensign Deltura.

Then he introduces Agent Hollis Copper as "the man who's going to fix all this shit. Isn't that right, Copper?"

Hollis blinks. Well, uh-oh. Thing is, he hasn't felt precisely *together* since all that bad news went down last year. The reason he brought in someone like Hannah is because he no longer feels properly equipped to handle the job.

He doesn't say all that, though. What he says is: "I'm an investigator. Not a problem solver. But one thing I am good at is getting the right people to figure things out."

He tells Cole he needs to get Ez Choi on the line. And then he needs to find Hannah Stander.

8:00 P.M.

Cole says no to sending anyone out to get Hannah. "We got a helluva storm brewing out that direction, Agent Copper. Can't go losing men and equipment in that. Right now they're saying it'll shift north by morning. We'll send someone then."

They try to get Ez on the line. A cop answers, and Hollis learns she's been attacked in her office. Unfortunately, whoever attacked her escaped.

Hollis now speaks to her in a quiet voice at the far side of the room, leaning up against a tall, him-sized stack of file cabinets. The others watch expectantly out of range. "You don't have to do this," he tells her.

"I'm okay," she says, even though she's clearly not. She's been crying. He can hear the nasal sound of her voice from swollen sinuses. But she's pulling it together, and that's what counts. "I'm looking at the e-mail now." A pause. "Jesus, Copper. These are how many died?"

"Uh-huh. And we've got more numbers coming in."

"You know where the ants came from?"

"Not really."

"What did Hannah say?"

"Hannah's off right now trying to find out whatever she can." He prays that his words are true.

Ez sighs and pops her lips, clearly thinking. "Can you get me locations? Addresses? Of the people who were hurt. Or better yet: *where* they got hurt."

"Sure. It'll take a few hours, but I can get some administrative folks on it." He pauses. "Listen, we have somebody here who might have a solution. Wanted to run it by you."

"Shoot."

"Woman here from EmpAg, she wants to spray the island—"

"No."

"You didn't even let me finish my sentence."

"You don't have to finish it. She wants to spray it down with some kind of hellacious chemical. Some high-octane pesticide. Lemme guess. A pyrethroid?"

"Yeah, that's right. Why? Is that bad?"

"It isn't good. No pesticide is really all that awesome, and what you're looking at here are long-term ecological effects."

"I think an invasion of killer ants is its own *much worse* ecological effect."

"Hawaii is a surprisingly unspoiled ecological niche. It's paradise for a reason, Copper. Spraying will hurt humans, too. You'll see cancer rates skyrocket. Birth defects. Hormonal imbalances and disorders. It's fucking *poison,* dude."

He sighs. "I know. But a little poison here is better than these ants."

"Can you hold off? Let me think about it."

"I can buy some time. Until morning, maybe."

"Not enough time."

"Gonna have to be, Dr. Choi."

"Shit. Shit! Okay. Just get me the information. I'll work on it." She hangs up on him.

10:00 P.M.

Young naval yeomen bust their butt-bones getting the data together. Some of it is already on the map there on the wall, but it's imperfect. They make it perfect.

Hollis sends it off to Ez Choi. Then he crosses his fingers.

11:45 P.M.

Hollis can barely keep his eyes open. But he's got reports. Each is the same but different, all over Kauai: a new injury, a new sighting, ants in Poipu, in Waimea, Lihue. Starting to come in from Princeville, Hanalei on the north side.

He runs the numbers in his head. Fewer than seventy-five thousand people live here on Kauai. Plus tourists of an incalculable number. What happens when they lose control of this thing? Hell, did they ever have control?

Cole clears his throat, and Hollis startles. "Phone, agent." Cole jabs the cell toward him like it's a knife.

It's Ez. As Cole walks off, she says, "There's a pattern."

"Tell me."

"The deaths and injuries cluster. Your people did me a favor by putting in times of the reports. It isn't perfect—I mean, reporting times and actual times are never the same—but you can see that there's a thing going on here that's like a bullet hole in glass. A center point, and then the cracks spreading out."

"So it has a start point."

"It has *multiple* starting points. Check your e-mail."

He heads over to the edge of the conference table and pivots a laptop toward him. He logs on to his e-mail. Ez has done this by hand, then scanned it in—probably with her phone. She tells him, "I would have done it at my computer, but I'm still at the police station. You're looking at five nexuses. They're at, let's see—"

But he sees them and starts rattling them off: "Waimea, Poipu, Lihue, Kapaa, then Princeville."

She says, "The highest concentration right now is in Poipu." That's the primary resort area in the south. "Then it's in descending order, counterclockwise around the island. The only outlier there is Waimea—but I think that's because it's not a huge population center."

"A boat," Hollis says. "Someone took a boat around and did this."

"That would be my best guess, yeah. That would keep whoever did it relatively safe from the ants onshore and allow him or her to move quickly and stealthily around the margins of the island."

"You think any more about our little problem?"

She hesitates. "Yes. If there were a way to evacuate the island, that would buy us time . . ."

"Is that an option? Be serious now. Because if even one of those things gets off this island . . ."

"A single worker ant getting off-island isn't apocalyptic because it wouldn't be able to start a new colony." She pauses. "Unless . . .

Some species of ant can turn existing workers into queens. Not exactly sure how, but a pheromone thing, I'm guessing. Like how in *Jurassic Park* the dinosaurs switch gender like frogs. What's the saying? *Life finds a way.*"

"This is a goddamn horror show, Ez."

"I know."

"We're gonna have to spray."

"Give me till morning. I'll find a solution."

"I'll try."

Midnight

Gabe Landry bobs on an inflatable raft in the middle of the hotel pool. He's soggy and cold. In his left hand he's got a pool skimmer—whenever he drifts closer to the edge of the pool, he pushes himself gently back to the center. In his right hand, he's got a water bottle. He takes the last few drops from it into his mouth. He's thirsty. And he's pretty sure he's not supposed to drink pool water but damn if he's not about to start soon.

A body floats nearby. A young woman. She's already starting to swell, her skin covered in little bites. She came running toward the pool as the sun was setting. Covered in little black specks. Shadows moving across her skin, undulating like waves. She slipped on the side, cracked her head on the ground, then rolled into the water. The ants drowned. She did, too.

The screams have mostly died down, though. So that's something.

Gabe looks toward the rising wall of the Outrigger Resort hotel. Balconies—sorry, *lanais*—face the pool and the parking lot beyond. One of those rooms was his. Didn't face the ocean. He and his girl didn't want to spend the money and now he wishes they had.

Sandy. Jesus, Sandy. He tries not to cry again, but the gulping sob comes out of his throat as he remembers her writhing on the floor of their hotel room, bitten up by those little motherfuckers. He ran away from her. He didn't try to help.

He's a bad person. He knows that now. A coward. This was supposed to be a nice vacation. He was going to propose to Sandy. The ring is still in his pocket. Hanging heavy there in its little box.

The ants came in just after noon. Nobody thought much of it at first other than how disgusting it was—an invasion of little buggies in a pricey Kauai hotel, well, you can be sure everyone was right away rushing to their phones and tablets to start leaving nasty one-star Yelp reviews. But the ants kept coming, and they didn't want crumbs.

In the moonlight, Gabe sees a body on a nearby pool chair. Face-down, ass up. Sometimes it looks like the body is moving, like it's breathing, but it isn't. It's *them.*

A little line of them marches near the edge of the pool, skin bits held aloft in their jaws.

Gabe thinks, *Maybe it'll be over soon.* Surely someone will come. He hears sirens sometimes. Yelling and screaming. Gunshots, too. Maybe people are killing themselves. Guns in mouths, triggers pulled. Leaving this world instead of watching it go like this.

He has things to live for, he tells himself. Friends, family. A dog named Beans. A nice car—okay, not *nice*-nice, but it's a four-door Hyundai and it's new and fuck you if you can't appreciate the power of a new car.

Gabe pisses clumsily into the pool. *I'm sanitizing it,* he thinks madly.

Of course, you can drink your own pee, can't you? He doesn't remember. Not that it matters much because he doesn't *want* to drink his own pee and again he reiterates: *It'll be over soon.* Someone will come. Cops. FEMA. The military. Christ, isn't there a big military base on the far side of the island? Got to be people there gearing up to help.

Once in a while, the ants come closer. He can see them there, lining up at the edge of the pool. In the quieter times, he can hear the faint clicking of their feet. Sounds almost like someone typing on a keyboard in another room.

Once in a while, they drop into the water. Whenever that happens, he thinks: *Drown, you little assholes. Drown.* Then he laughs so he doesn't cry.

Now, though, they're not just dropping into the water. He can see them climbing down the inside of the pool. Right to the top of the water but no farther.

"Get away!" he yells, and he takes the flat of his hand and makes a splashing wave. It hits the gathering ants. Some of them wash into the pool. Most, though, stay right where they are.

He blinks. Then he sees it: their tiny legs connecting to one another. New ants come to replace those washed away, and they climb over the others and begin to move into the water.

Where, he figures, they drown.

But even drowning, they stay floating. And as the dead ants accumulate, the others begin to use them to stand on so that *they* aren't in the water.

Gabe splashes at them again, and once more some go under while just as many stay buoyant. They're building a raft—which in turn is becoming a bridge. Right toward him. All the alarm bells go off in his head.

He starts formulating a plan: Go to the opposite end of the pool. Climb out. There's a fence, a tall bamboo fence so gawkers can't peer in at the pool. Beyond it is the parking lot. He can climb the fence, land in the lot. Then he can run, full speed, to the beach, which is only 200, maybe 250 yards the other way . . .

Gabe drops off the raft, the water up to his chin. He starts swimming toward the opposite end of the pool.

The ants are at that end, too.

He swims right—

Ants.

He swims left—

They're coming from all sides now. Creeping in over the edge. Dropping into the water and using their drowning comrades as rafts.

Gabe does all he can do. He goes the one direction they cannot. He dives down into the dark water. The chlorine burns his eyes. Bubbles flutter up from his nostrils. *I can hold my breath a long time,* he thinks, or he used to be able to when he was a kid. But the more he thinks about it, the more his lungs feel like they're on fire, the more his ribs hurt, the more his mind feels the way his dog acts during a thunderstorm—scrabbling at the door, clawing at the counters, shaking like a leaf . . .

He can't hold it anymore.

Gabe thrusts up out of the water. At first he thinks he's fine, they've gone. But as he draws in a deep, gasping breath—something's in his mouth. A clot of crawling things, working their way down his throat. He begins to choke. And thrash. They're on his face. His ears.

He tries to vomit—

A pinch. A sting.

His body stiffens.

I love you, Sandy. I'm sorry I ran.

As Gabe's body begins to spasm and he takes water into his lungs with a sudden hitching gulp, one last thought swims up out of the dark to meet him on his way down:

Sandy, will you marry me?

1:30 A.M.

The CBRN suit is ill-fitting. Hollis feels like he's wrapped in butcher paper and bagged like meat. He steps out of the back of the Jeep, and the two sailors, Hurwitch and Hornshaw, get on either side of him.

It's quiet here. Ahead, the masts of boats stand like sentinels, lit by the watery glow of old streetlights. They walk down past the Waikaea Canal toward the docks and the little ramshackle hut. Hollis sees no ants, but that's because he doesn't see any *people.* The little monsters are as single-minded as they come. Ez told him they have antennae that can pick up human frequencies like a shark sniffing blood from a mile off. He hopes like hell he's not radiating the stink of sweat or cologne or bad breath just because the suit doesn't fit right.

"Agent," Hurwitch—or maybe it's Hornshaw—says. "This way."

Hollis nods (the suit squeaks and rasps), and they walk along past the fishing boats parked here. Ahead, the hut is old wood with a roof made to look like thatch, but underneath all the grassy bits are wood shingles. A customer service window has been cut out of the front. A body lies slumped there. Half across the counter. Arms dangling out over the edge. Glistening red in the moonlight.

Hollis steps over. Most of the hair is gone. White bone shines. Flies take flight as he gets closer, but they don't stay away for long; they will not be dissuaded from a perfectly good meal. *The age of the insect,* he thinks. *The meek truly shall inherit the earth.*

"Sir," Hornshaw—or is it Hurwitch?—says. "Here's the camera."

It's on a pole adjacent to the hut. All the docks have security cameras. Part of Homeland Security law. And this one, like all the others, is old, decrepit, an antique rimed with salt.

And with a bullet hole in the dead center of the glass. Just like at the last three fishing harbors.

"Someone took this one out, too," Hollis says.

"Sorry," Hurwitch says, and he knows it's Hurwitch because Hurwitch is the nicer of the two and apologizes for everything like it's his fault.

Hollis goes back to the hut and leans over the customer service window. Looks again at the body. The last three joints didn't have anybody there. They were closed for business. The dead they found were on boats moored to the dock, not behind the counter. Here a rust-pocked sign says they're open twenty-four hours. Makes sense. Fishing boats want to go out early.

Hollis reaches over, puts the flat of his fingers under the dead man's forehead, and lifts. The man's face pulls away from the counter with the sound of ripping wallpaper. Ants spill out of the man's mouth, nose—

And from a hole in the center of his forehead.

Hollis barks a wordless alarm and launches himself backward. The man's head thuds forward again, shaking more ants free. They patter against the ground. Some aren't black. They're white. *No,* Hollis thinks, the ants are carrying something white.

"Eggs," Hornshaw/Hurwitch says. "They're carrying little eggs."

"They were making a nest in the man's head?" Hollis asks.

"Looks like."

Hollis has to try very hard not to throw up in his suit. When he's composed himself, he again lifts the dead man's head. Sure enough, he saw what he thought he saw. A bullet hole right in the middle of the man's skull. Never came out the back of the head. Low-caliber pistol. Maybe a .22. Though he's seen times when a .25 or .32 didn't make an exit wound, either—smaller caliber means a softer punch.

And there, over the man's shoulder—in the shack behind—Hollis spies a winking green light. He heads around to the door next to the customer service window. Finding it locked, one of the two sailors pulls a pistol and—*bang, bang*—barks two shots against the knob. *That's one way to do it.* The door drifts open.

Hornshaw (Hollis is pretty sure) says to Hurwitch, "You didn't have to fire your damn gun. We could've kicked it down. Shoot. My ears are ringing."

"Whatever, man."

"Warn me next time."

"I said whatever."

Hollis steps inside, and there, on a bench full of fishing supplies, he finds a laptop computer. At the top of the screen is the winking green light. And it's right next to a camera.

Bingo.

* * *

Back at the Roc, they pull up the video archive. Looks like the camera is pretty much always on. Then the man who owned it, a man named Jed Freeman (also the name on the business lease), diced those videos up into their own feeds. Looks like he was capturing videos of pretty girls going out on booze cruises—girls in bikinis, thongs, and the like. All the videos are like that.

All the videos but the one from last night. That one plays thusly:

Just before sunrise. 6:15 A.M. time stamp. No sound.

Boat pulls up in the distance.

In view is, presumably, Jed Freeman. Just past him is another man, unidentified—tall, maybe Chinese. Wispy goatee. Trucker hat turned around.

Suddenly, the two of them startle. They look around. Not quite panicked, but definitely confused. The man in the trucker hat points up toward the camera on the pole next to the hut.

They look at each other, talking—but there's no sound, so no way to hear what they're saying. (Hollis wonders if it's worth getting a lip-reading expert. The video is grainy, though. Lots of visual artifacts.)

Jed and Trucker Hat are still talking to each other, looking up at the camera. They don't see, in the distance, the boat sidling up to the dock. There's the blur of a rope lashing around a post. Someone in all black steps off.

A gangplank down. The person goes back on the boat.

Then the person is back again. Walking backward and pulling a hand truck with a barrel resting against it.

Barrel down. The stranger begins to walk down the dock. Toward Jed and Trucker Hat.

The stranger is a woman. Long hair. White skin. Too grainy to make out much else yet. One arm looks funny, Hollis realizes—but wait, no, that's not her arm. It's something looped over her shoulder, next to her arm. A rifle.

She doesn't need it, though, because in her hand she's got a pistol.

Trucker Hat turns, sees what's coming. He pivots, tries to run—

A red puff near his head and he goes down.

Jed has his arms up, waving them like, *No, no, no*— The gun muzzle flashes again. His head shimmies left and right, the motion of the bullet entering the head and bopping around inside without coming out. Then his head drops forward.

The shooter brings the barrel forward, then cracks it open down the middle. And then she leaves.

For a while, nothing.

Hollis asks Yeoman Stroop to fast-forward. She does. "Stop," he says.

He sees something spilling out of the bottom. Like it's leaking oil or ink. But it's not liquid. It's the ants.

* * *

Hollis sleeps in tiny increments on a cot near the conference table. Fifteen minutes here. Another fifteen there. Punctuated by reports. And radio crackles. And police scanners. Sometimes, though, his sleep is bitten in half by his own nightmares rising up out of his resting mind.

MORNING BRIEFING

6:00 A.M.

Cole gives the rundown. All the emergency shelters are bursting at the seams. Here the shelters are used for hurricanes and tsunamis (and in rare instances, earthquakes). They're set up at schools, homeless shelters, humane society buildings, a few neighborhood centers. Hotels have some shelters, too, in their basements, and a lot of tourists have holed up there.

"How are they keeping the ants out?" Hollis asks.

Cole says, "Jeff there had the idea that ants won't cross certain materials. Cinnamon. Chalk. Vinegar. Dish soap. Problem is, we have reports of that failing. Either the ants find a new way in—even a crack in the wall is an opportunity for these little bastards—or they've been adapting. Building bridges with their own bodies over the obstacles. So I just told folks: cans of goddamn Raid will do the trick."

The associate entomologist gives a sheepish half smile. "That'll do."

Hollis thinks, *This dipshit doesn't know dip from shit.*

"But these monsters *are* learning to adapt," Cole says. "Figuring out how to get over bodies of water, for one. And they climb into trees and then let themselves free-fall onto people passing underneath." He sighs. "We're gonna have a hellacious time cleaning up these bodies when—if—we get this sorted. There are already reports of some shelters that failed entirely—swarmed by these damn things. Rooms full of bodies."

They're flying in medical supplies and they're sending out rescue teams of sailors in CBRN suits, carrying either tanks full of pyrethroids or plain old Raid bug spray. Some, Cole says, are carrying flamethrowers—a joke suggestion at first, but sure enough, it "flames 'em up real good." Cole notes that in the north end of the island, where it's pretty wet, there's little danger of setting anything on fire.

"What's next?" Hollis asks.

Roston, the woman from EmpAg, says, "We spray."

Hollis gives a look to Cole. Cole says, "What do you want, Agent Copper? You want these things dead or alive? Hell, man, this spray is the same thing pest control guys use. Same thing for home use."

Copper nods. "Just let me talk to Dr. Choi first. Okay?"

"You go ahead. But they're loading up the sprayers now. Our boys fly in thirty. You better bring me something big if you figure on stopping 'em."

* * *

"I got nothing," Ez says. She sounds on the verge of tears. "Do you know how hard it is to kill ants? Fuck, man, Argentine ants have formed a supercolony that spans three continents and has more than half a billion members. Even the smallest colony has to be wiped out down to the queen or you just don't know. I mean, these colonies aren't established yet, so if you could find *each* colony and target them individually—"

"We don't have that kind of time."

For a little while, she says nothing. At last she says, "Okay. *Okay.* You do what you gotta do. But, hey. Before you go, they got a lead on the guy who attacked me. I guess he checked into a hospital because he thought he was dying. Cops came for him and he busted his way back out of the hospital—went out a window, landed on an HVAC unit, and then hobbled off. But they got him on video."

"I'll talk to the police. See if we can't get an image of his face. I have some friends who can maybe do something with that." *Some friends who are not necessarily in the Bureau.*

"Thanks, Copper."

"Get some sleep, Dr. Choi. And a meal. And a week's vacation."

* * *

The C-130H flew in from Hickam on Oahu. It is fitted with a MASS—Modular Aerial Spray System. The sprayer can dispense chemicals over a wide area. They use it to disperse oil spills. And to eradicate invasive plants.

And to spray pesticides meant to kill an insect population.

The two pilots, Pam Jaffe and Llewellyn McCoy, joke sometimes—as they do right now during precheck—that they're the ones spraying chemtrails. Mind-controlling the masses. Turning them all gay with their gay spray. Or whatever something-something global-warming anti-Christian CIA NSA conspiracy wank you feel like going on about, because all those New World Order junkies think that the chemtrails in the sky are something sinister, and they froth about it on the same Internet forums that play home to the nutballs who think the moon landing was faked and that 9/11 was an inside job.

Pam and Llewellyn like to joke a lot. They also like to fuck each other. They're planning on getting married in the fall, but nobody knows that yet—they're not going to make a big thing of it. A beachside ceremony. Not much family. A local hippie minister. It'll be cool. Except for the part where they probably won't be allowed to fly together anymore. And if she gets pregnant—"I want six kids," she told him, "because I had five brothers and I think it's good to have a big family"—then everything will change anyway.

For now, everything's going as planned. At least, as much as it can be, given that they're having to spray an island to kill off some weird-ass invasion of legit killer ants. "Sounds like a B-movie," Llewellyn remarked.

But the two of them have seen their share of the apocalypse in the last few years. And not just the two of them. The C-130H has a respected crew comprising a pilot, a copilot, a navigator, a flight engineer, and two load masters (though today, only one load master is present because of short notice, and no flight engineer). Llewellyn and Pam have another joke about who is the pilot and who is the copilot, and then they also like to say it really doesn't matter (but Pam is the pilot). Today the crew is Pam, Llewellyn, Deshaun Michaels (the navigator), and "Red" Robins (the load master). They were together when the shit hit the fan at the *Deepwater Horizon* spill. Goddamn BP. And they flew over New Orleans after Katrina, spraying for mosquitoes. That was its own special brand of scary: rivers where roads should have been, boats broken against one another, pleas for help scrawled across bedsheets on rooftops by people who knew they had been forgotten.

They do their prechecks. Everything looks good. The truck out there is filling up the sprayer with the help of Red. Deshaun's got their course plotted out for most efficient coverage of the island and so he's taking a quick snooze.

Pam and Llewellyn give each other's hands a little squeeze.

* * *

Hollis rushes to the radio. They've found Hannah.

Cole's been talking to a pilot, apparently. Maybe Einar's own pilot, he's not sure. Someone named Sullivan. Hollis gets on the mic, asks to talk to Hannah. Cole says he gave the pilot the scoop.

And then Hannah gets on the line. "I've never been so glad to hear from you," she tells him.

"I'm glad to hear from you, too, Stander. Where the hell are you?"

Hannah gives him a quick rundown: they left Kolohe about a half hour ago. Island overrun by the Myrmidons—the ants. Most of the people at the lab are gone. The colonies have been stolen.

That's where it started, he thinks. Arca Labs. And yet he still feels like he doesn't have a clear picture of what's going on. Who did this? Einar? A competitor? Someone inside the company or outside it? Everything feels slippery.

Hollis tells Hannah the ants are here on the island and that he's here, that people are dying—

The radio crackles. Her voice starts to break up.

"Hannah? Hannah?"

"—opper—there?"

"Hannah, stay with me. Ez was attacked. The island here is overrun. People are sheltering in place and there's an island-wide quarantine. Don't land here. Land somewhere else, *anywhere* else. I can get you clearance at Oahu, I can—"

But she's gone. All that's left is the whisper-hiss of low static.

Cole says, "Could be the storm. Interference. Wouldn't think too much about it. If they're about two hundred miles out, won't be long before they set down on one of the other islands."

"Yeah. You're right." Hollis nods like he believes that. His gut, though, has gone sour. *Something's off. Something ain't right.*

That's when he hears the explosion.

* * *

All clear. Llewellyn goes to wake up Deshaun. He tries to shake his crewmate awake—

And Deshaun falls to the side. Blood pools around him from a bullet wound in his chest.

Llew is about to open his mouth and yell for Pam, but a man in a black mask and fatigues appears from behind the corner and fires two silenced rounds into his chest and one into his head.

The man is joined by a second, also in all black. They shoot Pam in the back of the head before she can even stand up. Her blood and brains spatter the console.

The two men then leave, but not before lifting Pam's head and placing a small brick of Semtex underneath it. It is not the only present they leave behind: they have already planted three other similar devices.

As they head toward their boat on the Barking Sands beach, the man on the right holsters his pistol and removes the detonator.

His thumb hooks around the trigger and—

8:30 A.M.

The toxic cloud has yet to disperse, though it has lessened. The black plumes rising from the ruins of the C-130H have dissipated to a gray, eye-burning haze. The fires have at least gone out.

At the Roc, two rooms down, they've got two bodies laid out on tables. Two dead men in black fatigues. They were caught moving toward a boat that, in the chaos of an island under siege and in the fawn light of the morning, everyone had missed. Their egress was denied. A firefight ensued. The men were shot, killed.

Hollis sits forward, his hands planted on his knees, pressing down so hard he half expects the kneecaps to grind to dust. Their chance to spray is gone for at least twelve hours, until another MASS-equipped plane shows up and the pyrethroid can be mixed and loaded onto it. All the while, more death, more ants, more nests, more panic and madness and uncertainty.

It's almost no surprise when Cole shows up with bad news. His eyes are wide as moons and his voice has gone hoarse—in part from yelling at men to do their jobs and in part from breathing in that stuff outside. He says, "You gotta see this."

Hollis stands up. He moves in a way that feels disconnected from himself, like he's a passenger inside his own body.

Outside, at first he doesn't see it. The haze of burning pesticide has made everything gauzy, and it hurts his eyes and his throat, but it's fading with the wind coming in off the sea. Soon, though, something flits by him. Something small.

Then another. And another.

Dozens. Hundreds. Hollis watches the little flying things flit past. Some of them are flying through the haze just fine. Others are dropping to the ground onto their backs, tiny legs kicking the air as the pyrethroid fog kills them.

"The hell are these things?" Cole asks. He holds up his hand, and one lands on the back of it before flying away.

"Wasps, maybe," Hollis says. *Shit, now we got a wasp problem, too?*

But then a new voice behind them says, with no small amount of wonder, "It's a nuptial flight." It's Jeff, the entomologist. He coughs into his fist.

"What?" Cole asks him. "Speak English."

"They're ants. This is their nuptial flight. Queens looking to mate and settle down to make new colonies."

Horror strikes at Hollis's heart. He starts swatting at the air, but the entomologist catches his arm. "No. Don't attack. They won't bite if they don't feel threatened. Ants on a nuptial flight are only interested in mating. They're not aggressive, only defensive."

Keep it together, Hollis thinks, even as the air around him is suffused with flying things. He moves slowly toward Cole, who looks panic-stricken, then says: "We get inside, then order an evacuation. *Now.*"

35

The sound of the ocean is the sound of breathing. The rise and fall of waves, the inhale-exhale of oxygen. The lift of the sea mirroring the swell of one's chest.

The raft bobs and dips. Kit pukes over the side again.

Hannah pulls back from the edge of the craft—an eight-person emergency life raft, yellow as a goldfinch—and goes to Kit's side. She pats the woman's back as she dry heaves into the waves.

Behind them, the storm is a wretched, dark thing. But ahead: blue skies and feathery clouds. "The storm is turning north," Einar says.

"Good" is the only response Hannah can muster.

"I saw you watching it. I saw the fear in your eyes. I seek to reassure you."

The fear isn't just in my eyes, she thinks. It's everywhere. All parts of her, every cell, sings a song of dread.

Ray says, "I don't think now's the time for reassurance. We're floating in the middle of the fucking ocean. We don't know where we are."

"We know exactly where we are," Hannah says. She holds up the GPS—it came with the survival kit moored to the underside of the raft. It is both a beacon locator and an admittedly primitive GPS system. But it's enough.

They're about fifty miles off Kauai. The gear will come in helpful: fishing kit, medical kit, sunscreen, flares, flashlights, hand-crank radio, strobe light, signal mirror, and so on. Some of this would have come in handy on Kolohe—the radio especially, even though

it's one-way. Hannah knows her way around survival gear, and the raft is a high-end one. It's built for long hauls at sea. It covers over in storms. It's built so it won't overturn even in the most violent churn. It came with a pair of oars, too. Not that anybody's rowing yet.

For now, they sit. And float. Every time Hannah closes her eyes, she flashes back—

Rotor cutting the sea—

Water rushing up and rushing in—

Her head, bleeding plumes of red—

She swims, reaching for someone's hand—

They sink—

A flurry of bubbles—

Caught in the downward drag of the helicopter, and Hannah struggles against it—

Someone nearby, struggling with something yellow and bright—

She swims over, dizzy, sick, screaming inside—

Together she and Ray get it inflated—

Einar says, "We should all be happy that we are alive. Life is a gift."

"Tell that to the dead," Barry says. His face is gray with something worse than seasickness: it's gone pale with despair. "Nancy. Captain Dan. *Buffy.*"

"We need to get to Kauai," Hannah says. The time to mourn will come, but it isn't now. "We need to move, so that means we need to row."

"Kauai?" Kit says, peeling herself away from the edge of the raft. She wipes spit bubbles from her saggy lower lip. "We can't go there. You said—"

"I know. Hollis said the island might be compromised."

"Those ants . . ." Kit's eyes pinch shut, hard. "We can't go there if the ants are there. We have to go somewhere safe. One of the other islands."

"The other islands are too far," Hannah snaps. She hears it in her own voice: the anxiety, the fear, the uncertainty. She takes a deep breath and tries again. "Oahu is another eighty miles easy from the eastern side of Kauai, and we'll be coming up on the west."

"We could go to Niihau—"

"It's too close to Kauai. It could be compromised. Besides, we need to handle this. We have information. Nobody there knows what we know. It's up to us to help. We have a responsibility."

Kit is about to say something, but Einar interjects: "Hannah is right. We are obligated. And I believe in the team here. I believe we can make a difference. If these creatures make it to the other islands, it is likely they will make it to the mainland. And if they make it to the mainland—imagine that."

Silence all around. Grim faces stare.

Eventually Ray sniffs loudly and says, "Then we better get rowing."

* * *

Hannah does the calculations as best as she can in her head: a rowboat at a good clip will travel eight to ten miles an hour. This isn't that. They're a big, clumsy life raft in the ocean, where the current does not favor them. And they're using manpower that is pushed to its limit and near exhausted. They're traveling three miles an hour, tops.

Fifty miles out: given no other hiccups, and given their maintaining that speed (which is unlikely), they'll get to Kauai in seventeen hours. Impatience threatens to choke her. The longer they're away, the more the island will fall to disaster. The more people will die. And the chance that the ants will find their way off that island only increases.

Barry says, "Maybe they'll send someone. We have the GPS locator."

"We can't count on that," Hannah says. "Even if they send anyone, who's to say they'll find us? The GPS locator assumes someone is looking for this particular device." She looks to Einar. "Should we assume that?"

"I confess," he says, "I never established much of a protocol in that way, no. I was not even aware that the locator was part of this raft. If anyone knows to be looking for it, I don't know who they are."

"So," she says, putting her back into rowing. "We keep on."

Einar is next to her, also rowing. He leans toward her. "I've been thinking. We lost Ajay's notes in the crash. But we are not without recourse. Will is still out there."

"He is. And I aim to find him."

"As do I. Once we have his notes, I can counter this plague of ants. We can work to undo the damage he has done. Much as we did with the *Aedes aegypti* mosquito, we will breed a second Myrmidon ant—this one a terminator species. We can wipe them out in a generation."

"It won't be that easy," Barry protests. "Ants are eusocial. Their life cycle is complicated."

"Mosquitoes are one-and-done," Kit adds. She and Barry are huddled together. "Male and female mate, female lays eggs, the genes are carried on. Ants are different. Every *species* of ant is a little different. Usually, mating flights establish new colonies with virginal queens. One of those queens mates with ants of other nests and goes off to lay the first eggs of her new colony. Problem is, queens don't mate constantly. They store the sperm and can produce a thousand eggs a day until they die—and many queens can live five, even ten years. That's why ants suck to get rid of. You can wipe out the colony, but as long as the queen survives she just keeps pumping out eggs, boom, boom, boom."

Einar thinks. "We breed a mating flight, then. New queens. Winged virgins. They contain the terminator gene. They fly, they mate, and the new colony that results becomes a dead one."

"That'll limit the growth of new colonies," Barry says. "It stops the spread of the Myrmidons. But it won't do anything for the ones that exist."

"So, think," Einar says. "Get your teeth around it. Use your brains. How could we counter the existing colonies? What is our solution?"

"Poison," Barry says.

"*No,*" Einar snaps. "That is not an acceptable answer. That's the answer we already have. Poison is the brute's choice. It works if you're some local *pest control technician.* You want to kill a single colony, maybe poison. We need bigger. We need innovation. You are geniuses. Act like it."

"The yeast," Kit says. "We engineer a new yeast. Yeasts are simple enough eukaryotes. It can be pathogenic for humans—especially immunocompromised people. But if we can feed the colonies a yeast that is pathogenic for *ants* . . ."

Barry sits forward. "That's it! Ants are fundamentally predictable little jerks, right? You drop food at a picnic and they swarm it—but they're not eating it. Not really. They're ingesting it, taking it into their stomach to carry it back to the colony, where they actually spit it back up out of their mouths or something through their, ahem, *back doors,* and they use it to feed the larvae, the males, or—" He points to Hannah expectantly.

"The . . . queen?" she tries.

"Bingo! Give the lady a stuffed panda. They feed *the queen.* First and foremost, the queen must get fed. So we take this new yeast, this pathogenic yeast, and we just spray that stuff everywhere. Long as it's harmless to people and the environment. The ants start nibbling on it, picking it up, taking it to her, and it kills her. And them. Slowly but surely. God, if you really want to go gonzo with it, you do a *Cordyceps* thing with it—turn it into a zombie maker. But I don't think we have that kind of time . . ."

Hannah says, "That means you wouldn't even need to produce new ants. No need to create a terminator version."

"I disagree," Einar says. "The terminator will be our first offensive. We cannot guarantee, given the sheer numbers of Myrmidons created by Will, that they will not have some way to adapt to the yeast—a yeast we have not even created yet. The ants will be easier to replicate immediately *provided* we find Will—or, at least, take hold of his research."

Kit nods. "It'll take a while to cook up the yeast. Simple is simple, but it's still something entirely new."

Hannah notes that Kit looks much improved. The scientists are excited to have a solution. It's the perfect distraction. And Hannah notes how Einar engineered this moment—not as some crass team-building exercise, but shepherding his people to do something greater. It's clear to see why he's a leader. Not just a leader—a visionary.

The visionary speaks: "That is the plan, then. We reach Kauai. We seek Will swiftly. I know where he lives, so Hannah and I will go to find him—"

Hannah interrupts. "I don't think we should strike out on our own. We should find Hollis. We head to Barking Sands, to the base."

"Once there, what?" Einar asks. "We wait for the ants to come? We wait for the dead to be counted? That base is overrun by not just the military—an organization driven into the ground by its bureaucracy—but dozens of competing companies who surely each have their own solution to this crisis and will be squabbling to decide who can be the hero. Meanwhile, our hands will be bound with all that red tape. We must seize actionable evidence while we can."

"Let's not forget," Ray says, "that if you show your face, they'll want to put you in a room for questioning."

Hannah knows that Ray is right. And she agrees with him. She doesn't say it aloud, but she'll do anything to get Einar in that room.

"They will," says Einar. "They will seek the source of this thing and will hold me responsible." He hesitates. A small bit of emotion enters his voice, surprising Hannah. Is it real? Or just artifice? "And they should. I am responsible. This was my company. Will and Ajay were my hires. So, yes. I admit it. I want to be the one to solve this problem because that is how I pay this debt. Not by sitting in some room, questioned by an imbecile too dumb for university but just smart enough for military service."

Behind them, thunder rolls across the open sea. And ahead, the distant sliver of an island—their destination, it seems. Dread crawls across her skin on delicate legs as Hannah fears what they'll find when they arrive.

36

Night. The moon caught in the waves receding back to the Pacific.

The raft rolls atop the waves toward the beach, and the five of them piston their legs in the water, dragging it up the sand to where the sea cannot reach it.

Hannah is glad to not be sitting anymore. Even though her arms and shoulders ache and tremble, she feels suddenly, inexplicably alive.

"Where the fuck are we?" Ray asks.

Einar has the GPS. He taps the screen. "Pakala. Just southeast of Waimea." In the glow from the GPS, his face brightens with that trademark smile. "And good news: we have a phone signal. Cell towers remain intact."

Einar walks off, dialing a number.

Ray says, "Island's awful dark. No power."

"The ants don't have the ability to take down a power grid, do they?" Hannah asks.

Kit's words are sleepy as she reminds her, "Well, crazy ants do it at the localized level. But this is a lot bigger than that."

"Maybe the island is dark because it's night," Ray says.

"Or maybe," Hannah says, "it's because these Myrmidons are smarter than the average ant."

"No one ant is smart," Barry says. "Their intelligence is in the colony. A superintelligence."

Kit shrugs. "Still, Will and Ajay made a real Frankenstein's monster. Who knows what these ants can do? They sure killed our ride," she says, referring to the helicopter.

It's then that Hannah decides: Kit and Barry had nothing to do with the Myrmidons. It's a hasty call. She knows that. But she has to pick someone here to trust, and these two—they just aren't the type. She can't see either of them having a hand in the creation of the Myrmidon ants.

Now, though, a larger question: Do the two of them stay or do they go? If they stay, they can be an on-site resource, helping her or Hollis. They know a lot. They would be valuable. But then the longer game presents itself. If this thing ever goes to a trial, she needs them on the stand. Expert witnesses providing meaningful testimony as to what happened here. She can't have them dead on this island because she thrust them into the thick of it.

It's a hard call, but she makes it:

"You two," Hannah says to Kit and Barry. "You need to get to safety somewhere off this island."

Barry laughs. "And where is safe? Here? Another island?" He sits up with a groan. Sand sprinkles from the back of his head. "I'm not getting on another boat."

"You get back in the raft. Take it parallel to the coast. At least down to one of the docks. You can probably find a snack bar or something for food."

"We are not survival gurus like you," Kit says. "We go out there, we die."

Hannah winces. They're probably right.

Einar walks back toward them, talking into the phone: "Hello, hello? Yes." His smile returns. "Yes, that's right. We are near Pakala. I can't say where, precisely. Near the point. Yes. Yes. We can do that. Thank you, Pono." He puts the phone into his back pocket; then to the others he says: "We have a ride."

"May I have the phone?" Hannah asks, putting out her hand. Einar hesitates for just a moment, then gives it to her. She files that little moment away: Why did he hesitate? What is he afraid of? No time to worry about that now. Hannah takes the phone, tries to remember Hollis's number. She dials it.

It rings and rings, goes right to his voice mail.

Damn it. Maybe the base, then?

She calls information. They would have a number for Barking Sands.

A tone plays and a voice recording follows: *Your call could not be completed, please check the number.*

A deep, anxious breath in. Hannah feels besieged by uncertainty. Einar says, "We should walk to meet our ride."

To Barry and Kit, Hannah says: "You're going to walk, too. Just in the other direction."

"Wait, what?" Kit asks.

"Barking Sands is on the southwest side of the island. We're not far. If this is near Waimea, then it's a . . ." To Einar she says, "How far is it?"

Einar shrugs. "Ten miles. Fifteen at most."

"You're going to walk there. It'll be safer if you stay in the water. Even if you just keep your feet covered, the ants . . . they shouldn't be able to reach you."

"And if we get there and the whole place has gone tits up?" Barry asks.

Hannah's honest answer would be: *Then I don't know.* Instead she says: "Then find a boat. Stay in the water. Wait for help."

They nod. Their faces make it clear: Kit and Barry are not sure about this. They're tired. Beaten down. And most of all, they're afraid. But acquiescence sweeps over them, as it must, because no other choice exists.

So they say their good-byes. And all the while, Hannah prays she's not condemning them to death. It's one prayer to a God she doesn't believe in, one prayer in a line of many: she prays Hollis is still alive, that they can find Will, that the ants don't kill them, that all this is just a dream and soon she'll awake.

Hannah, Einar, and Ray head north.

* * *

They creep through the dark under the cover of tall tulip trees and scraggly ohi'a lehua trees—the branches black against the blue-dark sky, against the spray of stars and moon-painted clouds. Hard earth and twigs crunch under their feet, mosquitoes take their blood, and once Ray steps face-first into a spider's web, freaking out as he pinwheels his arms against the invisible silk.

All the way, though, Hannah isn't worried about the mosquitoes or the spiders. All she can think about is *them.* Creeping, crawling underneath. Have they gone underground? Are they hiding in the dirt now? The darkness of the island—gone deeper here under the trees—is like the darkness of her knowledge. Everything is an unknown quantity. Have they killed everyone? Have they gone on to other islands? Her short conversation with Hollis was almost twenty hours ago, and what little she heard strikes terror in her heart even now. *They're everywhere. People have died. Shelter in place. Quarantine.*

She shivers. She's wet. She's cold. She's terrified.

"Look," Einar says.

Lights. Bleeding through the trees. It takes a moment for Hannah's eyes to adjust, but there it is—a house. No, an *estate.* Houses don't have wings, don't have pool houses and in-law suites and multiple decks and massive garages, but this one does. Hannah's first thought is to march over, throw a rock through the window, and find food.

That inclination gives her pause. *How quickly we descend,* she thinks. She's a law-abiding person. She works for the Federal Bureau of Investigation. And her response during the start of a crisis is to break into a rich person's house with nary a thought? Steal? Pillage? Kill?

Maybe her parents were right. If society collapses, even the most law-abiding will find their eyes and hands wandering. Morality and civilization are facades that crumble quickly, exposing the raw rock and jagged stone of mankind's true nature underneath.

Ray says, "We could go inside, get food—"

"No," Hannah interrupts. *Hold the line. Maintain civilization. Do not become your mother.* "We keep moving. We have a car to catch."

* * *

Highway 50 is a dead line carved through quiet black space. Guardrails stand rimed with the red dust that Hannah remembers from what seems like a lifetime ago but was only a handful of days before. Grasses sway in a gentle breeze.

Everything is quiet. It is the quiet of corpses. The quiet of graveyards. Power lines above hum and buzz, but otherwise there is no sound of traffic, no planes or helicopters. Though they cannot see them from here, she knows that the sea is home to boats—coming in on the raft, they saw twinkling lights out there on the water. A smart refuge, she thinks, from the scourge of the Myrmidon colonies.

For now, they stand and they wait.

It's Ray who breaks the silence. "Whoever your driver is, he's not coming."

"He'll be here."

"We should think of an alternate plan."

"We don't need one."

"That house back there. We'll go, break in, get some food—maybe we can find the keys to one of the cars. Maybe—"

Hannah interrupts, her tone sharp. "The driver will be here. If Einar says he's coming, then he's coming."

"So, now we all just trust Einar."

Einar pivots. Smirking. Amused by the outburst.

"You don't?" Einar asks. "Even still?"

Ray looks cornered. Like he's not sure he should keep going down this rabbit hole. Hannah's not sure he should, either. Now's not the time. She's not sure she trusts Einar, but this is a battle best fought later. They're tired and hungry and their nerves are frayed like old carpet. With that, Ray says: "I'm just saying, the oversight here hasn't exactly been top-notch. This all happened because he didn't keep control over his own people. He let psychopaths play in his big money playground and, surprise, surprise, they went psycho. Besides, how do we know he's not trying to play us? Maximize his profits? He said he didn't want other companies involved because this is his responsibility. But maybe it's also his payday he cares about."

"My payday?" Einar asks, then laughs. He extends both arms out like he's beseeching the heavens. "You above others know how my companies work, Ramon. I lose money on nearly every transaction. The batteries? The wind farms? I'm trying to change the world, not get rich." He says that last sentence like the very idea tastes like bile. "The world is *run* by the rich. *Over*run by them. My home country was almost ruined by the wealthy. The disparity between those with all the money and those with none is a widening chasm and we're all *tumbling* into it. I'm trying to save the world and you're here doubting my intentions? *Farðu í rassgat!* Fuck. You."

"Fuck you," Ray mutters.

"Guys," Hannah says. "Our ride."

Down the highway: headlights.

* * *

The Lincoln Town Car is prepped for the end times. Pono went buck wild with duct tape, covering dashboard cracks and vents, plus all along the exterior of the vehicle (covering up the gaps caused by trunk and hood). And the whole thing stinks of bug spray.

In the backseat sit Hannah and Einar, with Ray crammed between them.

Moana, Pono's sister, stares balefully at them from the front seat. Her jowls are tight, and her scowl hangs between them. "You da richie-rich one," she says to Einar. He smiles politely and nods. "You pay big for this ride."

"I will, yes."

"Moana. Shush," Pono hisses. He laughs pleadingly. He's nervous.

Like he doesn't want to upset anybody, even though for all intents and purposes it's the apocalypse out there. "Don't you worry, Mr. Einar, we got you covered. Where we headed today?"

"North Shore," Einar says. "Wainiha."

"Ha, okay, sure. You know," Pono says, licking his lips, "*wainiha* in our language means 'unfriendly waters.'"

"That's pretty fuckin' appropriate," Ray grouses, then shifts uncomfortably between the other two in the back.

"Shush," Hannah says to him. Now isn't the time. She can't have anything derail their current mission: Get to the north end of the island and find Will. And, hopefully, find the rest of the ant colonies, too.

Moana, still staring at them from the front, narrows her eyes. "You three better fix dis. People are dead. Ants took over island like on that zombie show on the TV, except these aren't zombies, they're ants. They bite you and you go down, boom. Then they eat your face, your hands, your balls. Some people go to shelters, but some of the shelters, they get overrun. The hotels got the rich people protecting them. The shelters got closed off by the *pakalolo* dealers. Out here it's fend for yourself. For a while we had helicopters coming in and bringing us medical supplies and food, but now they stopped, too. People startin' to whisper. Saying they gonna drop a bomb on us. Big boom." She sniffs. "First I thought, maybe these ants, they give us back our island from the *haoles*. But they come at us, too. We just *ono grinds* for the little anties. We too tasty to resist." Then, with a smile, "They still bettah than you tourists."

Her laugh is a mad bellow.

* * *

They drive through a dead island. Past houses sealed up with plastic and boards in such a way that Hannah can't tell if they're serving as shelters or as tombs. Cars sit on the side of the road. Some crashed into trees, guardrails, poles. Others abandoned. Others still occupied, their owners dead at the wheel, red faces glistening. Pono eases the car past and rattles the can of Raid as a demonstration. “Don’t worry, they won’t get in here.”

Pono rambles as they drive. Hannah lies back and closes her eyes for a little while, not to sleep, but just to try to find her center. Some calm in the fury of the storm raging inside her. Pono goes on, mostly just telling stories about when he was a kid, like that time he got bit by a little fish but told everyone it was a shark, or the time he lost his hat down in some ocean geyser called Spouting Horn. But as she listens to him talk, she hears the fear in his voice. He’s worried for his family. He says they’re safe somewhere—on a boat—but she can tell he doesn’t believe it. Nor should he. Because none of them are safe. But a boat is better than on land, and she tells him so.

Eventually she asks for the GPS tracker again to see if she can try another call to Hollis, but the battery is dead.

The road turns north through Koloa. She sees a lone building under a cone of light and says, “Is that a general store up ahead?”

“Koloa Town Store,” Pono says. “Yeah, sure. We shouldn’t stop.”

“Would they have pharmacy items? Or grocery?” She thinks, it’d be great to have some kind of defense against the ants. Coconut oil would provide the oleic acid. And if she could find antifungal spray . . .

Something would be better than nothing.

“Sure. Maybe. Some over-the-counter stuff. Definitely some food stuff.”

“I’d like to stop.”

“Bad idea,” Ray says. “We keep going.”

“We need some kind of defensc,” she says. She tells them about the oleic acid and fungal spray combo. Ajay thought that’s what Will was using to hold off the ants. “And they might have food. I know I’m hungry.”

Einar says, “I’ll agree. We can all go.”

"I'll do it alone," she says. "I don't want to put anyone at risk."

"I'll stop just outside," Pono says. "Then I drive the loop a couple times. We'll catch you on one of the go-arounds, okay?"

She nods. He eases the car up outside.

Hannah pops the door and exits.

* * *

The store is humid and dimly lit. The front half is full of kitschy Hawaii tourist stuff: grass skirts and coconut shell bras, tiki mugs and shot glasses.

She takes her first step toward the back of the store, then listens. A faint sound rises. Like Rice Krispies crackling in fresh milk.

Hannah peers around the one shelf toward the counter. A corpse is slumped backward in a chair. The face is a dark, clotted mask—flies twitch, flitting from cheek to cheek, from nose hole to forehead. The eyes are a bulging, bold white. Teeth, too. The head shifts slightly back and forth.

The smell hits her nose: the pungent, all-too-familiar whiff. This is a nest. She has to move quickly. What takes priority? Food or defense? Her stomach has its answer as it growls, and on the list of survival priorities, eating is definitely top of the list. But if there are ants in here . . .

On the floor sit a few small plastic shopping baskets. Hannah scoops up one and bolts toward the back of the store. There's only one pharmacy aisle, and for a moment she fears she won't be able to find what she's looking for. But her bet pays off. This is a hot, wet island. If ever there's a place you're going to get athlete's foot, it's here. Which means there are two cans of Tinactin antifungal spray for sale. She grabs them both. Then she hurries around to the two grocery aisles and starts using her forearm to swipe food into the basket. Granola bars, bags of chips, chocolate. It's just junk calories, but it'll do the trick, and her stomach tightens like a coiling snake to remind her how hungry she is. Then she spies a jar of coconut oil, and she tosses that in, too. Now if she can just find an empty spray bottle, she can make her own mix of the stuff.

She turns to head back to the front—

A black line of ants half a foot wide has crossed in front of the door. Their little antennae have caught her scent. They know she's here. They just don't know where yet.

The moment they detect her is as clear as a tolling bell. The river suddenly breaks in the middle—and both halves begin streaming toward her.

There has to be a back door. *Has to be.* Hannah curses herself for not looking when she was there, but now she has no choice. She turns tail, bolts toward the back of the store. There's a small hallway. An office, a restroom and—

EXIT.

She slams up against it, twists the knob. It won't open. She checks the knob, looks for a dead bolt . . . but nothing. The door opens a little when she pushes on it, though. Something's blocking it from the other side.

She looks for a window. Another door. Any way out.

But this is the only one.

The river of ants has broken apart. They're streaming up the walls, across the ceiling, and over the floor. The larger ants shepherding the smaller ones, or maybe protecting them. Their jaws lift in the air, tilting toward her like some kind of mad, insectile salute—like a promise, like a *threat.*

They're ten feet away now.

Nine.

Eight.

With her shoulder, Hannah rams the door again and again. It budges a little more—she can now see a dark line through the lower half of the door crack: the shape of whatever is blocking her egress.

Seven feet, six feet . . .

Hannah quickly reaches into the basket, digging through

the food until she finds one of the cans of Tinactin. It's not mixed with the oil, but it's not like she has the time for that. She wrenches the cap off, then begins to spray herself down. A cloud of acrid chemical stink fills the air in front of her. She suppresses her urge to cough even as her eyes water. Up and down her body she sprays—

Five feet. Four. *Three.*

She winces her eyes shut and blasts herself in the face and all over her hair. All the muscles in her body tense up. She knows what's coming. The tickle of their little feet. The clamping pinch of their jaws. The needle-stick of their stingers.

But that never comes. The ants gather only inches away from her feet. They have stopped in their tracks. Jaws in the air. Antennae twitching and turning like satellite dishes that have lost their signal.

It worked. The spray *worked.* She's not sure if it's because the chemical scent is too overpowering or if it has already begun to undercut whatever *Candida* she has growing on her body. Either way, the mob of ants begins to break up. They recede like a tide, going back into the store.

When the ants are truly gone, she stabs out at the door with a hard kick, targeting the area around the hinges. The door won't bust outward, so that means the whole damn thing has to come off.

The wood is weak. The hinges are old. It takes only a few kicks before the lower hinge squeaks and hangs loose, and Hannah can get her hands in the gap and wrench it off. She leans it up against the wall.

There, behind the store, is a car. An old Ford Escort. Its hood is pressed right up against the door—but it didn't break the wall, so whoever hit it wasn't going fast. She sees the shape of a body slumped over the steering wheel. Skull hairless, stripped down to meat and bone.

Hannah grabs her bounty from the store and climbs up over the hood and drops down the other side of it. As she does, she sees a few ants wandering on the inside of the windshield glass. They don't see her; she pretends not to see them.

She heads back to the road to wait for the Lincoln. The can of antifungal meds did the trick, so she needs to get that information to Hollis. (*If he's still alive,* she thinks.) But first, they will go to Will's house on the North Shore. That is priority one. He designed these ants. He knows how to stop them. He *must.*

Moments pass. She thinks she hears an engine, but then—nothing. Impatience gnaws at her like a rat chewing bone. A few flies swarm dead birds nearby—chickens with neither flesh nor feather.

Across the road, she spies something. A dark heap. Another body, she realizes. Human. All black clothing. She thinks, *Are those fatigues?* A military man, maybe. Navy or Army. But wouldn't they be wearing hazmat suits? Or at least be in the traditional camo?

Another ten seconds, twenty, thirty, and she thinks, *Hell with it,* then crosses the road.

Sure enough, it's a dead body in head-to-toe fatigues. A black balaclava sits pulled down over his face, too—though what little of his face she can see is skinless, glistening red like raw beef. At his hip hangs a holster. Hannah reaches down, frees the pistol that nests there. Looks like a black HK45 Tactical.

The holster has a smaller side sleeve, likely for a suppressor. It's empty.

The guy's not military. He's PMC: a private military contractor.

And just who sits on the board of a PMC corporation? Archer Stevens. Was this dead man one of the Blackhearts? That could mean Archer is involved.

Which would mean . . . Einar isn't.

Hannah takes the pistol and tucks it in the back of her pants, then pulls her shirt down over it just as a pair of headlights shortens the dark. *Better safe than sorry,* she thinks. Mom always said that when the shit hits the fan, your biggest enemy won't be the thing that caused the cataclysm—it'll be all the people around you. *People are what will really end this world,* she used to say. Cynical, but there it is.

She waves her hands, and as she jogs over, the Lincoln slows for her.

When she gets in, she doesn't tell them about the gun. An echo from her mother, herself something of a gun collector:

Never tell them you're packing heat, Hannah.

37

Hannah may not tell them about the gun, but she certainly tells them about the body. If only to see what their reaction is. Does it mean anything to them? When she describes it, Einar and Ray share a look.

"What is it?" she asks.

"Sounds like a PMC," Ray says.

"I believe that's accurate," she says.

"A mercenary?" Einar asks. "Why would a mercenary have any interest in an island overtaken by a plague of ants?"

"I don't know," she says. And she means it. She neglects to mention, however, that it may very well connect to Archer Stevens.

"It certainly complicates the puzzle." Einar leans forward. "Now is perhaps the time to mention that my competitor Archer Stevens sat on the board for a private military group. The Blackhearts."

Sat on the board.

Past tense. A slipup? Accidental? Intentional? Simple language-barrier issue? She bites her tongue. But suspicion creeps in at the margins. Hannah wants to believe that Einar is telling them this because it's relevant. But she also knows that interrogators use techniques to elicit confessions—sometimes false admissions of guilt—from criminals by leading them into information, stringing them along, and pushing them into conclusions.

"Stevens is a very rich man," Ray says. He shifts uncomfortably in his seat. "The fuck's that mean for Will, though? You think he and Ajay were in on it? Like, bought and sold?"

"With enough money, anything is possible," Einar says.

Hannah frowns. "Will didn't seem the type, though. This is different for him. Not about money. It's about a message. The same way a serial killer kills to complete a moral or emotional mission."

"Perhaps he is simply an excellent liar," Einar offers. "Consider how well he fooled us in the first place. He is a chess player. It is possible he anticipated the need for that lie and orchestrated a narrative that would fit your view from within the FBI: a consultant familiar with criminal profiling."

Though, Hannah thinks, that's not really her specialty. Hers is futurism—how the future could spell humanity's end. Will knew that. So if he did tailor his message for her—if he did craft a special deception—then would this be it? His language did speak to her life, her upbringing, her fears . . .

"One thing is certain," Hannah says. "We need to find Will Galassi."

Moana looks back. "Only thing I know for sure is I can't wait to have you jabberjaws out the back of my bruddah's car."

* * *

The drive to the North Shore of Kauai takes them up the eastern coast—past abandoned cars and bodies in the road, past a blocky elementary school with bedsheets painted with HELP US hanging out the windows, past the smoking wreck of a Navy UH-1 Huey helicopter. In the distance, another fire burns. They hear occasional screams and gunfire. Windows are broken or boarded up. Doors are shattered off their hinges or covered over. Sometimes as they drive past, Hannah sees shadows flitting about. Survivors? Military contractors? Or the more likely answer: just tricks of the eye.

Pono stays quiet as he weaves around dead cars. They round the northeastern bend of the island. Through Kapaa, Anahola, Kilauea. Here, it's quieter. The growth is thicker. More trees. More shadow. They drive past dark rocks and crashing surf. The car eases under canopies of rain forest trees and drooping palms. Eventually Einar tells them to take a turn down a narrow, ill-paved road. Then he signals toward a rutted driveway.

"This is Will's home," he says.

* * *

It's a little bungalow the color of coral. A set of rickety steps off the driveway leads to a dark wooden porch at the front of the house. The property is surrounded by dark, swaying trees.

A warm glow of light shines from inside. Hannah sees someone move past one of the front windows—it's fast, and then gone. "Someone's here," she says. She hands out the Tinactin. They all hose themselves down with the stuff.

Einar tells Pono, "Keep the engine running, please, Pono." He, Ray, and Hannah step out of the car. The air is cool and damp. The trees and bushes hiss and whisper in the breeze. From inside the house, Hannah hears the crackle of static and an interrupted radio broadcast swallowed beneath it. At her back, the gun feels heavy with purpose.

Ray takes the lead without asking. He steps up to the screened-in porch, the wooden boards groaning under his weight. He looks toward a small gardening shovel leaning up against the latticework underside, then leans back and picks it up before heading toward the screen door.

Hannah can't see any ants. But a smell tickles her nose and jogs the memory of being down in Special Projects back on the atoll. It's the smell of whatever concoction Will uses to keep the ants at bay.

Ray gives her and Einar a look. Einar nods.

The screen door opens with an obnoxious creak. Every inch of Hannah's body tenses, waiting for an attack to come: a gunshot, a scream, a knife, a rain of ants. But through the light of the door Hannah sees Ray look to his right, then his left, then back to his right.

He's looking at somebody. "Who are you?" she hears him ask.

Inside, a woman sits at a small breakfast nook table. She idly bats a Kleenex box back and forth. A cairn of used tissues is built off to the side. She regards the sudden trespassers with raw, red eyes.

An emergency radio crackles and hisses: *—ation—land—ency—ants—ilitary—*

The woman's dark hair is pulled back in a sloppy ponytail. She's pretty, Hannah notes. She scans the corners. The windows. The doors. Ahead is a pair of double glass doors going out to what must be the backyard. Beyond them, a corner leading to a hallway. Behind them is a well-worn kitchen, and it's wide open enough to show that nobody is hiding in there.

"You're him," the woman says to Einar.

"I am," he says in a way that is somehow both entirely devoid of ego and yet entirely given over to the inevitability of that question. Hannah wonders what that must be like: to be a person people know, to be someone about whom they have strong opinions.

"Will isn't here," the woman says, then blows her nose.

"Where is the little fucker?" Ray asks.

Hannah pulls up a chair next to the woman. "I'm Hannah Stander. I'm a consultant for the FBI. What's your name?"

"Rachel. Rachel Kelley."

"Rachel, do you know what's going on?"

New tears form at the corners of her eyes.

Hannah says, "Will is involved in something. We don't know what yet, but we do know that what's going on here, on Kauai, is in part his responsibility. But maybe it's not all his responsibility. Can you help us understand? Is there anything you can give us? Any information at all?"

"I don't know much," the woman says. Her words are sticky with spit. Her voice has gone nasal behind her stuffed-up nose. Hannah wonders if she knew all along who or what Will was. Does she even know now, or is she only just glimpsing it? As if reading Hannah's thoughts, Rachel gives a bitter, mirthless laugh. "Except I know the wedding's off."

Hannah forces a smile as she takes Rachel's hand. She gives Ray a look. Ray nods and disappears into the house. Einar stays rooted behind Rachel.

"Rachel, do you know where Will is?"

Rachel hesitates, and in that moment Hannah knows she does.

"Rachel, if Will is involved, we need to know as much as you can tell us. If you want him safe, then this is how that happens. He may be in possession of the Myrmidon ant colonies—ants we both know are very dangerous. We're not out on a witch hunt. We're here to understand the situation and find Will *and* bring him home. But that puts it all on you. That's a heavy weight on your shoulders, I know. It doesn't change the fact that if you want to save Will—if you *love* him—then you need to tell us where he's gone so we can go after him."

Rachel swallows and blinks back tears. She turns her head away, and Hannah is sure in that moment that she lost the chance, that the woman will only dig in deeper. But then she sighs and it all comes out: "He packed up some gear. Hiking gear. He took his laptop. He told me he'd be back someday and I told him not to bother and that seemed to hurt him, like I really *hurt* him, you know? Then he left. He just took off."

Hiking gear, Hannah thinks. He's trying to hike the interior of Kauai, or he's headed to the western shore of the island. Which means he's hiking the Na Pali coast, taking the popular—and dangerous—Kalalau Trail. "Does he know Na Pali well?"

Rachel nods. "He hikes it at least once a year."

"Do you know hiking, too? The gear?"

"Yeah. Yes. A little."

"Did he take a water filter with him?"

"I think so."

"Climbing gear?"

"No. I think that's still in the shed. You can check . . ."

He's hiking Na Pali. He's got to be. People can disappear up there. It's eleven miles of trail, but that's assuming he stays on the trail and doesn't go beyond it. If he was hiking the interior, he'd be climbing. And going to the wild margins of the island makes sense. Even if he's protected from his own monsters for a time, going to where few people are means the ants will have little reason to be there.

Einar asks, "He has all his research with him, doesn't he?"

A stiff, reserved nod from Rachel. Tears now creeping down her cheeks.

"Did he use something on you?" Hannah asks. "A spray. I don't see the ants here, but surely you know what's happening on the island."

"I do." Those two words are a struggle for Rachel. Like she feels complicit. Why wouldn't she? She's probably asking herself right now: *How did I not see this? How did I not know I was about to marry a madman?*

"And did he? Spray you with something?"

"Mm-hmm. It's over there." She gestures toward the kitchen. Sitting on the counter, under a dangling rack of pots and pans, is a small non-aerosol spray bottle. "I don't know what it is, but he said they wouldn't come for me if I used it. Twice a day to be sure . . ."

And then it's over. She crumbles like a clod of dry sand held in the hand. Hair forming a mop around her as she melts into her folded arms. Shoulders hitching with every sob.

Hannah gets up, goes to the small spray bottle. What's inside sloshes around, and bubbles of oil separate. She shakes it, emulsifying it, then gives it a little spray onto the palm of her hand. The smell is familiar. It's the same mix of oleic acid and antifungal. Will's special brew. "Does the phone work?" she asks Rachel, spying a portable on the wall. "Rachel, answer me, please."

"No," the other woman bleats from inside the cavern of her arms. "It's dead."

"What about a cell?"

Another bleat: "Will took it."

"We're going to have to go after him," Hannah says to Einar. "If he has the colonies, then we need to get them back."

"Even if he doesn't, he has information. He knows more about these ants than anyone. Do you agree that he's hiking the coast?"

"I agree. You hike?"

He smiles. "I do."

Ray appears around the corner. "No sign of him. No sign of a laptop, either, but there's a desktop in there he tore apart—boards broken, hard drives ripped out. And a file box that's open but empty. Where's the little slug gone?"

"He's hiking the coast," Hannah says. "Kalalau Trail, I'd guess. You hike?"

"Sure," Ray says, but the way he says it, she can tell it's just bravado.

"Ray, just stay here with Rachel. Keep searching the house."

He throws up his hands. "Whoa, whoa, I've hiked. I can *hike*." Now he's just trying to talk himself into it, Hannah thinks. He takes one step forward—

Kssh.

Behind him, a sharp crack runs up the glass of the patio door like a bolt of lightning frozen in place. Ray stands there for a second, his lips forming soundless words. Then he falls. Behind him, the glass is punctured by a single hole, spreading into jagged cracks.

Hannah moves fast—she plants her hand on Rachel's chest and pushes at the same time that she drives the side of her forearm hard into the crook behind Einar's knee. The chair tips and the woman screams as she slams flat on her back. Einar's leg jerks and he falls to the ground.

Just as the rest of the glass door shatters. The emergency radio hops off the table like a spooked toad, sending up a shower of broken plastic even before it hits the ground and breaks into pieces.

Rachel screams, a howl that drowns out any other sound. Hannah tries to shush her because it's messing with her situational awareness, and still the woman keeps shrieking and wailing, a siren of panic. Hannah snakes an arm around her head and cups a hand over her mouth. The scream continues, but muffled, at least.

Then: The sound of glass crunching. A shadow in the room.

Hannah looks up, sees a broad-shouldered man in a balaclava and black fatigues raise a rifle—an AR-15 by the look of it. She rolls out of the way as the shot perforates Rachel's back. A little spray of blood and the woman's scream is cut short.

Hannah scrambles to stand. Einar is already up, launching his hands in the air. "Wait, wait, wait," he is saying. "Stop. Don't shoot."

"Slowly," the man says, gesturing at Hannah with the gun. "Up. Up!"

She stands just behind Einar. The man has no clean shot on her.

He gestures again with the rifle. "Move. I said, *move*!"

He could just shoot. But that would mean hitting Einar. And the way he's got that rifle pointed, he's making a concerted effort *not* to point it in Einar's direction. No, there's a bullet in that gun and it is reserved for her and her alone.

The realization is like a kick to the chest. The man doesn't want to hurt Einar. *He doesn't want to hurt Einar.* Why would that be, exactly?

In the time it takes her to blink, she knows what she has to do.

Hannah moves behind Einar, pulling her own pistol. She presses the barrel hard against Einar's temple.

"Hannah," Einar says. "I don't understand."

"He wants to shoot, he can take his shot," she says loud enough so the shooter can hear it. "He guns you down, he can gun me down."

But the shooter keeps his gun trained to Einar's margins.

"You figured it out," Einar says.

"Far too late," she says.

The shooter stands, confused as to what to do. Hannah presses the HK45 harder into Einar's temple. "Why?" she hisses in Einar's ear. "*Why?*"

"Now is not the time to dissect that," Einar says. "Now is the time to negotiate. What will it cost?"

Her mind is frantic. Negotiate? He's cool and ever the consummate businessman; her mind feels like a tangle of sparking wires. "What?"

"How much this will cost me is what I am asking you, Hannah. What I want is for you to leave me out of this. What I want is for you to go back to the Bureau and tell them that it was Archer Stevens all along. You can do that. You can pinch their noses and lead them along like good little doggies."

"I can't—"

"You can, and I'm asking you how much this privilege costs me. You have me at a loss. I am, as the saying goes, *bent over a barrel.* We make a good team. I like you. You're smart. *Tenacious.* What if you and I go to find Will together? Just you and me. When we find him, we help heal the world."

"You helped cause this."

He sighs. "The story is more complex than you know. Will did most of this without me. He designed these monsters. I am merely capitalizing on his error. Trying to turn a *frown upside down,* as it were, Hannah."

Moments pass. Breathe in, breathe out. Her hand on the gun shakes. Sweat slicks her brow. She looks to the side of Einar's face, then to the gunman.

The gunman's gaze is flitting from Einar to the door behind her.

Then she hears it—the faint *creak.* Einar has just been stalling her. Someone else is coming up behind. On the porch *right now.*

Hannah yanks Einar backward, pivoting so that she's out of the line of fire—just as the screen door kicks off its hinges and someone else steps into the room, gun up.

It's Venla Normi.

Because of course it is. She never died on the island, did she? Hannah goes through the last forty-eight hours. Venla was the one, wasn't she? The one who took the colonies off the atoll. The one who brought them *here.*

Hannah lets her guard slip just long enough for Einar to pull his head away from the barrel of the gun and drive a sharp elbow into her solar plexus. The air pops out of her lungs in a hard burst and the sharp pain goes fast into a dull ache—

Venla's pistol is up. Hannah stagger-steps left, just behind Einar again.

The woman doesn't take the shot. Einar spins, going for Hannah's gun. His hand catches hers. His thumb presses hard into the soft spot of her wrist. She growls and as the gun passes by his ear—

She squeezes the trigger. The weapon discharging is loud. It's like a hammer driving a nail into her ear—and so close to Einar, it's far worse for him.

He winces, shaking his head like a bee-stung dog as he pulls away from her—

Leaving a clean shot for the first gunman.

The gunman raises the rifle—

But there's sudden movement behind him. *Ray.* Ray launches himself into the man with the elegance of a falling piano. But it works—the rifle goes off, pinging off pots and pans, as the gunman goes down.

As Hannah flinches from the rifle shot, Einar scowls and throws a straight punch. Hannah turns her head aside at the last minute and the knuckled blow crashes against her cheek, staggering her. Again he's on her, air hissing through his teeth as he goes for the gun. She pistons a knee into his gut. He slams the side of his head into the side of hers. She tastes blood. She sees stars. The gun is slipping from her grip as he mauls it, crushing her knuckles against the steel receiver . . .

You're a survivor. So survive.

Hannah yanks the gun toward her own face. Einar's resistance braced him in the other direction, so this comes as a surprise to him. Soon as it's close enough, she sinks her teeth into the back of his hand. She feels his flesh part. Blood wells into her mouth.

Einar rips his hand away. Blood spatters the cabinets. He shoves her backward hard. Hannah slams into the counter, a geyser of pain shooting up from the bottom of her spine to the base of her skull.

Already Einar's running—bolting from the room, his hand cradled by his chest. Venla's got her gun back up, but Hannah isn't about to go down like that. As she ducks and scurries, she points her own piece and fires off two more shots in their direction. Bullets chip the door frame and punch through the screen as Venla and Einar dart outside.

Hannah checks herself. She hasn't been shot. Which she's pretty sure qualifies her for miraculous canonization.

The sounds of a scuffle at the other side of the room draw her attention. The gunman has Ray pinned, rifle held fast across the man's throat. Ray's face is red and going purple—swollen like a balloon about to burst. The gunman turns at the sound of her—

She puts a bullet between his eyes.

Guilt surges against her like the sea against sand, battering her. Her knees go weak and it threatens to drag her down—but outside, the sound of an engine roaring to life draws her out of it. That followed by the noise of tires chewing driveway.

"Go," Ray gasps.

She races outside, but it's too late. Through the trees, she spies the blur of taillights. And there on the ground are two more bodies: Pono and Moana. Blood made black in the moonlight pools beneath their slit necks.

* * *

The bullet went through Ray. If he were a whitetail deer or a pheasant or even a goat, Hannah would have a fairly precise clue where the projectile went and what it hit on its way through, but she's not an expert on human anatomy. Best she can tell is that it passed through the middle of his torso. Entered just to the right of the spine and came out just above his stomach somewhere.

His middle is sloppy with blood. His face has gone a ghostly green-gray. She wrapped up his middle with towels and bandages from a first aid kid she found under the sink, secured them with his own belt cinched tight.

It isn't much.

"Fucking Einar," he says. His words are wet. "I knew it. *I knew it.* That thing he said to you . . ."

"Shh, don't strain. What thing?"

"He said a couple Icelandic sayings, right? The one thing about being stubborn enough to win and the other thing—"

"About survival being king."

"Yeah, except that's not what that meant."

"You speak Icelandic?"

"A little. He was my boss. I was trying to kiss up."

"What was it he said?"

"Something about, *I'll show you the two worlds.* And I thought, that doesn't have anything to do with survival. First I thought maybe it was some kind of threat. Then I excused it—figured maybe I just got the translation goofed up. Now I figure it was some kind of threat."

She looks down at her own blood-slick hands. Already the red has begun to dry to brown. The HK45 sits nearby.

"You're going after him, right?" Ray asks.

"I'm going after Will. But I figure that's where Einar is headed, too."

"I'm coming with you," Ray says, and then laughs as he slumps back down because no, he isn't.

"I think you need to rest."

"I think I'm probably dead and my body just doesn't know it yet."

She suspects he's right. A shot through the middle isn't good. If the bullet hit the liver, he might be bleeding bad on the inside. If it hit the stomach, it could lead to a fast infection. (These things learned from her survivalist mother as a child.) Injures of that sort are fixable *if* he gets to a hospital quickly. But that's not much of an option out here. The hospitals aren't open during the end of the world.

The memory appears, unasked for: Bucky the goat, the knife in her hand, Dad taking the .22 and killing the goat she accidentally mauled.

"Hey," he says, interrupting the show going on behind her eyes. "I figure this is as good a time as any to ask: If I live, will you go out on a date with me?"

A doomed request. But she nods and forces a smile. "Sure. You survive, I'll go out with you."

"Great. You, me, Miami South Beach. Drinks. A Cuban place. Cuban coffee and lime pie afterward. It's gonna be good."

"I bet."

"You better go. Catch the bad guys."

"I will."

"I'm gonna rest."

"You rest." She kisses his brow: an odd gesture from her. It feels warm, familiar, and comfortable in its discomfort—nice in how it feels like something someone else would do. Someone human. Someone who isn't Hannah.

His eyes shut gently. His chest rises and falls as blood wets the towels.

Hannah packs what little gear she can muster, then leaves.

38

Hannah has never hiked the Kalalau Trail. But she knows of it. The eleven-mile hike starts at the North Shore of Kauai, with a trailhead at Kee Beach, and goes around the Na Pali coast on the western side, winding across a series of peaks and valleys, over streams and past waterfalls. It is renowned for being one of the world's most beautiful hikes.

Also, one of its most dangerous.

It's dangerous for a lot of reasons. An experienced hiker will be okay, most likely, but a lot of inexperienced hikers want to take the trip, and underestimate what the hike entails. They don't know about Crawler's Ledge at the seventh mile. They don't know to bring enough water. They don't realize that with just a little rain, conditions can change in the breadth of a heartbeat—streams can become rivers, cliffs can become mudslides, visibility can go to hell and leave you blind and stranded. People have to be airlifted from the trail every year. And every year, people die. They fall off the cliffs. They get swept away by a sudden flash flood. They die from exposure.

It doesn't help that the trail has a handful of permanent—and illegal—residents. Trail weirdos and wanderers who hit the coast and aim to disappear. Hannah has encountered the same kinds of people at various points of the Appalachian Trail. Some of them are nice enough, castoffs from the world who have exiled themselves. Some of them are creepers, stalkers, maybe worse.

As morning bleeds across the horizon, she stands at the trailhead on Ke'e Beach—from here, everything looks peaceful and

the sound of the sea does its best to shush her dread, but it's futile. Hannah feels none of the excitement she would harbor if this were recreational. This isn't a choice. And she's ill-prepared. Not enough water. Not enough food. She's already tired and beaten down—not to mention the ghost of injury in her ankle. All parts of her feel like a rotten tooth whose middle has been scraped out. She stands there, stretching, trying to talk herself out of going. *Just turn around. Go home. Let someone else fix this.* She almost has to laugh. *You're just a consultant.*

But the others already have their head start. She wonders how many of the Blackhearts mercs are here with Einar. She wonders how exactly it is that he ended up working with the Blackhearts in the first place, given that they seemed beholden to Archer Stevens. But they are mercenaries, after all. They work for whoever pays them.

* * *

The first mile.

Hannah hikes up overlooking Ke'e Beach as the sun's light eases across the wide expanse of brilliant blue. The serpentine curves of reef can be seen under the slowly rolling tides. Plum trees bloom. A pair of red honeycreepers chase each other from branch to branch. The breeze kicks up to a buffeting wind.

It's beautiful out here. Hannah feels suddenly small, in the best way possible. It absolves her, somehow. The world will go on. People will do as people will do. She can change none of it.

It's almost enough to make her turn around.

Almost.

She has to do this. She has to end it, get answers. This is in her power. She is alone out here, which means it's all up to her.

Her absolution blows away like dust off the trail ahead.

* * *

On the second mile, the hike begins to show its teeth. The trail begins to rise up as the pinnacle Na Pali peaks push up against the banner of the wide sky.

It's at a small stream that she sees it. There, on the ground: boot prints in the dirt.

The wind shifts then, and she smells the cigarette smoke.

Hannah reaches behind her and draws the pistol, then creeps forward, trying to suss out the direction of the smoke. The wind is coming in from the coast—the ocean now unseen behind vegetation—and the stream heads that direction. She ducks behind a tree and scans the foliage. The sharp bite of nicotine hits her nose.

A sound hits her ears, too. At first she thinks it's just the noise of the stream burbling along, but it's something else, something separate.

Psssshhh.

Then she makes him: A black shape standing just behind a hala tree. One of the soldiers. She's pretty sure he's pissing. That means she has to move fast *and* quietly.

Part of her thinks that the best bet is to hurry past him. But she doesn't want some armed and dangerous variable coming up on her back. She'll never stop looking over her shoulder.

And he may know something.

She spies a fast path right alongside the stream—flat stones and dirt. No sticks to break underfoot, no foliage to crunch and snap. She moves, light on her feet despite a twinge in her ankle, gun up. She can see the soldier's shoulder next to the tree. His body jostles—*shake, shake, shake*—and then the sound of his zipper zipping.

Her foot knocks a rock bounding down toward the stream.

The man pivots around the tree, his hand going to the gun in his holster. But Hannah meets him there, her own weapon already drawn and pointed at his head. "No," she says. "Don't."

He has his balaclava pulled up over his head. Dark hair is stuck to the sweat on his pale forehead. He's got his sleeves rolled up and his dark pants pulled up to his knees, too. His face is heavy, round.

Stubbled cheeks. Dark eyes. Tongue sliding over little teeth. At his feet, ghosts of smoke rise from a heel-smashed cigarette.

"Take it easy," he says.

"What's your name?" she asks.

"Chuck U. Farley." Then he smiles the way a little boy smiles after he wipes a booger in a girl's hair. Puckish and mean.

"Where's Einar?"

"Don't know an Einar."

She thumbs the hammer back on the HK45. "Take a look at this pistol. Heckler & Koch. Look familiar? Look like one that belonged to one of your own? Bet it matches the one in your holster. I've already killed one of you," she says. "I won't hesitate to kill another. Where's Einar?"

The man's throat works in a nervous swallow. "Ahead."

"By how far?"

"I don't know."

"Guess."

"I don't know. I don't know!"

She tries another tack. "How long have you been here?"

"About five hours."

If they move one to two miles an hour, they're probably at mile seven already. That's far enough ahead that despair plucks at her strings.

"How many of them?"

"Three."

"Who? Einar, Venla—who else?"

"One other PMC."

He's lying. She can tell. The way he flinches when he says the number. The way he licks his lips when he tells her who.

"What's their plan?"

"Find Galassi, find his research, get out."

"And you? How about you? You here to kill me?"

He clamps shut. He's starting to get twitchy.

She says, "You're here as a distraction. Einar sent you back here to fail. He was cutting deadweight. You're out of shape. I bet you travel slow. I bet—"

He moves fast. Going for his weapon.

Her eyes squeeze shut at the same time her finger squeezes the trigger.

Ears ringing. The devil-stink smell of gunsmoke.

When she opens her eyes again, he's on the ground. One leg kicking out, heel tapping against a flat rock. The stream burbling nearby as blood runs from the back of his head into the water.

She wants to take the gun and pitch it into the brush.

But she doesn't.

Instead, Hannah swallows her disgust and searches the body. She finds an extra magazine for the pistol, and also a suppressor. She takes them both. The gunshot echoed out loud, and it's a good bet that Einar and Venla and whoever else is out there heard it—which means they know she's either dead or on her way for them. She'll want any more shots silenced. The ammo in the magazine looks to be subsonic—even with the suppressor, she'll never get a shot to be as whisper quiet as they appear in the movies, but it'll dampen any echo and drop the decibel level.

Nearby where he was pissing, she finds a black bag. She takes a water bottle out of it and drinks a good bit, then wolfs down a protein bar before getting back on the trail.

* * *

Mile three.

Over the wider Hanakapiai Stream—the water soaks her boots and socks as she crosses—to the beach beyond.

A tent sits on the beach. Its flaps rustle in the wind. Sticking out of the entrance of the tent is a socked foot, and just past it, a hiking boot.

Hannah feels the breath catch in her chest as she creeps up to the tent and finds the two bodies inside: a man and a woman. Young.

Maybe midtwenties. She in a bikini, he in board shorts and a tank top. She's shot in the chest, he in the temple. Blood and flies. The smell of voided bowels.

Hannah backs out of the tent, gagging. The blood is still fresh enough that this was not the work of Will Galassi.

She wonders if the couple even knew what was going on around the rest of the island. Did they come here to get away from the ants, or were they already so far away from the world that they never knew what the Myrmidons had wrought?

* * *

The seventh mile is thought to be one of the hardest.

This is in part because after Hanakapiai Beach the trail goes from sea level to eight hundred feet in just over a mile. Then down again, then up again. Through another stream. Down through trees where the ground is covered in slippery scree—here Hannah takes a tumble and skins her knee. *At least,* she thinks, *I didn't screw up my ankle again.* The wind fights her the whole way. The ground is rough and uneven. The sun beats down.

By the time she gets to the seventh mile, she is worn to a nub. She moves up a series of ascending switchbacks—round, tight bends in the trail like loops of kinked bowel. Up and around, up and around.

That's when Crawler's Ledge begins.

The ledge is narrow. Two people across in the widest of spots, but for much of it, it'll accommodate only one person. On one side is rock. On the other, a drop down into a rocky valley and the gnashing waves of the Pacific.

Hannah shuffles, planting her hands on the edge of the rock. Every time she secures some rough semblance of a hold, an eerie frequency runs through her: a sudden self-destructive urge to simply *push* like a swimmer kicking off the pool wall, and fall down, down, down. Of course, maybe she won't have to—the wind whips hard enough she thinks it might pick her up and fling her into the abyss, where the sea may swallow her.

Progress is slow and arduous. She hopes like hell to see her quarry ahead in the off-chance that she's beating them to the punch, but she doesn't. She expects to be shot. But she isn't. Then she begins to wonder: Did they leave the trail? They could have. They could have gone inward, toward one of the waterfalls. Or could she have passed them? Maybe they were back there at the beach, hiding.

Fear and worry are like ropes lashing around her neck. Her foot skids out, kicking a rain of stones off the cliff. She watches them tumble downward to the point she can't even make them out when they hit the sea.

Deep breath. *You can do this.* She winds around the outer bulge of a massive cliff, and then the narrow path tucks inward again toward the island.

At the end of Crawler's Ledge is a respite: a small stream, a grassy bluff, a circle of red stones. Hannah doesn't step into this clearing so much as fall into it, onto her hands and knees. She presses her forehead against the earth. She finds her water bottle and takes a greedy sip. She wants to cry, but doesn't.

She's not sure how long she stays like that. Too long, she knows. She should be up. Moving fast. The others will be. If they're even out here . . .

When she finally lifts her head, she sees that she is not alone.

Will Galassi is here.

39

He's dead. His face is the color of ash. His chest is dark with blood—the soaked-through shirt perforated with a small hole. His hands are curled up in his lap, fingers barely touching.

"That you?" he asks. Then his lids lift. The whites of his eyes are not white at all, but so shot through with red they look like cherry tomatoes gone ripe and ready to split.

"Will," she says.

"Hannah." The last syllable dragged out in a rattling, gurgling wheeze.

"Where is Einar?"

"Gone."

"Gone where?"

"Water," he says, and she thinks, *Einar is going to a boat.* But then Will's hands lift a few inches off his belly and feebly caress the air. "Drink."

Hannah hesitates, but cruelty seems to have no value here. Any anger she may have felt toward Will has dissolved. She pulls the water from her bag and takes it to him. He sips messily, greedily. Most of it goes down his chin.

"Gone where, Will?" she asks, more insistently.

"Red Hill. Heli . . ." He coughs and some of the water burbles back up over his lips. It's tinged with threads of red. "Helicopter."

That means they got what they came for. They don't need Will anymore. "They got your laptop? With all your notes?"

He offers a small nod and a waxen smile.

"How many of them are there?"

He whispers, "Ffff. Five."

"Einar, Venla, and three mercs?"

Another nod. She knew the other PMC was lying.

"Glad you're . . . alive," he says. He reaches out and holds her hand. His grip is brittle. His fingers are cold.

What to say to that? How to respond? *I'm glad I'm alive, too. Sorry about you.* She offers a stiff, forced smile. "Why, Will? Why did you do it?"

"Why . . . wouldn't I? People are people. You ever . . . look at a YouTube comments section? You'd . . . want everyone dead . . . too." A spark of mirth dances in his bloodshot eyes. "B-besides. I . . . didn't do this. I just . . . made the monster. Einar . . . set it *free*." He leans forward with a grunt. Fresh blood drenches his shirt. He stares at her with an intense gaze, lifts one finger, and she realizes he's about to give her a lecture. It would be funny if it weren't so grim. His pedagogical tone begins: "And do you know . . . why Einar did . . . what he did, Hannah?"

Thing is, Hannah has had time to contemplate this. Time on this hike. Time over streams and under blooming plums, time in the dust and the dirt. Time snaking her way across the dreaded ledge.

"The mosquito," she says. "*Aedes aegypti*."

He nods and grins—a reaper's rictus, that grin.

"Einar knew that despite its success elsewhere, the politics in the U.S. would never allow him to bring his mosquitoes here. But if his hand was forced . . ."

"If he was made to fix his own . . . mistake . . ."

"Then he would demonstrate that the only way to fight these intrusions by nature—be they natural or unnatural—is to implement opposition through genetic modification. We would let the barbarian through the gate because we would need the barbarian to fight for us. A risky gambit, but he could claim that Archer Stevens was the one who forced his hand. And the government would trust him. And then the people would trust him. And he would again change the world."

Will chuckles: a muddy gurgle. He makes the "okay" gesture with his hand, and says, "Thus endeth . . . the lecture." He stares off at an unfixed point, until his stare unmoors. It's like it disconnects, suddenly. And she realizes: *He's not here anymore.*

Hannah steps back. Takes a few deep breaths. There's a part of her that gets it. She cannot on the surface acknowledge any nobility in what he did, no, but she understands. The world is a strange place. It's full of beauty and wisdom. But sometimes it feels like finding those gems means wading through human waste first. Reaching into the muck and slurry in the hopes of finding something good, something pretty. People are a mess. And they're making a mess of the planet. Why not return it to a time when humans were just a fingerprint upon its surface and ants ruled the world?

She has to catch Einar before he leaves. Though part of her thinks, *I could just go. Head back. My existence is enough to cause him trouble.* If his plan is to return to the world and be its woeful, obligated savior, her narrative will directly contradict his. But what evidence does she have? It'd be her word against his. He has Will's research. He has lawyers and money. Then there's Kit and Barry. Does he have them, too? Already they think Archer Stevens is behind it. Already they believe their job is to return to the world and fix what's broken.

It's too uncertain. She has to finish what she began.

Before she leaves, she looks around for supplies—anything Will may have left behind. No bag. They probably took it along with the laptop. Though she finds the act detestable—*I'm not some vulture picking bones,* she thinks—she pats down Will to see if he has something, anything, that can help her.

She finds a bulge in each of the side pockets of his cargo shorts. In each she finds a black disc. Like a hockey puck—a hole on one end sealed with a tight plug of pale wax. Two Myrmidon colonies. She almost drops them like they're burning her hands. She imagines the ants spilling out all over her, biting, stinging.

But somehow, she maintains her grip. And she remembers: *I have the spray.* Will's special concoction.

Einar and the others either missed these or didn't bring them on purpose—maybe they saw the colonies as a liability. After all, they reached their goal. No need to bring more ants with them.

Hannah pockets the colonies.

It's time to go and finish this.

40

The Red Hill is a mound framed by green spires behind. The ground rises up sharply—a few hundred feet over a quarter of a mile—and the earth is as red as a penny. Scrub and grass stick up everywhere.

Hannah crosses down into the valley, staying in the few shadows afforded by the hala trees. She's tired. Her legs ache. Her feet hurt. *Everything* hurts. Her mouth is dry even though the air is wet. Her greatest desire right now is to sit down and lie back and let the sun warm her skin and pretend like it's her alone in a problem-free world with a future that's fearless and uncomplicated.

But then, up ahead—small shapes move in the distance, like dolls on a child's stage. *It's them.* Einar and the others. Her heart starts tumbling in her chest like a boulder down a hill. *I'm almost there. Just a little farther.*

She thinks to charge hard ahead—

And yet, her quarry isn't moving. Milling about the apex of that hill, yes. But moving past it? No. They're staying in place. Why?

The sun has risen up over Hannah's head and is now dropping back down over the other side of the sky, easing toward the horizon. Evening will be in a few hours. Hannah wonders: Is that what they're waiting for? It makes sense. If there is a quarantine in place and nobody is allowed to leave the island, a black helicopter flying under the cover of darkness gives them a greater chance of escaping uncontested.

Which means she has a few hours to plan her attack. Hannah hunkers down against the rough bark of a bottle palm. She drinks

water. Eats a protein bar. Checks the pistol, changes the magazine to the one she stole from the dead PMC in the stream.

The horizon claims the sun. Evening bleeds. Hannah removes her shoes. She coats herself in the spray, head to toe. It's a greasy mist, hanging on her, oily and slick. The smell is not unlike cooking spray.

At last she creeps down the hiking trail, up the hill. She puts as much speed in her step while moving along as silently as she can.

It's slow going, and for a while it feels like she'll never get there—like this is some absurd optical illusion where her destination continues to stretch out away from her, always drifting just out of range. But soon her targets begin to become larger shapes, shadows on the horizon of the hill, and though it takes a half hour of darting from cover to cover, their voices become clear.

An unfamiliar voice: ". . . this raghead piece of shit comes up on me, he's got a kid with him, and a fucking goat—"

Another: "Always goats. Do they not eat cows there? I swear to fucking Christ, I would've killed for a cheeseburger."

"I think I *did* kill for a cheeseburger, but shit, Barnes, let me finish my story, will ya? So he's got a goat and—"

"Shh," says a woman's voice. Venla. The two men keep muttering and she hisses at them: "I said *shut up*."

Hannah thinks, *She heard me.* Her hand scrambles into her pocket and extracts one of the discs. Her nails find the wax plug and she prays: *Please let this work, please let this work,* and for a moment she can't bring herself to do it. The fear is too great. The memory too strong. Ants, swarming all over her. Biting her . . .

She swallows the fear. She drowns the memory. *You applied the spray. You're safe. They're your weapon now.* With her thumb, she pops the plug, gives the colony a good shake, then sets it down and hurries perpendicular to the trail, darting behind a shrub that looks like a series of sword blades jammed in the ground at a central point. She skids to a halt and lowers her head, peering through the V between bladed leaves.

Two shapes crest the hill and walk down toward her. Broad shoulders. Pistols drawn. Mercs, the both of them. One of them kicks into the puck. "The hell?" He bends down.

And suddenly he's shaking his arm like it's covered in fire. "Jesus Christ, Jesus shit, they're here—"

But his words begin to catch in his throat as his esophagus tightens.

Hannah remembers the feeling all too well. The tightness in the throat and the chest. The itching. The swollen tongue. The Myrmidons, doing their work.

The man's knees bend and he starts to sink to the ground even as the other man moves to help him—a mistake, but an understandable one.

Soon, the second man is down, too. Crying out. Gargling his own spit.

The third merc crests the hill.

Hannah springs from cover, gun up. While that third man is distracted, she moves fast, charging across the hard ground. He turns toward her too late. She takes no chances: three shots from the pistol spin him on his heel and drop him. For a moment she considers taking out the other two: one shot apiece to their heads would put them out of their misery fast and save them from the ants. But she has no time, and they are out of her way.

The real prize is on that hill.

Her legs carry her forward with long strides, the stones of the hill threatening to cause her to slip and fall, which only invigorates the pain in her ankle. Acknowledging the pain is not an option. Later, she will have time to recognize it. If she survives.

At the top of the hill, leaning up against a rock, is Einar. Arms crossed in front of him. "Hello, Hannah."

Shoot him, she thinks. Her finger tightens on the trigger—

Bang.

Something hits Hannah hard from the side. Her right foot takes a step forward, but it's like her leg has no strength in it. Like it's just a rubber band with the tension let go. Her knee pops out of joint and she falls to the side. Her gun clatters away into the rust-red dust.

She tries to prop herself back up, but her left arm is a dead slab of meat—for a moment, it's a vacuum of any feeling at all. Then, as she tries to breathe, the pain comes in sharply. A bullet in her arm, in the biceps. *Through* it. Into the shoulder and collarbone beyond. The pain now reaching out with greedy tentacles, seizing the space under her jaw, under her armpit, all the way into her chest. It feels like with every breath she's sucking in razors.

Two shapes stand in front of her.

"Wait," one of them says. Einar. His hand out, staying someone familiar: Venla.

"No talking," Venla says, her words like cobra venom. "Let me end this. Aron will be here soon with the helicopter."

"I like to talk," he says. "It is my way." He moves toward Hannah. "You have been shot. I hate to see you like this, Hannah. You impress me. I would love to have you working for me. Is that even possible? Can we get past all this?"

"Of course," she says, scooting backward so that her back is against a rock. She thinks, *Just keep him talking. Buy yourself time.* She can tell that the bullet has done some damage. If she's out here long enough, it'll claim her. But if she could just think of something . . . "But I don't think you can afford me."

He laughs. "I'm sure I can pay more than your meager salary at the FBI, Hannah. I did a background check on you. I know about your house, if you can call it that. Your car. Your life. It's very empty, that life. I could help you fill it. We could change the world, you and I. I could use a mind like yours. It's not just that you're smart. You're tenacious. A *survivor.*"

"Einar," Venla cautions, but he silences her in Icelandic.

"If this is your idea," Hannah says, the words suddenly lost in a flurry of painful coughs. She tries again, blinking back tears: "If this is your idea of changing the world, I don't want to live in it anymore."

"I was just making do. You don't see that yet, do you? A problem presented itself in the form of Will Galassi, Ajay Bhatnagar, and their Myrmidon ant. But I am fond of turning problems into solutions."

"The *Aedes aegypti,*" she says. Even speaking those three words sends new waves of misery through her. Her injury is getting worse. She wonders how far the bullet went in. Is the pain just from bone splinters? She feels a lot of blood—can see it, too, shining in the moonlit dark. Did the bullet hit an artery?

"Very good. Yes. That was a problem for me. This problem solves that problem. Pitting two abstract enemies against one another on the field of battle."

"And the Blackhearts?"

"I have money. They are mercenaries. I paid."

"You're a genius," she says. She means it.

"I am."

"You're also a monster."

His silhouette tenses and recoils. The words that follow are bitter. "I am not. Not anymore. I am a better man than I once was."

Her arm is ruined, she fears. It'll never work again. But she has to make it work. *Has to.* Right now. She wills her limb to respond—she attempts to summon something almost supernatural. God, a ghost, a magic spell. Or maybe, just maybe, her own adrenaline. *Push, push, push.* Her hand twitches.

Her fingers begin to crawl along like a reticent spider.

"I am feeling confessional," Einar says. "You know the story I told you? About the Ethiopian man I saved from the two skinheads?"

She nods and wishes she hadn't. Fresh pain. More blood.

Her fingers at the end of her left hand—at the end of her shattered left arm—tease open her pocket.

"I was one of those skinheads. I killed the male prostitute, Hannah. With a broken bottle to the neck. He propositioned me and I felt such *rage* at that. My father . . . well. That's a story for another time, but the rage I felt was like a blast furnace. And the man I killed, I still see his face. I knew then and there how awful mankind could be because I myself had manifested that awfulness. But I resolved to do better. To *be* better. To make this a better place for men like him and men like me. I wanted to change the circumstances. I wanted to save the world."

Hannah's left hand finds the second and last black disc. Her thumb begins to wander blindly along its edge. Once it finds the soft wax, she begins to work. *Scrape, scrape, scrape.*

"I have my own confession," she says.

"*Einar,*" Venla says.

"Shush!" he chastens her. "Let the dying woman confess her sins. I respect her. I owe her that much. Go on, Hannah. Please. *Confess.*"

"The man . . ." She coughs again. Spit flecking her lips. She doesn't taste blood. Not yet, anyway. "The man who came onto our property when I was a girl? The vagrant. Roy Peffer. My father didn't shoot him. *I* shot him."

Scrape, scrape, scrape.

Inside the pocket, the wax pops off into her hand.

"I had my rifle. He kept coming toward me. He was saying things, strange things, and he wasn't right in the head. I shot him. I just did it. I didn't hesitate. My father took the blame. Because that's who he was. The kind of *man* he was. A good man. Not like you."

Einar sighs. "No, not like me. But I'm here, and he is not. I'm sorry, Hannah." He looks to Venla. "Do it."

Venla steps closer, teeth bared, gun raised.

"*Wait,*" Hannah says—a desperate, fear-tinged word. In the palm of her hand, ants crawl. One wanders onto her fingers, and she remembers Will standing there on the other side of the glass. The Myrmidons swarming his fist.

She pinches. An ant *pops* under the pressure. Squish.

Alarm. Alert. The Myrmidons swarm in the darkness—

"I have another confession," she says.

Einar eases back Venla's pistol again, but sighs as he does so. "Hannah, we have each told one another our sins. That is as it must be. Do not make this harder."

"The ants . . ." Hannah grits her teeth and pushes past the anguish to draw her hand back out of her pocket. She can feel the bones inside her shoulder grinding. Every movement pumps new blood down her shirt.

She darts out her hand and catches Venla's ankle. The closest thing she can grab. "The ants are *here*," she says.

"Yes, we know," Einar says. "They will have their meal and by the time they come to us, we will be gone. Venla. Now."

The tall, dagger-edged woman points the gun.

And then she flinches, crying out. Venla takes a step back, wrenching her ankle out of Hannah's weak grip.

"Venla?" Einar asks.

But the woman's face, even in the growing dark, cannot conceal the sudden panic. Her features freeze. Mouth open in a worried *oh*. Eyes so wide.

Something crawls across Venla's cheek. She screams—a scream fast stifled—and swallows as she begins to claw at herself with stiffening limbs. Ants crawl from Hannah's pocket in a trail toward her, their little bodies gleaming in the moonlight.

Einar wastes no time. He bolts in the other direction.

Hannah gets the elbow of her right arm under her, and using her legs she launches herself forward. Not toward him, but toward the HK45. She crashes against it, fumbling for the weapon as he darts toward the far side of the hill.

Hannah gets up on one knee. Trembling arm out. Gun heavy, so heavy. She remembers the same lesson she conjured from memory on the day she shot Roy Peffer. Her mother was worthless when it came to teaching Hannah things; the woman was too impatient, too angry at Hannah's immediate lack of comprehension and demonstration of skill.

So her father taught her how to shoot—she was ten at the time, though Mom wanted her to learn much earlier. He said, "Here's what you do, Hannah. Think about what you want to hit." In that case, she wanted to hit a Dr Pepper can on a fence rail. "You breathe in, then you breathe out. All the way out, like you're trying to push all the air from your lungs. When it's gone, don't think about anything. Don't think about the target. Don't think about that can. Don't think about me or your mom or any of the world's troubles. Empty your head and pull the trigger and I promise you—that can will jump like a frog who got his ass bit."

That's what she did then. The can did indeed jump.

And it's what she does now.

Bang.

Einar goes down.

Hannah gets up. Hobbles over to him. Einar is pushing himself up. His one leg hangs there, limp and dead. Which means she hit where she was aiming: right behind his knee.

He starts to hop forward on his one good leg. She shoots that one, too. Einar screams and drops. He curls up into a ball, sobbing.

Hannah sits down on a rock. Her body moves in waves of pain and numbness. A cold icy nothing washes over her, and then a hot, acid burn. Then back to the cold nothing again. The start of shock.

She centers herself. If she's going to live, she needs to move now. She knows that somewhere around this camp, they have a way to make a call.

To Einar, she says: "You have a phone somewhere here. Satphone or GPS tracker or something. I need it."

He curses at her in what she presumes is Icelandic.

His breathing is fast. Which means the pain is bad. She knows because *her* pain is bad and *her* lungs are like a rabbit's. "You want to sit here in pain, fine."

"My legs are a mess," he says. His voice sounds weepy.

"Good."

"You did a number on me."

"I know." She bites her lip to distract from the pain in her shoulder. "The ants will finish with Venla soon. And then they'll come for you. With your legs injured, you won't even be able to run from the monsters you loosed on the world. I don't know if you're a fan of irony, Einar, but if you are . . ."

"I have a chopper coming." He says that like a petulant child.

"And which do you think will get here first? Your friends? Or the ants? I have spray. I can use it to help you. But I *need* that phone."

Moments pass. All she hears is the sound of the wind and his breathing. No chopper yet. No rescue for him. That silence must break him, because finally he cries out in frustration. He says: "Venla has it. She has the phone."

Sure enough, when Hannah crawls over there, she pats down the woman's body—which now teems with ants, ants carrying away little bits of her to God knows where—and finds the phone in her back pocket.

The ants crawl up her hand as she pulls out the phone. Panic seizes her and she has to calm herself down in order to wipe them off. They go willingly. None bite. Hannah still crawls away as fast as she can.

In the moonlight, she sees Einar propping himself up with his arms. He stares at her, feral. Like he could come at her at any second.

Hannah feels around for the gun. "Don't. You can get the bullet, or you can get the spray."

The fight goes out of him. His chin drops.

"Throw me the spray."

She does.

And then she tries to make a call.

41

Three months later

Hannah Stander and Hollis Copper stand in a courtyard of bright crepe myrtles. "This is not a prison," she says.

"Oh, but it is," Hollis answers. "Minimum security prison for the wealthy. Guys like Bernie Madoff stay here. It's *pay-to-stay*. You pay in and you get to live like a king. A king imprisoned by his own court, maybe, but a king just the same."

"Figures." She adjusts her arm in its sling.

"How's the arm?"

"Hurts. Itches." The cast goes all the way up her shoulder. Her arm was propped up on a truss for a while, but now it's allowed to hang somewhat. The bullet shattered her bones. She's got pins in there now—making her feel at least a little bit like a Terminator. "Cast comes off today, actually."

"Enjoy your returned mobility."

"Thanks." She draws a deep breath. "I never did thank you properly."

"For what?"

"For saving me that day."

"I didn't save you. I sent a helicopter to pick up you and the Icelandic prick is all I did. It's you who needs to be thanked, Hannah."

That day, she really thought she was dead. After getting the phone from Venla, it took her a while to get in touch with *anybody*. Local information didn't work. Hollis wasn't answering his

cell. Eventually she tried Ez's cell phone—and lo and behold, she answered. Turned out, Hollis and the others had retreated from Barking Sands and were on board a littoral combat ship—the USS *Independence*. From there, Hollis sent a chopper—a chopper that dissuaded Einar's own ride from landing (though later Einar's pilot was tracked down overseas under a false name, and was thrown into the basket with the rest of the Blackhearts contractors, all of them presently undergoing litigation and imprisonment).

Hannah spent a month in a hospital on Oahu. If you're going to convalesce somewhere, Honolulu is a fine choice. Every morning the smell from the plumeria blooms wafted in across her balcony—or, rather, her *lanai*. It didn't hurt that Ez came to Hawaii, too, for a while. She took a week, had a TA handle her job at the university. It was good just to sit and . . . be with someone. She spoke to her mom every day, too. The time difference made it hard, and every time she wanted to get on the phone with Dad, he was too tired, or wasn't having a good day, and Mom kept up that same refrain: *Come home, come home, you need to come home.*

Hannah wanted to be more involved in the case, but Hollis said no. He explained to her that she had done enough. He said *he* wasn't even involved anymore aside from giving testimony. Forces beyond their control were working with Einar to "rectify the situation."

Speak of the Devil and the Devil shall appear—

There, walking out the door into the courtyard, is Einar Geirsson. Well, not walking. Hobbling on two trembling legs, using a cane. She and he share a look and a long silence. His mouth is fishhooked into a mean smirk.

"Can you give us some privacy?" she asks Hollis.

Hollis Copper arches an eyebrow, but silently he acquiesces. As he passes Einar on the way in he offers the billionaire a cold knife-in-the-front stare.

"He's *quite* the friendly one," Einar says once Copper is gone. The caged billionaire is smiling, but the smile is fake. He's angry with her. Disgusted with the way things turned out. She can see it on his

face, a face covered by a resentful, contemptuous mask. His gaze is practically bestial.

It gives her some satisfaction. "It worked," she says.

"I know."

"The island of Kauai is free of the menace you made. Kit and Barry helped produce both the new strain of terminator ant and the engineered *Candida*."

He sniffs. "I am told also that your friend Dr. Choi was involved."

"They needed help and she had value as an entomologist familiar with the species Will Galassi created. Besides, she deserved the rather significant payout afforded by working for Arca Labs." Labs that remain in operation under Einar's board of directors—independent of the Icelandic billionaire.

"Maybe I will whisper a word to the board to hire her."

"She won't take the job."

Einar shrugs—a dismissive *who the fuck really cares* kind of gesture. He looks her up and down. In that gaze, she can feel how much he's changed. Gone is any pretense of civility. He's stripping her down. Like a man looking at a woman he's imagining unclothed and splayed out before him. "You look well."

"And you look comfortable here. In your cage."

Silence between them. He finally says, "I am told that the release of the *Aedes aegypti* will proceed apace in the Florida Keys. As a test."

"You got your wish." All along, this was his plan. To use Kauai as proof of concept for genetically modified insects—a dangerous gambit, considering how the Myrmidon ants were themselves a GM species. But Einar's gambit was the correct one: Using the terminator ants to halt the march of the Myrmidons convinced Congress and the American people that it was time to be the master of the world's genetic destiny rather than its slave. And with that came the sweeping approval of using Arca's own *Aedes aegypti* mosquito to help combat dengue fever in Florida, Hawaii, and anywhere else it pops up in the United States.

Einar smiles. "Just as Icarus got his wish of flying very high in the sky."

"They found Archer Stevens."

"Did they?"

"Suicide."

"He was a troubled man, I hear."

"She did it, didn't she? Venla. And it was her who delivered the ants to Scottie Stevens there in that cabin. The second set of prints—it was her wearing the same exact type of Lowa boots." Hence, she thinks, the lean to the prints—those shoes were a hair too big for her. Their poor fit led to strange footprints.

"Venla always was her own creature. I could never control her. I admired Archer. Scottie, the child, not so much." His face is an implacable veneer.

"They'll investigate you for it."

"Let them."

"There's also the matter of nearly five thousand dead on the island of Kauai," she says, her mouth a firm line. "I hope that haunts you. You turned those monsters loose on an island of people who had no way to protect themselves. Ten percent of the island's inhabitants—gone. Cut to pieces to feed your little soldiers. Does that bother you? Does it keep you up at night?"

A twitch at his lips. "A small price to pay for progress. Ten percent of the island's inhabitants—whether you're considering the tourist population there or not, I cannot say—is a *speck* compared to the seven billion people on this planet. Dengue fever sickens millions every year, killing twenty-five thousand. *Every. Year.* And that's not factoring in all the other mosquito-borne diseases, Hannah. Malaria. West Nile. Chikungunya in Central America. Zika in South America and now here in North America." He waves his hand in the air as if dismissing a moth. "Five thousand dead? A sadness. Regrettable. But as the buy-in to allow us to save five times that many annually? Ten times that? A fleeting, forgettable price to pay so we may teach mankind that science is not our enemy."

"*You* made science our enemy."

"Only in the short term."

"You're a sick man."

"And you're a deluded woman. The world needs visionaries like me, Hannah. If men like me are not willing to be so bold, we will lose the race against ourselves. You know that. You've looked into the eye of the future."

"If you're the hero we deserve, we have already lost that race, Einar."

"I'm sorry you feel that way."

She nods. "You could have been someone important. Instead, you're just another ego-fed maniac. A man who can't help but push his hand into wet concrete to leave his ugly mark. Good luck. Enjoy prison."

"Where will you go, Hannah?"

"Where else? Home."

* * *

She goes home. Her mother leads her into the bedroom without saying a word, and there under the covers is her father. He talks to Hannah, but the words he uses aren't words at all. They sound like another language, some gabbled alien tongue that makes sense to him but no one else at all.

"He had a stroke," her mother says.

"When?"

"Months ago. Before you left for the island."

Hannah feels her eyes go wet. She kneels by the bedside and holds her father's hand. His skin is dry like the paper around a cigarette.

All that time, her mother wouldn't tell her this. She pretended nothing was wrong. "Why didn't you tell me?"

"Would it have mattered?"

That stings. Because of course it would've mattered. Wouldn't it?

Dad babbles, then laughs as if he just told a joke. Hannah tries to laugh with him as if she *understood* the joke. But her laugh rings hollow.

"How do you know it was a stroke?"

"I . . . had a doctor come."

"When?" She stands up, suddenly angry, because this is important. "When did you have a doctor come?"

"A few nights after it . . . happened."

Hannah's jaw clenches, and through her teeth she says, "Time *matters* with a stroke, Mom. How *fast* you act . . ." She pounds a fist into her own thigh, hard. "Damn it, you may have cost him his mind."

"Doctors don't know what they're talking about."

There it is. A burning ember in her heart, like a flung piece of meteorite scorched from atmospheric entry. She wants to strike her mother. Hannah wants to haul back and knock her into the next room.

She doesn't. She stays her hand. Instead she storms off into the kitchen and makes herself some tea: A comforting ritual. Meditative in its way. She picks out a teabag, gets the kettle on the stove.

Her mother follows, though, and she stands there like a bitter pill, saying: "You see now, I was right." She reaches past Hannah, taking out a mug that says BLACKMOORE TRACTOR SUPPLY and sliding it across the counter to her daughter. "If all this nonsense proves anything, it's that we're balanced right on the edge of things. Those ants? That European man? The future isn't a door. It's a wall. And we're headed right toward it. I hope you see that now."

"That's where you're wrong, Mom." She says these words as if she believes them, though honestly, she's not so sure. But Hannah keeps on: "If you want to be scared of anything, be scared of here and now. It's the present that's frightening. The future we can fix. If we want to. But we have to *really* want it. We can't just keep our heads down. *You* can't just keep your head down. You fucked me up. Now you fucked Dad up. Maybe he was always fucked up because of you. Things could've been different, but they weren't."

Mom looks worse than if Hannah *had* hauled off and hit her.

The kettle starts to whistle. Hannah pushes it aside and leaves. That night she sleeps in a motel about ten miles away. She has nightmares. The same ones she's had almost every night since the island. Nightmares about drowning. About being torn to ribbons by little teeth. About falling from a great height into the sea. And once in a while, not every night, she dreams about shooting Roy Peffer through the chest with a rifle. Blood sprayed on the windswept grass.

Sometimes she wakes up feeling like she's covered in ants. Or blood. Or both.

She spends the next week with her father.

She and her mother share no words.

MIAMI

A week later

It's hot. And so humid the air feels like it's gone gelatinous, like she's moving through warm Jell-O. She sits at the café, drinks an iced coffee.

He's late, but he shows.

Ray. Ray, the cocky jerk. Ray, the guy who survived a gut shot—a *miraculous* gut shot, the way it missed his vital organs. Ray, the guy who tricked her into going on a date by asking her out on what she assumed was his deathbed.

He smiles. He's lost some weight and some muscle. But his structure is all still there—broad, firm, tall.

Well, she thinks, *let's see how this goes.* Her own advice to her mother rings in her ears: *Maybe it's time to rejoin the world.*

"Hola," Ray says.

"Hey."

He sits down, and the date she owes him begins.

ACKNOWLEDGMENTS

This story contains *bugs* and *science,* and I tried getting those two things right (even though I know I'm getting it all mostly wrong), and I have to thank some folks who helped me do it: Gwen Pearson and the rest of the Purdue University Bug Barn, Bert Hölldobler and Edward Wilson (seriously, go read *Journey to the Ants,* it's rad), and Alex Wild (whose macro ant photography is elegant and beautiful).

Thanks, too, to the other writers who joined me on the Bug Barn expedition: Max Gladstone, Stephen Blackmoore, Delilah S. Dawson.

Also, thanks to my agent, Stacia Decker, and to the great folks at Harper for helping to put into your hands a book covered in ants—thanks Kate Nintzel, Margaux Weisman, David Pomerico, Caro Perny.

I guess I should also thank the carpenter ants for invading my shed while I wrote this book. I'll assume they're fans. Also, sorry to the few I squished. Your sacrifice will be remembered.

ABOUT THE AUTHOR

Chuck Wendig is the *New York Times* bestselling author of the Miriam Black thrillers (which begin with *Blackbirds*) and numerous other works across books, comics, games, and more. A finalist for the John W. Campbell Award for Best New Writer and the cowriter of the Emmy-nominated digital narrative *Collapsus*, he is also known for his popular blog, terribleminds.com. He lives in Pennsylvania with his family.